Also by Angi Morgan

Ranger Protector
Ranger Defender
Ranger Guardian
Bulletproof Badge
Shotgun Justice
Gunslinger
Hard Core Law
The Sheriff
The Cattleman
The Ranger

Also by Jane Godman

Colton 911: Family Under Fire
Colton's Secret Bodyguard
Colton and the Single Mum
Covert Kisses
The Soldier's Seduction
Secret Baby, Second Chance

CRIMINAL ALLIANCE

ANGI MORGAN

COLTON MANHUNT

JANE GODMAN

MILLS & BOON

First Published in Great Britain 2020
by Mills & Boon, an imprint of HarperCollins*Publishers*
1 London Bridge Street, London, SE1 9GF

Special thanks and acknowledgement are given to Jane Godman for her contribution to *The Coltons of Mustang Valley* series.

ISBN: 978-0-263-28024-1

0320

MIX

SC™

green

CRIMINAL ALLIANCE

ANGI MORGAN

Thanks for the years of encouraging words and support, Therese! You deserve a great, capable heroine named after you. Lori, Amanda and Robin…couldn't have done it without you.

Prologue

Last year

"Dammit, Hamilton. It doesn't matter if you were right. You broke every rule we have. If it were up to me, I'd kick you to the curb like you deserve." Major Clements slapped his hand against his thigh as he paced in front of the door.

Wade Hamilton stood at attention, something he'd rarely done since becoming a Texas Ranger. Eyes straight ahead, he couldn't see his commander walking behind him. But hey, even if he stood directly in front, Wade couldn't focus on the major's expressions. His left eye was still swollen from the beating he'd taken a week ago and everything was blurry. He couldn't judge if this was the end…or just a very long reprimand.

Wade could feel Major Clements just over his right shoulder. Out of his peripheral vision, he saw the major's hand clenched in a fist, the knuckles white from the tight grip. His supervisor had been angry before.

Yeah, several times before.

But hopefully, he could remember that Wade had saved lives. Didn't that count for something? His partner had reminded him often enough that Wade trusted his gut too much. But this time Jack was grateful for it.

"It seems that I don't have a final say," the major continued. "Seems that someone at headquarters put in a good word. Who knows, maybe the woman you helped save talked with someone. Or maybe the top brass doesn't want to have to explain why a Texas Ranger from Company B was fired after saving someone from the state fire marshal's office. Hell, I have no idea."

Major Clements's boots struck the floor, paused and pivoted again.

It wasn't the first time the major had given him a lecture. It *was* the first time he hadn't been looking at Wade when he delivered it. No matter the words about how lucky he was and unknown friends at headquarters, Wade still wasn't too sure about job security.

"I drew the line at the suggestion you be given a commendation. Rule breakers should not be rewarded. The example you've set is not a good one. I'm very disappointed in you, Lieutenant." The major's voice was tempered with sadness instead of anger.

"I understand, sir."

"Good." He walked back to his desk, putting both fists knuckle down on the polished wood and leaning toward Wade. "And yet, I don't hear an apology or simple words like *it won't happen again*."

"That goes without saying, sir."

"Do you really believe that, Wade? I hope you'll at least try not to play the hero. You barely survived this time. But since I can't fire you, in order to rein you in a bit…" He sat. A good sign that Wade hadn't lost his job. "You're benched."

"Excuse me, sir?" Wade's eyes moved to make contact with the major. One stern look was enough to have him back at attention. "I'm not sure I understand."

"Desk duty, Lieutenant. You'll report here every day.

And every day there will be files for you to work on. You are not to leave this office from the hours of nine to five. I don't want to hear about you even going for lunch. You got me?"

"Loud and clear, sir."

"Dismissed."

"But what about the case, sir?" Wade looked just above the major's head, concentrating on keeping his eyes from pleading with the man in charge of his fate. "We only touched the surface of what crimes Rushdan Reval is behind. This is our way into that scumbag's organization."

"We've been ordered to stand down, Lieutenant. I said dismissed."

Wade left the office barely able to swallow, feeling grateful that he had a job, wondering how he'd survive sifting through files—especially paperwork that wasn't even his—and disappointed in himself that he'd been close to accessing Reval's group and had messed up... bad.

His partner, Jack MacKinnon, gave him a "what's up" look from across the room. Slate Thompson and Heath Murray, along with the other Company B Rangers, gave him a wide berth and no eye contact. They all probably thought he was heading to his desk to clean it out. No one really expected him to keep his job, his rank or his anything.

He made it to his desk, still using the crutch the hospital had forced on him. Honestly, he could barely see his chair since his left eye was killing him. It was the roll-y thing behind the big block of wood. Yeah, he could joke but not laugh—the cracked ribs were too painful.

The doctors had been straight about the headaches that wouldn't go away for a while. Even straighter about the possibility his sight might not ever be 100 percent again.

Rest—sitting-down-and-not-moving kind of rest, to be more specific—was what they demanded.

They hadn't cleared him for anything. But after two days of sitting inside his house, he'd finagled his recovering body behind the wheel of his truck and driven the fifteen minutes to headquarters. It had been more painful sliding out and hitting the ground with both feet.

He sat, putting the crutch on the floor next to the wall his desk was pushed against. He heard himself suck air through his teeth as he rolled into place.

"You okay?" Jack patted him lightly on the back. "Looks like you're still employed."

Dammit, he hadn't seen Jack come up behind him. He jumped, then hissed again in pain.

"For the moment. And only at this wonderful desk." He petted it like a dog.

"Always the cutup. How long?" his partner asked before sitting on the corner of his desk.

"You got me." It hurt too much to shrug. And it hurt too much to focus across the aisle. Everything really was mostly a blur.

"Man, I'm not sure how long it'll take for him to trust you again." Jack rubbed his chin, then the back of his neck—or at least that was what it looked like through the fog. "I'm sort of surprised I'm not stuck here, too. On second thought, it was entirely your fault I was involved in the first place."

"Don't go there, man. Not only did you get to make a serious arrest because I asked for a favor, but you also got a girlfriend out of it. Who I should probably thank for saving my job with a word from her state-level boss. You can say that I'm responsible for setting you two lovebirds up."

"You could say that." Jack stood, removing his gun

from his desk drawer and placing it in its holster. "But if you do, I might just have to kick your butt." He laughed. "Your desk duty explains why I'm on loan to Dallas PD for a while."

"They're still shorthanded after the loss of their officers. You'd think the major would want me out there with you."

His partner raised his eyebrows almost into his hairline. "Get real. You know I trust you with my life. But man, you got to learn to play the game. Rangers have a specific duty and—"

"And are restricted to following the law. Yeah, I know. I heard that lecture for the past hour while standing at attention. I thought the major would go harder on me if I reminded him I'm having problems standing."

Jack clapped him on the shoulder. Wade tried not to wince. He was determined to force his body to at least stay upright.

"I was going to say," Jack continued, "that we have a proud tradition. Our motto might be 'One Riot, One Ranger,' but that doesn't mean it has to be us doing things alone. I'm here for you. Always will be. No matter what."

"Thanks, Jack. It's appreciated."

"Keep your head down and fly under the radar. Don't go looking for trouble."

"I never look, man. It just always seems to find me. Watch your back since I won't be there to protect you."

"Like you did by getting beat up so bad you can't stand?"

"Three cracked ribs isn't too bad." He squinted through his good eye. "Besides, they took me by surprise."

"Right."

Wade watched his partner leave the office without

him, passing one of the clerks on his way. A clerk with a box, heading straight toward his desk.

"Major Clements said you should go through these, Wade." She dropped the box on the floor next to his chair. "You need to verify that all the appropriate reports are in order and scanned or the data inputted. Basically, that everything's ready for trial or to turn over to headquarters. When you're done, I have the rest of the alphabet waiting." She turned to leave but pivoted back to his desk. "Remember that these files need to be locked up each night."

Wade lifted the lid and pulled the folder at the end… Carla Byrnhearst. "That's just great." One box got him through two letters. He shoved the file back inside and pulled the Ader file from the other end.

Keep his head down.

Do the time at his desk.

Accept the punishment.

Keep his job.

He could do this. He'd wanted to be a Texas Ranger for too long. One man had put everything on the line to keep him from a life of crime. After that, all his focus had been toward obtaining that goal. College, Texas DPS, the highway patrol, three long years near the border and finally an opening and assignment to Company B.

These men were his brothers now. His desk phone rang and he answered.

"Hey, sexy. Just checking up on you."

Therese. Trouble did have a habit of finding him.

God, just the woman's voice sent electricity shooting through his veins. Where had she been? Where was she now? Last week in the hospital, he'd forced another ranger to run Therese Ortis's name. She should have been awaiting trial for her involvement with Rushdan Reval, the Dallas crime syndicate leader who had just tried to kill him. But there had been nothing.

"I guess I owe you something—at least dinner—for saving my life." His mind was already following the steps to have the call traced.

He'd seen her once. Spoken to her fewer than half a dozen times. And he was caught, dangling at the end of her string. In fact, he'd swallowed her enticing voice and innuendos hook, line and sinker.

"Even though I'd enjoy that very much, I don't think it would help you get off desk duty," she purred.

"You're the one who kept me my job?"

"Ladies never kiss and tell, Wade." She paused long enough to let the words have their desired effect. "Gotta run, Ranger Big Man. Till next time."

"Wait…"

Too late. The line disconnected. He didn't have to inquire about the number—he knew it would be a dead end. Just like each time before. His mystery woman had a habit of swooping in for the save and disappearing until she needed him again.

He opened the file and started. With any luck, he could get through a letter each day. Twenty-six days stuck in a chair. Behind a desk. Watching his fellow rangers do the heavy lifting.

No playing hero.

Most investigating happened from a chair anyway. Sitting here would give him plenty of time to discover just what the mystery surrounding his lady was all about. Yeah, he could do this. Especially now that he was properly motivated.

And man oh man…he was definitely motivated to find Therese Ortis.

Chapter One

Present day

Just another two-for-one longneck Friday special. Wade sat on the same barstool he'd ended his nights on and had claimed for years. This particular stool was the last one next to the wall, located where no one could catch him by surprise. Only his right side was open to patrons. Better for his vision, especially now that it got fuzzy from time to time.

He should be somewhere else.

Maybe somewhere more respectable for a Texas Ranger. That wasn't here. Someplace he could share that he was a ranger. Or maybe be with his friends. But they all had girlfriends. Heath was back home with his wife. Slate might as well be married. And Jack—his so-called partner—was engaged.

He should find some other friends. Maybe some who liked to…to what? Watch a game? Play trivia over some chicken wings? It didn't matter where he went or what barstool he ended up on. He'd still be looking at every dark-haired woman who walked in the door to see if it was her.

Dammit. He couldn't keep this up. Six weeks was long

enough visiting bars on lower Greenville Avenue. His search for Agent Therese Ortis needed to end.

Soon. No. Tonight. He'd shown his face once too often in other dives. Earlier the barkeeps had waved him past their place, in a hurry to get the discouraged ranger on his way. His badge was far from good for their business.

So here he sat. His go-to joint that knew him from way back. The one place where they gave him a pass for having a badge.

Twisting the rest of his lime slice into his Mexican beer, he studied the peel—more interested in the citrus than in anyone around him. He needed to take Jack's advice. If Therese wanted to get in touch… Well, she knew how. She'd done it before to save Megan and a second time to save his hide before Rushdan Reval blew him up inside a building.

Across the room, the door banged open. Heads— including his—turned toward the noise.

What the hell?

"Wade!" The woman who had haunted his dreams crossed the sixty feet, dodging drunks and other happy-hour patrons who had quickly returned to their conversations.

"You have got…" she began, too loudly, before nervously looking around and landing next to him at the bar. "You've got to stop your…your inquiries. Are you listening to me? I'm furious."

No, he hadn't been listening. Dressed in the smallest bright yellow dress—more like a piece of a dress that could still be respectful—he barely noticed anything else. The color set off her dark brown hair.

The bling around her neck drew his eyes straight to the diving-low plunge between her breasts. How the hell was she walking in those heels?

Shoot. How did the dress stay in place?

The woman who'd actually 100 percent saved his life licked her lips and drew a deep breath. Trying to ignore her, he looked down at the bar, stabbing the three lime slices with a plastic sword.

"Hey, Wade, hon?" Her erotic voice whispered close to his ear while her feathery touch on his hand shot all sorts of feelings through him.

Six weeks without a word.

And she was mad. *At him?*

Even though she'd been caught working with crooks last year, he'd never believed she was on the wrong side of the law. Something in their sparse conversations had forbidden him from thinking badly of her. Then six weeks ago he'd found out—like a kick to the head—she was working with the FBI or something. Nobody talked. Lots of secrets. Had he forgiven her for taking away a major case?

Probably not.

There was no mistake who she spoke to. She'd stopped so close her breath of air brushed his bare neck, encouraging him to act. But he wouldn't. He didn't have the right. Even if she had called him *hon*.

"I like you in a T-shirt. It shows off these strong arms. But this button-up looks great on you, too. It brings out the steel blue in your eyes."

He could tell her he liked her dress. Or not.

Yeah, she squeezed his biceps. Yeah, she puckered her lips together like she waited for a kiss.

"No."

"Are you sure?" She eased onto the stool next to him, her long legs reaching sideways under his. Damn, that yellow silky thing climbed up to her hip. "I haven't even asked anything."

Wait. Were they talking about a kiss or the favor he thought she was about to ask? He should consider himself lucky that the stools weren't close enough for him to pull her onto his lap to find out. *Lucky?*

Therese twisted away from him to face the opening door and back again with a blank look. A big fella walked inside, propping the door open with his foot and calling to a buddy on the sidewalk. They both entered, finally shutting the door to keep the cooler air in and the blistering summer heat outside.

Everything about her demeanor changed. Where she'd been full of anger she was now soft. She closed her eyes, drawing a deep breath through her nose and making her breasts swell in the tight dress. Then she wet her lip gloss with the tip of her tongue. To stop his drool, he tipped the beer to his mouth, drinking her in with his eyes.

The fresh burst of lime made him lick his lips, or was he mirroring the seductress beside him? Then her dark red lips parted ever so slowly. Slower than necessary and very practiced. Hell, he could give in right then, doing whatever she asked, having no idea what it might be.

Instead he broke off his stare and looked around the intimate, off-the-beaten-path bar. Mostly regulars with the exception of the last two men. Every corner was shadowed and filled with secrets, but he didn't butt his nose in. He knew the ins and outs. Knew what to expect. He'd been coming here since college and it didn't hurt that no one broadcast that he was a Texas Ranger. He'd never had a need to show his badge. Not here.

"I know it's been a while since I've called. Please don't be annoyed with me." She swiveled on the stool, reaching for his limes, daring him not to look down the low-cut dress she flashed under his chin.

"I'd have to care to be angry. Or annoyed," he lied.

He didn't know the reason for her personality switch, but he'd play along.

"There's just been a lot going on, hon—" She pouted.

Pouted? Therese Ortis didn't seem the pouting kind. What the hell was going on? She knew he'd been looking for her and seemed pretty doggone upset about it less than five minutes ago.

"So you aren't angry, annoyed or even a little hurt, baby?" she smiled with a knowing smile, circling a deep red nail around the back of his hand.

Hon? Baby? What was she trying to pull? She reached out, taking his extra lime and swiping her tongue across it. She knew exactly how to make *him* nervous. But she was the one shaking like a leaf in a windstorm—the only thing that kept him from showing her just how angry he wasn't.

Yeah, he was succumbing to the seductress line. What man wouldn't? But it was the trembling that got him.

Her eyes darted in every direction, checking for trouble. The bartender walked to the other end of the room and she leaned in close.

"I need a big favor. I can explain everything if you give me a chance."

Even though the intensity changed from flirtatious to urgent, he still answered, "I'm all out."

Explain? Nice fantasy. Therese never explained. He poured more than a sip of beer down his throat. He tipped the bottle toward her, politely asking if she wanted something. She shook her head while he caught the bartender's eye and ordered two more.

"I promise not to land you on desk duty again. What do you say?" she asked in a low, sensual voice he had fallen prey to a few times already.

Wade had wanted to connect with her for over a year.

Why the hesitation? *Desk duty. Uncertainty. Tired of being used. Downright irritation at being ignored.*

"I say—" he grinned way too big "—that you haven't mentioned anything I haven't heard before."

"I'm sure that can't be true," she still whispered.

"Considering I can recall all seven conversations we've ever had… Yeah, I'm pretty sure I can clearly remember every word that you've said." *And exactly what you haven't.*

"I really, really think you're going to be interested in my favor, hon."

"Nope." He kept his voice low, matching hers.

He was done. Had nothing left. Finished. Kaput. Refused to get involved. *Remember?* And yet, completely curious.

"Is there anything I could do or say to change your mind?" She drew circles on his shoulder, dragging her long fingernail down his arm until she got to his hand.

She looked innocent. If he knew her better he might think she seemed desperate. But he didn't know her better. She came to him when she needed something. Case or no case, he didn't like being used.

And he hated giving in to her, to anybody.

Therese's eyes darted to the mirror.

The two large men moved away from the opposite end of the bar and Therese stiffened. Obvious to him since she held his hand. Probably not obvious to the men who had eyes for no one else in the room. They looked like typical guys, with the exception of the bulges under their jackets. Jackets worn for the simple reason of hiding the weapons.

They were there for her—obviously.

"Wade," she said way too loudly. "I'm so hungry."

"What?"

She dropped a finger across his lips to stop his next question. Her eyes moved to the mirror. His hand gently tugged hers from his face back to the bar and slid a longneck bottle into it.

"I guess I need to hear about that favor after all." He squeezed a lime slice and pushed it through the neck of the sweating bottle.

Chapter Two

Normally, Therese wouldn't have paid any attention to someone as good-looking as Texas Ranger Wade Hamilton. He was almost too good-looking.

Dark brown hair swooped back off his forehead. Dark blue eyes framed by masculine-shaped brows. And a sprinkle of chest hair. Just visible tonight with the open collar in his Texas-blue dress shirt. She'd seen the outline of that chest in a T-shirt a couple of times, too. Just like she'd admitted a few minutes ago.

Oh, yeah, she'd kept up with him. Back when she was in control. Right up to coming face-to-face with him at a crime scene six weeks ago.

She should have gone to him covertly and explained what she was doing. Wade would have left things alone then. When she'd told her handler her plan, he'd laughed and ordered her to stay clear of the ranger. Everyone had seen what they called "smoldering looks" from Wade. And they'd made it known they'd seen right through her attempt to act immune.

So she'd avoided the tall, handsome ranger and paid off the bars where he kept asking after her. But the damage was done. Wade had shown his badge one too many times. Rushdan was convinced she'd sold him out to the cops.

Of course she had. But he'd had no clue before Wade Hamilton kept asking everywhere for her.

The moment she'd seen Wade sitting on that very barstool last year she'd lost her breath. When he hadn't recognized her cowering in the corner, she'd just watched. She hadn't stopped thinking about him since that Friday night.

The very first time they'd met, he'd literally swept her off her feet while rescuing her teenage version. When he hadn't recognized her as an adult, it had stung a little, but it was totally understandable. A lot had gone down that night. And wouldn't you know it, now he was the only man she could trust to keep her alive.

Being alone would get her killed. Period.

If only she could wait or fill him in on why she needed him. Crossing her fingers that he'd be sitting on his barstool, she'd come here looking for him. Unlike how she'd avoided it every Friday night since she'd returned to Dallas. She'd been ordered not to speak to him or meet him under any circumstances.

Her last conversation with Rushdan had left her uncomfortable. He did the hinting thing, talking around her to only the men, asking why a certain Texas Ranger was asking all over Dallas for her. When she'd left the offices, the two thugs behind her had followed.

Okay, she felt desperate and her brain began to panic a little. Pretty sure those men had been sent to take her out. Three years of undercover work shot because she'd been ordered not to talk to the man beside her. Yeah, panic closed in, making the bar feel even smaller.

With one eye on the bar mirror, she watched Rushdan's men loitering just inside the bar's door. She pushed her nerves aside and daringly placed her palm on Wade's thick-muscled thigh. He actually jumped a little. How sweet.

"This seat taken?" Rushdan's head hit man knew it wasn't. He knew she'd come in alone. And knew she didn't carry a weapon. Or at least thought he knew.

Leaning away from Wade, she tried to give the man following her a brilliant, reassuring smile. "We're on a date, sugar. Please don't try to pick me up."

Please go with it, Wade. Don't yell at me for acting like we're lovers. It is *all your fault.*

"As a matter of fact…we were about to leave." Wade tipped the remains of his beer between perfectly handsome lips. "We're meeting friends for dinner."

"Then you're not drinking that longneck?" Rushdan's guy slanted his body, blocking her view of the entrance. He moved so close to her as he reached for the beer she hadn't touched that she was afraid she'd slide off the stool trying to avoid him. Wade's legs connected with her body, effectively catching her. Too bad there wasn't more time to flirt. As nervous as he seemed, she could have had some fun.

"Go for it. The little lady's afraid she'll spoil her appetite." Wade stood, dropping money on the bar before sliding his hands back onto her shoulders, his body next to her back, steadying her. "You can have our stools just as soon as we go."

His gentle twang could melt her heart under different circumstances.

"We'll never make our reservation, hon. Not if you do anything…to slow us down." She licked her lips and knew they appeared sexy. She had much too much practice at flirting and yet it still made her uncomfortable.

Give her a 9mm and a target at fifty yards and she'd be completely at ease. She mentally demanded her nerves to settle. Otherwise she'd need a bucket to catch the sweat from her palms.

The dumb blonde routine—even if she was a brunette—had never been her dream assignment for undercover work. But she was stuck with it. Her carefully constructed identity called on her to be soft, vulnerable and not too smart. At least Rushdan Reval considered her soft.

Leaving the stool, she deliberately fell into the side of Reval's man, letting her hands play across his flabby chest and lifting his weapon from his holster.

Rushdan's second goon took a quick step toward them. She backed up quickly, passing the gun to Wade, who aimed straight at their assailants. The bartender jerked to a halt along with the rest of those in the bar.

"Uh-uh-uh." She waved a finger at Rushdan's hired help. "What will your friends say if they knew you lost your weapon? I won't tell if you don't."

Wade jerked her back to his side.

Damn, he's a rock. She dropped the thoughts about Wade's body and planned their walk past Rushdan's men. Wade acted like she'd been his for a decade—not two minutes. Maybe he was used to women throwing themselves at his feet, but she wasn't used to being held.

She might play the part of easy…but she hadn't had a real relationship since college. Undercover work had major pitfalls.

Her stomach did a double backflip when Wade's hands darted a little lower on her waist than she'd intended. She didn't change their direction. She needed to leave this bar and take him with her. How else could she explain her presence on lower Greenville and try to salvage three years of undercover work?

Lying to Rushdan about why Wade had been looking

for her bought her time this afternoon. Time to find him. Granted, it had been spur of the moment and she'd been unable to contact her team for backup. But something—or someone—had made Rushdan suspicious. When the crime boss sent these guys to follow her, it was for one reason…elimination.

She began the longest walk of her career. Wade's long fingers slid over her hip and back up around her waist, distracting her with their heat. Her hands flew to fan her face—half acting and half needing to cool her hot cheeks.

Wade pulled the door open, waiting for her to go through. She wanted one last look at the men chasing her and turned. The movement brought them closer, making her aware of Wade's body, the complete maleness of him.

A sparkle in his eye caught her attention. *The jerk. He's laughing at me.* Maybe she'd been flirting a little too much and couldn't stop herself. It was as if the sensual woman in her—although scarcely unleashed—chose that very moment to take control.

She turned completely into Wade and the slinky thing the salesgirl called a dress rose higher along her thigh. His fingertips brushed the bare skin just below the hem. She froze.

Something happened.

The look in his eyes turned volcanic.

Somewhere in the back of her mind she was aware they stood just inside the doorway of a semi-crowded bar. Somewhere in her nonfunctioning gray matter she knew she'd only spoken a handful of sentences to this man. But somewhere in a part of her soul that had never been touched, a magnet flipped on and pulled her to this unselfish ranger.

When their lips connected, she forgot everything. She forgot the reason she was on lower Greenville. The reason she needed to leave. The reason she shouldn't be standing there kissing her escape plan.

Soft, firm lips grabbed hers, gently sucking and pulling. She parted her own. What should have been a strange invasion felt…perfect. His wonderfully strong arms reached around her body, pulling her into his hard angles. This wasn't kissing. It was more than fabulous. A simple lip-lock shouldn't make her weak in the knees.

"Get a room," someone in the bar shouted, followed by erupting laughter.

Wade's dark blue eyes watched her face as he pulled slightly away, his breathing just as rapid as hers. "Yours or mine?" he whispered, but the entire room listened.

Then she remembered the necessity to leave. Could the kiss have convinced Rushdan's men she'd really met her lover? Would sticking with him for a while save her life?

"Yours. Mine's too far," she heard herself say.

He didn't let her pull away. He kept her safely tucked into his side as they let the door close and headed toward a parking lot. That in itself was unusual… She wasn't used to someone else keeping *her* safe.

It had been a long time since she'd been nervous. What if they jumped them? Her Beretta was hidden in her car. The car several miles away. And now she'd involved an innocent man who had no idea what he'd just agreed to.

A slight laugh escaped. *Innocent?* The hunger in his eyes made her doubt her strong hero had ever been innocent.

Either way, she shouldn't involve him. It was against orders. She'd get to his truck and find another way out of this mess. But as they got outside, she looked up just as he glanced down. If she'd wanted to be heroic, she'd made a fatal mistake.

It happened again.

Raw energy pulled her to his mouth for a second time. He plunged between her lips, molded his hands to her butt and brought her into his instant hardness.

Someone cleared their throat. The sound jerked Wade away from her mouth, but not from her body. He kept her close, whispering what he wanted…what they'd eventually do. Small tremors shook from her into him. He skimmed her ear with his teeth.

There wasn't any doubt what would ultimately happen.

What they both needed.

Wade dug in his front pocket and shoved bills into the parking lot attendant's extended hand. Keeping his arm around her waist, he brought them both at a fast walk to his truck, forcing her to stay in step with him. Then he opened the driver's door and lifted her inside. She began slipping across the front seat, but spying Rushdan's men rounding the corner stopped her.

Before Wade could get the key in the ignition, she pulled his face to hers, kissing him again but keeping her eyes on the men. Just like him.

Her rescuer pulled away, leaving both of them breathing hard. "I swear…if you keep kissing me like that, it won't matter what kind of favor you need me to do. We really will be heading straight for my place."

Chapter Three

Hell's bells, what was all that about? Wade couldn't wait for answers. The men following Therese were outside. Probably the reason Therese had kissed him again. And again.

She began to slide to the passenger side, but he stopped her, tugging her back to his hip. "Nope. You're staying right here. You aren't going anywhere without me. No disappearing acts."

"I was only getting a seat belt. We can't afford to be stopped by the police."

He reached to the far side of her, remembering the silky feel of her thigh. He took pleasure in skimming her hip while he dug between the seats for the middle belt, then fastened it, pulling it tight across her lap.

He put the truck in gear and pulled past the men she obviously knew. "So what's the problem? Or should I refer to it as a favor?"

"Oh, I think you noticed." She waved to the men. "I hate it when they think I need protection."

"Hold on a minute," he interrupted while pulling from the parking lot. "You might as well come clean, Therese. You chose to bring me into this. Now give it to me straight. No sidestepping the truth. Those guys were not a protection detail."

"I understood when you indicated that you didn't want to get involved. You can't have it both ways. I respect that. If you drop me at a corner, I'll call a rideshare to get back to my apartment." She tried to put space between them. It didn't work.

"You aren't going anywhere. And I *am* involved. They just took pictures of me and my truck." He pointed to the last man to head to their vehicle. "It won't be long before they know who I am, where I live and what I do."

"Oh, God. I forgot you'd be in your truck instead of a government vehicle. I can fix this before anything happens. I promise."

"No fixes. I need the truth for once, without any stalls." They were still near the bar as he watched the men get into a car double-parked on the street.

They crept along at a snail's pace. If you were driving to a bar on Greenville, you couldn't get upset about not getting anywhere fast. It was just part of coming to this part of town on a Friday night. Everyone expected to be stuck and frustrated in happy-hour traffic. But it guaranteed that the two cars would be sticking close to his tail. Something he didn't mind for the moment.

Not if it finally got him information about Therese.

"Turn on a side street, speed up and lose them," she said, stretching a little closer so she could see out of the rearview mirror.

But he'd made up his mind. He deserved answers. He made a couple of turns and headed into downtown.

"Where are you going? Wade? Are you… Are you trying to keep them in sight?"

"I thought you said you were hungry." It was a stall, pure and simple. Not fooling her a lick, judging by the roll of her eyes.

"Right. So now you're interested?"

He couldn't see her face. She sat next to him, one arm around her waist and leaning into the other—fingers against her forehead. He had no gauge—no history—to know if she was serious or not.

"About what? Being hungry? I happen to eat regularly."

She turned to look behind her. "They're not even bothering to hide that they're following." She tugged her cell phone from a small pocket he hadn't noticed before.

Feeling like a kid on his first real date, he dropped his arm around Therese's shoulders at the next stoplight. He looked back and counted how many cars behind him the two threats were.

"Where did you want to go?"

"A fancy hotel?" She rubbed his knee, causing his mind to detour.

He kept driving. Proud that he didn't run off the road with all the distracting images he had running though his head. A protection detail or hit men? Could he keep her safe if they went to a… He swallowed hard and replayed her words.

Dammit—too much sarcasm.

"Okay. Enough games and put away that phone." He pulled through the light, slowing enough to make certain he was still followed until he had answers. "Maybe you should just tell me what's going on? And I mean everything, Therese. Don't leave out anything. You should consider me part of whatever operation you're running."

"I can tell you part of the story." She turned slightly, scraping her fingernails across his after-hours scruff.

"First." He squeezed her shoulder, tugging her slightly back to him. "You should probably know that if you invite me to a hotel again, I'm heading straight there. And don't plan on me sleeping anywhere except next to you."

She smiled. It might have even been genuine instead of completely calculated to capture his attention.

"And second?" she asked, outlining his ear with the tip of her finger.

He pulled to a stop at a red light. Her *friends* had moved closer—as in the car was now beside the truck. She looked at him and he prepared. The sultry lips were in front of his face, and her lips connected to his in slow motion. She kissed him deeply, deliberately and for longer than it took the light to turn green.

Horns honked. Both cars blocked a full one-way downtown street in Friday night traffic. Horns honked more. It registered in his mind, but he didn't want to let her go.

She slipped from his arms with a very satisfied grin. "They blinked."

"What?" He pulled forward on autopilot after the cars behind him veered around his truck.

"Drive slow and they'll have to pull through the next light. Then we're in the clear."

Oh, yeah, the men following her—them. Dammit, he'd completely lost focus. He couldn't blame anything except holding her—the only woman he'd thought about more than twice since meeting her.

"I think all the kissing fooled them," she said. "Oh great. They're pulling over to wait on us."

"We should use their following to our advantage," he threw out. How? He wasn't sure.

"What do you mean?"

"Tell me what's going on, beginning with the thugs behind us." He kept heading west on Commerce, past downtown, past the county jail. They stayed close on his tail, not trying to hide. "Are you in danger?"

"Short version?"

"We'll start with a simple yes or no."

"How about an *I think so*?"

"You've got to be kidding me. I need some answers, Therese. Or I'm making a U-turn back to County and a hundred police officers. You can try explaining to one of them. What will your friends do then?"

"No. Good grief, you don't have any right to make demands." She unfastened her seat belt, turned and brought a bare leg up next to his, dropping a hand in her lap and using the other to twirl her hair. "You know this is all your fault."

"My fault?" He couldn't let all that bare skin get under his. But it was definitely getting harder to concentrate. He should make her turn back around and refasten the belt.

"Asking around town for me actually got these guys all in my face. I wasn't prepared with answers and had to come up with some type of excuse."

"What the hell are you sidestepping, Therese?" Maybe his words could have been a little less confrontational, a little less loud. *Not really.* "Dammit, I need some answers."

"The truth is I've been on this case for over three years."

Case? Three years on a *case*? "I knew it." He slowed to a stop, wanting to caress all that silkiness. "You're undercover FBI. That's why you were with Steve Woods that day."

Her hands waved him to silence even as her lips puckered sexily again. "Shh. Don't say it aloud even if we're alone. When you started asking around town for me, I shrugged it off. But then you kept asking and it's made my 'boss'—" she shrugged, using air quotes to stress the word "—a little angsty."

"Angsty enough to send your um…protection detail?"

Hit men, more like it. God, he wanted to pull her to him and kiss her. He shook it off. Men. Guns. Undercover. Favor. Focus.

"Last chance, Therese. Who is your boss?"

"What I'm working on isn't important."

"It is to me. I can keep my mouth shut. Secrets are easy."

"You can't mess this up, Wade. It took me over a year to work my way into Rushdan Reval's confidence. I just need you to stop asking—"

"You're working with Reval's group? So that's what you were doing when we arrested him last year? Have you been in Dallas this whole time without contacting me?"

"No…not…really." She stared him down like he was insane if he thought she'd hide from him.

"Don't try that look on me again, Therese. You have a successful disappearing act."

"I wanted to reach out, but I was given a direct order to avoid contact. It might have ruined my cover. After he was arrested, Rushdan pushed me off on one of his side gigs in San Antonio. I've been waiting for him to clear the charges you brought before I could continue here." She waved him forward with a finger. "You should probably keep driving even if we don't know where."

He'd sat through the light twice. Reval's men were hanging farther back, and as he moved forward through the yellow glow, they raced to catch him but got stuck instead.

"I know where I'm going. We need backup."

"No. Believe me. If they were going to attack, they would have by now," she said, looking back over his hand, still around her shoulder.

He retrieved his phone from his back pocket, reluctantly losing contact with Therese. "I need to take care of some cover issues before we go forward." He dialed Company B headquarters.

"Wade, seriously. I've been at this a long time. You've helped enough. I can't put you in danger again. Reval's going to recognize you as the Texas Ranger from last year." She sat straight on the seat, scooting toward the passenger door.

No!

"Dammit, Therese, there's no reason for you to jump out in the middle of nowhere. I can hide us for a few days until we sort out what to do."

He reached out to grab her arm and missed before she opened the door. Therese could probably jump—he'd slowed for a curve—but he slammed on the brakes so she wouldn't have to.

"Just keep driving, Wade. They won't bother you if I'm not here."

Out in a flash, she passed the truck and ran for a path between the trees. He couldn't follow her before he parked. And as soon as he did, they'd know they were out of the truck. Speeding up, he was far enough ahead of the men following that he could whip into a warehouse lot and cut his engine before he was seen.

"Dammit. Razor wire." He couldn't go over and had to go out through the same gate he'd come in. They'd probably see him if he did. *You are not disappearing on me again, Therese Ortis.* "Not this time."

He couldn't make his customized truck disappear or blend in with the others taking up the spaces. The built-in compartments made it impossible to mistake. And Therese was right, several of Reval's men would recognize it as belonging to the ranger they'd captured last year after he'd taken out one of their men.

There was an upside to him being in his truck—the built-in gun safe holding his weapon. But if he pursued Therese on foot without notifying headquarters… If things went haywire… If he messed up an FBI undercover operation…

No more being a Texas Ranger. He was done.

Was she worth it? He didn't need a thoughtful reflection. There wasn't a choice. He needed her safe.

"If I didn't owe her my life, I could drive away and do nothing." He eased from the truck. "Hell."

The longer he took to make a decision, the farther Therese got ahead of him.

So be it. There were a lot of *ifs* in his life. *If* he hadn't made a couple of scenes looking for her during the past six weeks…she would have blown him off forever. And *if* Therese hadn't come to his rescue by contacting Jack last year… Well, he wouldn't be here now, needing to make a decision.

Keeping his head down, he retrieved his weapon. He couldn't go over the eight-foot fence, or around it. Not with the thug car just outside the gate—not without the thugs seeing and following. Okay. Then he'd just have to go through the building and find a rear exit. He could make it to the open loading dock door.

That was all. Cross an open parking lot directly in front of the two cars and jump onto the four-foot loading dock without being seen. He didn't trust Therese's opinion about being safe. He couldn't get caught. Once these yahoos realized who he was…he'd be dead. Therese, too. When they caught her.

One step at a time. A honk from a big rig made the car that had followed them pull to the side of the road closest to the lot.

But the eighteen-wheeler pulled inside the gate, effectively allowing him to cross the lot without the thugs seeing him. He kept running until he passed two building doors. The third had the street view blocked by a box truck. Once he made it there, it was easy to enter the loading bay. He casually walked through the manufacturing company's warehouse. Few people were around as he made his way to the west side of the building, which backed up to the railroad.

He needed wire cutters or something to get through the fence. Nothing. Noticing a man taking his cigarettes from his pocket and heading to an outside door, Wade followed and took a look.

There was a gate. So instead of sulking around kicking himself, he made his job work for him. He headed straight to the office.

"Man, am I glad you're open twenty-four hours," he entered. "Texas Rangers, ma'am." He flipped open his creds. "Would you happen to have a key to your back gate?"

Chapter Four

The evening hour had made it easy for Therese to hide. Unfortunately, it made it terribly difficult to move through the brush. The heels didn't help, either. She pulled them off, looping a finger in each strap to carry them. They were too expensive to leave behind and a pair of her favorites. Slowly picking her way from one oak to the next, she carefully walked through the dirt and debris, hoping for a path.

Far from a Dallas city park, the two ruts were about the same distance apart as a four-wheeler. Nothing was around. Even the ambient light from the city was getting scarce. As scarce as her dress that snagged on every tree she passed.

Another rip and she groaned. "Shoot. What a night to wear the sexiest thing I own."

"It is really sexy."

Her heart leaped into her throat. She totally understood what that meant now as her pulse beat at an insane pace. "Oh my God, Wade. You scared me. What are you doing here?"

"Right. I scared you." Wade grabbed her hand. "What the hell, Therese? You jumped out of my truck."

"If you get involved with this—"

"I already am."

"I admit that it was stupid to march into that bar and ask you for anything. Whatever you're thinking, you don't owe me. You have no obligation. Nothing. Do you hear me?"

"Everybody will hear you if you don't keep your voice down. Your friends found my truck and caught on that we're out here in the trees."

"And if you'd kept driving like I meant for you to... they would have followed you until it was too late to realize I was no longer there."

"Pardon me, but you didn't ask me to keep driving. What you did was apologize."

"I don't apologize."

"Well, you did to me." His voice was louder.

"Shh." She couldn't kiss him into silence this time.

It didn't matter. He took her hand, leading her away from the sounds of men tromping through the brush somewhere behind her. They ran and the sounds of the men searching for them grew fainter, but Wade kept pushing forward.

"How did you find me?" she whispered. "Ow. Hey, slow down."

"What's wrong?"

She pushed her high heels into his chest. He pushed them right back, then bent in half. Oh, Lord. He stifled her gasp when his hands touched her backside as he lifted her, with the pressure of his shoulder cutting off a lot of her air.

Hearing above the truck traffic on the nearby road grew more difficult, but voices seemed to carry. She had an unusual view behind them to see if they were being followed. No one seemed to be around.

"Um... Wade, honey?" she chastised as his fingers slid under her dress to stabilize her on his shoulder.

"Oh, pardon me." He laughed.

The thong only covered so much. Embarrassingly, he'd found a whole lot of nothing. He continued to carry her toward the open railroad tracks. No cover put them at a greater risk.

She tapped on his back. "Come on, put me down. No one's following."

"Are you sure you can walk?"

He did a deep knee bend, pulling her dress down, then smoothing it over both hips as her feet hit the ground. After all the kisses she'd laid on him, she deserved whatever teasing he dished out. The playfulness between them had been there since the very first phone call.

This was all her fault. She couldn't stop encouraging him. She slipped her shoes back on her feet, admitting two things. No matter how expensive the shoes were, they could never be worn in public again. And she didn't want to stop whatever attraction she had for this man.

"I really shouldn't have involved you in this."

"Better than paperwork." He shrugged. "No need to beat a dead horse, Therese. I'm here. I'm involved. Let's deal with it and get out of here."

They'd both been talking in a loud whisper, but noises from the trees had them shutting their mouths and running—even in heels along the train tracks. Hitting the old wood slats was much faster than trudging through the washed-out gravel, and they could avoid the risk of stepping in a hole and turning an ankle.

"We're almost at Westmoreland Road," she told him over her shoulder.

"Your friends are catching up. Will they shoot?" Wade's question was answered with a couple of rounds from a handgun.

"Head for the far trees," Wade yelled.

To hell with the shoes. She kicked them off, leaving them as they ran full out for the trees to their right. She couldn't be bothered with how much the gravel hurt her feet. If she stopped, Rushdan's men would capture her. She might survive to be taken back to the slimy pig, but Wade probably wouldn't. He'd die before he let those men take her.

That was the kind of guy he was. Honorable. Trustworthy.

"Stop whatever you're thinking and head down the tracks. We'll never make those trees," he said. "I've got this."

"How?"

"I came prepared. Just run to the right once you hit the street." He pulled his phone from his back pocket.

More shots.

The industrial area allowed them only one direction left to run. They were boxed in by the grove of trees behind and on either side businesses with eight-foot fences and razor wire on top.

Rushdan's men were too close behind them. The only direction left was the open area along the railroad tracks until they crossed Westmoreland Street. Then where?

She hit the sidewalk and turned right as Wade instructed. He stopped at the fence pole—as if that would stop a bullet—and fiddled with his phone.

"Keep moving to the intersection!" he told her.

The men following shot again. "Come on." She tugged on his elbow.

"Get going. I'm right behind you." He waved his hand holding the cell and leaned around the poll.

She was out of breath and her feet were hurting enough to make her scream, but she ran the long block to the intersection. Still half a block behind her, Wade waved her forward.

"Go on! Cross!"

The light was in her favor, so she ran…again. And kept running to the brick wall of the small convenience store. Wade received honks from the cars he darted in front of. Rushdan's men didn't follow him.

"Where to now?" She gulped air into her lungs. "Were you calling for backup or 911? Do you think anyone else did?"

"Our ride's here." He waved his phone at a sedan pulling into a parking space.

"This is a bad idea. We can't involve a ride-for-hire driver."

"It's only a short distance. Or would you rather run? Your *friends* are probably getting into their cars now."

"This is really dangerous."

He blocked her from view and tilted her face to look at him. "Do we blow your cover?" he asked in a whisper.

"Over three years of undercover work…" She hesitated.

"I don't think anyone has seen us, but we've got to go. Now." He drew her to him and gave her lips a quick kiss as if they'd known each other for years.

"Take the car and get as far away from me as possible. Leave town. Go on vacation. Let me talk my way out of this with Rushdan."

"Isn't he the one who sent these guys to take you out? You gotta let me help with this, Therese." He laced his fingers through hers and opened the car door, helping her inside.

"Evenin'," the driver said. "You going to the Westin at the Galleria mall?"

"That's right," Wade answered.

"Wait a minute. Isn't that a hotel?" She remembered his promise. And by the twinkle in his eye, so did he.

"Funny you should mention that." Wade winked.

"They're going to find out where we've gone," she told him.

"I'm counting on it. But to give us a little time…" He tapped the front seat to get the driver's attention, then showed him his credentials. "This is going to sound weird. I need you to take the long way through downtown."

"Whatever you want, but it'll cost more."

"If someone asks where you dropped us, just tell them. There's no reason to be a hero. Okay?"

"You got it. But how long of a ride are you talking?"

Wade tugged her securely into his arms and tilted her lips to his. "As long as it takes."

"Sure, man. Anything for law enforcement."

"This is insane," she whispered against his lips. "Are you seriously going to neck with me in the back seat of a rideshare car while Rushdan's men try to find us?"

"As soon as I use the credit card in my wallet, they'll know where we are. Besides…when's the last time you had some fun in the back seat?" He pulled her onto his lap and devoured her mouth until she gently pushed against his chest.

"You know we'll most likely be dead tomorrow. Since this is the last bit of pleasure either of us will ever enjoy… I'm in."

Chapter Five

"This won't work," Jack MacKinnon yelled through the phone.

"Sure it will. You're mainly angry because you'll have to work all night to make it happen. Give me some bad debt, add a couple of reprimands to my file— Okay, a couple more reprimands. It'll give me a reason to need money. I've got the setup from last year when that stuff with Megan went down."

"I think they hit you one too many times on your head. That *stuff* is when they tried to kill you. Remember how these same people were going to drop a building on top of you as your tomb?"

He rubbed his ribs. "It's hard to forget."

"This is a bad idea."

"I keep telling him that," Therese said from beside him.

"You're on speaker. She insisted on listening in," he told his partner. "I've got a hunch that you're giving in, Jack. You know it's a good idea. It's logical and if you get the finances falsified, Rushdan Reval will be completely suckered in."

"Your hunches have been close to getting us both killed, pal."

"You'll do it?"

"You two can't be serious. You're both crazy." Therese walked away from the phone, throwing up her hands and heading to the bath. "You *are* crazy, Wade. Major Clements will never go for this," Jack said.

"He will if you plead the case. What can I do? She's the woman who saved your girlfriend and me. Remember? Don't you think you owe her?"

A long, indecisive sigh from his partner filled the dead air. "You know that favor you owe me, Wade?"

"What favor?" Yeah, he knew full well what Jack meant.

"Remember when you asked me to pick a woman up from the airport. No big deal, you said. Keep her out of trouble, you said. Out of sight until I hear from you again. No big deal."

Wade took him off speaker. He knew exactly what Jack was recounting. Therese did, too, since she was the person who'd asked him to protect her friend.

Out of the blue, Therese had asked for a strange favor. After all was said and done, the Company B Rangers had discovered that Megan Harper's life had been in danger. Jack had saved her. Sure that Therese had been in trouble, Wade had searched for her, gotten caught and been beaten within an inch of his life.

"Look how good that turned out for you, Jack. You met your future wife."

Wade's occasional banter and favors for Therese had become an obsession to find her. But she'd really disappeared.

"Ha. I think it's time for me to redeem a favor from you."

"Yeah, I remember owing you a favor. But I thought you'd ask me to pay for the limo at your wedding or something." He had to dig deep in order to convince

Jack to help. Time to make the big man feel indebted. "Okay, I sort of promised I'd never mention this again. But Therese is the one who saved you from MS-13 when your dad blew your cover."

"How? I thought you said… Dammit, Wade. You never mentioned where that helicopter came from. Therese was the one who arranged it?"

"I didn't ask who it belonged to. She didn't say. I just found out she has access to privileged information. That's when I knew. Now you do, too."

"She saved my hide and then Megan's." Jack sighed again. "And yours."

Wade looked around at the closed bathroom door. "She won't admit it, but I think she's in trouble. Big trouble. She's afraid to go to the FBI or any other backup she has."

"Is she afraid of a breach?"

"Jack, why else would she have come to me?"

"Right. She trusts you. I get it. I'll get Heath onto your finances. He's going to love working all night. What kind of problem do you want? Gambling would be the easiest."

Gambling. It hit a nerve he'd kept buried for a decade. He didn't want to slip back into the familiar world. But he could to save their lives.

On their way to the hotel they'd shared a lot of kisses and a few whispers of how to convince Reval not to kill them. It was up to him—and a fake financial background—to prove he was dirty. A dirty Texas Ranger who needed quick cash and was willing to do anything for anybody. Including the man who'd ordered his death last year.

It turned his stomach, but it would work.

"Sure. Just as long as Heath can—and will—make it all go away. I'm going silent. I'm locking my stuff in the safe. Send someone to pick it up."

"Watch your back."

Wade turned his phone off. It was the best he could do.

"About that explanation..." He poked his head between the bathroom door and the frame.

Therese was under the streaming water, naked like she should be for a shower, her long hair flowing down her back. Her arms were raised to her face just enough for him to see the curve of her breast and lots of smooth skin.

"Sorry." He averted his eyes to the bottom of the towel hanging on the wall rack. "I heard the water running and expected the shower curtain. Not clear doors."

"No need to be embarrassed. I think our relationship is far beyond professional. Don't you?" She turned the interesting parts of her body toward the back wall.

He could see the outline of her legs and her beautifully shaped derriere. Had he just thought all the interesting parts were facing the other way?

"You know that I didn't mean that stuff about the hotel. Right? I'm fine sleeping in the chair." He stepped backward to give her privacy and to stop acting like an ogling lecher.

"Maybe we should talk about this in a minute? You're letting in a cold draft." She laughed at him.

"Got it. I'll order us some food."

"Or you could join me," she teased.

Against every desire he had, he managed to close the door. The first time he made love to Therese, it wouldn't be while they waited on Reval's men to take them to the second-rate crime boss. He ordered two steaks and the works, hoping that the woman he'd been kissing for the past hour wasn't a vegetarian. He didn't know a thing about her.

"Oh, man, I feel better." She was wrapped in a towel, her wet hair slicked back, and her bare arms raised to pat the long strands dry with a second towel. "I am so starved. I had to skip lunch today."

She looked at the dress, now with several tears on the sides. The towel slipped. He lost his concentration as she caught it, tugging the end back into place.

"What food did you order?" she asked, laughing as she sat on the edge of the bed next to him.

He jumped up. "We should probably keep some distance between us." He pulled his dress shirt from his shoulders and handed it to her.

How did she stay cool about being naked under that towel? A little towel that would drop from her body with a gentle tug.

"Such unusual modesty as he takes his shirt off. This coming from the guy who just necked with me for the half-hour drive." She bent her arm and hooked her long hair that was beginning to curl behind her ear.

Did she have curly hair?

"This is different," he finally got out.

"You could have fooled me. Our rideshare driver had a lot of fun watching."

God, he loved her laugh. She didn't do that enough. He turned his back, shutting his eyes tight while she put his shirt on.

"Maybe you should tell me about Reval and how he fits in with Public Exposure? Yeah, I connected those dots. Last time I saw you we just took down part of that domestic terrorism group. Is Reval working for them or vice versa?"

"You're right. We've had credible intel for quite a while—"

"The beginning, remember?" he interrupted. He wanted every piece of information she had. "Who's 'we'? And how long have you been under, working with that scumbag?"

"I'll save the real beginning for another time. Sharing this amount of the intel will probably get me fired."

"Hey, it won't matter if we're dead like you keep telling me." He wished room service would knock on the door. He wanted a beer in his hand.

"That's true. But since you've put yourself in the middle of everything, you probably should know what's going on." She covered her face with her hands, then crossed her fingers on both sides of her face with a very fake smile. "I sure hope you're a good liar, Wade Hamilton."

"I can fake it when necessary."

"Great. If you can't, we really don't stand a chance." She stood. "Turn around."

He obliged but saw an arm extend through a blue sleeve.

"All done." She wandered around the room examining fliers and hotel info, straightened the lamp and discovered robes in the closet. A robe she didn't put on until room service arrived.

When the robe was safely around her body, relief washed over him along with thc smcll of food. His stomach growled as he signed for the feast. They settled on either side of the bed with two trays set between them.

"Back to our story," he urged. "From the beginning."

"I was at the police academy in San Antonio. I guess I fit the profile of someone the FBI needed. Honestly, I don't know why they chose me over anyone else," Therese said between bites.

"Is that where you met Jack's girlfriend, Megan?"

"Yes. Everyone was told that I was forced to drop out after cheating or something. The Bureau used that when Rushdan—or anyone else—checked out my background."

He knew that partly from Megan, partly because it was so prominent in any report on her that he'd initiated. "So you went to work for the FBI?"

"They wanted to discover where Rushdan's money came from and who his contacts were."

"Let me guess, a little drug running, real estate fraud, night clubs, prostitution and money laundering."

"You did your homework." She clapped softly.

"I have a tendency to obsess over people who try to kill me." Was it too soon to say he'd actually been looking for her?

"Did your research mention that Rushdan Reval has been brokering illegal deals? I never discovered how he got into it. But last year, when his real estate fraud fell apart, he began contact with Public Exposure."

"That's how a low-level fraud group got into the domestic terrorism business?"

"When Megan and Jack stumbled on Rushdan's real estate fraud, it stalled my involvement. At least with his Dallas group. I mainly played go-between on the phone with several of his *business* representatives in San Antonio."

"That's stating it nicely."

"True." She stuffed a yeast roll in her mouth, swishing it down with a cola—not the beer.

"Let me guess… Enter FBI agent Kendall Barlow and her husband Texas Ranger Heath Murray, investigating claims about Public Exposure's fraud."

She pointed at him. "Yes! Bonus points for the man without a shirt. They really are a good team. Almost too good, since they practically dismantled the Brantley Lourdes end of this thing."

"Brantley Lourdes. Isn't he the guy in charge of Public Exposure? And what do you mean *almost*? We retrieved the algorithm, obtained confessions and nothing happened after all the threats that Dallas citizens would die."

"That's the problem. Rushdan just brokered the deal for Public Exposure. He only had a copy. Someone else developed the algorithm. Sources have verified that he's improved it and bidding for the improved version has begun. We're no longer certain what the algorithm is capable of."

"Son of a biscuit eater!" He picked up his roll. "Lourdes wouldn't tell you who created it? I thought this case was wrapped up. I haven't seen any alerts from local, state or national authorities. Why are your bosses being so secretive?"

"Do you really not know after one of the FBI's Dallas agents was caught in the middle of this?"

"I get it. There might be another traitor around. But you trust me, right? I could have been helping discover who Reval plans to sell to."

"I've already explained why working with you wasn't possible. Besides that information isn't what we're after. We need to discover what it does now. In addition to capturing the geeks who designed an algorithm that can take down a city's electrical grid."

"Every city's worst nightmare."

"Country's worst nightmare. I've been attempting to get back in Rushdan's good graces. He's accused me of helping you escape, but he seems to overlook it."

"Why's that?"

"Maybe he's hoping I'll hang myself and he won't have to give the order to get rid of me. Like other people I won't name..." Therese reached over the tray and brushed crumbs from the corner of his mouth, seductively raising an eyebrow in his direction "...he's sort of sweet on me."

Man alive, he no longer wanted to talk about Rushdan

Reval or the FBI or algorithms that could bring down cities or countries. At her touch, he just wanted to pull her to the bed and finish a different discussion.

"You know, it's not too late for you to go back to your regular duties as a Texas Ranger. I can clean this up."

"No. We talked about this." He stood, removing the remnants of dinner to the desk. "I'm going with you and we'll find the threat. I've spoken with Jack. I'll call back. Who should he speak with at the FBI to confirm my involvement?"

"Steve Woods. He's the only person I can trust there who knows about the threat. He's working with Homeland and only providing 'as needed' info to them."

"You don't trust very easily, do you?"

"No," she answered with a whisper. "Rushdan will have a hard time believing a big ol' Texas Ranger is willing to get his hands dirty. Why is that exactly?"

"Money. It's always about money."

"We'll have to convince him you need a lot…and fast."

"Right. Heath will be set before Reval looks into my background." He pushed down the old feelings from his youth. Fright had no place here. He needed confidence and arrogance. "Think I have time for a shower before our location is discovered?"

"Probably. I think I'll try to catch some sleep. After they get here, it might be rough." She draped the robe across the end of the bed, then pulled back the covers. "Thank you."

"For what?" he asked from the bathroom door.

The urge to bring her close was overwhelming. His knuckles turned white as he gripped the door trim and tried to keep himself there instead of at her side. She smiled—completely sexy in his blue shirt that looked better on her than him. That was all she did, but he understood.

He took a quick shower, thinking about the impossible situation the FBI and Homeland had placed on her shoulders. Therese needed help whether anyone admitted it or not.

Her eyes were closed when he locked his phone, gun and creds inside the safe. He called Jack from the hotel line—not only to check in, but to tell him the combination so he could send one of the guys to grab his things.

He scrambled back into his jeans since he knew that at some point a gun would be aimed and they'd be taken to Reval's headquarters. Therese shivered in her sleep. He smoothed the covers and she backed her body close to his. They lay in each other's arms, fitfully resting. He woke with every movement and could tell that she hadn't fallen into a deep sleep, either. He kept her close, whispering again what he would eventually do.

Around four in the morning, Reval's men arrived for the next phase of their undertaking. It was going to be a very long day.

Chapter Six

Rushdan's men used a key to enter the hotel room. Wade covered Therese with the robe as the door burst open, so he hadn't been taken by surprise.

He'd held on to her body until they were yanked apart and his hands tied behind his back, angled to grab her robe before she was shoved through the door.

Therese had never worked with a partner and oddly enjoyed the thought of her first being this tall Texas Ranger. She liked him. A lot.

All those sexy words he'd whispered in her ear as she'd tried to go to sleep still had her body burning. She hadn't dare tell him she wanted the same. She wouldn't have held back. If they survived, being with Wade would be a genuine pleasure.

But one that would wait.

It was infuriating not to be tied up like Wade, not to be considered a threat. But she'd worked hard over the last years not to reveal her strength or quickness to these men. She walked freely as they were taken down the service elevator and escorted into the back of an SUV.

Once they were at Rushdan's new office, one of his hired goons punched Wade hard enough to make him lose his breath. "That was for the six months I served in the county jail."

What had she done by involving Wade? How could she have let her judgment lapse so badly not once but several times? She'd completely lost her mind and would probably lose her job for disclosing everything about her undercover assignment.

But worse…if they beat Wade or tortured him? Would she be able to hold her tongue?

"Just take us to Rushdan," she instructed, stepping in front of Wade. "If you touch my boyfriend again, I guarantee you won't be around tomorrow to regret it."

Therese held her breath, preparing for the punch that never came—not to her and not a second one to Wade, either. Both of them knew the risks. Talking his way into the Reval organization was a long shot. They were both flanked by two men who yanked them through rooms and eventually stood them in front of Rushdan Reval.

"Therese, my darling. Come, let me see you. Untie our guest." Reval instructed his men. "Are you barbarians or something just as awful?"

The goons released her arms when she gave them a shrug. She approached Reval's desk wearing the robe over Wade's shirt, which covered her skimpy underwear.

"Come closer. You know what I want." The pig tugged at the belt at her waist, inching her closer to his chair. She could see his hope of anticipation that she'd let the robe fall open. She dug her fingers into the cotton sides, barely keeping it closed.

Somehow she managed to get into character, the part she played of a dingy woman who was slightly incompetent. The character that all these men thought so little about that they didn't bother to tie her hands.

Tonight was different. Wade watched, as well. His strength could be felt across the room. She saw the worry on the men's faces. Gritting her teeth, she forced herself to tolerate Rushdan as he unbuttoned the top two buttons of the dark blue dress shirt. He skimmed the back of his fingers against her cleavage to cop a filthy feel. She desperately wanted to slap his hands away from her, but she took it.

Just like always.

The men gripping Wade attempted to hold him, but he broke free. He yanked her back to his arms just before the robe fell open.

"So it's true. Our ranger friend has a thing for you. After all this time of you saying no to me, you said yes to someone who can put you behind bars? Do you think he really cares for you?"

"He got me out of jail last year."

"So you finally admit that you had someone with pull to help you. Why not just tell me the multiple times I've asked?"

"He said it was a secret, Rushy, baby. And you told me secrets were important," she sounded more like the confused ditz they were used to. "I told you I was meeting someone last night and you had me followed. I don't understand what I did wrong."

"They ran." The bigger-than-big man tsked at them.

"Only after they began shooting at us," Wade threw out.

"I didn't ask you, ranger boy." Rushdan dug his fingernail into his mouth, picking food from his teeth, then gestured as if shooing a fly. "Take him from my sight while I decide what to do with him. Did you think to bring their clothes?"

"Rushdan, baby." Therese turned and took steps back to her "boss," letting the robe fall open, and purposely tugging the shirt to where it left little to the pig's imagination. "I've been working on this guy for months. I thought you could use his help."

All the men in the room could barely raise their eyes. She had them mesmerized and hoping the shirt would fall completely open. Rushdan had the best seat.

The pig.

"I spent nearly six months in that filthy cell, wearing orange." He shuddered. "Why would you think you could bring your pet in here for me to adopt? I have no use for a Texas Ranger. He can't do anything for me. Even if I thought he really would." Rushdan tried for a whimsical, light voice, but it was countered by the evil in his eyes.

"You're right. I didn't believe Wade at first, either. Now I mainly want the money he owes me." She leaned forward to whisper. Rushdan bent to look down her shirt. "He has a gambling problem, baby. You can use that against him," she suggested.

"Therese." Once again Wade tugged on her arm to pull her to his side. "I can speak for myself."

"Not if he won't listen, sugar."

"Aww, how sweet. The two lovebirds are fighting," Rushdan said.

"We aren't fighting." Wade buttoned the shirt to cover her cleavage. She spun around while he kept his hands on her shoulders.

"I do so enjoy your little shows, Therese. Too bad it seems your champion has ended this one." He nodded to his men. "I'm busy. Go put them somewhere until I'm not."

"But," she began again.

"By the way, I love the boots. Sal, remind me I need to get me some real Texas boots." He pointed at Wade's Western footwear.

"Yes, sir." Sal pushed at them with a gun.

Rushdan looked at the men in the room. "I said put them somewhere until I can think up an appropriate punishment."

Therese forced Wade to let go of her. "Really, Rushdan. I do a good job for you. Even while you were gone I ran the San Antonio clubs like you wanted. Wade is a fun time, but you know I'm loyal to you. I really thought we could use his connections to widen our prospects."

"Why would you think that?" Rushdan said, smacking his lips after another bite of breakfast. "Or should I ask why you try to think at all?"

"I thought I could help."

"Therese, you are such a nice-looking broad. But why do you bother?" Rushdan backhanded her, sending her stumbling barefoot against Wade.

She quickly turned around and stopped the ranger from roaring forward. "I warned you about this, Wade," she whispered. "Rushdan is always right and never wrong."

"I can't let him—"

She locked both his hands with hers. But he still managed to swoosh her around and protect her, absorbing Rushdan's next blow across his back.

"I need the money," Wade managed after a couple of seconds. "I admit that. Thing is, Texas Rangers are squeaky clean, man. No one thinks of us as being dishonest. It doesn't happen. You're throwing something special away here, Reval. I'm a one-of-a kind opportunity. Whatever you think up, I can do."

"Wait, wait, wait," Therese said as Sal began pushing them from the room. "Please listen. He can get inside places even the cops you own can't get into. Wade literally works with every agency. Right?"

"All right. Wait. Can you really get inside every building or restricted area?"

Yes! They'd found a reason Wade was unique.

"Sure. No problem." Wade shrugged.

"How do I know this isn't just a very good acting job?" Rushdan swiveled his huge body to sit in his chair. His house slippers slid across the marble floor.

Only the best for Rushdan Reval.

Wade slipped his arm around her waist. "I can't help it. No way can I walk away from this lady. I'm crazy about her. Thing is, she doesn't come cheap. I need money, Reval. If I don't work for you, I'll be working for someone else to get it."

Oh, God, he was about to kiss her. She recognized that smoldering longing in his eyes. How in the world could he do that with threats and guns hanging over them?

"This just might work, but what type of collateral can you give me?" Her enemy interrupted.

"Collateral, sir?"

"Aren't you quaint. *Sir?*" Rushdan looked around at his men. "Listen to that, he called me *sir* and actually means it. Yes, collateral. You don't think I'm going to invest in you so you can steal from me when you're entrusted with something valuable, do you? I don't work that way."

"Me," she answered for Wade. "I'll be his collateral."

"Isn't that sweet." Rushdan used his pinky to pick something from his teeth again, making the nice words turn sour. "Unfortunately Therese, you're already mine. Neither important nor valuable."

"She is to me. I love her."

The words struck something deep inside her. Even

knowing they were said in order to save their lives. Coming from his lips after the beautiful night in the hotel… she realized just how much she wanted them to be true.

Chapter Seven

"Take them somewhere." Rushdan shooed his crew away like they were flies. The thud of someone being shoved reminded him to say, "And no punching. At least not yet. Pretty boy might have a job to do."

He caught Sal's look, which certainly questioned his temporary decision. He hated anyone questioning him. What was the harm of considering the ranger's proposition? If he didn't, he'd lose Therese, too.

One person could give him the confirmation he needed. Andrew was faster with a computer than Rushdan was at making money. He silently laughed at his own joke and picked up his normal phone. Then dialed the number on the hidden cell phone in his desk.

The key to everything was right there in plain sight for anyone who wanted to see it. But they wouldn't know what it was and they wouldn't know what to say even if they found a reason to search.

"Money is a pitiless master but a zealous servant." The code quote seemed both stupid and cryptic.

"P.T. Barnum," the voice answered. "Andrew, it's for you," the voice called from a distance a few seconds later.

He looked around the new office, so close in style to his last. A shame he'd blown up the previous one. All because that badass ranger had brought others to try and take him down. Perhaps this was a mistake and he should just kill him and be done with it.

Therese would need to die, too.

He tapped on the fish tank full of smaller versions of the inhabitants of the one he'd had last year. They'd gain in size, just like his bank roll would after this deal was brokered. The biggest deal of his life.

"Yeah?" Andrew finally said.

"This is Rushdan Reval. I need information on Wade Hamilton. He's a Texas Ranger in Dallas." Rushdan waited for some type of acknowledgment.

"Who is this? JK, I mean…just kidding, Reval. What did you want?" Andrew asked.

"I need information. Today."

"Yeah, on a Texas Ranger. You said that. Why are you bothering, Reval? Does it have anything to do with our deal?"

"As a matter of fact, I either need to kill him or I can use him to help facilitate the exchange."

"I'll get back to you."

The phone went dead. "Thank you, I look forward to hearing from you," he said into the phone, refusing to let anyone working for him know that someone had hung up on him.

Andrew was a rude young man who continued to call him by his last name. No matter how many times he insisted on being called Rushdan.

"What now?" Sal asked. "I locked them in the sixth-floor storage room."

"Do you have surveillance in that room?"

"That's not up and running yet, boss."

"Dammit, Sal, make that a priority. I want to know if anyone is following our two guests or approaching our building."

"You got it, boss."

"Did anyone pick up his vehicle?"

"Nope."

Rushdan tapped on the glass. He didn't allow anyone else to bother his fish that way, but he loved it. They all swam toward him, expecting food.

"I guess a little more won't hurt you," he said to his fish. "Did you keep someone at the hotel room?"

"No. Want me to send someone back?"

"Why do I surround myself with idiots?"

The exception was Therese. Smart. Competent. Reliable. Even though she pretended to be all too stupid around his men. She had all the qualities that made him question why she worked for him. Even if she did try to hide behind the dumb broad persona she portrayed. He didn't understand why she played that part. It didn't make sense. And that was exactly the reason his men had been following her tonight.

He had suspicions. Too many coincidences for his peace of mind.

If he dwelled on it or questioned her motives too much, he might let his paranoia get rid of her. But he wanted her in every way.

He should kill the ranger and be done with that specific problem. Sal and others had wanted him to deal with Therese after the Public Exposure episode but he'd ignored them.

The problem with Therese… She was good with the details. He needed her back in the fold and she might leave if anything happened to her "boyfriend."

"Oh, well," he mumbled to the blue fish with dots. "I shall call you Dotty."

If Wade Hamilton hadn't stuck his nose where it didn't

belong last year, Rushdan would have his lovely office building, and the program would be complete for the new buyers. The money he would rake in from this deal would easily make up for the past six months of being shut down.

If he had a way to keep the ranger under his control, to assure that he'd behave, then he'd control Therese at the same time.

He tapped on the fish tank glass again. A beautiful blue-and-pink wrasse came to his finger. The blue reminded him of Therese's eyes. He'd have to ask her to streak that dark brown hair of hers pink. That would be interesting…very interesting.

Perhaps keeping the ranger alive could get him benefits of a different, more intimate nature with the smart beauty. Even if it didn't, having someone to offer his new clients assistance with their government endeavors would only help the real operation get up and running again. An inside man always paid off.

"Yes," he answered his beeping cell.

"Your ranger is in debt up to his eyeballs," Andrew said without any greeting. "That should be enough for your purposes. But I went a little deeper, just to make sure. Back to a sealed court case when he was fifteen. Seems he had a very big bad gambler dude for a daddy."

"Is he still alive?"

"Naw. Died in prison. But get why he was in the pen. The dude pulled the trigger on a Texas Ranger when a scam went south."

Blackmail. How convenient.

"Send me details. Everything."

"Look, Reval. My boss overheard the convo. Is the date firm yet?"

"Definitely. I'll have details first thing in the morning. It seems I have a new knight to insert into the game."

"Info is on its way. Did I mention my boss is getting impatient?"

And once again, Andrew disconnected without a proper goodbye, taking him by surprise. It didn't matter since he was alone. Sal had backed out of the room at his earlier irritation. A few arrangements and he'd get his gambling ranger involved so deep that the success of the deal would be guaranteed.

Chapter Eight

One dim yellow light in the back ceiling gave the small room an eerie feel. She sat next to Wade on the unfinished floor. At least it was cool against her bare legs. She pulled the belt on the robe tight again. Thank God Wade had given her his shirt or she might be even more exposed.

"Who has a storage closet that's completely empty?" she asked to break the silence.

"Reval seems to like 'em," Wade said quietly. "I was locked in one just like this."

"Oh, right. Sorry. That's where they kept you in the building that exploded."

"Don't forget I nearly exploded with it." He looped his fingers through hers, drawing her hand to his lips. "I should have said thanks as soon as I saw you again. You know…for getting me rescued."

"Are you really angry about me not calling you?"

"Did behaving like a hurt kid give me away?"

"Sort of." She patted his thigh like they'd been together for months, not hours. "So how do we get out of here?"

The electrical charge she associated with him filled the air as he leaned close enough to kiss her. His warm breath shifted to her neck and close to her ear. "We don't. Remember? We want to be right where we are."

"Don't we need a backup plan or something?"

"Shh." He placed a finger across her lips. "Your boss might be listening."

"I feel like we're wasting time," she whispered back, as close to his ear as he'd been to hers.

"I know a lot of things we can do in the dark."

His whisper sent one of those delicious tingles down her spine, landing in all the right spots.

"You already passed on that, remember?"

"Postponed," he breathed intimately across the top of her ear.

One word of encouragement from him and she melted in anticipation. About to give in, she came to her senses when two unknown somebodies walked past the door. "You're right. They may be watching us. I know surveillance and security increased since you brought the building down. Literally."

"To be fair, I was in no shape to destroy anything." Wade twisted her hair around his finger, trapping her ear close to his face.

"Never mind, you know exactly what I mean." Breathy words escaped and a gasp of expectation as his lips passed across hers once more.

"As a matter of fact, I do," he said louder, leaning away from her.

"Don't sound so surprised." She cut an anxious giggle short, changing it to a worried tap on his shoulder. *Why am I more nervous with him than the criminal I work for?*

"I am surprised."

"Why? This happens when two people know each other. It's natural."

He laughed so hard he began to choke, coughing into his hand like a man with asthma.

"Why is that so funny?" she asked before she laughed with him.

"Therese, we don't know each other." He shook his head, laughing more. "We have this thing—believe me, it's an attractive thing and I like it. But I don't know if anything about you is even real."

God, he was right. Wade Hamilton was absolutely right. *He* didn't know her, but she'd kept tabs on him, researched him, knew a lot about him.

Not like a stalker or anything—or at least that was what she told herself. But every once in a while she'd see where he was or what he'd been working on. He did good work. He was a good man. The one-sided relationship she'd forged was the main reason she trusted him.

"What do you want to know?" she blurted into the darkness, unafraid of who might hear.

"They're probably listening," he reminded her. "Why not pass the time another way?"

His hand slid around her back, circling her waist, scooting her even closer to him. He didn't have to hit her over the head with the fact that he was attracted. But her real emotions got the best of her and crept through. She wanted a genuine relationship with him. Not a one-sided almost-stalker thing.

"There's no telling how long we'll be left here," she said, trying to play it cool. A real relationship. So that involved talking and not just necking as soon as they were alone. Right?

"To be honest, sitting in the dark next to you—practically naked like you are—isn't that bad." He put space between their hips. "It's not the worst situation I've ever been caught in. This doesn't make the top ten."

She bit back a laugh. “I don’t know what possessed me to involve you.”

“It’s okay. Everybody panics occasionally.” He rubbed the back of his neck, then his side.

“Not me.”

“I’m not sure I believe you—” He slid a hand across her bare leg. “Instead of debating the ways people react to stress…why don’t we just get back to what we can do in a dark room?”

Of all the sexy voices in the world, the owner of the one that affected her in the best way possible flirted with her. In a closet. In a dire situation where they may very well be killed. He bent his head and gave her a perfect kiss. Just enough pressure to suggest to her lips he didn’t want to stop. But he did.

“I guess I deserve that after—”

His lips connected again. When they both were breathing extra fast he paused. “After all the teasing?”

“Teasing is what someone does who has no intention of following through,” she pointed out.

Both of his strong arms wrapped around her and pulled her across his lap. “I have to say this is the most unusual date I’ve been on.”

“Do you go on many?” She knew the answer.

After checking the bars for her, he sat on the same stool every Friday night for hours. She’d been so tempted to meet him there and talk. Deep down she’d known it would end like this. Okay, not necessarily sitting on a concrete floor as hostages. But definitely sitting on his lap…somewhere.

“I’ve been doing a lot of late night filing. It’s kept me busy.”

Huh? Oh, right, they’d been talking about his dating life. She let a nail wander across his collarbone and leaned forward to whisper in *his* ear.

"If we can't really do anything or make *plans*, let's get to know each other for real. Tell me one truth about yourself."

"Like…?"

"Your choice. It can be anything as long as it's the absolute truth," she continued whispering.

"Absolute?" he whispered back.

"No sugarcoating or stretching to make it fit first-date parameters."

He tapped her just above her heart. "Okay, but you go first."

"I hate alarm clocks."

"Doesn't count." He shook his head. "Everybody hates alarm clocks. Getting up in the morning isn't my favorite thing, either."

"Point taken." It had to be more intimate, something she wouldn't share with others. It had been so long since she shared something real. "I love running. Physical training. Give me a long path with no one else around and I'm in heaven. Your turn."

She tapped his knee next to her, afraid to glance directly at him and see an "are you serious?" look on his face. It hadn't been that intimate a gesture. His knee was covered with worn blue denim. Dragging her finger across his chest…*that* was intimate. Kissing him, sitting on his lap…intimate.

So why did she finally feel naked and vulnerable?

Dangerous territory.

She needed a distraction and fingered the strong black rope braided around Wade's left wrist, holding his watch. "I've always wondered about this strange watchband."

"Always?"

"You know what I mean."

She'd noticed it six weeks ago when he'd seen her at the FBI bust. But recognized it from when they'd first met. It wasn't the right time or place to remind him of that meeting. He'd definitely think she was a stalker. Shoot, she was having to convince herself she wasn't.

"I began wearing it again full-time after my capture last year. It's a little insurance policy. It might come in handy one day. Your turn."

"Oh no. It's still round one. That is definitely the same level as my alarm clock and totally not intimate."

"I have a better idea. Let's warm up a little."

One-handedly he unbuttoned the top two buttons of her borrowed shirt, causing her to shiver. Still sorting the emotion shooting through her, she forced herself to return to their lighthearted flirting. "So your motive is purely to get me warm?"

"Warm is good," he teased, winking before his lips captured hers again.

Kissing him was a little bit of heaven.

He behaved, keeping his hands in place, cupping her shoulder with his fingers to entice her to get closer. She tried to be careful not to sweep them up to the next level of desire—which would have been easy to do anywhere else. But he was quickly warming her inside and out. An unshaven cheek tickled a little before he abruptly brought his face away.

The bright light flooded the room when she opened her eyes. Wade quickly helped her to her feet and tucked her close to his side before walking through the hallway to meet Rushdan.

"Well, well, well." Rushdan smiled. "Welcome to the

dark side, Ranger Wade." As he looked at their hands and snickered at Wade's obvious protectiveness.

"You came to a decision?" she asked, knowing the answer.

He splayed his hands and shrugged.

"Come on, Rushy, honey. If you intended to kill us, you would never have set eyes on us again." She turned to Wade. "He's sort of squeamish that way."

Wade cleared his throat, but his lips curved in the beginnings of a smile. "What do you want me to do?" he asked, dropping both his head and his voice, then covering his face with his hand.

Rushdan might actually believe the whole pensive act. But that was all it was with Wade…just an act. He cleared his throat several times like he had after laughing himself into a coughing fit.

"Let's chat while Sal retrieves your first assignment." Rushdan placed his hand on Wade's shoulder.

The ranger stood taller, Rushdan's hand slid down and soon returned to his pocket. Wade continued to hold her hand. She yanked on it, hoping to remind him that Rushdan Reval was in charge. And that they wanted him to be.

If Wade continued to tower over the little fat man, it didn't matter what Wade *might* be able to do for him. When Wade didn't react, she squeezed a little harder and thrust her shoulder into his ribs.

"Rushdan, why not just tell us what you need us to do? Why all the drama and suspense?" she asked.

"Oh, allow me to have a little fun, darling Therese. And you should know by now I never discuss business with witnesses. Sal will inform you of where Texas Ranger man is going and what he'll need to do."

"You mean where *we're* going." She pointed to Wade

and then herself. "I go where he goes. What do we need to do? And by when?"

"Today, my darling Therese."

"So it's last-minute, not well planned and no big deal if it goes wrong." She tapped one finger on the back of Wade's hand, hoping he got the message to let her go.

No luck. He squeezed her hand but didn't release it.

Finding and stopping the terrorists—her real assignment—was probably the most important thing she'd ever done. But keeping Wade alive ran a close second.

"Darling, this will be so easy for your boyfriend. It seems he has a very sordid past. At least in his youth. It's admirable that he turned his occupation around to work for him. Using his instinct and certain…skills." Her undercover employer stared again at their hands, fingers laced together.

"Do us all a favor, Rushdan, and stop talking in riddles. We already know Wade has a gambling problem."

"Yes, but do you know about his father?"

"Those records are sealed," Wade said, squeezing her hand tighter.

It was his cover. He didn't have to give her any sign. Had she worried about his ability to act before? Wade was a statue, stiff and unmoving. His eyes were hard like he wanted to rip Rushdan's head off.

"Dear, dear lover boy," Rushdan continued. "Everything can be found if you know how to look."

"I haven't run a game in years. I wouldn't know where to begin," Wade told him.

"Game?" she asked, trying to keep up.

"That's the beauty of today. It's waiting for you. All put together…just waiting." Rushdan clapped his hands together with excitement. "Give yourself credit. You know your way around a track. Who to look for. Where to look. This will be second nature for you."

"What's Rushdan talking about?" she asked, playing her part. "What records were sealed?"

"Mine. My childhood and teen years were filled by feeding my dad's gambling addiction." Wade rubbed his forehead with his free hand. "That is, until we were caught."

"You were in jail?" She heard the amazement in her voice. Not disappointment…more like wonder.

Why would she feel a kinship with him? They barely knew each other. Wait. They didn't know each other at all. And this was a perfect example. He was cute and had been helpful. And somehow she felt closer knowing he had more flaws than just following a hunch and jumping into situations.

Rushdan practically giggled like a girl. "Tell her all of it. Knock all the stars from her eyes."

It wouldn't help. She knew what Rushdan attempted to do. Crime boss Reval wouldn't ever make her his, no matter what she thought of Wade or what he shared from his past. She tucked herself closer into her ranger's side, more comfortable there by the minute.

She'd assumed Wade was an honorable man because of his occupation. But no modern Texas Ranger had been accused of something like this. They were the keepers of law.

"You look betrayed, my darling. Did you think you were the first to lead this one—" he gestured as if dusting Wade's chest "—off the righteous path?"

Rushdan laughed, dabbing at the corner of his eyes as if tearing up.

"Aw, that's sweet. You were a delinquent, Wade."

She rested her head on his arm. "How perfect. Where were you—"

"You've got more skills than I gave you credit," Wade said, finally dropping her hand, circling her waist instead. He hid the surprise of his past being revealed or kept a poker face for another reason.

Oh, Lord. She'd fallen for the fake background his partner had created. She should have known immediately that this man wouldn't have had a gambler for a father.

"That's enough reminiscing about sordid youths," Rushdan commanded. "We need this done quickly. Sal will give you the instructions and will be there to capture it all on video."

"Blackmail?" she asked.

"Insurance policy," Rushdan answered sharply.

"And Sal has all the details? Details that I had nothing to do with." She faced Rushdan straight on, keeping Wade's hand plastered across her stomach. "When are you going to accept me back?"

"If you weren't back, my darling, you wouldn't be in my building." Rushdan's voice held a menacing threat as he swept the bottom of her chin with his pointer finger. "Perk up, Ranger Wade. This should be old hat for you if you remember the racetrack. You do, don't you?"

Wade shrugged. She didn't know if that meant no, yes, or a big fat he-had-no-clue.

Rushdan sped up his short-legged steps and grabbed her upper arm as he began to pass, spinning her to face him. "This money is important, Therese. Don't screw it up." His anger literally spit through the gap in his front teeth.

Chapter Nine

Wade caught Therese as her "boss" thrust her away. Sal tried to grab her, but Wade stepped between them, blocking his reach. A leather bag hit the top of his boots.

"Everything's inside. Cash, names, bets and payoffs." Sal didn't appear happy at the change of events. "Take the back exit." He glared at Wade before taking a long stare down Therese's robe. "You aren't decent enough for the front."

He drew his arm back ready to throw a punch but stopped himself. Therese stared at his chest, which quickly rose and fell as she tugged a little to get him headed in the right direction. He'd almost lost it from the disgusting look Reval's right-hand man had sent toward Therese.

Dressed like they'd gotten thrown out of a cheap hotel—no money of their own or phones—they watched Sal draw the door closed. "Remember we're watching the whole thing," Sal said through the thick steel.

"No ride?" Wade unzipped the bag, revealing stacks of cash. "Do they expect us to walk to Lone Star Park?"

"We'll have a ride in a few minutes." She patted his chest with her palm.

Loving the feel of her hand sliding up and around his neck, he didn't wait for her to pull his lips down. He didn't mind kissing her at any time. But he did arch an eyebrow, questioning her timing.

"I could get used to this." He really could.

"You're so cute." She darted her eyes up and to the side of the building. He found the surveillance camera. Right. She was still acting.

"Cute? Not sure anyone's called me that since junior high." He winked and scooped up the bag of cash. "About that ride…"

"It'll require a little walking. At least it's eventually a sidewalk." She led the way out of the alley to a major street, then stepped into a large field.

"The building that looks like a bird's nest…that's the Irving Convention Center? Reval set up shop in Las Colinas. I hope you don't mind waiting a bit to get back to an open restaurant or fast-food joint."

"I think Sal will send a car. And if not, there's a hotel only ten minutes up the street." She pointed south toward the lake. "He's ultimately responsible for that bag you're carrying. I don't think he'll let us out of his sight for long."

To avoid parts of the dirt path, Therese jumped onto the curb occasionally. The late June sun hadn't heated the day completely but probably had made the pavement hot, so she couldn't use the street.

"You were pretty good back there," he said, shifting the bag to rest on his bare back. "Watch out for the broken beer bottles."

"Got it." She sidestepped onto the street, picking her feet up faster.

He could offer to carry her to the hotel, but he didn't think she'd go for it. She hadn't liked him throwing her over his shoulder last night.

He kept searching, but no cars were heading their direction—either from Reval's building or a Company B Ranger. He knew Jack or one of the men had followed them from the hotel. But they would keep out of sight until they were certain no one followed. That meant out of view from the building, leaving them a long walk.

Therese detoured into the street again, hopping from one foot to the other.

"Sure you don't want me to carry you?"

"Did you ask?" She shook her head. "But no thanks. Keeping the robe closed while I'm walking is a challenge. Besides, I think you explored my backside enough last night."

She laughed. He smiled, keeping an eye open for his team. It went without saying that they were close. Jack wouldn't have it any other way. So they were around here somewhere.

"Tell me about Reval." He needed to know more. "Not the paper version. What have you learned about him? Was today a normal reaction? Did he look desperate?"

"You want to know if he'd normally give us a bag of cash?" She fast-walked a little down the street, avoiding more broken glass, rocks and trash.

"Exactly."

Another hundred yards and the apartments would block anyone watching from Reval's building. They hit the sidewalk and Therese winced, popping her feet up and down off the hot concrete. Wade scooped her up in his arms to get her under some shade a bit farther.

She kissed his cheek, not objecting to being carried. "Short answer…yes. Everything he's done in the past couple of days is within his character. And I promise you, Sal isn't far away. By now, he's in front of us somewhere, just waiting and watching."

"Like at the hotel."

"Probably." She locked her arms around his neck.

"Damn."

"Tell me what I'm missing, please."

Years of approaching vehicles as a highway patrolman had him searching between cars and behind the tiny things considered trees that they passed.

"Let's put the questions on hold a minute." He set her on the manicured grass of the apartment buildings along the road leading to the hotel. He pointed to the bag of money, shook his head, then covered her lips with his finger.

Therese pulled the robe tighter around her body, knelt and helped him look through the entire bag for a listening or tracking device. She also blocked their search from a couple of cars passing by.

"Looks like it's all clear. I'm pretty sure that Jack's at the hotel. At least, I would be there."

"How would he have known—" She put up a hand, realization plainly dawning on her face. "He followed us. That was risky. Why didn't you tell me?"

She lifted the gym bag and took off back to the main road. Wade caught her free arm, spinning her back to face him. The force caught her off balance and she fell into his chest. He slid the bag's strap off her shoulder and onto his own.

"It'll be okay. Trust me." He planted a quick kiss on her lips, receiving a small response. "My partners and I are good. Jack won't do anything to jeopardize putting Rushdan Reval back in jail. For good."

"I don't see Sal," she said.

"It doesn't mean you're wrong." He didn't miss that she hadn't said she trusted him.

Not a lot of vehicles went up and down the street, but he recognized one that pulled into the area reserved for those not staying long. Major Clements was one of the few Company B Rangers who actually drove a car instead of a truck.

He started toward the hotel entrance, but a strong tug on his arm pulled him in another direction.

"Maybe we shouldn't walk in through the *front* door?" Therese laced her fingers through his, heading across the street and into the hotel's parking garage.

She squeezed herself between the oak tree and hedge, waiting for him on the other side. He followed, stepped down from the retaining wall and into the coolness of the covered garage.

He lifted her down, not embarrassed that he drew her body close, wanting the athletic suppleness of her next to him as she slid to reach the concrete.

Her hands remained at his shoulders as she slightly tilted her gorgeous face up to his. "If we go to the lakeside, I think we can sneak over the fence and look like we're on our way to the hotel pool."

"Good idea."

They stayed put, not going where they needed to be. Not looking to see who was around or if anyone followed. It had been a long time since he'd stared into the eyes of a beautiful woman. An equally long time since he'd admired one so completely. Longer than both of those put together since he'd *wanted* to do either.

And whose fault was that?

"Not mine."

"Do all the ideas need to be yours?"

Dammit. The question had been so loud in his head that he'd answered out loud. "Nothing. We should probably get going."

The unbelievable sexual tension passed from his head

but left his knees slightly wobbly. Right up to the point he heard the tires squealing on an upper garage floor.

"If it's Sal, we should just wait here."

"Not sure that's a great idea," he answered, securing the gym bag's shoulder strap across his body.

Therese stepped in front of him, stop-signing his chest for him to quit or give up. "Even if your friends are inside, there's no way for us to explain how they might help us. Rushdan told Sal to give us a ride. He *is* coming and will expect us to be exactly like this, with no money, no cells and basically no clothing."

"And if he finds anything different, he'll be suspicious," he agreed.

"Basically he has permission to kill us and let Rushdan move forward with other plans."

"About those plans—" Wade saw movement out of the corner of his eye at the staircase. A silver-haired man resembling Major Clements.

"He hasn't told me a thing. That's why I risked following him last night," she said.

"Then it's agreed. We stay put and see who's about to drive around the corner any second." He raised his voice so his boss could hear, then tried to angle Therese behind him, but she wouldn't have it.

"I can take care of myself, Ranger."

"I've noticed that."

The car approaching from the upper floor could be a hotel patron, security, his partner or Reval's man, Sal.

"That's him," Therese said, stepping into the open. "Things just got a little bit easier."

Wade didn't have a chance to ask how.

Sal was already next to them, smoke curling from his open window. "Took you long enough. I ran out of cigarettes waiting on you."

"Then maybe you should have given us a ride at Rushdan's office," Therese said before opening the door and scooting across the seat.

"You know I had to make sure your new boyfriend here wasn't being followed."

"And?" Therese asked.

Sal was silent as he inhaled his last drag on the butt, then threw it out the window.

"And nothing." Wade shoved the money bag between his feet. "Just like I said."

Sal drove too fast out the parking garage and away from the hotel.

At least nothing Sal could spot.

Major Clements dipped his head, hiding his face as they passed. Rushdan and Sal might recognize Jack and Slate, but the major was a different story. Today he looked like a faded old cowboy with a giant belt buckle and an old-fashioned snap shirt.

The tension between his shoulders eased at the knowledge the Rangers were there, trailing them, just out of sight.

"Take us to my apartment," Therese said as if Sal were her chauffer waiting for instructions.

"The boss said I need to—"

"Don't give any excuses, Sal. We all know I can't go to the track dressed in a robe. It's ridiculous to even suggest that Rushdan expects me to go like this." She tugged the hotel robe closed over her knee.

"What about him?" Sal asked. "You giving him back his shirt?"

"I can handle things after you drop us off."

"The boss ain't going to like that."

Wade listened to Therese handle Reval's right-hand man like she'd been ordering him around for years. Come to think about it, she probably had. So he stayed out of it and forced himself to look forward and not see if one of his friends followed.

Traffic was light early Saturday mornings. Sal turned off Northwest Highway and onto a side street soon after. He stopped at the corner, not bothering to take them to the gate. When Therese opened her door, Wade slid across the seat, following her, dragging the money bag with him.

Sal pulled away before the door closed.

Therese pulled the belt tighter and pushed the robe's collar higher on her neck. Wade stuck his head through the strap of the bag and shifted its bulk to his bare back.

"Lead the way. I'm starved. Your friends didn't provide breakfast."

"That's too bad. I don't cook, so I never go to the store." Therese kept a hand at her throat, holding the robe closed. She was actually more covered than she'd been in that yellow dress the night before.

"Not a problem. I know how to order pizza." It was sort of cute watching her be modest in case one of her apartment neighbors looked out their window.

"Pizza? For breakfast? Aren't we a little old for that?" She looked like she believed her words.

"We're not old and pizza delivers. Order the cinnamon breadsticks and it's like having those bite-size things you get at the airport. Shoot, it's too early for delivery. Maybe we could head to a restaurant?"

"I hate to disappoint you, but we don't have time to go out to eat. We have a lot of things to get done before we head out to the races." She passed by the pedestrian gate and crossed the drive toward the leasing office.

"If you're too old for pizza, we can still clean up and grab something. If I'm remembering correctly, there's a mom-and-pop diner back on Webb Chapel. They have terrific breakfast burritos they serve all day—" He grabbed her hand and turned her back to face him. "Isn't your apartment through there?"

"Yes—" Therese arched her eyebrows, waiting for him to catch on "—but I dôn't have my keys. I need management to unlock my door."

He tugged her toward the pedestrian gate. "Which apartment?"

She pointed to their left. "Twelve twenty-four. We should go to the office. I don't keep a key under the doormat. I don't even have a doormat."

"It'll be unlocked." He pulled her closer, kissing her quickly before she leaned back, trying to see their surroundings.

"Are you implying that one of your colleagues is waiting inside my apartment?"

"If we're lucky, there might even be breakfast. Then again..." He waggled his eyebrows at her while sliding his hands around her waist. "I might be luckier if there's not anyone around."

Chapter Ten

Was there time to get sidetracked? The gorgeous shirtless man caressing Therese around her waist sent an invitation with his eyes that she understood very well.

Wade made her forget about his implication that someone was inside her apartment. Her mind calculated how long they'd need to get ready and get to Lone Star Park. And then flooded with the disappointment that there would people expecting information. Or Sal demanding he escort them to the track.

Shoot! Wade's closeness was a problem…a huge distraction.

She turned the knob and walked inside without preparing herself defensively. Good grief, the door had been unlocked. They weren't alone. Just like Wade had said it would be. Her only thought had been…

Oh, God, she'd been hoping they'd have enough time to satisfy some of those teasing promises they'd been making.

Yeah, huge distraction.

"Did you bring something to eat?" Wade asked the man dressed in an apartment complex work shirt. They clearly knew each other and Wade had expected him to be here.

"No time."

"I was about to ask how you got in, but you must have picked up our things from the safe. Including my keys." Their phones sat on the coffee table along with her scuffed strappy shoes.

"Jack MacKinnon." He extended his hand and she took it. "I'm Wade's partner, mostly errand boy. At least to him."

"Therese Ortis, but you already know that. Normally my apartment is a little bit neater than this."

"Oh, yeah. I brought some of Wade's stuff and made it easy to find if someone checked you out. I also swept for bugs. You're clear, which I didn't think possible." He stuck electronic gear into a workman's bag, holding the straps in his hand.

"I see." She deliberately looked at the small suitcase and three pairs of men's shoes. Her small apartment was even smaller with both men standing in it.

Wade pulled open every cheap cabinet door in the small kitchen, looking inside. "Man, Therese. You really don't have any food here. Not even peanut butter. Who doesn't have peanut butter?"

Jack reached into the bag and brought out two weapons. He set them on the kitchen bar and tried to look casual, leaning against the wall. "Brother, I'm not going to tell you what we've gone through to make this operation happen and cover your you-know-what. After this one's finished, we're going to have a little talk."

"I figured Major Clements would be talking the loudest. I didn't really have a choice. The opportunity happened." His eyes cut to her and back to the fridge. "Once you guys discovered who and what we were dealing with...did you have a problem?" Wade stared into the freezer. "Man alive. There's not even any frozen dinners or ice?"

"Sorry to say you have some very bad friends, ma'am," Jack said, shaking his head at Wade. "Come on, man, contribute to the conversation."

"What?" Wade shrugged and let the freezer shut.

Therese answered with a shrug and mouthed, "I told you so."

"We probably don't have much time," Jack continued. "Slate is keeping an eye on Rushdan's man who dropped you off." He looked at his phone as if expecting an update. "After dropping you, he went to a 7-Eleven. I think the team is getting up to speed on the situation. Anything happen after we spoke last night? That is, anything I should know?"

"The bag I brought in is full of cash and we're due at Lone Star Park as soon as possible," Wade threw out casually. "A lot of cash that Rushdan Reval wants to increase."

"So I guess you don't need any cash. Your truck's back at your place. If anyone was watching it, we had it towed."

Wade gave a few more details but left out how he'd been used as a punching bag or how she'd tried to leave him in the truck.

"Did you set up the phone to listen in?" Wade asked.

"Yours, yes. The FBI had a few dozen choice words when we tried Miss Ortis's. Yours should be enough to keep tabs on you." Jack pointed to their phones at the end of the kitchen bar.

Wade's partner lifted his cell phone from his back pocket and read a message. "Gotta run. You've got company coming."

Then Texas Ranger Jack MacKinnon slid open the patio door and hopped over the four-foot patio fence with grace.

He'd cut it close.

Sal barely knocked, turned the knob and came inside. "Boss sent me for a walk-through. Believe me, this ain't my idea."

Rushdan's man picked up a pair of slacks from the back of the couch, dropping them immediately. He went as far as to look inside the bathroom cabinet, finding a slightly used toothbrush that didn't belong to her. Their weapons along with a Texas Rangers badge were on the two-person dining table.

"You shouldn't leave those just lying around anywhere," he said, pointing to the credentials and weapons. "You don't know who's going to sneak inside and lift stuff." When he was satisfied, he tossed an envelope in Wade's direction and left, slamming the door.

"Well, that was interesting," Wade said, dropping onto her couch the minute the door closed.

Therese turned the two bolts she'd installed herself, locking everyone out. She wasn't used to anyone being in the small apartment. No one had ever been there other than a maintenance man.

And yet, having Wade there didn't feel strange or awkward.

No distractions. And no thoughts of them together. They had work to do.

She scooped up his clothes, draping them over the end of the couch before reaching for the envelope. But Wade gently tugged on her hand, pulling her onto his lap.

"Don't you think we should open that?" she asked before glancing at the clock radio on the kitchen bar.

He skimmed the side of her knee with one large hand. And kept the envelope behind her back. He pulled her close enough to kiss her neck.

"Maybe you should read what's inside the envelope before we get sidetracked?" she asked while he nibbled.

"You don't think it's the same instructions that are in with the money?" He dropped the sealed brown envelope onto her lap but didn't relinquish his hold.

"I've never done anything like this for Rushdan before, so I really don't know." She ripped the edge open, then slid her finger, opening up the long side. She tipped it up and a cheap cell phone along with a piece of paper fell to her lap. "Maybe I should sit—"

"We can read it together if you stay where you are. Unless you don't feel comfortable?"

"I'm plenty comfortable. Too comfortable." Her arm brushed the bare skin of his chest, sending her stomach flipping wildly. She got up quickly before she could change her mind about getting even more comfortable.

There would be plenty of time to get to know Wade better. Plenty of time when they weren't due at the racetrack. She flipped the one typewritten page open, holding it by the corner just in case there were fingerprints to process.

"I don't know why I'm being careful. Rushdan doesn't run his *business* with any connections to himself. It's the reason he's out of jail, rebuilding his empire. Lots of nonprosecutable people do the dirty work."

"His cronies don't know what they're writing or what piece of the puzzle they might be acting on. We discovered that last year after he tried to kill me."

"Rushdan is the only person who has an inkling what the whole picture looks like." She stood by the sliding door, searching the edges of buildings to see if anyone lurked about.

"What's it say?" Wade asked.

"These instructions are different than those in the money bag," she said, handing the note to him as he joined her. "Everything he's done so far is part of a test to see where we'd go or who we'd call."

"And who stopped to help," he pointed out, tugging her to the couch again. He flipped the paper to the side table. "Seems awful risky to be switching the plans around from us placing bets to being the ones who pay out the bribes—at least in this version. Damn risky."

"I should grab a quick shower and get some real clothes on. Unless you want to go first?" She stood, tossed the cheap cell phone with the others and tried to pass by Wade. He didn't let her.

He tugged a little on her hand—too gently for her to blame him for keeping her there.

He shook his head. "I want a kiss." He guided her back to his lap, then placed a fingertip under her chin, drawing her lips to his.

The kiss was good, fulfilling, sexy. Long enough for him to maneuver his hands behind her back and press her breasts against his strong chest. More than enough to shoot her senses into overdrive. More than enough for her to potentially forget why they needed to be anywhere else.

Feeling safe within his arms, she found it hard to ease away. Especially when she wanted more of him. Her longing was getting harder and harder to control. And why was she thinking about feeling safe?

Safety wasn't one of her priorities. Putting Reval in prison for good, discovering who the cash was behind Public Exposure and getting the algorithm off the streets—those were her priorities.

Three things that would make a lot of people safe.

She scooted off his lap, pulled his shirt down around her thighs and tightened the sash around her waist. "We can take my car unless you think that's a bad idea. Jack said your truck was at your place. Is it far?"

Liar! It wasn't far at all. About three miles. She'd known exactly where he lived when she'd agreed to rent this place. Being alone, working alone like she had been for so long isolated her. Getting an apartment close to someone she knew—okay, knew of—was her one gift to herself.

She'd given up a lot to work with Homeland. Her parents may have died when she was eighteen, but she had lots of family in the San Antonio area. Tons of relatives who all thought she'd cheated on a test while at the police academy and had been kicked out. Several knew she worked with a small-time crime boss. Not that she worked for the FBI on loan to the Department of Homeland Security.

Shoot. Wade didn't even know that part.

Wade's steel blue eyes searched hers. "Thinking of something you need to tell me? Another truth-or-dare question?"

"I don't remember any dares." She shook her head. "I thought we were getting to know each other."

He tugged on the long lapels of the hotel robe until her hands were supporting her weight, split on either side of his face against the couch. It brought their lips close. So close she could feel him move to form his next words.

"There's another way for us to get to know each other better," he whispered against her lips.

"Do you…ah…want a shower?"

"You go ahead, I need some air." He took a deep breath and exaggeratedly shifted his seating position.

After that kiss, she needed some air, too. She ran to the bathroom, throwing her back against the door to save herself.

Pure oxygen might help clear her head. She opened the bathroom window and overheard Wade. He was on the small patio, talking into his phone. She had a sneaking suspicion he didn't need *air* as much as a discussion with his fellow Rangers.

So why not just tell her that?

Because he didn't trust her. Not completely.

She gently shut the window to give him his privacy, twisted the lock and began the shower. This time he couldn't "accidentally" open the door and see her in her birthday suit. A girl should leave some mystery. She hadn't last night, but Ranger Wade Hamilton still remained a gentleman. A teasing gentleman, but a gentleman just the same.

After the past two years of being in his life but not being *in* his life… Well, she'd given him no reason to trust her at all. How could she blame him for being hesitant?

The opportunity to come clean, to tell him *why* she trusted him had come and gone. Maybe they would continue the game about getting to know each other. But what if it was just a game for him?

She rinsed out her hair and dropped her forehead to the tile, letting the stream of water pound the back of her neck. It wasn't really sore, she just needed to think. Or think about another subject that wasn't Wade.

They should both be dead.

What was Rushdan Reval really up to? Why did he need Wade for his plans? He wasn't the sort of guy who easily forgave anyone. Everything he did had a selfish reason attached to it. Everything.

For weeks he'd had his people searching for someone with access to public facilities. Rushdan had never hinted that it had anything to do with Public Exposure. But the speed at which he'd acted today made her think it did.

Wade would help her find out why the domestic terrorism group wanted the algorithm and how it had been improved or upgraded. He was her way inside Rushdan's inner circle. Wade. Again unknowingly playing the part of her hero. But no longer in the teenage-crush way she'd fantasized about for too long.

No, this was worse. He was a nice guy. A considerate person. A competent lawman. Distracting. She could actually fall for the real person she'd discovered him to be.

Chapter Eleven

Wade awoke from the nudge Therese gave him as they exited the highway close to the racetrack. He hadn't slept—or napped—long, but it had been deep and reviving. Something he'd needed after staying awake most of the previous night.

"I think I'm getting too old for hands-on law work," he said.

"Why's that?"

"Maybe too many days behind my desk recently." He stretched and yawned. "I could have stayed up two nights in a row back in my highway patrol days."

Therese looked sort of funny, paused like she was about to speak, and then she looked out her window. What had he missed?

She hadn't complained when he suggested a nap. In fact, she'd told him to close his eyes. He didn't regret it. There was no telling when he'd get the real thing again and he needed to be on his toes.

A long line of cars was turning into Lone Star Park and it was almost ten o'clock. They were running a few minutes behind but it shouldn't be a big deal. She hadn't seemed anxious in any of the life-threatening situations they'd been in before.

He couldn't pin it down. Was she thinking about Reval's elusive comment about his past? Was she catching on? Would it change her opinion if she knew that he'd run scams like this for real until he was fifteen?

"Will it be easy to find the guy the instructions told us to find? Do you think he'll leave if we're a couple of minutes late? I could drop you off and park the car alone if it will save time." Therese tapped her thumbs against the steering wheel, waiting on the light to turn green.

"Are you nervous or something?" he asked, hoping it didn't really have anything to do with his youth.

"I guess. Aren't you? We didn't really talk about what we were going to do to find the guy, bribe him or even get the money inside the park." She paused for traffic and looked at him. "I mean, that's an awful lot of money in that bag. Who pays off a bribe with cash at the actual race track? Our odds of succeeding are not high."

"Trust me. It'll go fine." He shook his head, but some weird business was happening with his stomach. It had nothing to do with pulling off the bribe. He'd taken care of that with a phone call while Therese had showered.

He didn't have to think too hard about what caused his anxiety. It had been in the background since hearing Reval's words that morning. Having the crook tell him to come to the track had his insides bobbing around like a cork on a fishing line.

Every distraction he'd tried at the apartment had been countered by Therese. There had been a new professionalism in her since she'd showered. He'd ordered food while she dried her hair. They ate in separate rooms and hadn't really talked since he'd fallen asleep soon after getting in her car.

Therese signaled and turned into the racing complex, reading all the signs aloud. He pointed to the left lane away from the regular parking area. It was pretty obvious she'd never been to the races before. But he had. A major portion of his misspent youth had been running behind those gates.

But after he'd returned to Dallas as a ranger, he'd avoided setting foot in the place. No concerts. No nights out with the guys. No Triple-A ballgames at the stadium next door. No cases associated with anything to do with racing or betting.

Hell, he didn't even allow himself to drive on the frontage road around the entertainment complex. He'd done pretty good not looking back for his entire adult life. But now…

Now it rushed him like speeding down the hill of the Titan at Six Flags. Riding a roller coaster wasn't something he'd done since he was a kid, either. He had to control the sickening anticipation of what needed to be done. He had to rein it in, use it to his advantage.

This wasn't a theme park with a fake shoot-out in the Wild West. If he screwed up…

He rolled his shoulders—stretching, relaxing, shaking off the nerves. He wouldn't screw up. He wouldn't let Therese down. He wrestled the fifteen-year-old's memories back behind that locked door in his mind.

Therese pulled behind a line of cars for the parking lot. He remembered exactly where he needed to go for the bribes and broke out of his funk. He put a hand on Therese's shoulder, then pointed for her to head straight.

"Keep heading down this road. Enter through the owner/trainer gate. Then we get to the stables and jockey quarters without any real questions."

"Are you sure, the note said to—"

"What if that's just another test? Look, Therese. I've forgotten more about this track than other people can possibly discover. Trust me. If you want to drop off a bribe, you don't take it through the front gate."

"Forgotten? You've done this before?"

She passed the patron parking lots and main entrance of the park, continuing around the curve to an entrance he remembered all too well.

"What do I tell Sal?" she asked.

"Maybe exactly what I just told you. Or you just let me handle it."

She pulled over, parking just inside, next to the fence. The cell given to them in the envelope rang. Wade pressed the speaker button so Therese could hear.

"Where are you?" Sal yelled.

"We're doing what you instructed," she answered before he could open his mouth.

"I'm supposed to be with you," Sal complained.

"Bribing a jockey is going to be a little conspicuous if someone's on our tail with their phone pointed in our direction." Wade covered her hand when she reached for the cell. "We'll catch up with you after we're done."

He clicked the phone off while Therese tried to swipe it from him.

"I'm not sure that was such a great idea," she said.

"Trust me. We'd be arrested within a couple of minutes his way. Come on, let's get this over with."

They might be arrested any way they tried to pull this off. He reached over the seat, grabbed the bag of money and slid out the door. He kept walking. Not waiting on Therese. Not turning around to see if she even followed.

The car lock and beep of her horn told him he could keep striding between the trucks and trailers. But all of a sudden he doubled over, unable to catch his breath.

"Wade? Are you okay? What happened?"

Therese's questions swam through his head. He heard

them but something kept him from answering. He stood straight, catching the end of a horse trailer before he fell over a second time.

"Oh my God, what's wrong with you?" Therese rubbed his back and gripped his upper arm so tight it just might have held him up.

What's wrong? Images swam in front of his eyes, obliterating the real parking lot in front of him. Years drifted away and he was a lanky teenager with his hair hanging in his eyes, jeans he barely kept around his hips and a T-shirt that was sure to have some foul writing.

"I'm…uh…not sure." But he knew. He was having a flashback.

"If you can't—"

"I can. I'm okay." He pushed himself to his full height again as he shoved the thoughts of his father's arrest back to the place they'd been locked before.

They didn't stay. But he couldn't allow those memories to interfere with today. Everything he saw, smelled…hell, even the sizzle of excitement was like stepping back in time. He was fifteen again and throwing up while they cuffed his father and hauled him to jail.

It was the last time he'd seen his father before the trials. The first one had convicted his dad of everything from petty larceny to organized crime. His father never made eye contact during the second trial for child endangerment. Terrence Hamilton had given up his paternal rights and Wade had never seen him again.

"Never look back," he heard himself mumble his father's mantra.

"What? Wade, you've got to clue me in on what's going on." She stopped him from stepping around her by a gentle touch to his chest.

He could see where he needed to go, knew what he

needed to do. It was all right there if he kept looking over her head. She softly cupped his cheek and his knees shook.

"We're going to be late," he squeaked out.

"Better late than dead."

"Everything's okay, Therese. I won't let you down." Dammit, she caught his gaze and locked eyes with him.

It felt like she could see through his lies. Her X-ray vision into his soul made her eyes crinkle around the corners. The hand she had on his chest slid to his belt loop and shook him while she released an exasperated "errr."

"You're a very frustrating man. What did you mean when you said you'd forgotten more about this place than others could discover?"

If another woman had been in front of him, he wasn't certain what he would have done. But their get-to-know-each-other game of truthful facts tugged at him to tell her everything, to not hold back.

"I know my way around."

"You didn't have a real gambling problem. Did you?"

"No. Do you think I'd be a ranger— Hell, I'd be out of a job so fast."

"Then what is it?"

His hands found their way to each side of her waist. He was about to physically move her out of his path. But he looked into her eyes and realized his breathing was normal. His knees were rock steady.

The formidable memories of witnessing his father's arrest faded as he looked at a beautiful dark-haired woman. Dressed in lots of…sequins? He hadn't noticed until the sunlight bounced off a couple, making him blink back to reality.

"We need to get moving. Remember that whole thing about our real objective?"

"Hard for me to forget after three years." She stepped aside so they could continue. "You sure you're all right?"

"One of those punches caught up with me, that's all. A momentary thing."

The opportunity to come clean passed by without a second thought. Okay, so he was thinking about it as they walked between the vehicles. It wasn't a big deal. No one in his current world would care.

The guys would slap him on the back and might ask a question or two. He'd proven himself to Company B. He belonged there. They already knew he had their backs and was willing to put himself at risk.

But did Therese? Did she know?

More important, would *she* still trust him or think he'd been lying?

Just say it, man!

"This is probably going to sound funny." Therese laced her fingers through his. "I heard if you want a sure way to tell which horse will win the race, you should watch them before they're saddled. Then bet on the last one that went pee."

"Where the hell did you hear that crock?" He laughed.

She laughed. "My dentist. It's exactly what he does."

"And it works?"

"He swears by it."

"In my experience there's only one sure way that a horse wins." He patted the bag of money. "Bribery."

Chapter Twelve

Not many people gave them a second look as they walked between the buildings housing the horses, jockeys and owners. Therese looked everywhere, taking it in, still hyperaware that Sal could be around any corner. Sal or the police. Getting arrested would blow everything.

She also watched Wade. He didn't seem sick and didn't act like getting punched in the gut hours ago had anything to do with what had happened in the parking lot. Honestly, it seemed like he'd seen a ghost.

She wasn't used to seeing strong men like him stumble. One minute he stood tall and the next he was practically on the ground.

"Any idea where to find this guy we're supposed to pay off?" she whispered.

Wade pointed to a stall where an older cowboy tightened a buckle on a saddle.

"Are you sure? He looks too…tall." Wade arched both of his brows, waiting for her to explain. So she continued in a whisper, "I thought we'd be paying off the jockey like the instructions say."

"We'd be caught faster than any of these horses can run. The jockeys are watched a lot closer than the stable hands. We slip this guy the money, then he'll slip a jigger into the race."

"I have no idea what you just said." He tried to step around her, but she moved in front of him. She needed an answer. "He's also not the man Rushdan wants us to contact. Why not just do things his way?"

"A jigger is kind of like a small cattle prod they use to get extra speed at the last minute." His confidence looked to be back. "This is something I know, Therese. Trust me."

Wade took a step forward again, but she latched on to his arm to stop him. *Trust him?* Everything she'd sacrificed clawed its way to the surface from somewhere deep down where it had been buried for years.

Fear. Apprehension. Doubt. Especially doubt…

The self-assured character she presented to the world shrank back, giving way to the lonely undercover agent. The real her sat alone way too often, questioning every move she made.

What in the world was wrong with her? She'd never hesitated as much as in the past twenty-four hours.

"Oh sssugar!"

Yeah, she'd said it loud enough for everyone around them to hear. She got a confused expression from Wade and had startled the man he'd been watching. The stall cleaner's face changed from surprise to recognition when he concentrated on Wade.

"Well, I'll be a horse's patootie. As I live and breathe. Is that you, Wade? You've kind of filled out." He carefully tipped the pitchfork behind him and spread his arms wide.

"It has been fifteen years, Joey. I remember you as older." Wade walked into the old man's embrace.

"True. Every word, true."

Therese watched in silence and wonder. Wade Hamilton had a past. A real one with…regular people. People who matched the sealed files Rushdan had discovered. The Rangers hadn't built this background. It was real. Wade Hamilton had a sealed juvie record. The fact sort of stunned her. No wonder he'd laughed so hard when she'd said they'd known each other.

"Who's your friend?" Joey asked as the two men separated.

"This is Therese."

She stepped forward to shake his hand but he held it up to stop her.

"Mind your step, Miss Therese. Maybe I should come your direction."

Therese mumbled a "nice to meet you" and stayed put just inside the stall's entrance. But as Joey took a step, her new partner reached in front of him, grabbing the pitchfork.

"We should stand over here, out of sight." He quickly moved the horse poo to the far wall, making room for them.

There was a story there. Some bond between the two men that she really wanted to understand. It was a story for another time. Joey was more than just Wade's friend. But her curiosity would have to wait.

"You in trouble again?"

"No, sir, but I have a favor that might bring some your way."

"I heard you'd gotten out of the game, gone straight, were making something of yourself."

There was suddenly a great deal of tension charging the musky air. She sensed Wade respected the older man and wanted to be straight with him. His jaw muscles visibly flexed. But he knew they couldn't. It would put everything at risk…including Joey.

Someone out there had an algorithm that could potentially harm thousands. The organizers they'd caught from the domestic terrorist group Public Exposure had promised a catastrophe would happen in Dallas. That specific threat had been thwarted by capturing the group's FBI contact six weeks ago. Only a copy of the program had been found…not the original or the person who had developed it.

The programmer put the algorithm on the market again. Rushdan Reval was facilitating a new sale to the highest bidder. He claimed this version was more destructive than the original.

If Wade couldn't guarantee a win for one of these races Rushdan wouldn't get the cash he needed to proceed. Or he wouldn't have the leverage he wanted to include Wade in the plan.

Then they'd be back to square one.

"I wish I could explain, sir."

The older man shook his head.

"It's a matter of life and death." She heard the words fly from her lips.

Joey's eyes grew big and round in his weathered face. He shifted from foot to foot, clearly conflicted about lending aid.

She moved closer and took Joey's hand between hers. "Wade says you're the one who can help, I know you can. You probably think I'm exaggerating. I mean, life and death, who even says that? You have absolutely no reason to trust me. Please help us."

God, she hoped he would.

They needed a break.

"I suppose that's a lot of cash in that bag," Joey said.

Wade nodded.

"I hate to ask—"

"To tell the truth I had high hopes for you, son. I

thought that lawman straightened you out. I've been on a narrow path of redemption for a while myself."

"This is a bad idea," Wade said flatly.

"I won't tell you the thought hasn't crossed my mind once or twice. Make a killin' and retire on some island paradise. I wouldn't go up against the real mobsters out here. Look at what happened to your old man."

"You're right. It's too dangerous," Wade said. "I don't know what I was thinking. Forget it."

Therese watched the genuine emotion on both men's faces. The admiration, then sadness in Wade's eyes. The disappointment in Joey's. She wanted to jump in and tell Joey about the good man Wade had become.

Had she been worried about Wade's ability to keep their objective secret? He was about to let this man think the worst possible things about him.

She pressed herself into the stable wall covering her mouth with her hand. It was the only way she could keep herself from blurting out the real reason they were there.

"Well, I can't rightly do that," Joey pushed his hat off his forehead and smiled. "Thankfully, no one will be expecting me to rig anything."

He walked to the stall door and stuck his head out, looking both directions.

"You'll help us?" she asked, surprised by the man's agreement.

"Rightly so, little lady. I should have helped this boy when he was twelve and didn't. No way am I standing around like a wallflower again." He shut the door behind him as he spoke, enclosing them in the tight space. He sniffed a little—not at the smell but wiped away the sign of a tear—before cupping Wade's shoulder in a manly acknowledgment.

Joey claimed to be an upstanding citizen, but he knew

exactly which jockey or horse owner was open to accepting a bribe. In a few short sentences he laid it all out for Wade. It was a shorthand she couldn't completely follow, but something Wade had no problem deciphering.

After accepting a couple of stacks of the cash to bribe the jockey, Joey pushed them both out of the stall.

"I'll send note when everything's set. You know it'll be best if I disappear for a while 'til things are cleared up."

"Take this," Wade said trying to give Joey another stack of cash.

"No thanks. Favors don't come with price tags. Come back around when all the dust settles. Don't be a stranger." He patted them both on the back before he swaggered bowlegged past the other open stalls.

Wade took her hand in his and led them in the opposite direction.

"That's it?"

"Yeah. Well, we still have to place some bets. And I know right where to find the people we need."

"I bet you do." She had a long stride, but she practically ran to keep up with Wade. "You weren't kidding when you said you've done this before. If I didn't know better, I'd say you have real-life experience as a gambler. You have the lingo down perfect. No wonder they established your background so quickly."

Was that what Rushdan had been hinting at? Did Wade have some sort of juvie record? Joey had spoken of letting Wade down when he was twelve.

"Therese, if we had more time I'd explain. But we don't."

"I know. I know. I'll have to *trust* you."

Her words didn't get any reaction. They reached a corner close to where the crowds clamored around and he dropped the bag on her shoulder.

"Stay back where those two hallways meet, out of the line of cameras. I'll be sending several people to you. They'll all say I did. You give them a couple of grand each."

"Tell me one thing that's personal—and relevant—and I promise not to bombard you with questions of how this is possibly going to work."

She swore his eyes rolled as he tipped his white felt hat to the crown of his head.

"One thing." He held up his index finger before leaning in close next to her ear. "It's true. My father was a gambler and con artist. He was in jail several years and I put him there when I was fifteen."

He pivoted and hurried away before she could draw breath to whisper, "Wow."

The bundles of cash weren't in stacks of thousands, so she darted into the closest family restroom and locked the door. She counted quickly, not allowing herself to think about a fifteen-year-old Wade turning his father in to the police.

Of course she thought about it. But she got the money ready and took her place to wait. Several minutes passed before the first person stood next to her against the wall and said, "Wade sent me."

Nine men and women stopped next to her and inconspicuously flattened their palm to collect the money just out of view of the cameras monitoring everything. She gave it to them without questions or even direct eye contact.

"Well, lookie here." Sal stepped from around the corner. "You're finally showing up and you still got the money? What the hell are you playing at? You're going to get us both killed."

He reached for the almost empty bag but she twisted

the strap around her wrist. If he pulled at it, he'd make a scene.

"We've got it under control." Her calm, confident voice didn't reflect her jumping insides. She tried to see past Sal but he blocked her view of the main area where Wade and the people he'd been sending were located.

Sal turned quickly, pinning her to the wall, his finger poking deep into the fleshy part of her shoulder.

"I've never understood why the boss keeps you around. You ain't smarter than any of the rest of us. Just remember that this cop's severed head rests on your shoulders. Totally your fault when he disappears."

She let him poke her. Let him push her back into the wall until her bare skin pinched. Let him get in her face without loosening her grip on the bag. She stood firm, raising her chin a little more defiantly while staring into his watery, sad eyes and smelling his bad breath.

Whatever doubt had been tugging at her brain had fled. She was once again in the moment and remembering that she *had* done this job alone for a very long time. Wade might have the upper hand on fixing a horse race but she could navigate Rushdan's men.

An arm dropped across Sal's shoulders. He immediately stepped back but he couldn't free himself from Wade's embrace.

"Funny seeing you here, Sal. Checking up on us?"

Sal ducked his head, slipping from Wade's grip. "Man, you don't know who you're messin' with!"

"Calm down, Sal." Wade shifted his weight, draping his arm around her shoulders. "Babe, this is my buddy, Dale Beauchamp. He'll be taking that bag off our hands. Don't worry. He also placed our bet for us."

She didn't want to give Sal any reason to report to Rushdan that something was wrong. She swallowed her nerves—the ones that increased her breathing each time Wade stood next to her.

The strap of the bag slid off her shoulder and into the hands of a good-looking man about the same build and age as Wade. If he was from her partner's time here as a child she couldn't tell. More likely he was another part of the rangers' plan that she didn't know.

Dale eased the bag from her, holding the handle as he smiled and winked. "See you 'round, Hamilton."

Sal took a step in the same direction. Just one step before Wade slammed his palm into his chest, stopping him cold.

"You should hang around for the fun, Sal. Winning big calls for a celebration."

"You better win big, Hamilton. The boss expects his investment to mature. Keep the phone. Someone will be in touch." Sal walked away, obviously searching for the direction Dale Beauchamp had gone with the cash before lifting his hand to hide his face from the cameras.

Therese couldn't believe so much had happened in such a short time. Whatever respect she'd held for the Texas Rangers before, it didn't compare to how high she held them now.

They worked fast. About as fast as she was falling for the strong man beside her.

Chapter Thirteen

Wade saw the security guard passing to Sal's right. He remembered the old familiar rush, felt the adrenaline surge through him again.

"Well, that was easy," Therese said, heading toward the track.

Wade stood there a moment, tamping down the shakiness in his arms and legs. He snapped a picture of Dale walking away, fingers gripped around the bag handle. No one was taking the rest of the money from that Texas Ranger.

How many times had Wade been the handoff, receiving his father's payoff. Or more accurately the winnings of whatever group his dad was fronting for. Wade should make certain Therese understood the truth. He'd confessed haphazardly. He made this operation seem easy because it was second nature to him.

Still. Even after all this time.

Calling upon that cocky kid who carried around thousands of dollars, afraid of nothing, had been too easy.

"Wade? Are you coming? Do we get to watch which horse wins? I mean…we *are* here." Therese asked.

"Sure."

She waited until he stood beside her again. Lacing her fingers through his, she smiled at him as they headed through the crowd, back to the track's rail. They looked like any other couple betting a few bucks on a few horse races. He didn't have to work at keeping her close to his side. He wanted her there.

Dammit. Why had he allowed being here to hit him so hard? He'd controlled the emotions associated with this part of his life for years.

For a couple of panicked minutes he'd actually become that lost fifteen-year-old kid. But he didn't care about the old man who'd taught him to steal and cheat. He didn't. Terrence hadn't been a father to him.

Fred Snell was the only real man who had taken on that role.

Therese tugged on his arm. "Are you feeling sick again? You're looking sort of sick."

He shook his head, dropping his hand on top of hers, gathering warmth for his icy fingers. "I'm good."

"This is so exciting. Even if I know one jockey is—" she dropped her voice so only he could hear through the crowd noise "—you know, going to do whatever to win."

They stood through a couple of races. Each time his sequined companion would turn her face to his and he'd ask her who she'd thought would win. She actually chose one who placed, but not the winner. Then it was time. She asked. He nodded.

Therese didn't need to know specific details. Didn't need to know that the one wearing purple dot silks would send a shock through his horse at the last minute to make it run faster.

The crowd was happy and unworried, waiting for the start of the race as the horses lined up in the gate. The boards reflected great—but not too great—odds for Texas T.

The gates opened and hooves pounded the ground, dirt

flew and muscles rippled through the beautiful horseflesh of each mount. Memories of other races rushed through his mind, keeping him silent. Back then he hadn't wanted to draw attention to himself.

Authorities questioned the race when they'd seen him or his father or his father's cronies. It was one of the reasons he'd been so active in delivering money and messages when he was younger, smaller. Then overnight he'd grown tall enough to be spotted.

Then caught.

Therese waved her fingers in front of his nose. "Hey, did we win?"

Damn, it was over? He looked at the board and verified the race results. "Reval will get his money."

"So we're done? I'm sort of confused how we're going to collect the winnings since we didn't place the bets."

"Right." He glanced around. "I don't see anyone watching us, but it's probably better to have this conversation when no one can overhear."

They'd barely closed the car doors when the phone Sal gave them buzzed inside his back pocket. He pushed the speaker button in time to hear "Money. Mustangs. Las Colinas Boulevard. One hour."

"That's not going to happen. It'll take my guy twenty-four hours to get the cash together for that sum." For the Rangers or Homeland or some other government bureaucracy.

"That wasn't what you were supposed to do," Sal screamed.

"Oh yeah? Neither was going to jail, which is what would have happened if I'd bet that much cash. But that was the real test, right?"

"What?" Therese mouthed.

He waved her off, pointing to the phone. Waiting for a response from Reval's crony.

"Keep the phone handy. The boss will be in touch." The call blinked with a disconnection.

Eyes forward, Therese started the engine, put the car in gear and spun the tires a little as she pulled from the lot full of horse trailers and trucks. He'd read about people's knuckles turning white as they gripped the steering wheel. Therese had a death grip on the plastic and it was hard to miss.

She also wove in and out of traffic like a racing pro. Otherwise anyone watching wouldn't be able to tell she was upset. Her expression was…expressionless. The beautiful smile he'd grown accustomed to in such a short time in just twenty-four hours… That smile hadn't been there since they'd gotten inside the car.

They seemed to be headed toward her apartment when the route changed, and two turns later they were close to his house. How did she know where he lived? A few minutes later, screeching to a halt, she threw the car into Park and smashed the door unlock button.

"I take it that's my cue," he opened the door, still wondering what he'd said or hadn't said as he stepped out.

"Wade?"

"Therese," he said, leaning to look inside.

She held her palm out and gestured for him to hand something over. "Leave the phone."

"We're not waiting together? Inside?"

She flipped her fingers again and he complied, handing over the phone.

"I'll be in touch." She revved the engine, waiting.

"Dammit, Therese. What did I do?" Had he pushed the "I know what I'm doing bit" too far? He could concede that he had. He'd tell her that if he knew they weren't being watched. Watched by either side—Reval's men or the rangers. "Come on inside and I'll explain."

"Don't try to smooth this over by throwing me your all-innocent look. It sounds petty when I say this is my operation. But dammit, Wade, it is. You can't unilaterally make decisions and think I'm okay with it. I'm not. My supervisors won't be. This is way too complicated. There's more at risk than just bringing Rushdan Reval to his knees."

THERESE WANTED TO peel out. Wanted to leave him standing curbside with that complete look of bewilderment on his face. But she couldn't. He'd made sure that they were tied together waiting for the operation's next move.

"You seriously don't get it?"

"What?" he asked, shrugging his sturdy shoulders up into his neck. "Come inside and let's…talk."

Right. Like talking was what he'd want to do if they were alone. Sure, she wanted answers. More than just one at a time from their little game. But more important, she had to make him understand how critical this assignment was. Its completion was her way back. Back to a normal life. Back to friends. Back home.

"We could continue the Q and A you began this morning. The place is clean. No bugs—at least electronic ones—so, it's safe to talk," he said in a persuasive tone. But he didn't look too thrilled about another round of talking. He shut the car door and ambled across his lawn anyway. Yeah, she'd just thought he "ambled" across his lawn.

Must be his boots.

Wade wasn't like any man she'd dealt with. Granted, most of the men in her adult life had been criminals—

were criminals. Then again, it turned out Wade had been, too.

So she followed.

Once inside, she took in the sparse surroundings as he set his hat on the rack near the door. She'd seen bachelor apartments with little furnishings before, but this was worse. There was a leather-looking recliner and a television wider than she was tall in the living room. A folding table with four folding chairs was near the kitchen.

"The first thing people ask is if I just moved in. Answer is no. I just don't need a lot of stuff. I only have the house for a tax break."

"Accumulating things takes time. You haven't even been here two years." He raised a questioning eyebrow and she realized her mistake. She shouldn't know that information.

"Speaking of where I live…how did you know? You drove straight here without my directions."

She fingered the closed blinds and peered between them to see if anyone was on the street. No one looked suspicious. A couple of men walked casually behind their self-propelled mowers on a Saturday afternoon, but no one else hung around.

"Oh, I keep tabs on people who owe me favors." That answer would have to do. But she needed to tell him how she really knew. Soon, but not now. She was still a little upset. "You aren't going to change the subject. I think you already know what I'm going to ask."

"Maybe. But why don't you ask anyway?" He brought one of the folding chairs from the kitchen and gestured for her to take the recliner. "We can go back and forth again like when you were sitting on my lap. That was fun."

Wade's tone was sort of casual, but she saw the curiosity in his eyes. She also didn't believe for a minute that it was the questions he found fun—maybe the sitting together. He was willing to share, but he wanted to know something. The look tempted her to spill everything before he could ask. But she had her own agenda and would have to take her chances.

"The world of gambling is more than familiar to you."

"That isn't a question, but the answer is yes. What I said at the track is true. Not a cover story."

His confession should have shocked her. But it fit him. Part of his charm was the way he talked people into situations. All three of the men he worked closely with had fallen for it. Shoot, she had fallen. It was why they were in this mess together.

"Like I said, I was raised by a gambler, a con man," he continued. "A bad one. A cheat. One who got caught. And caught often. Both by the law and the people he stole from."

Of all the things she'd imagined about him when she was younger or after he'd come back into her life again, the possibility of him being the son of a con artist had never ventured onto the radar. She had a thousand questions, but she sat silently and let him talk.

"When he wasn't picked up by the cops, we lived in cheap motels or crashed with one of his girlfriends. I wasn't much different. Not from him or the men who cheated him. That is, with the exception that when I got caught, I turned in my old man to stay out of jail. What does that make me?"

"Smart," she said without hesitation. "How did you get away?"

"From jail or the life?" He flipped the chair around and crossed his arms over the back. "An investigation that involved the state of Texas and a ranger who didn't give up. On anyone. Even me."

He looked relaxed now. Not ill like at the track, not anxious. Just comfortable.

"So that's why you applied to be a Texas Ranger?" It all made sense. "And that's how you got into law enforcement. Because the ranger who put your father in jail had your record sealed and raised you?"

He shook his head. "No." He sprang up and took down the only picture hanging on any wall.

"This is Fred and his wife, Faye." He tapped the people in the photo before handing it to her. "Somewhere they found money to send me to boarding school. It straightened me out. Changed that resentful fifteen-year-old kid to a man who wanted more. And yes, he wrote a letter of recommendation when I told him I wanted to make up for my misspent youth."

"That explains so much about you. Not this house, mind you." She looked around at all the space. "I still don't get why you don't have a couch."

"Are you going to tell me how you knew I lived here?" He'd sat backward on the chair again and tapped his fingers on his forearm, seemingly counting off the seconds until it was his turn to interrogate her.

"One more thing. Explain what happened at the track. Where's the money?" She'd almost been distracted enough to completely forget that she'd been upset regarding him taking over.

"Oh, yeah. Sorry I couldn't really explain everything when it was happening. But there was no way we could rig the race and actually collect that money."

"I wondered about that. So Dale Beauchamp works with you?"

"Yes. If Reval asks, we can say that we sort of cleaned

the cash by placing the bet outside of the law's eyes. Sort of like structuring money or exchanging it for money orders, keeping the limits under ten grand. You know the routine."

"I'm halfway glad I don't. I'll trust you that the next time he asks for the money your associates will have it ready. But the last part… What makes you think they were trying to get us caught?"

"There would be an awful lot of questions if we placed a large bet—in cash—and then we won. So that had to be the real test. If we placed the bet and *didn't* get thrown in jail or at least detained, Reval would have known I'm undercover."

"Next time fill me in on the details. You took a risk that could have blown more than three years of my life."

"Promise." He stood, moved in front of her chair and extended his hands. "This trust thing works both ways, you know."

She shamelessly placed her hands in his, letting him pull her to her feet. "Obviously I just proved that I trusted you by letting you take the lead at the track."

A good, solid answer. One that should deflect her earlier mistake about knowing where he lived. God, being in his arms sent shivers throughout her body. It was mind-blowing how primitively she reacted when he touched her.

He encircled her and tilted his head like he was about to kiss her, then raised it. This kiss might actually get them to the only real piece of furniture in the house… the bed.

Soft lips barely touched the sensitive skin where her neck met her shoulder. His teeth grazed her on the way to her earlobe. Then he stopped and so did the sizzle.

It was about to get real. Very real if he circled back to how she'd driven straight here without directions.

"Why do I have the feeling you know more about me than I do you?" he whispered. "Is Therese Ortis even your real name?"

Chapter Fourteen

Wade kept Therese close to him. He raised his head only long enough to ask his question. When she stiffened in his arms, he put his lips to work. Maybe the attempt to break through her resistance could be approached a different way. The direct questioning route sure wasn't working.

"My real name is Therese Maria Elisabeth Ortis. Born and raised in San Antonio." She stretched her neck back, giving him more access.

Wanting answers, but also wanting more of her bare skin against him, he continued his lips' quest across her shoulder.

"Is this going to be that back-and-forth thing you started? Am I supposed to admit something now?" He kept his words low and in between each nip along her skin.

"If you…want to," she said, sounding out of breath.

"You don't sound mad anymore."

"Concerned. I was…"

His fingertips found the edge of her shirt and quickly shot underneath, taking in her smooth skin, pressing her breasts even closer to his chest.

"I think—" he planted his lips in the curve of her neck again "—that I—"

He raked the edge of his teeth up to her ear, following it with circles on her back.

Therese shivered against him.

Who the hell was he kidding? His actions weren't an interrogation—as if he ever thought they could be. He wanted her. She knew the truth about his history and still wanted him, too.

Dammit, he'd never felt like this. Open. Real. Excited about what came next. He drew back, staring at her beautiful face, waiting for her eyes to open and acknowledge the real him.

God, he'd turned into a sap. That was what nearly a year of desk duty and seeing his best friends find the women they love had done.

Therese opened her eyes. He waited for her to kiss him or at least expose her neck for him to take up his teasing again.

"Is this a good idea?" she asked instead.

"Getting to…um…know each other?" He slid his fingertips over the clasp of her bra. "Honestly, I think it's been a little one-sided."

Smiling, she drug a fingernail across his neck, then up and around the edge of his ear. His muscles tensed.

"You know that's not what I meant."

"I think you're assuming I can still think." He lifted her off the floor, letting her body mold against him. "I am a man, you know."

Wade flexed his jaw along with other muscles as he tried to let Therese down. Her arms were around his shoulders, but she moved, resting more against him. She reached up to stroke his temple gently. He couldn't let her go.

"I think you're right about the talking. Let's chat with our bodies."

He was at a crossroads. The do-or-don't sign flashed on and off, on and off. One decision would keep him in a perpetual teasing state and the other led to sweet relief. But along with that relief came a commitment he'd never made or wanted before.

The pledge was right there, ready for him. The weight of Therese in his arms was less than the weight of that promise he wanted. Yeah, he wanted it all. Relief, connection, possible love.

Hell's bells, he had a beautiful woman in his arms and he was thinking about tomorrow. And the next day.

He shifted to keep her next to him, but with a little pop off the ground she lifted herself, wrapping her legs around him, and he kept her there. The movement hiked the small stretchy skirt she'd worn to the racetrack higher on her thighs. Closer to his face, she smiled before kissing him—winding her tongue around his.

Two seconds. That was all it took to make every bit of him rock-hard for her. It was like she'd read his thoughts and given her answer.

He was no longer questioning if he should or shouldn't. She'd made the decision when she settled her practically naked bottom against the skin of his forearm.

Wanting the bedroom, he stepped in its direction, but the lounge chair was closer. He got near and plopped his backside down, sinking into the leather. Therese stayed as close as possible until she shimmied onto her knees, placing them on either side of his thighs.

"Help me with this," she said, then laughed when she met his eyes.

He probably looked like a man who hadn't thought the chair all the way through. She continued to work at the zipper of her skirt, tugging, her arms behind her, thrusting her soft breasts closer to his face.

A man could only take so much cleavage that close before he had to…

Wade got out of the chair as fast as possible with Therese precariously balancing on his chest. Somehow in his rush, he scooped Therese into his arms instead of splaying her on the carpet. He bolted down the hallway, ready to drop her on the bed and devour every morsel of her delicious skin.

All of it. Every last inch of her.

"This is not good," he said stepping foot into the room.

With her arms around his neck, she burst out in a full-blown laugh. Her head dangled back, enticing him with more skin and sparkling eyes.

"I'm assuming there isn't a bed in the spare room with no clothes on top?"

Normally stacked inside his dresser, his clothes looked like they had all been upturned onto the unmade bed. *Jack.* "I don't keep it this way. Really."

"It doesn't matter."

"Jack or one of the other rangers grabbed stuff to leave at your place." He set Therese on her feet.

"It looks more like they took revenge on you for some reason." She spun around. "Unzip that, will you? I think there's a hook at the waistband."

He obliged and was mesmerized at how she gave the material a tug and it fell to her feet. She bent at the waist and picked it up, showing her heart-shaped derriere framed by a couple of strips of lace.

She folded her skirt and set it on the dresser next to his phone charging station. He watched her in the mirror as she crossed her arms and pulled off the matching top. Again he stared as she folded it and placed it with the skirt.

Wade took in her golden skin, the pale color of her

lacy bra—even the tiny bows between her cleavage and on each side of her hips.

Therese cleared her throat, “The sooner we get this stuff put away, the sooner we can…get back to where we were. Unless you’d rather go back to the chair.”

No chair. He shook his head.

But there was also no way he would wait until things were back where they belonged. No way.

He took giant steps to the end of the bed, pulled the side of the blanket up and over the clothes and yanked until everything was on the floor.

“That’s one way to take care of things.”

He had his shirt over his head before she finished speaking. The belt followed while he toed off his boots. Yeah, everything landed on top of the mass of blanket and clothes. He didn’t care.

The three triangles of lace beckoned. Teasing. Testing his limits of control. Ripping them off might be considered too…too something rude. His brain wasn’t working, so it was probably true.

Man, did he want underneath those triangles.

Chapter Fifteen

Wade reached out, grabbing her hand as he jumped onto the bed, pulling Therese down with him. She giggled like a teenager. Maybe more like a nervous college girl. But she wasn't nervous.

Wade was just…fun. Their circumstances aside, she loved being with him.

He drew her next to him on top of the cool sheets. One arm under her head, the other under his own. She stared at the ceiling fan, spinning and cooling her skin.

Suddenly feeling awkward and not nearly as brave as when she'd disrobed, she tried to cover some of her midriff. But she wasn't going there. She would be bold and decisive with this man. She threw her arm out, landing on his chest.

Still watching the fan spin its blades in a circle, she drew the same shape across Wade's tanned chest, inching lower.

He drew in a deep breath through his teeth and captured her hand in his. "Whoa, how can you be so chilly?" He rubbed the back of her hand, keeping her fingertips just at the top of his jeans.

"Hey, not fair. There's still a major portion of you covered up." She gave a quick tug on a belt loop.

"Right." He popped up and tugged his jeans and socks off like they were on fire.

Maybe he was. She certainly needed the fan to cool off as he sat on the edge of the bed and slipped out of his boxers. The slight darkening of bruises from where he'd been hit by Rushdan's men almost brought her back to reality.

But instead she lay back on the bed on her elbows, watching him. Then he joined her, tangling their bodies together. She marveled at his warm, naked flesh touching every inch of hers.

The warmth soon became volcanic heat as he used all of himself—skin, hands and mouth—to touch most of her. Her cursed underwear was still between them.

"Did you answer your question?" he said before another round of strokes across her good lace bra.

"What?" she barely got out.

"About whether this is a good idea or not." He kissed his way to her belly button.

It is a super good idea. She enjoyed every second of his attention and wanted to be serious. But she laughed. Partly because his fingers slightly tickled and partly because he just made her feel good.

"Yes, my…my own question." *Oh, man.* How could she still think, let alone speak, with what he was accomplishing?

Wade kissed and explored and didn't ask any more questions. Her entire body shattered with reaction and kept her from thinking. Feeling became everything. The man used his hands—belly, hips, top of the lace, sides, bottom, then back to repeat. When his thumbs hooked the edges of the lace across her breasts, she clapped her hands over his to keep them still.

He paused until she slid her hands up his forearms. Then he gently raised her until his teeth could tease her nipples through the lace. Again and again he kissed, nipped and laved. Until…

"Enough!" she shouted, her voice bouncing off the ceiling and four walls. "Enough."

She pushed at Wade's shoulders, rolling him to his back. Sitting up, she bent her arms behind her back and unlatched the device she'd forever remember as being pure torture. She looked back at her partner, hoping she hadn't hurt his feelings.

Wade shamelessly grinned as her bra uncupped her breasts and fell to the bed.

"You did that deliberately." She quickly moved, shoving him deeper into the mattress, then sat across his lap and pinned him to the bed. Her intention had been to tickle him until he begged for mercy but that plan soon changed as they both realized where she was now located.

Wade's laughter became a raspy, long release of breath. His hands reached for her breasts but she leaned back, pushing their bodies closer together. Then he sucked in a breath, holding it while she controlled their movements.

She allowed his thumbs to trace the remaining lace outline, closing her eyes before they gave away all the emotion she attempted to regulate. His breathing quickened as his hands skidded to her waist. She opened her eyes, seeing his closed as he spread his hands over her hips, pulling her down as his hips thrust upward.

She couldn't believe she was about to climax and technically they hadn't done… Well, technically. His jaw clenched as he kept them together but separate. Her hands slid across his chest, allowing her body to melt into his.

Then she exploded. An outburst that demanded all her energy and concentration. Wade used his body to keep her erupting. Weak with emotion, she collapsed onto his chest.

Wanting the same feeling for him, she pushed her panties aside, but he grabbed her hands, lacing his fingers through hers.

"Wait," he rasped. "We need…on the left."

How he kept his wits about him she'd never know. They needed protection. She rolled off him and scrambled to reach the nightstand. Wade didn't move. His breathing was still ragged or very controlled.

It was her turn to grin.

And drive him wild.

Already so close, she wondered just how long he'd last if she… She didn't need to think it through. Just do it.

She rolled the condom into place and stretched a leg across his, almost back where she'd enjoyed such tremendous pleasure. But she slid onto his thighs, teasing his belly with her fingers. Letting her long hair fall and caress until he swooped it into one hand and held one finger silently out to stop her.

"Therese," he pleaded in a whisper. "Forgive me."

Feeling and emotion rushed over her as Wade flipped her onto her back and they were one in an instant. But it wasn't over. Not for a while.

Wade had asked for forgiveness, but he didn't seem to be in a hurry. His body tensed and pulsed over her, around her, in her. She'd only thought she'd experienced pleasure minutes before.

Again and again he moved until they both reached a place she'd rarely been. They both stilled after one long appreciative kiss.

It was wonderful. Something she'd hold close to her soul for a very long time. She drifted off with the sweet thought of a lifetime of possibilities.

When she awoke, the room had gone from bright afternoon to a shadowy dusk. They'd slept for the past hour.

She'd lay there watching the same fan turn in circles, attempting not to truly think about what she wanted. Or how much she hoped the assignment with Rushdan Reval would soon be over.

"Wade?" Therese gently shook his shoulder. "We should probably get up."

"Did you fall asleep?" he mumbled from his pillow.

"A bit. Too much on my mind."

Instead of getting up, Wade lifted her arm, rolled to his stomach and laid his head on her shoulder. He had a perfect view of her breasts, but his eyes had closed again. To his credit, the man was running on less than a couple of hours' sleep.

"My God, is today only Saturday?" she asked.

"Mmm," he sort of agreed. "You hungry?"

"Starving."

"I say we clean up and order some Italian. You like pasta? You aren't afraid of some carbs, are you?"

"I love carbs and I love Italian."

"Nice." He moved his free hand next to her head and played with her hair, bringing it across his face. "God, you smell good. Makes me hungry all over again."

"That's wonderful to hear. I thought I smelled like horses."

"Nope. Like peach ice cream."

"That's my shampoo. Peaches and cream."

His movements stopped and his breathing evened out as he fell back to sleep. Minutes passed and she gently freed her hair and tried to slide from under Wade.

"I'm awake," he said, lifting his head, but quickly dropped it again to her chest along with a quick kiss. "I'll see if Heath can pick up from Mariano's around the corner. He needs to take a look at the phone Sal gave us."

"I should probably get up, then." She tried once again to slide free from Wade's weight.

He moved quickly, placing a hand on either side of her body and moving his over her completely. "You sure you're hungry?"

He lowered his mouth to hers, tangling their tongues as he tangled their legs. They kissed deeply, continuously as their bodies moved in an age-old rhythm again.

There was so much to talk about, so much to plan, to discover. But it could wait. She'd waited long enough for this human contact…however much he could give her, for however long.

Whatever happened between them, she could only hope it happened again and again.

Chapter Sixteen

Something had changed. Wade had a lump in his gut that had nothing to do with eating. The pasta he'd ordered for dinner had been fine. But somehow, something had changed.

He cared.

Before this afternoon, he had taken a beating to keep her safe. But now… The protectiveness that overwhelmed him could become a problem later on. Hell, he'd already gotten *the look* from Heath.

Heath had played the part of delivery boy. Italian food along with the necessary equipment to clone the burner phone Sal had given them. Not to mention his opinion about the unprecedented interagency cooperation he'd been observing.

But no one had any new information to clue them in on what Rushdan Reval, Public Exposure or another buyer would actually do with the algorithm. Everyone was still in the dark. By cloning the phone, the FBI, Homeland and the Texas Rangers could listen in and get up-to-the-minute knowledge about their movements and any instructions Reval sent.

The time frame Sal had originally set had long come and gone. The phone they'd been given sat between them on a TV tray. Every few minutes, Therese would pick it up, turn the screen on and then set it back down. No messages. No calls.

After Heath left, Wade tried to open his mouth a couple of times to ask what was wrong. Because things between them seemed awkward now. There were lots of reasons he should ask and one big one why he shouldn't. They were on the job. They couldn't afford to become any more distracted than they already were.

Right. No distractions.

Like watching her flip her hair off her shoulder or wanting to wrap the stray strand around his finger or use it to pull her to him for a kiss.

Therese was a helluva distraction. His mind was completely occupied by finding reasons not to take her back to bed. A great idea, but it had to wait until they no longer had to deal with Reval. Or find an algorithm before a domestic terrorist group bought it. An algorithm no one could speculate how dangerous it had become.

At least he hadn't thought about it. He hadn't had time. Since meeting up with Therese the day before, his sole focus had been making it through the next hour.

"What do you think this algorithm has morphed into?" he asked breaking the silence. "Six weeks ago it supposedly could take down an electrical grid."

"Chaos is the word most bandied about on the dark web."

"Chaos on what?"

"People paid a lot more than me only have theories. Most center around reasons terrorists would want a complicated algorithm. We interviewed all the members of Public Exposure without getting any closer. None of them knew specifics and their leader wasn't talking."

"Reval is just the go-between guy?" he asked.

She shook her head. "When he went to jail, I thought

my undercover days were done. But I hung around Reval's organization tying up loose ends. Then you guys arrested the leader of Public Exposure six weeks ago. Word got out that the creator of the algorithm was looking for a new buyer. Reval wasn't involved before that."

"Then why is he now?"

"Since I was officially still a part of Reval's group they already had eyes on him. The FBI released him, hoping he could broker a deal. Homeland pushed the potential buyers in his direction by arresting others." She shrugged. "I haven't had any luck discovering details of the sale or exactly what the algorithm is capable of now that the programmer has upgraded it. Rushdan is keeping it very close to his fat chest."

"You think whatever reason he needs me will give you answers."

"Fingers crossed." She made the gesture with both hands. "The team has checked out all his known contacts. All dead ends."

"Does the computer guy who got my juvie records have something to do with it? How do we track him down?"

"We don't."

"What do you mean? It should be easy enough to find the info in Reval's office. Don't you have a warrant for his phone records? Together we should be able to find something written down."

"That's not our job." She gave a little shrug of acceptance—not anxious to explain.

"Wait a minute." He had to be misunderstanding. What the hell was their job if not to put Reval behind bars...for good.

"The team has checked out all his known contacts. All dead ends. Finding who has developed the algorithm is my objective. My primary goal. It won't matter if we stop whatever show they have planned for Dallas if we can't find the programmer."

"Show?"

"That's what they've called it recently. I've overheard Rushdan refer to it that way. The team is certain it's Rushdan's term for the terrorist attack."

"On Dallas? Do the rangers know about this? Local police?"

"I'm not certain. Prevention and cleanup aren't my jobs." She reached for the burner phone, checking it again.

"Wait...what?" He shook his head, unable to clearly comprehend what she'd just said. "What exactly is our job then? I thought we were taking down Reval's organization and preventing the algorithm from being used."

"I tried to tell you this before, Wade. Sure, I want to put Rushdan Reval behind bars. But they may let his petty crimes go in exchange for the algorithm tech and developer."

"Petty? Rushdan's crime activities are no longer involved just locally. And attempting to kill me or others isn't what I'd call petty."

"You know what I mean. He's only a means for me to find the algorithm and the programmer. That's my objective. I have to find the person who created it. Hopefully before it's disbursed or sold."

The use of her singular "I" throughout her explanation didn't escape him. It stung like nothing he'd experienced before. She'd been in big trouble with Reval's men before she'd cozied up next to him at the bar.

Things like accomplishment credit usually rolled right off his back. Especially since he'd been sitting behind a desk while his fellow rangers had been stopping a serial killer, uncovering subversive FBI plots and keeping state analysts alive—a favor to this woman that had nearly gotten him killed.

Teamwork had resolved those cases and he'd been a part of getting the job done. Just like teamwork had gotten them farther along in this particular case. Or at least he'd thought it had. Dammit, were his feelings hurt? Or his ego?

Whatever it was, he had to let it go.

"I heard you say you were after the algorithm. I kind of thought that's what I was helping with. One good break and we could grab Reval before he sells anything. Stop the terrorist group before they get started."

"That might not happen." Therese checked the phone, then moved to the window. "You need to get used to that idea."

"I get it. You've been at this a long time and it's hard to accept that you've needed help or that someone might have a different way of doing things."

She squinted in confusion. "*I* needed help? Hard for *me* to accept? Oh, really?" She crossed her arms and pressed her lips together into a straight line.

Damn.

"I just meant that working with me—with the Texas Rangers—might accelerate things a little. And plans might change."

"And you think I don't want to what? Share the credit? Stop acting like a bimbo? Stop having Rushdan or his men leer, touch and pinch me?"

"I didn't mean it like that."

"Oh, I see. Then you think I *like* being undercover. Or maybe I'm afraid to explain to my family exactly what's been going on so they might speak to me again? Or stop wondering if they'll be proud of me for what I've done over the past three years instead of thinking that I cheated on my police academy exam?"

"That's rough. I had no idea your family didn't know." His sympathetic thoughts slipped out. Then he witnessed a reaction that he was familiar with but hadn't seen. The feelings he'd had for so many of the early years with Fred rippled across Therese's face.

"I don't need you to feel sorry for me. This is a job."

"Right. Just a job." He hoped she meant the operation and not what had happened in the other room. For him the other room had been life changing and it was hard to focus on *just the job.*

She backed up and rested on the arm of his lounger but at least her arms weren't crossed in anger. "The FBI and Homeland are after the big fish, Wade. Some of the little ones will be thrown back."

"Meaning, they're already prepared to offer Reval a deal like the last time. Like the jail time he didn't serve for ordering his men to kill me."

"I don't have anything to do with the decision-making. Neither do you."

"Why not arrest him and make him cough up the programmer now? Why are we going through the motions?"

"We did that six weeks ago. The men who call the shots are prepared for the consequences."

"Even if innocent civilians get caught in whatever *show*—" he air-quoted the word to remind her what they were calling a terrorist plot "—Reval's customers are planning?"

"Can you drop this now? As a favor to me."

His hand flew to the pounding pulse in his temple, right above his injured eye. "Another favor? I'm not sure I can afford to. If you kept tabs on me like you said, you'd know how much your favors cost me."

Except no one knew about his loss of vision. Not even the doctors knew how much his peripheral was actually gone because he'd never been back to check. He was afraid they'd bench him. So he'd kept the loss to himself.

"I'm very aware of what happened. And I know how frustrating it must be to hear this. But you have to try to see the big picture. The algorithm is more important than you or me."

"I don't get it, Therese. Why can't the aim be to get both?"

The phone rang as Therese shook her head.

"Preventing a national emergency doesn't take into consideration our personal preferences. I just wanted to warn you that Rushdan Reval might make a deal."

Wade watched Therese click the speaker button knowing they hadn't left their debate in a good place.

"He wants you at his club. Now," Sal's voice boomed through the little cell.

"Wade's proven he knows what he's doing, Sal. Give the phone to Rushdan." Therese had shifted to that bimbo-like tone, coaxing men to comply. "Come on, Rushy, I know you're listening."

"Get here within the hour, Therese," the greedy, double-chinned slob answered. "I have a job for you. Leave the phone with your new boyfriend. We're moving forward."

"But we don't have the money yet. Don't you need me to bring that to you?" Therese asked.

"The money doesn't matter. It never mattered other than I like to have an abundance. I had to make sure Ranger Wade was sincere and didn't hold any grudge for the boys trying to dispose of him last year."

"Then I'll keep it." Wade threw in to let the man know

he'd been listening. "That will just about get the guys I owe off my back."

"Probably. But you still need to earn it." Reval made a disgusting sound, like slurping through his teeth.

"No more tests, please. It's too risky, Rushy. Can't you just tell us what you need?" Therese coaxed.

Listening, someone might get the impression she actually believed those words. But watching her, Wade could see that her body language showed she hated saying them. She was good. Really good at what she did. But what was she up to?

"We ran to the track for you. Then we've been sitting here so long just waiting. There's only so much golf a girl can watch. I got things to do, Rush baby. You don't pay me to be a babysitter," Therese complained.

"Funny you should mention that, Therese. I have another chore for you. Sal will pick you up at the club."

"Is an hour soon enough? I need to swing by my place and change."

Wade stood, searching for a reason he should be going with Therese. They should stay together. Right? Didn't she realize that?

"That'll be fine. And Ranger Wade?" Reval said.

"Yeah?"

"Don't bother following Therese. When I send your instructions they'll be timed from your house. And yes, I know where you live." The phone disconnected.

"What the hell was that?" Wade demanded.

"My job."

"I thought your job was to find the algorithm."

"My job is to do anything Rushdan Reval tells me to do so we'll find the algorithm and programmer."

"You can't go. Not like this." He put his hands out, but she grabbed her purse instead.

"When I'm summoned, I go. That's my role in all this."

"I can call him back, demand that you stay with me. We're a team."

She arched a perfectly shaped eyebrow and pulled her keys from her small purse before hanging the strap across her shoulder. "If there's one thing I've learned being undercover, it's that you're out here on your own. You should get used to it."

She was out the door the next instant. What if that was the last time he saw her? What if she did her disappearing act again? What if Reval...? He yanked the door hard enough to bounce off the wall as he pounced onto the porch.

"Wait!"

By the surprised look on Therese's face, she hadn't thought he'd follow her. But he had—still unsure how to handle their differences and damn sure he didn't want this woman to disappear from his life.

"I took an oath to protect the people of Texas. And I don't take my promises lightly. It's hard for me to let harm come to anyone if I can prevent it. Stop the threat, then find the next. I don't think I can do what you're asking me."

"Don't worry about it, Wade. We aren't really a team but it was fun pretending while it lasted. I'll handle this my way. I can take care of myself." She continued to her car. "Don't forget to watch your back, hon. Since I won't be there to do it."

Smiling at him over the top of the sedan, she opened the door and slid behind the wheel like everything was perfect. Wade watched, completely dumbfounded. Sometime in the last fifteen minutes his heart had been ripped from his chest. There was a big gaping hole making him wonder if it could ever be the same.

Why didn't any of this seem to bother her as much as it bothered him?

Chapter Seventeen

Therese's hands shook so hard she couldn't fit the key in the ignition. She wanted to stay put in her apartment. For the first time, she was actually afraid to face Rushdan. Walking out Wade's door was the second hardest thing she'd ever done. Facing her siblings, aunts, uncles and other family after leaving the San Antonio police academy in disgrace had been the worst.

"I hate this," she shouted as she pounded the steering wheel.

Deciding to be a police officer had cost her all of her friends from high school and college. Being a hot shot at the academy hadn't gotten her any new ones. So leaving them behind for an undercover job had been easy at first. Until the lies became everything her life was based on.

After a while it gets hard to remember there was a different reality.

No one knew the truth except her handler, and that person had changed with each year. Currently it was Steve Woods and Megan who had been in her academy class. None of them really knew the person she'd been before this.

And now Wade. She'd wanted to be truthful with him for a long time. Now he knew. So why did it still feel like she was lying?

What had she expected? Gratitude for all her sacrifice? Maybe empathy or even a big "wow." Any of those would have been better than the stunned silence and pity she'd read on his face.

Dropping her head onto her arms, she wanted to cry. But there wasn't time. She needed to get to Rushdan's club instead of Sal taking her to the office. And only had half an hour to do it.

The end game was in sight and she'd soon be able to put all her own self-pity to rest. She drove quickly to the seedier side of Deep Ellum, close to Second Avenue. The Reveille wasn't the darkest, dankest dive around… but it was close.

Pulling into the gravel parking lot, she noticed several of the street lights were out again. It happened all the time. No big deal, but when she caught the kids throwing rocks at them, they normally received a hefty piece of her mind. That wouldn't be high on her priorities for long.

She glanced at her wrist. Among the many hoop bracelets she'd added to her outfit tonight was a watch. She was on time. Before she patted herself on the back, she noticed movement in the shadows to her left. She had to stay in character, had to ignore Sal and pretend to be oblivious.

Therese forced herself to shrink back when he finally showed himself. Good grief, she wanted to stand nose-to-nose with Rushdan's go-to man and take him down. Drawing on the desperateness she'd felt earlier, she pushed it to the top of her frayed nerves, faking a little scream.

"Oh my God, Sal. You scared the living daylights out of me."

Whatever Sal was doing, his real intention was to intimidate her, and she had to let him. At least a little. That was her part in all this mess. The end was near. She clung desperately to that.

She looked around for Wade's truck. She hated to confess that she had hoped it would be there. Even as much as she hated involving him the night before, she wanted him there by her side.

Upset, confused. A little scared for what was coming. It all mixed together inside her head, making it hard to think straight. Right. That was it. She didn't need Wade to protect her. But that wasn't the point. It wasn't her need. It was her want, her desire. She wanted Wade nearby and wanted to work with him.

"The boss is waiting inside. You know he don't like to wait." Sal puffed on a cigarette, then tossed it to the ground.

"I got here as quickly as I could. Put that silly thing away." She gestured to the 9mm he had pointed at her. "It might actually go off and hurt someone."

Carefully maneuvering the gravel in three-inch heels, she clicked the alarm on her car and headed to the club. She'd been treating Sal like that since she'd been promoted in Rushdan's organization two years ago.

Blunt force dead center in her back sent her tumbling to her knees. There was no way to stop it. Once on the ground, a booted foot across her shoulder blades kept her there.

Her face had landed on the solid slab of concrete at the club's back entrance instead of the gravel that bit into her flesh. She could feel the sting of scrapes on her knees and the palms of her hands.

Sal pressed his boot into her flesh. The barrel of his handgun pinched the base of her neck.

"You listen real close, bitch. I know something ain't right. You might have the boss wrapped around your finger but you're gonna give me more respect. If ya don't…" He twisted the barrel, tangling the long strands of hair behind her ear. "I'll be explainin' to the boss man how you met with an accident."

"Respect. Got it. May I get up now?"

The vibration through her body thrummed so loud in her ears she was certain Sal could hear it. She'd just thought her hands had been shaking with anger before. Maybe it was good that they physically moved as Sal helped her to her feet. It certainly let him know that he'd scared her.

The heels wobbled under her unsteady legs, forcing her to grab Sal's forearm. She hated to, but it was either that or fall to the gravel a second time. He laughed.

Please let it be me that slaps the cuffs on this waste of skin.

The jerk didn't open the door for her. She hadn't really expected him to, but this time she wrapped her hand around the doorknob and found it locked. Her stomach rolled with uncertainty. She nearly lost it as she bent over to pick up her keys. Sal's smackdown had her spooked.

"What will Rushdan say about this?" she asked, forcing her voice to remain steady and ooze confidence.

Lies and more lies. The barrel against her skin had her more shaken than she liked to admit.

Pull yourself together.

"Go ahead and ask him."

Oh my God. It was last night all over again. And this time, she couldn't run to Wade to save her. She had to face Rushdan and hope there was a reason he wouldn't listen to Sal and allow him to kill her.

Still with a gun pointed at her back, she rounded the corner and saw Rushdan holding court with the young women who served drinks. It was early enough in the evening that the bar wouldn't have very many customers, but she searched the room. The official manager was nowhere in sight.

No other staff. Just the girls. Another glance at the front door and she noticed the bolt.

Sal crossed his arms—gun still in his hand—and planted himself between her and the back exit. No one would get out of the bar unless Rushdan allowed it.

The other women probably didn't realize they were hostages. They were chatting away, fawning over the bar owner, vying for attention or his notice. Hoping they might be the next girl Rushdan brought up the ranks. Someone to be her replacement?

Oh, God. She'd played right into their hands. It wasn't an accident that she'd overheard Rushdan's phone conversation that he needed someone in law enforcement to make sure the show happened. Then the threat had come from the two last night and she'd sailed directly into Wade's arms.

He knew.

She'd been set up. Been used like the pawn she was supposed to be. As much as she hated Rushdan Reval, the man was smart. Now he'd separated them.

Whatever Rushdan needed Wade to do, it was about to happen and she wouldn't be there to make certain it did. Wouldn't be there to make certain Wade chose finding the program and programmer over saving the day. Joining him to follow through on her mission… By the look on Rushdan's face, that wasn't going to happen.

"Sit down, Therese. Join me in a drink."

"What's going on, Rushy?" Her heart raced along with her mind.

"You'll learn soon enough. Get my special phone, Sal." He snapped his fingers like he was summoning a waiter.

The snap brought Therese to focus. Everything she'd been thinking vanished with the look on Rushdan's face. Fury filled his eyes. What had happened?

The right-hand man left through the front door and a new minion Therese didn't know took his place at the back of the room.

"I thought you needed me for something special."

He stared at her skinned palms she'd placed on top of the table and then he smiled. She slowly drew her hands into her lap to keep his thoughts on the now instead of the previous night. But the two accomplices he'd sent to kill her or chase her into Wade's protection were at the front door.

"You don't think a night out with me is something special, my dear?"

"Of course. But if we're taking over one of your bars for the night, it feels kind of weird to keep all the waitresses around. I can get you whatever you need since I know where it is."

"They're staying." His voice turned dark with an angry vibration. It was one of the rare times she'd seen the horrible man Rushdan Reval actually was erupt to the surface.

"Are they… Rushy, they kind of look like…like hostages."

No. She couldn't let all these women be hurt because of his suspicions.

"They won't be as long as your boyfriend follows through. Right now they're my alibi."

"I could take care of that. You don't really need them."

"Don't test my patience, Therese. Keep everyone in line and you'll all be fine."

The menacing look in his eyes as he'd chimed that they weren't hostages shouted that they actually were. She'd been the only one to see it or it would have scared all the women. It verified one thing she'd known all along. Rushdan wasn't afraid to get rid of them all. Especially if Wade failed.

What if the Texas Ranger followed his conscience or his desire for revenge? What if he told the rangers about whatever Rushdan had planned? There were five souls depending on him and he didn't even know it.

She regretted not talking things through with Wade before she'd left. Her self-righteousness might have just gotten them all killed.

Chapter Eighteen

Go to the private entrance at Love Field Airport. You'll be met with instructions.

Great. Would it be Therese meeting him? Maybe Sal.

Wade drove past the entrance, searching from his truck for a possible ambush—nothing in sight, no one around. The entrance looked normal and deserted for a Saturday night. Deserted might be normal. He didn't know.

He parked across the street, keeping his eyes open for his backup. He could only assume all the agencies involved in this operation had listened in on the phone call that gave him the instructions. Major Clements wouldn't send him inside without backup. He just had to trust it would be there when he needed it.

Two men lurked at the edge of the building shadows. He lifted his hands slightly in the air, waiting on them to indicate which way he needed to go. One man he recognized from Reval's office building. The big guy who'd hit him a couple of times. The other wore glasses and cradled a laptop in his arms.

Was luck on his side today? Could this be the elusive programmer Therese was so hot to catch? He caught himself cracking a smile and stopped.

"You guys going to tell me what's going on?"

"Should we check him for a wire?" the big guy asked the nerd.

"We don't have time." He began walking to the gate. "Come on. Come on."

"To do what? I haven't been instructed—"

"You just need to get us inside. Then escort us to one of the planes owned by your group," the nerdy guy squeaked.

"Now hold on. You mean a DPS plane? I wouldn't know where the Department of Public Safety keeps part of its fleet. This is a little outside my comfort zone." He needed more information.

"Don't worry, just get us inside."

"Easy for you to say. I need to talk with your boss."

"Mr. Reval isn't available. Just do what you do and get us inside the airport." Rushdan's man pulled up the edge of his shirt, showing the handle of a handgun.

"Is that supposed to intimidate me?" Wade pushed his fingers through his hair, then smoothed it back down. "To get inside, I'll be forced to sign in. That means this is a one-time deal. I think your boss might want to know that."

"Everything's been planned, Hamilton. Just get us through those gates and past the guards," the little nerd demanded.

Wade shrugged. He still didn't have a clue about what would happen. If he had to take down these two, he could. Therese might be angry… Who was he kidding, she'd be furious and that would probably be the end to a relationship that had barely got off the ground. But he couldn't allow these clowns to launch an attack on Dallas.

Right?

With no concrete evidence, he had to play it by ear. Waiting to decide was a logical choice, not just an excuse to try to let it unfold Therese's way. Then why did he feel guilty that he'd be stealing all of Therese's glory?

They approached the gate and Wade took out his badge. The security guard turned out to be an excited kid.

"Evenin'," Wade said, holding his ID up and purposely keeping his fingers over his name. "Mind if we visit our hangar?" Hell, he didn't know if the Rangers had a hangar or not.

The kid pulled out a clipboard. "Not at all. I just need your names." He looked up, pen in hand, ready to write.

"That's the thing. It would be better if we didn't leave the reporters anything to report."

"But I might get into a lot of trouble."

Wade dropped a hand on the kid's shoulder. "I promise after this case breaks open to come back and update your log or talk with your supervisor. I'll be sure to let him know how helpful you were."

"Aw, man, that would be really nice of you. The hangar's a long way. Do you want to borrow the golf cart?"

"You're all right kid. Thanks," the big guy answered.

"No problem. Here's the key." He took a lanyard from around his neck and held it out.

The big guy snatched it with his thick hands while Wade put his ID away. His two companions got on the front bench, leaving him to sit backward. The big guy took off, pedal to the floor.

"Slow down, Nico. Don't draw attention to us," the nerdy guy insisted.

"That was too easy." What kind of a guard just handed everything over—even young inexperienced ones? "Yeah, way too easy," Wade muttered.

"Just go with the flow, Hamilton." Nico turned to look at him and forgot to steer, sending the cart—and them—swaying back and forth.

Bracing himself between the bars, Wade twisted around to look at the guard's booth. Sure enough, the kid was on the phone, pointing in their direction. *Good for you, kid.* But no luck for him tonight.

"We need to ditch this cart." He could see flashing lights from the opposite end of the airfield. "Ditch it now!"

Nico slammed the cart to a halt, drawing his weapon when his feet hit the ground.

"Put that thing away and get to the side of that hangar."

They ran to the metal hangar wall, Nico pounding into it and making enough noise to wake the dead—or alert Love Field police—whichever happened first. The nerd panted like he'd run a marathon.

"Take care of those cops," he huffed and puffed through his words, "while we do what we came to do."

Wade couldn't let these guys out of his sight. No way. He had to know what they were implementing with that laptop.

"No." He turned and used both hands to grab the nerd by his shirt collar. "Tell me what you need."

"I can't."

"You should have from the get-go and we wouldn't be in this mess. Now what do you need? What are you trying to do?"

The lights were getting closer. The little man's eyes darted back and forth under his glasses. Nico—the big guy who Wade owed a punch to the gut—tugged at Wade's hands.

"All right. I need to test some software."

"Give it to me. I can get in and out without the two of you slowing me down."

"I… I can't."

"It's either that or we all go to jail. You and Reval

should have been upfront about this and I would have come up with a plan. A much better plan." He released the man's collar and backed up. "I should hand you over to the cops and maybe I can talk my way out of this mess."

Nico chambered a round. He made a huge mistake by acting all tough guy and keeping it by Wade's ear. Wade whipped his elbow into Nico's gut, then as Reval's gunman doubled over, Wade shoved a fist into the thug's nose.

Nico dropped his weapon, grabbing his face and moaning.

"Sorry about that, tough guy, but I owed you one." Wade quickly knelt and hid the gun in his boot. "Instructions. Fast. Then get lost. If you're caught by the cops, it's trespassing and Reval can bail you out."

"You can't do this," the nerdy guy said as Wade pulled the laptop from his fingers. "You need my expertise."

"Watch me. Now what do you need?"

With blood smeared across the side of his face, Nico had a recognizable look in his eyes—revenge. But he reached into his pocket and pulled out a folded piece of paper. Nerdy guy watched him, shaking his head from side to side, mumbling something about Wade being not only a cop but a stupid one.

Wade crumpled the paper into his palm and ran. He made it to the corner of the building before looking around. The police cars split in two directions. The men he'd walked through the gate with were nowhere in sight.

Squinting at the paper in the dark shadow of the building, he could see that it was a list for the morons he'd parted ways with. Beginning with meeting him at the west airport gate.

Nerdy guy didn't seem to be the programmer. Wade wasn't lucky—unless he didn't get caught by the police currently circling around every building. He squatted at the corner and held the note in the edge of the light, barely making out Building Six.

Feeling like he was in a World War II POW movie, he avoided searchlights and the airport police. He finally made it to Building Six and parked himself between the recycling cans and some decorative bushes.

There was no way he had the algorithm on this laptop. The directions said nothing about any kind of attack or uploading any type of file. Waiting for the police searchlights to fade in the distance, he walked up to an unlocked door and went inside the dark office.

"Stay right where you are."

"Don't move."

"Freeze!" Laughter. "You know I've always wanted to say that."

Greeted by three familiar voices…music to his ears. Maybe his luck was holding after all.

Chapter Nineteen

Therese sat at the corner table with the other four women. Regulars came to the door, found it locked and would tap on the window close to her. She could only shrug and smile. She pretended to be just as clueless as to what was going on.

Rushdan had practically admitted that this was his alibi for whatever task he'd sent Wade to complete. So here she sat while he flipped the "special" phone Sal had brought to him. He hadn't used it yet.

It looked like any other cell phone as he dropped it inside his jacket pocket. In fact it was identical to the one he took from another pocket. The special phone could be what he used to contact the programmer. She needed that phone.

"God, I'm hungry. Do you think we could order a pizza, Therese?" Julie Anne asked.

"I'd go in on that," Rachel said.

Therese got up and wove through the empty tables to her boss. "Any chance we could order or have one of the guys pick us up a pizza from around the corner?"

With his back to her, she hadn't noticed he was on the phone.

Rushdan turned on a dime and Therese couldn't avoid the backhand that came along with it. She didn't fake the painful moan that escaped before she had control. The staggering blow was meant to hurt and intimidate. He raised his hand to hit her again but she blocked it.

"I'm not telling you what I want done. If the cops get their grubby paws on that laptop, I'll kill you myself." Rushdan's eyes were huge in his red, puffy face. He looked like he'd pop with the prick of a pin.

If only she had a pin.

Too late she realized that her arm still blocked his second blow. She wasn't supposed to be quick or competent enough to accomplish that. Still rubbing her face where his hand had connected, she tried to drop her arm to her side. It was caught by one of the men she didn't recognize.

"Why are you bothering me, Therese? What did you hope to gain besides irritating me?" Rushdan finally asked before putting his concentration back into his phone.

Therese yanked her arm free. "The girls need a restroom break. And if we're just sitting there, is it okay to order a pizza?"

"I don't have time for this! Your stupid boyfriend can't complete one task I give him. First the money and now this! I expected something. But this is outrageous. Get him on the phone. Now. Immediately."

Rushdan paced the length of the bar. Therese had never seen him frantic, ranting as he tossed his regular phone to one of the guys to dial. His plans must have gone wrong.

Her mind had been working on a way she could keep her cover if Wade stormed the bar and arrested everyone. He must have somehow stopped the attack. Why would Rushdan look so confused if everything had gone well?

Wade was willing to blow everything—including her cover—to bring down Rushdan. She had to be ready.

"Is there anything I can do to help?" she asked timidly while taking steps away from Rushdan.

"Get me a good shot of whiskey. The stuff that's behind the bar is terrible." It might be watered down, but Rushdan still finished what was in his tumbler.

"I'll need to go in the back for the good stuff."

Rushdan tossed his chin up, essentially giving her permission to walk around Sal. Therese tried to remain confident as she passed him in the narrow hallway that held the restrooms. But Sal stayed where he was as she entered the storeroom and secured the boss man's whiskey.

Wait. If Rushdan knew she and Wade were undercover—wasn't that the reason he was treating her this way? Then why would he be confused if Wade hadn't completed his assignment? Good grief. Wade hadn't thrown her assignment away…he'd completed it. That had to be the reason Rushdan was confused.

Wade had followed through.

She felt the outline of her phone in her trouser pocket and was tempted to call Wade. Tempted, but something didn't feel right. Rushdan was out in the open, something he never did.

She abandoned the idea of phoning Wade, deciding to wait it out. Whatever was going on, her instincts told her it wasn't the big "show." So she'd concentrate on getting the girls pizza and keeping them safe. Keeping her fingers crossed that Wade hadn't taken the easy arrest and would wait to get his revenge.

Bottle in hand, she reached behind the bar on her way past and grabbed a clean tumbler.

Rushdan was on the phone, looking into it like a video call. "Bring the laptop back to me, Hamilton, or I'm afraid Therese will…"

Rushdan pointed the phone at her. Sal stepped in front

of Therese and threw a right punch into her stomach. The tumbler rolled free from her hand on one side as the whiskey bottle shattered on the other when she hit the floor.

"You son of a bitch, leave her alone!"

Wade? Not here. Just the phone. He was on the phone.

No acting necessary. She hadn't seen the punch coming and sent a major shock through her body. Julie Anne rushed to her side, helping her into a chair. It took several seconds before she could breathe regularly again or talk.

It wasn't the first time she'd been hit. And from the reactions of the other women, they'd all seen something like it before. It was her fault they were all here. So she was glad to see them retreat farther into the corner. They looked a little more relaxed knowing it was Therese who would take the beating.

Now she knew why they were there…to keep her in line. She may be a hostage he would threaten to kill. But she was the leverage to ensure Wade behaved correctly.

Covered in whiskey, she turned to Julie Anne, "Snag me a couple of clean towels from behind that post, please."

Julie Anne did it in as small a way as possible. Therese didn't blame her. Sal stood close by, ready to attack. Once the towels were in her hands, she waved the young woman back to sit with the others. Dabbing up the whiskey around her face and neck, she hid her eyes and took in where all the men were.

Rushdan pushed a drink into her hands. "This will help, my dear."

She tried to fake some calm. She couldn't, but who would? So she acted naturally and swallowed the cheaper whiskey he'd poured in one long gulp. Then she looked into the face of evil… Rushdan.

"I should have killed that tin star bastard when he

showed back up last night. What made me think I could use him?" He paced a few seconds then looked directly at her. "Or you."

Rushdan marched to her and backhanded her again. Her head snapped from right to left but this time she concentrated, keeping her breathing even. At least both cheeks would be equally red and swollen.

"Put her in the car," Rushdan ordered, pulling a stack of cash from his money clip. "I'm sure the rest of you could use a couple of hundred in tips tonight to keep quiet."

At least the women would be okay. Sal tried to jerk her up from the chair. She didn't move. She took deep breaths, controlling the urge to rub the sting away. But it was more than just defiance. She needed to hear everything Rushdan said.

She couldn't do that from the car.

Had Wade called Rushdan or had it been the other way around? She forced herself to think. Right. Rushdan had been screaming for someone to get Wade on the phone. What had happened in those precious minutes she'd been thinking in the storeroom? "I said put her in the car." Rushdan seemed to have control of his voice again.

Sal shrugged as she jerked her elbow from his grasp.

"I can walk all by myself. I've been doing it for years. Even in heels." She stood, catching her hip on the nearby table, but keeping the "ouch" all to herself.

Sal walked closely behind her. She could see him in the bar mirror. Rushdan finished paying the women and hurried them out the front door. None of them picked up their purses from the top of the bar.

Therese raised a finger, trying to catch them, but couldn't say anything. It was hard just putting one foot in front of the other. Each upright step was a major accomplishment. Okay, maybe she was a bit more loopy from the gut punch or that shot of whiskey than she originally thought.

Before she made it to the hallway, Rushdan latched on to her elbow, pulling her to a stop. Her heels were slick on the floor as he spun her around.

"Feeling a bit tipsy, Therese?" he laughed.

She tried to nod, but her vision went a little wonky with a lot of blinking, before the world turned completely black. Wade wouldn't be storming the place coming to her rescue.

But the night was young.

"CAN'T YOU GO any faster?" Wade asked, knowing it was the fifth or sixth time since he'd seen Therese get punched.

"Creating a fake that looks as good as the real thing isn't as easy as I make it seem." The FBI computer specialist returned to clicking away at his keyboard on the other side of the office.

Jack dropped a hand on Wade's shoulder. "I know this is tough, but he's doing the best he can."

"He said I had an hour. I need over half that long to get to that address."

"Reval isn't going to hurt her." Jack grimaced. They all knew she'd been hurt with that punch.

"You're right." Wade continued to stare at his phone, watching the estimated arrival time change on his map app. "He's got guys to do it for him."

"Thinking like that is going to get in your way," Heath said, leaning back in a desk chair in the corner. "I can tell you that from recent experience."

"I think we all can," Slate added.

Wade put the phone in his back pocket. Reval wouldn't

call him again. He probably wouldn't hurt Therese. Or have Sal touch her. At least not until Wade arrived with the damn laptop.

Then he might kill them both.

Heath was right. Thinking like this was messing with his mind, his training and any plans that needed to be made to ensure he and Therese weren't killed.

"Look, guys. I appreciate that you're here supporting me. But is it necessary for *all* of you to hang around?"

"You're just lucky Major Clements was required to hang back at the task force headquarters. Talk about impatience. He'd be wondering why all of this wasn't done in advance." They all laughed at Jack's observation.

"I got to ask you guys." Wade looked at his three best friends in the world. "What would you have done if those other two clowns had shown up?"

"Arrested them," they said in unison.

His friends and partners all nodded their heads and stopped talking. Arms crossed, each leaning on something, all more worried than they were letting on. He didn't want to be dramatic, but none of the cases any of them had worked on were as important as this. He wouldn't say it aloud, but they all knew it.

The "show," as potential buyers on the dark web had been referring to it, had the potential to be another 9/11. Therese hadn't been exaggerating. She'd been right about its importance, but wrong that she wasn't a part of the team. There was a huge team of people working on this.

This team. His team.

That was why these men were all here for him. Waiting with him. Keeping him sane.

"Maybe you should go over what the task force has come up with one more time," Heath said, breaking the silence.

"I got it," Wade told him.

"It can't hurt. Remember, Heath couldn't recall which one of us he'd sent to find his daughter," Slate reminded them.

"It can't hurt." Jack slapped Wade's back again. "When the specialist over there is finished, you'll have a fake schedule for the private airplanes arriving at Love Field and the surrounding smaller airports. Reval just clued us in on his buyers and their arrival times."

"I don't get why he needed this. Wouldn't they all contact him?" Wade had listened and accepted the information and reasoning handed to him earlier. But the guys were right, hearing it and then processing it were different. This time around, parts just didn't add up.

"It might be that he doesn't have specific information," Jack told him. "Or maybe he's worried competition might be headed this way, too. Maybe you'll get him to fess up why he needed it."

"Aren't we tipping our hand if he does and knows this one is a fake?"

"Possibly," Jack agreed. "If that happens, we'll ride in to save you and your princess."

"I wouldn't let Therese hear you refer to her as a princess or even a lady in distress," Slate joked, bending his arm to show off his muscles. "Have you seen the guns on that woman's arms? I'm sure she's okay, man."

Heath got that what-if look on his face and raised a finger. "I'm going to have the computer specialist check something. Be right back."

That look—or thought process—had saved them on more than one occasion. If it saved his hide tonight, it would be saving Therese, too.

"What are the three of you going to be doing while I'm risking my neck?"

"Getting the job done," Slate told him with a straight face.

"Don't worry about our end—or the task force—we've got your back. Just like you've had ours," Jack told him.

The words meant more than he'd thought. *Damn.* Therese had never had that. She'd been completely isolated for the past three years. No friends, family or coworkers. It made it easier to accept that she'd walked away from him so quickly that afternoon.

Or at least he'd thought it had been easy for her. Maybe not.

The guys—his fellow Texas Rangers—had him covered. They'd penned him to the wall to keep him in that office after Therese had been hit by Sal. Maybe that was why two of them were still between him and the exit.

Needing to focus, he brought his phone back to his hand to stare at it once again. Focus evaded him except for one thought. Reval.

He'd been determined to bring Reval down before. There wouldn't be any deals for the common scum. He'd be in front of every judge and prosecutor to make certain that didn't happen.

A year ago he'd felt anger at nearly being blown up. Anger at how stupid he'd been to go at it alone and let Reval's men get the jump on him. But he'd gotten over it. Or at least he thought he had, until he'd found out Reval was out of jail.

The past six weeks hadn't just been about searching for Therese. In the back of his mind, he knew she wouldn't be far from Reval. Someday he'd let her know just how right she'd been to question what his true motivation was today.

Reval was going down. Away. For good. Without parole or deals.

But not before Wade got a piece of him. And not before Wade severely chastised Sal for hitting his girl.

Chapter Twenty

Therese awoke in the dark with a headache the size of Dallas. She was on a couch in Rushdan's office, blinds drawn. Alone. Where would he keep important, secret information? She let her eyes search for obvious cameras. None. Envisioned the sleek glass desk. Limited drawer storage only in the bookcase.

There had to be a safe in the wall, the floor, behind the books. That meant they needed a combination. Three years and she still didn't know. But what was most likely his special phone—as he'd called it—would still be in his pocket.

Swinging her feet to the floor, she slowly pushed herself up and staggered to the private bathroom. Even after shutting and locking the door, she could hear the fish tank gurgling as she examined her split lip and slightly discolored cheeks.

"You look absolutely terrible," she told her reflection.

She quickly washed the blood from her face and pulled her fingers through her hair. The bathroom had as little decor as Rushdan's office. No pictures with glass that she could break. No heavy statues to swing. Just the bare necessities.

"The Bare Necessities."

She returned to the couch, humming the Disney song

that had popped into her head. She didn't walk the room physically. It was too dangerous and she didn't know if she could. She should let Rushdan return and see her acting obedient.

God, she felt loopy. Light. No, it was more of a heavy feeling like she couldn't get up. Weird. Or drugged.

That was why she'd passed out so fast.

So she continued to hum and look around the room for any indication of a safe. It had to be here. Rushdan didn't have any other offices. She kept staring at the walls, but her headache distracted her.

The song earworm took her back home to San Antonio. She couldn't shake it out of her mind. She was certain there was something else she should be doing. Being the oldest, she'd been the resident babysitter when her parents took extra shifts or the rare times they went out. Her siblings had watched a ton of sing-along movies. The words drifted through her mind, urging her to close her eyes.

But instead of cartoons or animated images, she was suddenly in the passenger seat of a car. Eighteen. Stuck in her boyfriend's wrecked Camaro. The darkness surrounded her. No dashboard or streetlights. They'd been out in the country on a little known state highway when a deer ran across the road. They'd crashed.

Wade.

She hadn't known him. She didn't know his name until she'd read it in the paper. He wasn't a Texas Ranger at the time, just a Texas Department of Safety highway patrolman. It was the only time in her life she'd been rescued and she'd never forgotten his face. A couple of years later she'd seen it again with his promotion to the Company B Rangers and she'd been following his career ever since.

If it hadn't been for the hero crush she'd had on Wade she would never have joined the police academy or been recruited for this undercover position. So, in a way, all of this was Wade's fault. The bloody lip, the headache, the undercover life-threatening moment… *Yep, all of it.*

She laughed hysterically. Out of control, she couldn't stop.

"Therese, my dear. Wake up."

She opened her eyes from the strange, disturbed sleep. Rushdan had his hand on her shoulder. Sal had his hand on his gun.

"Are you okay, my darling?"

Now she was his darling? Hardly.

"I'm fine. Just a bad dream." She scooted across the white leather sofa, away from Rushdan.

Too late she remembered the phone. Back in his jacket pocket? Back in a safe? They needed that special phone. Before she could return to his side, he stood and went to his desk.

"You've been out for a long time, Therese. I had no idea you were so…delicate." He massaged the back of his hands, then dismissively waved at Sal. "Leave us."

She waited for the door to shut before saying, "You love doing that."

"Yes. I love being in charge and making everyone else scurry around trying to stay on my good side."

"Being the big, important man," she mumbled.

"Don't be afraid to speak up, Therese. Nothing can change our relationship."

Control. Focus. Change the subject.

"I'm afraid to ask, but has Wade returned?"

"We'll be joining everyone shortly. He failed, by the way. I don't know how he pulled off the racetrack, but he failed miserably at the airport."

"Airport?" she squeaked.

"Yes. It was fun discovering just how much you and

the authorities knew about the *show*. It seems there's an entire task force assigned to me." He dangled a phone between his fingers. "This is what you've wanted by the way. It has all my real contacts. Potential buyers. Sellers. Records. Secrets. You have that look about you now, Therese."

"What look?" she asked, her throat and mouth suddenly drier than dust.

"The look of desperation has settled in your eyes and caused a crease in your brow. Don't worry. I like you, darling Therese, and you've been a huge help over the years. But because of your betrayal, the end you're facing won't be quick and it definitely won't be painless. I intend for it to be long and humiliating, until you beg to join your ranger friend in death."

Long and humiliating. Beg to join...in death. The words echoed, bouncing from one side of her aching head to the other. He slid the phone back into his jacket and crossed to the door. She darted out, causing Sal to draw his weapon and Rushdan to jump in retreat.

"Sorry, sorry." She slowly reached for her boss's hand. "I trusted him and was duped just like you."

"Don't deny it, sweetheart. You helped him right into my inner circle. And I was never duped."

"When he contacted me weeks ago with his sob story, I had no reason to doubt him. Then Friday night he put it all out there to help me." She used one hand to cover her eyes and hitched her breath a little. "I don't know why I fell for it, Rushy."

"Give her the shot." His hand hesitated on the doorknob before he left. Had she made him doubt her guilt even a little?

Not a chance.

THE DIRECTIONS GIVEN to Wade on the burner phone took him north of Dallas. Straight highway gave him access to an express lane and made up some of the time he'd lost waiting on the FBI specialist to check out the computer.

With Heath's help, they'd discovered the laptop meant nothing to Reval. It was all a ruse. Something to keep him and the task force busy. *While he did what?*

Killed Therese. Sold the algorithm. Set up in a location where he couldn't legally be touched.

Wade had left the task force behind in Dallas waiting for a hint of what they needed to deploy to protect the cities in the metroplex area. The Rangers—his friends—were en route via helicopter to his destination. He still had the cloned phone from Reval and they could hear through it.

If he wasn't shot on sight and if he could get Reval to brag, then the others could relay the info to the rest of the team. They'd all agreed the plan had a lot of holes. Too many what-ifs for any of them to feel comfortable. And they'd all left the most important question unasked... would he be able to hold it together *if* Therese was dead?

He honestly didn't know. He kept telling himself not to go there. Kept repeating that he would be fine. He'd be able to do it for her. He'd finish the job she had begun. But he was also realistic.

Being there might change everything. Seeing her might...

The GPS indicated he should make a left turn, and he slowed to stop on the side of the road. The warehouse wasn't what he'd expected. Damn if it wasn't lit up like a strip mall parking lot. It wasn't old or broken down.

"Why the hell did Reval bring me out here?" He said it for the team to digest even though he couldn't hear their reply. "This place is brand spanking new. At least there seems to be a place for your chopper to land. Open parking lot, open fields around it. And completely in the middle of nowhere. See you on the other side, guys."

He turned into the lot, backing right up to the front door. *Why not?* He unlocked the gun safe built into a panel of his truck then tossed his keys in the cup holder. If they made it out of the building alive, it might help them escape.

Heading to the main door, laptop in hand, he gave it a tug and it opened. An electronic bell alerted anyone who could hear that he'd walked through the front. Security cameras followed him from the entryway down the empty hall of offices.

"Hello?" He raised the laptop over his head and shoved his shoulder into the last door.

Staying in the doorway, he searched the almost-empty warehouse.

"Walk straight ahead."

"They're waiting inside the office."

About halfway to the wall in the middle of the emptiness, the two who had spoken to him stepped from the darkness. One pointed an automatic weapon at his chest while the other frisked him, then pushed him forward again.

"Open the door and go inside."

Sure enough, the wall had a door. He hesitatingly opened it to find an exact replica of the office he'd stood in earlier that morning. Rushdan Reval sat behind his desk. Sal stood on the other side of the door. The two men from the chase the night before were on either end of a fish tank empty of fish.

Therese was on the couch. She sat with her head back

as if she'd fallen asleep. She didn't stir and seemed to be out cold.

"I guess the party can get started now that I'm here." Wade held the laptop out in front of him.

The nerdy guy from the airport stepped through the door after him and took it. He opened it on the desk, punched several keys and shook his head. "Just like we thought. Bogus info. No tracker. You still want him to do it?"

"I think with the proper motivation he'll do fine." Reval waved his hand toward the unconscious Therese.

Damn.

Chapter Twenty-One

Wade's mind got stuck on what Reval had done to Therese to keep her so solidly out of commission. He shifted gears to what the criminal who'd escaped the law too many times had planned for them both. Why here in this remote part of Denton County?

"I suppose a good investigator like yourself," Reval said, leaving the comfort of his chair, "wants to know why you're needed."

"You might say that."

"Access, access, access." Reval moved toward Therese, leaning on the arm of the couch closest to her. "I need to get in and out of a place without detection."

Reval flicked his finger in the air and the nerdy man at the laptop crossed the room and held out his hand in front of Wade.

"We'll take the phone back from the racetrack."

Wade pulled it free from his back pocket and handed it over. The younger man pulled a screwdriver from his hip, popped open the cover and removed both the battery and SIM card. One of the what-ifs had just happened.

Wade was cut off from the team. They'd be deaf and blind until they landed and set up some type of surveillance.

"Tell me how much of my plans does the Homeland task force know?"

"Homeland?" Wade tried to play dumb. "I don't work too much with those characters."

Reval slapped Therese's check, snapping her head to the left, but she didn't react.

"Wrong answer, Ranger Wade. You won't get very many, so you might want to be truthful."

"You drugged her. What did you give her?"

"You see my predicament, don't you, Hamilton? You're here and I'm certain you didn't come alone. But I still have a problem." He splayed his hands toward Therese. "I need to know if her task force has discovered my plans."

"There's no reason to hurt Therese. She didn't pass anything to me."

"Oh, she's not hurting. I promise she's not hurting… yet." He pulled a syringe from his jacket pocket. "But we could make certain. Just one more little push and she won't have any pain at all ever again. That the path you want to choose?"

Reval lifted Therese's arm. He'd do it. Wade didn't have any doubts.

"Okay, okay. I believe you. But I honestly don't know what you're talking about. I followed your directions at Love Field and brought the laptop back to you."

"Then why are you so disappointingly late?" He shifted the needle closer to her vein.

"I… I had to hide until the cops searched the entire airport because of your men. I got here as soon as I could get back to my truck. What more do you want me to say?" Dammit. Even he thought he sounded like he was lying.

"Maybe we should try to wake her up?" Reval stood, backed away and slashed a fat finger through the air. Sal and his armed companion moved across the room.

"I don't know anything. Nothing." Could Reval's computer guy tell that the FBI had searched what was on the laptop?

"Don't waste my time, Wade. This isn't a negotiation," Reval continued. "Tell me what I want to know, but you're right. An overdose is such an easy way out for Therese." Another flick of his finger sent Sal and the second man to either side of Therese.

"Wait. Look, I don't know what those two inept morons you sent to Love Field told you, but I followed your instructions. I'll do whatever you need me to get done." Wade's heartbeat skyrocketed. They were going to torture Therese.

He had no way to stop it or let anyone know it was happening. And she was still out cold.

They hooked an arm under Therese's arms, semistanding her, then dragged her to the fishless tank of water against the wall. Wade hadn't noticed that the tank stood just a little higher than waist level. Not before Therese's head lobbed forward and her long hair fell to drift in the circling water.

Therese was suspended between the two men.

"Stop! What do you want me to tell you? I wouldn't be here if the Rangers knew anything."

"Do it," Rushdan commanded.

They lifted her higher and shoved her head underwater.

"She'll drown. Are you trying to kill her?"

When Therese struggled and kicked to get air, Sal let her catch a short breath before shoving her down again.

"Come on, Reval. This is between us. If you don't believe me, then put my head underwater."

Reval nodded. Sal grabbed Therese's hair and wrenched upward. She spit out tank water as she sucked in air. She tossed her head, waking up from whatever drug Reval had given her.

Therese kicked and twisted to get free. Then they did it again.

And again.

Wade grabbed the edge of the couch and held his breath along with Therese. Each time she got close to getting a deep breath, Reval's men sent her under again.

Reval snapped his fingers and Sal grabbed a fist of her long hair, yanking her back. No one said anything as she slowly recovered.

"W… Wade?" Therese gasped.

"Reval, dammit, stop. I did what you asked. You want the money. I'll get the money I'll have it first thing in the morning. Just don't do this to her any longer."

The men allowed Therese to collapse on the floor. Wade watched her back rise and fall as they gave her a long break to recuperate.

Reval casually walked back and forth in front of the windows that looked out to an empty warehouse. He flipped his phone between two fingers, then tapped it against his chin.

"Here's the deal, Hamilton. I don't believe you, and Therese shouldn't have, either. If she's not a dirty undercover cop—which, looking back over the past three years, I think she is. Then, she's just plain bad luck. Either way, I need to get rid of her."

"His phone," Therese whispered.

"What was that, my love?" Reval bent and grabbed her hair himself, yanking her head back to see her face.

"Every…thing on phone. Forget me."

"Well, look at that. Seems she is a cop and willing to sacrifice herself for the better good. Are you Ranger Wade? Are you going to insist that you aren't here undercover and you aren't a part of the elite task force set up to stop my show?"

Therese was lifted and shoved under the water again. Once there, her face was jerked toward Wade. Eyes wide and scared, hair swirling around her face, she was upside down, holding whatever breath she could. Then Reval snapped his fingers and Sal grinned.

Sal pushed on her harder, lifting her feet off the soaking wet carpet. She was practically to the bottom of the tank when her air escaped in a large set of bubbles. Wade wouldn't let her die. Not like that. Not because of him.

"All right! Let her up!"

"And what?"

"I'll tell you what I know. But let her breathe."

Reval waited another long second before nodding his head to bring her out of the water. Sal didn't move fast enough. Wade jumped from the couch and shoved Reval's men out of the way. He lifted Therese and laid her on the floor, immediately pushing against her belly.

"God, she's not breathing." He needed to push properly on her diaphragm and get the water out of her lungs.

Wade situated his hands, ready to begin CPR, when both men grabbed his arms. He struggled, pushing them away. He shoved on Therese's chest once, twice. They grabbed him again.

"Enough!" Reval shouted. A weapon was fired into the ceiling, causing his men to freeze. Wade was finally unrestricted and forced pressure on Therese.

Therese coughed. Water spewed from her mouth. She turned on her side, still throwing up water. Wade gave a rough shake with his body when both men grabbed him again. They released him and he gently stroked the hair away from her face and tried to reassure Therese she would be okay.

He loved her so much he'd do anything to keep her alive. He had his answer. He chose her over everything.

"His…his phone," she struggled to say.

Wade understood. The information they needed was on the phone Rushdan Reval had in his pocket. He helped Therese sit up, his eyes falling to the burner phone left in pieces. Damn, the men of Company B wouldn't know.

Whatever happened, he and Therese were the only hope of stopping this man. Of stopping the terrorists who wanted the algorithm.

With her dying breath she'd been telling him what he needed. And with her dying breath, he'd discovered he'd tell Reval anything to keep it from being the last thing he heard her say.

"So, Ranger Wade, let's hear all about this task force the government has brought together to stop my little show."

Chapter Twenty-Two

They were waiting. At least half an hour. Maybe longer. Therese had no idea.

Rushdan's men had taken their watches and phones, locking them in this fake office. At least they had a working toilet. With Wade's help she'd even rinsed the fish and whiskey smell from her hair in the sink.

"What time was it when you arrived?"

"After ten at night." His eyes were closed as he lounged in the corner of the couch.

"I don't know how you can sleep."

"I'm not. You're doing a good job keeping me awake."

"How can you relax like that?"

Wade sat up, blinked rapidly and pushed his fingers through his hair, making it stick straight into the air. It would have been cute under different circumstances.

"Okay, I'm sitting up so you'll think I'm completely awake."

Shoot, it was cute. She quit her pacing directly in front of him. "You need to fix your hair."

"What's wrong with it?"

"Smooth it down."

He clasped her hand and tugged her to his lap. "Now you can fix it however you want."

"This isn't the time, Wade."

"Of course it is. I'm not going to fight with you, Therese. You can be mad at me, but I'm not flinching."

"I'm not mad at you. I'm…" She covered her bruised cheeks with her fingers, whispering underneath them, "Why aren't we trying to get out of here?"

"I had a good look at this box from the outside. We're covered by men with long guns and there's nothing to hide behind if we do manage to knock down one of the walls." He tugged her fingers from her face.

"Still…"

"You nearly died tonight, sweetheart. I wouldn't have… I mean…" He cleared his throat a couple of times and pulled her into his arms closer.

"I didn't die," she whispered, dropping her head to his shoulder. "How long until your partners come bursting in that door?"

"After they freak—because I'm not there to calm them down," he answered softly into her ear. "They'll find a way to discover what's going on. Then they'll wait because we're all taking our orders from your boss."

"And they're after the programmer."

"And none of them know we could get that information right now off his phone."

"Right." Reluctantly, Therese pushed back to look into Wade's eyes again.

She had no clue what he thought. After being undercover for three lonely years, she still couldn't get a read on this man. Even with time on their hands, she couldn't broach the subject of their differences. Too risky.

"I should probably…" She began to move from his lap. "You know, if they come in… Oh wait, your hair."

Wade used both hands to smooth it down.

The door opened with a grunt from Sal. "Time to go. Hands behind your backs."

They were both handcuffed and walked out the back of the warehouse. Wade had filled her in on their location and his curiosity about it. When they walked outside, why they were there was explained with one word…helicopter.

"We'll make an emergency landing at DFW. Flashing your badge around will get my men where they can have access to the systems they need. After we're done, we'll take off, leaving the two of you behind to do whatever you want."

"That's it? You think I can flash my badge and no one will call for confirmation?"

"If they try, it'll be up to you to make sure they don't." Reval climbed inside next to the pilot. "Let's speak plainly. If I don't get what I want Hamilton, neither do you."

"You'd kill her?"

"You know I will."

Sal placed duct tape over both their mouths. They climbed up and were strapped tightly in.

It wouldn't be a long flight to DFW. The control lights put off enough light for her to watch Wade's eyes move around the small bubble they sat in. She was wedged between the guy with glasses and Wade. Sal on his other side.

The helicopter bobbed up and down and around. She'd never been affected by things like this before, so it was probably the drug Rushdan had given her earlier. Her head spun and she wanted to be sick with the hopelessness consuming her.

Right up to the moment that Wade tapped on her bare foot to get her attention. Just looking in his eyes gave her strength. He gestured with his shoulder and eyes. Looking at his strap and then the pilot. This time she had no trouble discerning what he thought. He wanted to crash the helicopter.

Crash it. Stopping the potential attack. Probably killing everyone on board. She shook her head. No. They needed the programmer. Sure, one of their team members might find an extra phone on Rushdan. But the programmer would be gone as soon as he didn't get his information tonight.

Wade bent his ear to her mouth.

"Too risky," she said under the restrictive tape. "No."

The sounds from the helicopter were extremely loud without a headset, which the others were wearing. But he understood the no. Or at least she hoped he did.

Therese stretched her mouth to loosen the tape around her bottom lip and chin. Then she pulled at it by scraping the corner against Wade's shoulder. He copied her movements until they both had it free enough to talk. No one noticed the loose tape since it still connected on the top.

"Can you hear me okay?" she asked directly in his ear.

He nodded and then turned his mouth to her ear. "So we're not going down in a blaze of glory?"

She shook her head. She'd been willing to die in that fish tank, but knowingly dropping out of the sky… Maybe the drugs had clouded her mind enough then, to where she'd given up hope. But now it was different with Wade next to her.

"We can find a way through this without killing ourselves." She truly believed that.

Wade responded with a raised eyebrow and a look toward the pilot.

She used her chin to get his attention again. "I know what you're thinking," she said, continuing their dialogue directly into his ear. "But circumstances change."

He drew his eyebrows together questioningly before

leaning to her. "You didn't do your mind-reading trick. I'm waiting." Then put his ear back to her lips.

Explaining what had been in her mind during the time she'd been struggling to breathe would take longer than a helicopter ride. And maybe fewer restraints. She wanted to kiss him and tell him how glad she was to still be alive.

It didn't make sense to go there. To tell him how she felt—especially about him. Or did it? Would she get another chance?

"Okay, I'm not a mind reader. But I need to tell you how grateful I am that I found you last night. Sorry to get you involved, but once you were, I've been truly grateful not to be alone."

He nodded but didn't turn to speak.

"You know we actually met a long time ago," she continued.

The young man sitting next to her pulled a white Stetson from a gym bag at his feet.

"What the hell?" Wade shouted.

Apparently it was loud enough for everyone to hear. Rushdan's man slapped his hand across the duct tape again—first hers, then Wade's. It was the first time she'd looked at what the younger man with glasses wore. White dress shirt, slacks, Western boots and a silver star inside a circle. Wade's Texas Ranger badge.

Add the Stetson and people would assume…

So why hadn't they killed her and Wade back at the warehouse? Why did they still need them alive?

The helicopter changed directions. Fast. Then began a spiral. It was dark, but she could tell they were close to DFW. No one around her looked panicked. They were staging an emergency landing. They would be on the ground and all have their weapons inside the airport perimeter.

Staged or not, it felt real, like an out-of-control roller coaster stuck on the same loop.

The man next to her dropped his headset, placed the Stetson on his head and then loaded a round into the chamber of his handgun.

It seemed like forever but actually only took a few seconds before they landed with a hard thud. Rushdan was out first and opened the door closest to Wade. The man dressed like a Texas Ranger ripped the tape from their mouths and unbuckled her. He tugged until she was sprawled face first on the pavement. Sal did the same with Wade.

The sound of the helicopter winding down was accompanied by the smell of smoke. Nothing was wrong mechanically. They'd just covered their tracks.

"Either of you say a word and we shoot your partner," Rushdan said.

"I would have remembered meeting you, Therese. So what are you talking about?"

She wanted to laugh at what Wade had chosen to whisper next to her. But the boot in her back kept her quiet. That and knowing Rushdan would kill Wade.

"Howdy," the fake Wade greeted the emergency crews. "Sorry for the bit of excitement."

Wade tapped his boot against her leg. "I've never said howdy in my entire life."

Chapter Twenty-Three

Wade had been pulled to his knees. If he'd wanted to tell someone what was going on, he couldn't have. There was no one to tell. Since the helicopter hadn't been on fire, the airport first responders left. Two cop cars were between him and any law enforcement officers.

Reval's plan to get into DFW Airport had worked. The pilot stayed with the helicopter. The computer guy impersonating him—something he'd make sure charges were brought about—stood guard with a handgun and a long gun. They'd done a good job separating him from Therese, who now sat in the locked back seat cage of a black-and-white.

"I'm sorry but our transport can't get here for another fifteen," Reval explained. "I wish we could get out of your way."

"No problem, Deputy," an officer said.

Cargo planes passing by on the local runway drowned out the rest. Reval shook hands and rejoined the computer nerd.

"When are they leaving?" the nerd asked. "Our window is closing."

Reval took the long gun from him, propping it on his hip. "The car with Therese is staying. Make your move after the other one departs."

"Got it."

Wade pulled at the cuffs. Whoever gave the movies the idea that it was easy to dislocate your thumb to slip handcuffs off had to have been crazy. He tried and didn't succeed.

The second unit pulled away and computer nerd removed his handgun, shifting it, ready to bring it up to take aim. He'd obviously had some type of training, and looked military calm. Wade moved slowly, trying not to be seen, shifting one foot from back to front, ready to stand.

The remaining police officer turned to face the computer nerd, who raised his weapon.

"Take cover!" Wade yelled too late.

The officer went down as Wade threw himself into the computer nerd, trying to stop him. The nerd moved but was able to recover before Wade took him to the ground.

Wade ended on his back with a gun barrel under his chin.

"Andrew, put that away and get him up," Reval said, jabbing the long gun and forcing Wade's neck to stretch.

Andrew the nerd guy pulled Wade to his feet and immediately punched him in the kidney. "You can't save anyone, Hamilton."

"Now, Andrew, you know he might be able to save Therese if he does as he's told," Reval said, pointing the gun at the police car.

Getting their attention back on himself, Wade said, "Why do you need me? Not that I'm in a hurry to leave this world, but Andrew thinks he looks pretty good in that hat."

"Make sure Andrew gets what he needs and there's a chance I'll let you both go."

"You really think I believe that?"

"I think *she* does. I don't understand how you turned her after last year. She was so loyal."

He'd let Reval think that was what happened. It would just get bloody sooner if the criminal knew Therese had been undercover this entire time.

"Let her go now and I'll give you my word."

"Your word means nothing to me. And I don't want to let her go." Reval stuck the long gun under his arm and used the nail on his little finger to pick something from between his teeth. "You can earn her freedom or she comes with me. Think about that while you help Andrew."

"At least let me say goodbye."

"No way. We need to get this over with. We've wasted too much time talking," Sal said from behind them.

"I think you might really care about our Therese." Reval used his hands once again and made a sweeping sign toward the police car. "Make it quick."

With a vocal protest heard under the engine of a freight airliner, Andrew unlocked the back door. Therese got out, but the kid kept a hand on her shoulder.

"So this is goodbye?" she asked.

"I still think you're pulling my leg about our first meeting."

"Really? That's all you have to say?" She laughed a little even as Andrew pushed her back inside the car.

"You go first," he encouraged.

"All right… I love you. Keep yourself alive."

"You owe me an explanation," he shouted as the door slammed.

He could have said he loved her, too. The words were in his heart and on the tip of his tongue. But not like this. Maybe he should, since her admission gave him courage he didn't realize he'd been missing.

Therese placed her forehead against the window. Her long dark hair fell to either side, hiding most of her face. If she looked up…made eye contact with him… But she turned, dropping her head to the back of the seat.

THERESE'S BLOOD PUMPED through her veins, making her lightheaded. She'd said it. Admitted that she loved him in the least romantic setting ever. Captured.

She blinked rapidly to keep away the tears. Yeah, she wasn't a girl who cried. Even when the love crush of her life didn't say he loved her back. *Blink. Blink. Blink.*

There are more important things on our plate. Like how do we get free and prevent a domestic terrorist strike. Yeah. That.

Rushdan Reval took the keys and opened the driver's door. "You both have twenty minutes. Deploy and get back to Hangar Four," Reval told Sal and the kid. "You know we won't wait for you, Andrew."

Deploy what?

"Don't worry. I could do this in my sleep," Andrew answered.

Deploy what?

The algorithm, naturally. Andrew must be the programmer. She'd already pushed and twisted the handcuffs, making her wrists raw. There was nothing in the back seat of a police vehicle to help her. She wasn't wearing anything useful—not even shoes.

Andrew shoved Wade to get him moving. To where? Too many unanswered questions. After nearly drowning, admitting that she worked with Wade and that she loved him…there was little chance Rushdan would release her.

She needed the handcuff key and had no idea even where to look. The kid Andrew had snapped the metal bracelets on her, but maybe—just maybe—Rushdan had kept the actual key on his person.

Rushdan got behind the wheel and was joined by the pilot. *Curious.* Andrew and Wade ran across the field to a group of buildings.

"Where are we going?" she asked through the police cage.

"We're leaving. For good. After this *show* there won't be a need for any more petty moneymaking schemes. My clients will know what we can do and will be paying anything I ask."

"Aren't we leaving in the helicopter?"

"Why would we do that, my dear? It's so much nicer to fly in a private jet. Especially to South America. You'll love it there."

"You aren't going to kill me?"

They didn't travel far. Across a large parking lot from the building where Wade and the kid were entering. It was too dark and too far to read the name on that building. But by looking above it as she was escorted from the car, she could see a tower.

It must be a control tower for private and cargo planes. By accessing this system, Rushdan could gain access to the main air traffic control network for DFW.

"You're going to crash planes? Are you crazy?"

"By your standards, most definitely." He yanked her along with him through a small door the pilot had already unlocked.

"Please don't do this, Rushdan. So many people could be killed."

"I won't be doing anything except living the high life in Costa Rica or Buenos Aires or the Mediterranean. I haven't really decided." He made his signature disgusting sound as he sucked his teeth open to a smile.

SHOWING THAT HE was entirely out of shape, Andrew uncuffed Wade's hands while continuing to huff, puff and curse as they ran. They waited on a security guard to open the door and then the nerd placed the white Stetson on Wade's head. It sat on the crown instead of his forehead, obviously not fitting.

"Doesn't seem to be my size."

"No one cares. You tell the guard we're here to serve this warrant." The kid pulled a piece of paper from his back pocket. "Don't worry. It looks real and is for one of their people on duty tonight."

"And what if he says no?"

Andrew fingered the handgun holstered on his hip. "Convince him or he dies now. And then your girlfriend, of course."

"You feel like a tough guy? A big shot? Shooting that cop back there is the action of a coward." He waited for his words to rile Andrew.

They apparently did, but as the kid started to unholster his weapon, the door opened. Andrew held up the fake warrant, but he remained silent.

"I'm Texas Ranger Wade Hamilton and this is my partner. We're here to serve a warrant on..."

"David Liteman." Andrew flicked the fake warrant.

"Before you object," Wade cautioned the guard and took a step inside, removing the ill-fitting hat. "We know this is a highly unusual situation. But we wouldn't have been allowed on the grounds if it wasn't all cleared. Right?"

"Somebody should have called me," the guard grumbled. "But hey, it's only my job. What do I know about protocol?" He turned his back on them and went to his desk. "Nobody ever tells me anything."

Wade entered, followed by Andrew. He could take

this kid at any point. There wasn't anything tough about him. He was just plain more experienced and knew what opportunities to watch for. The kid didn't.

Point in fact, he could have disarmed the kid coming through the door.

"Is he upstairs?" Andrew asked.

"Yeah. Where did you think he worked, here at my desk? Elevator is around the corner, but if you don't want him to see you coming, the stairs are back this way." The guard pointed back over his shoulder.

Andrew walked into Wade's back. Okay, that was another place to disarm him. Throw one punch and the kid would be out cold. He steadied him, waited for him to turn around and followed him to the stairwell.

Yeah, kid, I'm following you, not the other way around.

Once in the stairwell, Andrew seemed to realize he was vulnerable. He waited until Wade passed him and then left two stairs between them.

"What do you need access to?" Wade asked. "Are we going up to the control windows?"

"Not if there's computer access outside the room."

"Like from the supervisor?" Wade pointed to the sign just under the second-floor symbol.

"That should work."

"Where did you get the idea for this malware thing anyway? You that smart, Andrew?" Wade held the door open, hat still in his hand and waited for the kid. "I mean, you seem smart and all. But no one does stuff like that alone. Right?"

"Smart?" He waited at the top step. "I take exception to that description. I opened your sealed court records in less than a minute. This algorithm took me years to develop. The sophistication of the decryption capability is insane."

"You developed it all by yourself? That's hard to believe."

Andrew pulled his handgun. "Oh no, you don't." He waved the barrel, indicating Wade should go through the door first. "Why do you want to know about me?"

"Hey kid, I have no clue about computer viruses. Nothing like that. None of it's my cup of coffee." He shrugged, taking a step into the second-floor hallway.

"Coffee? It's your cup of *tea*, you ignorant cowboy." Andrew relaxed his direction with the gun, dropping the barrel toward the floor.

Just another opportunity for someone of Wade's experience. And now that he knew Andrew was the programmer…

Wade tossed the Stetson to the kid, whose natural reaction was to catch it. Then Wade grabbed the kid's arm and used his momentum to flip the gun backward behind Andrew. He turned, pinning him to the open stairwell door, lifted his elbow hard into the man's chin and heard the gun drop to the floor.

Then for good measure, Wade pounded his fist twice into the kid's solar plexus, knocking his breath from him. He dropped him facedown to the floor. Out cold. Wade rolled the kid over, grabbed hold of his collar and slid him across the slick linoleum floor to the elevator.

"But I don't drink tea."

He frisked the kid, looking for a phone. Nothing except a flash drive, which he pocketed. He pulled Andrew onto the elevator. He hated doing it, but if was going to save Therese, leaving this guy with the incompetent guard was his only option.

"What the hell is going on? Did he fall?"

The guard stood and moved while Wade jerked on the kid, sliding him through the elevator doors. He'd seen an empty office on the way to the stairs, which would be a good place to lock this terrorist up.

"Look, I don't have time to explain. Call 911 and get this man to a secure—"

"Help me," Andrew whimpered.

Wade couldn't finish the sentence. Words and thought left him as something slammed into the side of his head. He hadn't seen it coming. Nothing.

Chapter Twenty-Four

Damn blind spot floated through Wade's mind as he rolled in pain. Blurred vision. Pain. Cool floor against his skin. More pain.

"Yeah, this is Randy Allister in the northwest tower. I need help. I ain't kidding. This is the real thing."

Wade used his arms in an attempt to push himself to an upright position. It didn't work.

"Tell 'em not to come in hot. A woman's life depends on it," Wade said. But he didn't know if the guard listened to him.

Randy Allister seemed to be dancing around the room, gun drawn in one hand, radio in the other. Wade managed to roll over and the guard seemed to move faster or maybe there were two of him. He lifted his hands, trying to calm the inexperienced guard down.

"Listen to me, please." Wade covered his left eye, eliminating the double vision. "Randy, I've got to get to Hangar Four."

"You ain't going anywhere, man. I brought you down, imposter."

"You brought down an authentic Texas Ranger. But I'll forget all that if you just let me get to Hangar Four."

"No way. Capturing you might save my job."

"You mean because you let us in the building to begin with."

"Yeah, well. They'll forget that part when I show 'em I captured you."

Wade rubbed the side of his head, vision clearing a little. "I doubt that. You're letting the real bad guys get away."

"Don't listen to him," Andrew screamed, trying to get up and away from Wade.

"Tell you what, Randy. We'll both sit here in your custody if you just get on the horn and ask the cops to check out Hangar Four." If Wade couldn't get to Therese, maybe other cops could.

"No! You can't!" shouted Andrew. "He's…he's trying to trick you. I watched him shoot one of you in cold blood. He's still lying out there."

Wade used his heels to slowly push himself to the wall next to the desk during Andrew's yelling. He didn't want to injure the guard, but he had to get to Therese.

"You can both stay right where you are until the DFW cops get here. They can decide which of you is lying and which is telling the truth."

"Listen, Randy. What would it hurt to ask your friends not to flash their lights on the way here? I'll wait." He stuck his hands behind his head. "I won't give you any trouble."

"He's right, Randy," Andrew moved to the same position. "Be the hero and save this woman's life. She'll die if the terrorists see the cops."

"Terrorists? What kind of terrorists? Is something going to blow up?" Randy began nervously shifting back and forth, mumbling the word *terrorist* with each step. His movements and chanting made Wade's headache grow exponentially.

"Just get on your radio and call it in."

"No! Don't listen to him," Andrew shouted, drawing Randy's attention. "They'll kill her."

Wade took advantage of the moment and pulled his jeans leg up over the boot with the Love Field guard's weapon. He'd grown used to the weight and almost forgotten it was there until feeling it while lying next to Therese earlier.

If he was lucky, neither the guard nor Andrew would see him remove the handgun. Not that his luck had been holding during the past two days.

The radio squawked and Wade used the distraction to pull the gun. Andrew jumped up, sliding feet first, using the guard's ankles like second base. He popped back to a standing position gun in hand.

Wade stood covering his bad eye to search for the radio.

Andrew roared, dipped his head and charged. He crashed into Wade. The force took both of them rolling into a watercooler stand but they both managed to hold on to their guns.

Back on the floor, they were at a standoff, pointing the guns at each other.

"Find your radio, Randy!" Wade shouted, keeping his gun on Andrew. Then told the kid who pointed the gun at the guard, "Don't do it. Put it down."

The guard crawled on all fours. Andrew's barrel vacillated between Wade's head and the back of the guard.

"Got it!" Randy raised the radio in the air.

The reverb of the shot rang in Wade's ears as he saw the poor guard spinning to the side from the force of the bullet. Wade pulled the trigger. He couldn't allow Andrew to fire again.

Wade's aim was true.

Andrew's eyes were wide and fixed, staring at him as if he didn't understand what had happened.

"Oh my God. I've been shot. I've been shot," Randy kept chanting.

Wade stood and removed the gun from Andrew's death grip. He went to the guard's side, taking the man's free hand and placing it on the wound.

"Keep pressure on it like that. Good. I'm sure someone heard the shot and will be downstairs to help you."

"Are you guys really terrorists?" Randy asked.

Wade grabbed the radio and turned for the door. "He was." He stopped and pulled his badge from Andrew's belt. "This is mine."

He pushed the door open with his shoulder. "This is Texas Ranger Wade Hamilton. Cars approaching northwest DFW, refrain from lights and sirens. Possible terrorist with hostage at Hangar Four. Be aware am on foot and armed. Ambulance needed at tower. Officer down. I repeat, officer down. Don't run code."

"Hamilton, stand down. Team is on the way," a voice he recognized told him. Recognized as one of the men making decisions about this operation. But Steve Woods had no clue what was actually going on.

Wade dropped the radio and covered his bad eye to limit the double vision. He couldn't be sure which hangar was number four, but directly across the concrete lot—large enough for two 747s to pass—sat an empty police car.

He had to get to her. So he ran.

THERESE PROPPED HERSELF on an old desk in the corner of the cramped hangar. The airplane took up most of the room. Rushdan and the pilot hadn't threatened her since she'd gotten inside.

They also hadn't seen her pick up a paper clip before she parked herself here. While she fiddled with the handcuffs behind her back, she watched the clock above the door click off the seconds toward twenty minutes.

Maybe they'd forget about her. She wished.

"What happens if the kid can't get it done?" the pilot asked while removing the blocks from in front of the wheels of the plane.

"He'll do it. This is his crowning achievement. He'll get it done or die trying." Rushdan leaned against the plane's stairs.

"That's what I'm afraid of. The kid is a bit trigger-happy."

"He does get a bit…excited."

"It's getting close to time. We going to wait?"

"No. I have what I need. Tested or not, my copy of the algorithm will bring me millions." He laughed. "I told him twenty minutes. If we wait longer, the authorities might find his mistake near the helicopter. Go ahead and open the doors. Let's get in the air."

The pilot pushed a button and the doors began to creak open.

"And don't forget Therese," Rushdan added before climbing the steps.

The pilot waved his hand at her like he was directing traffic. It was her signal to join them on the plane. She stared at him.

"Move it."

"You don't have to do this. There's no reason to take me with you."

"The boss wants you around, so you're going. Now get up the stairs and buckle in."

"Kind of hard to do with the handcuffs." She popped off the corner of the desk and turned around to show him.

"Nice try. It'll give the boss a reason to get close. Come on." He gave her a hard push toward the plane.

The metal rungs of the ladder hurt her bare feet and keeping her balance wasn't easy without her hands. But she stepped inside the small plane, climbing into the seat closest to the door.

God, she hated feeling helpless. Or maybe it was hopeless. She'd had her fair share of pity parties, but she'd never felt as alone and lost as at this moment. If they took off...

The pilot crawled in behind her, then into the seat to fly.

"Is this it?"

"What do you mean, my dear?" Rushdan answered as if it were any ordinary day. He moved past her to the front.

"You're just going to fly away, taking me along for the ride? Why?"

"I have patiently waited for you to come around, Therese. I hate that you allowed yourself to be taken in by the ranger. I guess he fits every girl's idea of a dream man, doesn't he. I can see why you liked him, so I'll forgive you."

"Forgive me?"

"You're mine now. You belong to me. Wherever I go, you go." He moved from the front of the plane, stopping at the seat opposite her.

"You're crazy," she whispered. And then a little louder, "I don't *belong* to anyone. Especially you."

"I disagree. Once we get to South America, you'll be dependent on me for everything. Water, food, clothes, protection. You'll be grateful then."

"I'll never be grateful, you sicko. Who would be grateful to their kidnapper?"

A loud noise from outside the plane got their attention.

"That must be Sal or Andrew. Looks like you'll have company back here after all."

Body slams, crashes and sounds of a fight grew louder as Therese searched out the windows of both sides of the plane. It had to be Wade. More thuds and metallic slams—someone being thrown into the hangar door.

"Sal? Andrew? What's going on?" Rushdan yelled.

"Pull up the steps, boss. We gotta get out of here," the pilot yelled from up front.

Therese Ortis's family had not raised a helpless girl. She'd never be a woman who was dependent on any man's whim. Especially this terrible, sick man. Her eyes met Rushdan's across the aisle, then darted to the staircase.

The plane rolled forward, leaving the brightness of the hangar, only the dim lights from the controls illuminating the cabin. Rushdan reached for her seat belt. Therese scooted forward in her seat, blocking his hands.

This is going to hurt.

Chapter Twenty-Five

The plane taxied forward from the hangar. Wade had run across the giant parking lot. He was about to pull the door open when someone slammed into him. He hadn't seen anything out his bad eye.

Sal was all over him. Wade kicked out, shoving the crazy man off. Sal turned, jumping on him, forcing the gun from his hand. They both fell to the cement floor and rolled, only stopping when they hit the metal hangar wall.

Wade landed on top and got in the first punch. Sal no longer had a smirk on his face to wipe off. He shoved with both hands and Wade's injured head banged against the wall. Hard. Wade thrust the pain aside and threw his weight into pinning the bigger man down.

The plane kept moving. He could see Reval through the doorway as it passed. Could see Therese through the window.

Sal freed himself by rolling. He wanted on that plane.

"Not so fast." Wade jerked on his legs. Sal kicked out, keeping Wade a leg length away, then rolled and twisted to his feet.

The man's eyes were narrow slits as he used the back of his hand to remove the blood dropping from the smirky tilt to his mouth.

"You want a rematch? Come on. I'll teach you a thing or two." Sal gestured for Wade to come at him. Taunting.

Wade didn't want to engage. He needed to stop that plane from taking off. He needed to save Therese's life. But this man was in his way.

His fingers curled into fists. Then he relaxed, steadied his breathing, found his center and waited for Sal to advance.

"You think you can beat me?" Sal danced from side to side like they had all the time in the world.

Wade kept his good eye focused on his opponent. He watched for the first kick and deflected it with one of his own. He followed with two punches that connected with the center of Sal's chest. Sal absorbed some of the momentum when he took steps backward but quickly charged.

Wade received a right cross that he hadn't seen coming. It stunned him enough that he staggered, giving Sal time to run to the back corner of the hangar.

RUSHDAN MUST HAVE seen the direction of her gaze and made a move to restrain her. She stood slightly, shoving her shoulder into the fat man, keeping him off balance. She took a step forward and he fell back to the seat he'd been occupying.

She stepped over his sprawled legs and leaned against the doorway. She'd nearly fallen trying to step up. How would she get down now that the plane was on the move?

Worrying about how to get down the gangway was a bit bizarre. She had no way to grip anything, with her hands cuffed behind her back. The plane would only gain in speed. She had to go now.

Two men fought at the edge of light from the hangar. She recognized Wade as he swung, connected with the other man's ribs, spinning him sideways. But the other man countered by slamming the back of Wade's thigh, forcing his knee to the ground.

"Therese," Wade shouted between defensive grunts. "Get out of the plane! Now!"

The other man—Sal—removed something shiny from his waist.

"He has a knife!" she shouted to warn Wade.

It was ridiculous to wait for a better opportunity. Each second seemed to flash by. A huff behind her let her know Rushdan was on the move. She took the first two steps. Then the madman was at the door, trying to grab her.

Sal suddenly soared away from Wade, running to catch up with the plane. Therese took another step down. Sal's arm stretched toward the ramp.

One more step. Just one more step. She had to jump. Before she could, her body lurched in reverse, her back falling across the steps. Rushdan jerked her hair, pulling while she screamed.

Having completed its turn, the plane revved its engine and sped up. Therese had no way to hang on. The handcuffs on her wrists were caught on the metal rungs as she twisted, trying to get free. She tugged and pulled her hair from Rushdan's grasp.

The plane sped up a fraction more and she lost her regained footing. She slid free, slamming to the concrete, taking Sal with her.

He landed an arm's length away. In the time it took for her to get her bearings, he straddled her and had the knife raised.

The knife descended while she rolled to her side, trying to deflect the blade from her chest as much as possible. Pain. Her own hiss and scream blocked out all the other sound.

Then a deep shout of pure rage echoed around her. Sal took it as a warning, jumped up and pulled the knife. Coming out was worse than going in. She screamed again, twisting in pain, blinking away the wetness in her eyes.

"You okay?" Wade asked, his hands gently cupping her face. "You're bleeding. Bad."

"Catch him," she gritted through her teeth.

"I think the help can take care of him," Wade knelt next to her. "I need something to put pressure on the wound. Now, don't think I'm trying to be sexy." He joked as he took off his shirt and stuffed it between her arm and ribs.

Each time she opened her eyes, she could see the flashing lights of the emergency vehicles. She had to convince Wade to go after Rushdan. "I'm fine. Go. They don't know him," she got out after a groan. "He's crazy."

"The plane's surrounded, sweetheart. He's not going anywhere. Dammit, No one can see us. I need help getting these cuffs off."

"He has a copy of the algorithm." She squeezed her hands into fists, trying to control the stinging pain. "You've got to find it."

"Stay conscious, Therese. You need to tell me when we supposedly met."

WADE RAN AFTER the plane to get help. It was the only reason he left Therese lying alone in front of the hangar. He caught up with the cars that had brought it to a halt and caught his breath on the hood.

"My partner. She's bleeding. Need ambulance." He

pointed behind him. "The man…armed with a knife somewhere around that building."

"You Hamilton with the Rangers?"

He nodded. "Yes. Can you take me back? Got a handcuff key and med kit?"

"Your team is almost here."

"I can't wait, man. Get her an ambulance."

"Hello out there," Rushdan called from the plane. "We'll surrender, but only to Ranger Hamilton."

"Aw, hell."

Therese needed him. Rushdan Reval was crazy. She'd said it. He agreed. What could he possibly accomplish by going to that plane and taking the man into custody?

He might be able to save lives. And if he didn't try, he was totally sure about one thing… Therese would never forgive him.

He pulled the DFW police officer in close. "You take this car and find my partner. You get her to the hospital no matter what she says. Got it?"

"Yes, sir."

"I need your restraints and your weapon."

"Ranger Hamilton?" Reval shouted.

"I can't—"

"Yes!" Wade nearly grabbed the officer by his shirt front, but dipped his head and regained control. "Please. I'm trusting you with her life."

The officer moved and moved quickly, handing Wade what he needed and jumping in his car. He pulled away like the plane was about to blow.

Oh, damn. What if the plane was rigged to blow?

Chapter Twenty-Six

Wade stuffed the gun down the back of his pants and slapped together the Velcro of the protective vest the officer had shoved at him. He walked with his hands raised toward the stairs of the plane.

"I'm here. You can come out and surrender. Pull off your jacket, hands on your head so we can see you're unarmed."

"Wade, I can't say it's good to see you alive. Come on in."

"Not gonna happen," Jack said from Wade's right side.

"I guarantee you that ain't happening," Slate said from his left.

Heath nodded from his position, pointing a long gun at the nose of the plane. The pilot cut the engine and placed his hands on his head.

"Time to join the party, Reval!" Wade called out. He had to focus on getting Reval out of the plane and finding the second copy of the algorithm. Get this done. But his real attention was on the ambulance that had pulled next to the police car at Hangar Four. If he could just finish this, he could center his attention on Therese.

"You are surrounded," a voice called through a bullhorn. "Come to the door with your hands on your head."

Wade took a step forward. Jack and Slate pulled him back.

"Don't, Wade," one of them said.

Wade's mind was with Therese. He looked at the blood on his hands. The man in the plane had caused all this.

"If she dies..." he ground out in anger, marching forward before his fellow Rangers could stop him. "Get out here, you filthy coward."

He stopped at the bottom of the stairway, one hand on the rope that would have pulled them closed, one foot on the bottom rung. Rushdan Reval appeared in the doorway, hands in the air and no longer smiling.

"Get out."

"I'm on my way. Don't let them shoot me." Reval took his time, handling the steps carefully.

A lot more carefully than Therese had been able to manage. If she hadn't fallen onto Sal, she might just have a few scrapes and bruises instead of a deep knife wound.

Wade jerked him from the last step, spun him around and raised his fist. "If anyone was going to shoot you, it would have been me."

"Whoa, buddy," Jack said, blocking Wade's right hand. "I'll take it from here. You go see about your girl."

Jack placed the restraints around Reval's wrists. Then turned him, searching his pockets, pulling the shoulders of his jacket down to limit his movements more.

"Where is it?" Wade shouted.

"What?" all the men asked, including Reval.

"He has a copy of the algorithm. Therese said it was on the plane. And there's a second phone with all his terrorist contacts. He had it on his person before we left in the chopper. So where is it?" Wade demanded of Reval. Dammit, he wanted to leave.

Jack found a phone but not a second. Wade remembered Therese's dying declaration that they needed the phone.

"We'll take it from here." Steve Woods, Therese's handler, stepped forward to take Reval off his hands.

"He's been using a second phone. It's probably hidden somewhere on that plane. I wouldn't trust anyone else to look for it if I were you."

"You're right," Steve answered, handing off their domestic terrorist to another ranger. Then he slapped Wade on the back. "Great job. I'll meet you at the hospital."

"She lost a lot of blood. The officer said they're moving her to Baylor Grapevine. We cleared to go?" Heath asked behind them.

His friends stared at him and he stared at Therese across the parking lot as they strapped her to the gurney. Jack's hand came down on one shoulder, Heath's on the other.

"She'll make it," one of them said.

Wade couldn't speak. He was willing her to beat the odds and survive. She had to live. They were a good team. She thought so, right?

The ambulance doors shut. God, he could only assume she was still alive, because they were rushing away. Lights flashing, sirens loud and fierce.

The idea that she might die hit him. His knees buckled. If his friends hadn't been on either side of him, he would have fallen to the ground.

He fought the emotion to keep it from his voice, "Get me out of here."

"Sure, man. We got a car waiting."

They walked him to a vehicle. At some point during the ride to the hospital, one of them peeled the vest off him and handed him a T-shirt. Major Clements met them at the emergency entrance and told him the tower security guard was fine. He'd be reprimanded, but he would live.

"She's going to be okay, Wade," Clements said.

Sometime in his haze and daze, he began believing they'd both be fine. Even if the eye injury kept him from working as a ranger in the field, things would be great if Therese was with him.

God, he really was in love. They barely knew anything about each other, but they knew enough. She was definitely the woman for him.

Therese would live. He deserved some good luck. They both did.

"IT'S ABOUT TIME you woke up, sleepyhead." Wade's face filled Therese's vision.

"I think that's the first sound sleep I've had in years. Painful but sound. What time is it?"

They were both alive. Wade raised a straw to her lips and she took a long sip. The cool water felt almost as good as his skin next to hers. It was just his arm, but she used her hand to rub it comfortingly.

"You should ask what day. It's been two." Wade scratched his chin covered in stubble. "You're going to be okay. Sal missed everything vital."

"Doesn't feel like it." She tried to joke but the words sounded rough.

"I bet. But before you convince me to play that question and answer game… Or before the nurse comes in here and they kick me out… You'll want to know what happened after you lost consciousness."

"I didn't pass out."

"I assure you that you did." He kissed her quickly on the lips and sat back down, taking her hand into his. "Reval surrendered and they caught Sal trying to climb out over the barbed wire fence of the airport. Steve searched the plane, found the phone with all the contacts and the algorithm. I had Andrew's copy. Reval swears there were only two. Homeland's priority is to verify that."

"That's good, but—"

"Turns out Andrew was the sole programmer—according to him. Something else DHS is checking into. It looks like his algorithm was just a fancy word for a highly capable decryption code that was designed and modified to take over air traffic control stations. If terrorists had gotten their hands on it, they would have brought down planes, or worse. Unfortunately, Andrew didn't make it. He fired on the tower guard and I had to shoot."

"Can we get back to what's important?"

"I can give you more details later. All you need to know is that Reval is going away for a very long time. No deals."

"I'm glad we managed to succeed with both of our goals. Now you owe me..." She couldn't believe he looked puzzled. "You don't remember our first fight? Come on. You wanted him put away. And I wanted the programmer?"

"Oh, yeah. That conversation seems like a lifetime ago. Your lifetime, to be exact."

"I wasn't going to die. Not when I finally have the chance to live," she whispered. "Speaking of which. It's your turn."

Wade's face relaxed into a smile. He knew exactly what it was his turn to say.

"And you have a story to finish. Talk about drama. You tell me we met years ago and then you promptly get abducted." He picked up her hand and kissed the back of it.

"You first," she prompted.

"Sorry. When did we meet? Did I pull you over when I was with the highway patrol and issue a ticket?"

"Actually, you pulled me out of a wrecked vehicle nine years ago. It was May 31, near San Antonio."

"Damn. You must have just been a kid. That was a long time ago. And you knew where I lived because you were keeping tabs on me?"

"I would never," she lied.

"I bet you would, Therese Ortis. I bet you would." He leaned forward to kiss her properly on the lips, then sat again. "I wish I could remember you from back then. How come you kept it a secret? Did you have braces or something like that you didn't want me to remember?"

"I thought I'd find you here. Ranger Hamilton, you have to spend some time in your room for us to check on you," a nurse said, walking to a whiteboard to write.

"But Debbie, she just woke up," Wade whined dramatically and winked at Therese.

"Oh my goodness, you are awake. Fantastic. I'll page your doctor as soon as I get your vitals." The nurse wrapped a blood pressure cuff around Therese's arm but looked at Wade. "Seriously, Ranger Hamilton, they're debating if they should add restraints to your bed. You'll have to go back to your room now." She put her hands on her hips but she still didn't look very authoritative.

"Room?"

"We kept him for observation," the nurse supplied.

"I have a little concussion. Nothing's wrong."

Debbie smiled at Therese. "And yet they've kept him here for two days."

"Two days? Were you shot? You've really been here for two days?"

"Yeah, but you didn't miss anything by getting some

rest. And they're kicking me out today so I can officially sleep on your chair."

Did he really think she was more interested in the task force operation than him?

"I'll be back after the day shift does their poking and prodding." Wade stood and kissed Therese sweetly on her forehead and then her lips. "Don't go anywhere without me this time."

He smiled and left before she could get a word out.

The nurse pumped the blood pressure cuff, shaking her head. "That man is too stubborn for—"

"Oh, yeah." He stuck his head through the door opening. "I love you, too. Hell, I'll even buy a couch."

TRUE TO HIS WORD, Wade brought his cell phone with him when he returned to Therese's room. She didn't realize how touch and go it had been that first night. One day he'd tell her. But today was for celebrating that they were both alive.

"You look different," Therese said groggily when she awoke a second time.

"Yeah, the nurses thought you might like me better if I cleaned up. I told them that was impossible—for you to like me more—but they insisted."

"I think the same thing about me. I must look horrible."

"Well, I won't ever lie to you, sweetheart. The bruising is pretty bad. But I'm good with it." He ran his thumb along the line of deep purple discoloration on her shoulder. "But the nurses might be right about cleaning up. I had the guys stop by your place and get some things."

"I don't know if I'm up for that."

"Come on, honey. There are a couple of big surprises

you're going to want your hair combed for." He pointed to her bag.

"Can't it wait?"

"You've got about an hour."

"Wade? What's going on?"

"I had a long talk with Agent Woods. He agreed that your undercover days are done. I mean, our pictures have been all over the news and it wouldn't really work any longer."

"And…"

"There are some very important people on their way to be with you."

Therese's eyes filled with unshed tears. "You called my family?"

"Not me, but I'll take some credit."

"He threatened a lot of people to make it happen," Steve said from the doorway. "If it's something you don't want, blame him."

"Oh, I want it," she whispered. "Thank you, Wade."

"Come on, Wade. The nurses are ready to do their thing."

Wade gently kissed a very happy Therese, reluctantly leaving her room.

He stuck his hands in his jeans pockets and wandered to a pillar to wait. Steve followed.

"Thanks for getting the Ortis family up here. It's the best way you could have thanked her for the sacrifice she made for this country." Wade stuck out his hand for Steve to shake.

"I heard what you said. It was the very least we could do. I also heard your physical didn't go so well."

"You heard right. I've got some permanent eye damage." He dropped his head, staring at the floor. "Looks like a spot will be opening up in Company B."

"Are they transferring you?"

"I resigned."

"Got something in mind?"

Wade looked up at Steve. "You offering?"

"Actually, Homeland wondered if you and Therese would be interested."

"I don't know. I just bought a couch."

Steve looked confused. "They move those along with the other furniture."

"Honestly, I'd be happy sitting around a pool for a while. Whatever she wants. You know? I'm not willing to give her up yet."

"I bet you aren't. Same thing happened to me a long time ago. I made that mistake. Let her walk away. Worst day of my life."

"But you're married now, right?"

"That I am. But this is your story and you've got time to think about it." Steve shook his hand again and Wade watched as the agent walked down the hall to the exit.

The nurses came out of Therese's room, leaving the door open. Wade's phone vibrated with a message that the family had arrived. He didn't have much time.

He knocked before entering. Therese sat up in bed, ready for visitors.

"They're on their way up," Wade told her. "It took them an extra day to get here. I think Heath told me one of your younger brothers attends Washington State."

"I know." She grinned. "I kept tabs on all the people I loved."

"So you are a stalker." He crept over to her side.

"I said you were more like a hero crush." She held her hand out, wiggling her fingers for him to take hold. Which he did.

"That does sound a lot better than stalker," he teased.

"Why don't we just keep that as our little secret." She slid her finger down his nose, landing across his lips.

"I won't ever tell. But I will be exacting blackmail on a regular basis." He leaned in for the long, extended kiss he'd wanted for days.

She wrapped her arms around him, bringing him to sit on the bed next to her, ending their kiss in each other's arms. He could have stayed there. Finally resting because she was awake. And safe.

But her family was on their way. Jack had picked them up personally. Wade sat back, wondering how he would tell her he'd had to resign. But he had a feeling she wouldn't mind. That she'd support him in whatever he decided to do.

Life after being a Texas Ranger…

"Hey, I ordered a couch."

"Really? That's what you think is important right now."

He turned off all the outward charm and stared at her. It was one of the few times in his life he actually tried to be serious. "I never had a reason to buy a couch before. This is a pretty big deal."

"Wade Hamilton, are you asking me out?"

"Well, I do have a couch we can make out on now."

Therese wrapped her arms around his neck, tugged him close and kissed him again.

"Now we have to rescue a dog."

"Oh no. No animals. This thing is plush leather. The real stuff. Not that fake pleather."

Epilogue

Six weeks later

Wade's heart pounded in his chest. It could probably be heard by the people sitting at the next table. He'd never been this nervous in his life. Time was running out to change his mind. But he didn't want to change his mind.

Nope.

He was frightened about the upcoming situation he let himself be talked into. What had he been thinking?

"Are you okay?" Therese asked, reaching around her now empty plate to grab his hand. "Should we go to the hotel instead of trying to see a late movie?"

"No. No. I'm good. Sorry. I've just been thinking."

"Well, that's obvious. I don't mind heading back if you're tired. You did drive me to Fort Worth for a lovely weekend and brought me here for a very fancy dinner." She squeezed his hand tighter. "You *are* springing for dinner, right? Did you forget your wallet?"

To answer, he drew his hand away, pulled his credit card from his wallet and held it in the air, signaling to the waiter. Therese leaned back, wiping the corner of her luscious mouth one last time with her napkin.

"I didn't need dessert anyway."

"Did you see something you wanted?" He barely

got the words out when her foot connected with his. He mouthed an "ouch" but it hadn't hurt.

"No, silly. I'd love to head back, too." She winked.

The waiter came and went with the card and Wade took her hand back into his. Things were good. Great, in fact. But they needed this weekend before he headed out for Homeland training.

All their spare time had been spent together, but that had been limited. Between wrapping up the case, grand jury testimony, paperwork, applications, more interviews… Well, they'd barely seen each other. So, yeah, he got the hint about heading back to the hotel.

But first…

They walked hand in hand from the restaurant toward the hotel.

"Hey, what's up?" She dropped his hand, wrapping both around his biceps and giving him a squeeze. "Are you worried about training? They said your blind spot wouldn't be a problem in your new analyst position."

He shook his head, shrugging, and mumbled that he was fine. He could feel her disappointment as she loosened her grip, letting her hands fall to her sides.

Damn…he could barely swallow and his knees really felt weak. He was just nervous. He hated to admit it, but if he wasn't careful he would blow all the elaborate plans.

Maybe he should tell her and not find out if she enjoyed surprises. He'd been assured by his best friends' girlfriends, Vivian, Kendall and Megan, that *all* women liked this kind of surprise.

Wade scooped up Therese's hand, raising her arm above her head and forcing her into a twirl in the middle of the sidewalk. She laughed. He did it again until they were both smiling and he could forget his nerves.

A minute later they were there.

Sundance Square.

The fountains glowed with a gold light. He'd been told by Megan, Vivian and Kendall it was the perfect backdrop. Beautiful. Great for pictures. Something they all said was important. New traditions and all that.

Tradition?

He'd never had much of that but wanted it now. Even if Therese hadn't mentioned it. Not once. A sign the major and Fred had both warned him of.

Their friends were all around them. He recognized the men from their hats and the women who ducked behind them. But the one woman he loved hadn't noticed. Or at least she didn't give him any indication she had.

Too enthralled with the kids running through the plaza fountain, she didn't seem to pay attention to anything behind them. She was focused only on walking and being happy. Maybe on seeing the show she'd mentioned or just getting back to their hotel.

He wanted to scoop up Therese and run with her over his shoulder back to the truck. What if she said no? God, what if she said yes?

Before he could confuse himself any further, he dropped down to one knee. Strangers pointed. Mothers pulled their kids from splashing through the fountain. And Therese turned around to stare at him, covering her mouth with her fingers.

"Wade? Are you—"

"Why's everyone looking like that? Can't a guy scratch his leg?" He pulled up his dress jeans and reached inside his best boot. That was a clue for all of their friends to get a little closer. Her family sat just a little behind and Therese hadn't noticed them yet.

Therese released a long breath and spun away from him. He snagged the ring tucked safely inside his sock and worked it onto his little finger before pulling his pants leg over his boot.

He didn't move even as she took a couple of steps away from him.

"Oh, thank God. I thought you were going to pro—"

He stayed put, his arm outstretched with an engagement ring on display to everyone except the one it was intended for. When the woman with a kid in her arms pointed in his direction Therese stopped, hesitatingly turning back toward him.

Her beautiful eyes were huge, and the tips of her fingers covered her lips, which were open and in the shape of an O. She stared into his eyes, then at the ring, then back again. Her unblinking orbs filled with tears, making them sparkle.

"Is this a bad idea? Do I need to put this back in my boot?"

He spoke as softly as he could. If she was going to say no, he didn't need all of Fort Worth along with their family and friends hearing.

"Therese?"

She blinked and the tears swiftly slid down her cheeks.

Crying. She was crying. Of all the scenarios that had played through his head…*this* wasn't one of them. He began shifting, preparing to get to his feet.

He wanted to wipe her tears away, but he was stuck kneeling and quickly feeling like an idiot. All the doubts his friends had talked him out of after buying the ring slammed into him again.

"Wait!" Her hands extended to keep him where he was. "If there's a question in there somewhere… I might have an answer."

Hadn't he asked?

"Damn. Therese Ortis, would you marry me?"

"When you put it like that, how could a girl say no?" She smiled and offered him her hand.

He slipped the ring onto the appropriate finger and got up off his knee. He barely kissed her before his friends were slapping him on the back and welcoming Therese to the fold.

She began crying again when she saw her family along with Fred and his wife. Everyone was there for the important moment. Wade had never felt blessed before, but he did now.

"You had all of us worried there for a minute," Jack said.

"I was totally caught off guard." Therese smiled at Wade again.

He was still recovering from her answer and couldn't really think straight to reply. He could only feel and this…*this* was completely right. No doubts. He hugged Therese and spun around.

"I love you," he whispered into her ear. "You're not alone in life. I'll always have your back."

"I love you, too. You're the best partner I've ever had."

"I'm the only partner you've ever had. And for this—" he kissed her finger with the diamond "—the only partner you'll ever need."

* * * * *

COLTON MANHUNT

JANE GODMAN

For my lovely husband, Stewart, who is gone but never forgotten. We don't say "goodbye."

Chapter One

The last ten minutes of every puppy class was off-leash time. The dogs, who were all three months old, had spent almost an hour involved in an intense training session. Now was their chance to release some energy and socialize.

Katrina Perry, owner and head trainer at the Look Who's Walking dog-training center, knew this informal period would be more stressful for the human clients than the canines. Let their precious babies go free around these other dogs? What if they ran away, got scared, or were bitten by the class bully? Since this was the first session in an eight-week program, she outlined a few rules.

"I need you to remain seated at all times while the pups interact. If you see your pet engaging in something that looks like aggression, don't be alarmed. Play fighting is a natural behavior and the way they engage with the world." She gestured to Suzie Calles, her assistant trainer. "If there is a genuine problem, one of us will intervene. If your pup, or any other one, appears shy around the others and comes to you, please don't pet them or pick them up. The aim is to get them to relate to the other animals, not the humans."

There were eight dogs in class today, and Katrina had already figured out what would happen. The vocal German shepherd would fall silent the instant another pup approached him. The hyperactive rottweiler would tear around the training ground without even noticing the other dogs. The timid Siberian husky would find somewhere to hide. The others would make some noise before starting to play.

She had been working with dogs since she had volunteered at the local kennels in high school. Initially, her only qualification had been her love of animals but, as her skills had increased, she'd known that this was the only career for her. Yes, she had an intuition where her canine clients were concerned, but she also had years of experience to back up her instincts. Her business had a good name and that had been built on trust.

There was only one pup she had any worries about, and her concern centered more on his looks than his behavior. The little mutt reminded Katrina of another dog she knew, one she hadn't seen for a while.

"Hey, the brown-and-white one looks just like—"

"I know." Cutting off Suzie in midsentence made her feel mean, but she didn't want to have this conversation in the middle of a workday. If she started to have the conversation Suzie wanted, she'd inevitably get upset. The little dog she was thinking of and its owner meant too much to her, and, anyway… "Whoa. Bulldog emergency." Katrina was glad of the distraction.

Drummond, the English bulldog, unable to keep up

with his speedier classmates, had decided to slow them down by sitting on them.

"After a count of three," Katrina said, then she and Suzie lifted the muscle-bound little guy. Their actions released a Yorkshire terrier and a bichon frise, both of whom barked delightedly and tried to encourage Drummond into a repeat performance of sitting on them. As if wounded by the affront to his dignity, the bulldog ignored them and strutted away to gnaw on a fence post.

Minutes later, Katrina brought the session to a close. As they cleared the training ground and set up for the advanced obedience class after lunch, she was conscious of Suzie sending troubled sidelong glances in her direction.

Eventually, she sighed. "You're right. The little brown-and-white mutt reminded me of Dobby."

She sensed Suzie relax slightly. They'd worked together for nearly four years and had become good friends. Until now, there had never been any tension between them. And Katrina didn't have enough friends to let it become an issue. "Have you heard from Eliza recently?" Suzie asked.

"That obvious, huh?" Katrina asked. "I thought I was doing a good job of covering up how worried I am about my troubled twin."

"Maybe someone who doesn't know you well wouldn't have noticed," Suzie said. "But you don't usually check your cell phone every two minutes. And, now and then, I've had to call your name twice because you've been lost in your own world. But your reaction to the Dobby look-alike was what clinched it for me."

"Poor Dobby." Katrina managed a smile. "With looks like his, I always found it doubly sad that he had such a fondness for the ladies."

Dobby was her twin sister's dog. With his big, floppy ears, sparse hair and lopsided jaw, he would never win a beauty contest. What he lacked in looks, he made up for in charm. Dobby was the happiest, most self-confident dog Katrina had ever known. But Dobby wasn't the problem…

"I hadn't heard from Eliza for months prior to the earthquake. That wasn't unusual. She's never been great at keeping in touch."

Suzie knew all about Katrina's sister's checkered past. There was no point in trying to hide it. Not when Eliza could turn up at the training center at any time, either down on her luck, or high on drugs…or both. Or when Katrina might get a call from the police or a hospital and have to drop everything. Eliza claimed to have been clean for over a year, but that was a familiar story.

Then, two months ago, Mustang Valley had been hit by an earthquake. The area was rural and spread out, limiting the overall impact, but many homes and buildings in the small downtown district had been damaged. Since she hadn't known where Eliza was living at the time, Katrina had fired off a series of increasingly frantic messages to her sister, hearing back from Eliza after a few days.

"I didn't know if she was even in Mustang Valley

when the quake hit." Having finished setting up for the afternoon session, they went through to the small staff area to clean up before snatching a quick lunch. "I considered reporting her missing again, but this time I had no evidence that she *was*."

Suzie shook her head. "I wish you'd told me you were dealing with all of this."

Katrina shrugged a shoulder. "This is what it's been like all our adult lives. And it was the same with our mom when she was alive." She sucked in a breath. Although she didn't talk about it, she figured Suzie could guess how hard it had been for her. Her mother's drug and alcohol dependency had shaped her life, and Eliza's, in different ways. In Katrina's case, it had made her view close relationships as something to be avoided.

"Addiction makes people selfish. Eventually, after a day or two of almost constant messaging on my part, Eliza replied to say she was fine. She was still drug-free. Her apartment had been destroyed, but I was to stop worrying because she'd found a wonderful relief organization called the Affirmation Alliance Group. They had given her somewhere to stay and were helping her find her best self."

"I've seen the AAG out and about since the earthquake," Suzie said. "They seem to be doing some wonderful relief work. Everyone in town speaks highly of them."

"I know." Katrina moved toward the coffee machine. "They have a guest ranch about ten miles outside of the town center and, from everything I hear, it's very warm and welcoming. At first, I was pleased that Eliza had gone there."

"At first?"

"She hasn't answered any of my other messages. And..." She wrinkled her nose. "'Find my best self'? That just didn't sound like Eliza."

"Why don't you drive out there and see how she's doing?"

When Suzie put it like that, it seemed so simple. With anyone other than Eliza, maybe it would have been. But Katrina had always handled her twin with caution. Eliza was volatile and vulnerable. It would only take one wrong word to turn their fragile relationship into a nonexistent one.

If she took action and things went wrong, it would be her fault. Remaining passive had become her default position, her approach to life. So what if it was a dull, lonely place to be? Having friends, relationships, a social life... Those things were overrated.

"Yeah. Maybe one evening—"

"No." Suzie took her gently by the shoulders and turned her toward the door. "I meant, why don't you go *now*?"

"Because we have a class in twenty minutes?" Katrina dug her heels in like one of her own problem pups.

"Laurence has nothing on his timetable until six. He can leave the paperwork he has planned and assist me with this class. Tomorrow, I'll help him catch up." She handed Katrina a sandwich and a bottle of water. "You can eat in the car and thank me later."

Spencer Colton pinched the bridge of his nose, trying to relieve the slight headache that was forming behind his eyes. From beneath the desk, a faint rhythmic snoring was evidence that Boris, his two-year-old chocolate Labrador retriever, was sleeping off their strenuous, early morning training session. Not for the first time, he envied his canine partner's ability to relax in between jobs. As the human half of the team, Spencer had read and reread the file into the shooting of Payne Colton so many times he knew most of the details by heart.

But they still weren't getting any closer to catching the shooter.

Although Spencer was a distant cousin to Payne, chairman of the board of Colton Oil and owner of the prosperous Rattlesnake Ridge Ranch, the two branches of the family weren't close. The thought caused Spencer a moment's distraction. Close? His own upbringing had been a world away from the luxurious lifestyle of that enjoyed by Payne's family.

Despite his riches, Payne had been going through a rough patch prior to the shooting that had left him in a coma. Back in January, an anonymous email had been sent to the six board members of Colton Oil informing them that the company CEO, and Payne's oldest son, Asa "Ace" Colton, was not a Colton by blood. Subsequent DNA testing proved that the bombshell claim was true.

Although Spencer didn't know them well, he felt for the family unit that had been shattered by the email. The news was bad enough, and no one deserved to hear it in such a horrible way. The anonymous sender had clearly intended it to cause maximum devastation. It was his job to investigate, and he would do it with understanding toward any family in the same situation, but the Colton link made him even more sympathetic.

The family, torn apart at the news, had been in the process of investigating what could have happened. A mystery unfolded around the events in the hospital on Christmas Eve forty years ago, when Ace was born. It appeared that there was a nurse who'd quit on Christmas day after giving birth to a baby son, and there was a possibility that she'd switched infants. But there were so many unanswered questions around that scenario. The baby boy of Payne and his then wife, Tessa, had been born sickly. Why would anyone have switched a healthy child with a sick one?

Events took another dramatic turn when Payne was working late at the Colton Oil building one night. A cleaning woman had heard a gunshot, footsteps, then a stairwell door shoved open and banging against the wall, followed by silence. She ran toward where the gunshot originated and found Payne on his back on the floor of his office, bleeding from two wounds in his chest. He was rushed to Mustang Valley General Hospital, but had not regained consciousness. Doctors were uncertain if he ever would.

"Sergeant?" Spencer looked up from his reflections to find Kerry Wilder, the rookie detective who had been involved in the case right from the start, standing close to his desk. "You wanted to talk to me about the Colton shooting?"

He leaned back, glad of a chance to straighten his spine. "Just prior to the attempt on Payne Colton's life, Ace issued a threat against him, is that right? Please remind me of the circumstances."

"When it turned out that Ace really wasn't a Colton, Payne ousted him as CEO of the company. It's in the bylaws that the CEO must be a Colton by blood. Ace was devastated and told Payne, 'You'll regret this, *Dad*!' There has been speculation about whether it was intended as a threat. Ace Colton swears it wasn't."

"You interviewed Ace soon after the shooting. What was your impression of him?"

"He was very upset about everything that had happened, and being the suspect in an attempted murder added to his emotional turmoil," Kerry said. "My fiancé, Rafe, is Ace's adopted brother."

"Is Chief Barco aware of that potential conflict of interest?" Spencer asked. He knew Kerry would play things by the book, but he needed to double-check.

"Yes, and he's happy for me to be part of the investigation," Kerry confirmed. "For what it's worth, Rafe doesn't believe Ace is capable of attempting to kill their father."

Privately, Spencer didn't think the opinion of a sibling counted for much of a character reference, but he kept his thoughts to himself.

"In your report, you've stated that security camera footage from Colton Oil shows the shooter appears to be of slight build, five-eight or five-nine, in a black ski mask and covered head to toe in black."

He flicked through the pages of Kerry's report, refreshing his memory.

"That means there was no way to tell gender or age."

It also meant they couldn't rule Ace Colton in or out of the list of suspects. It was frustrating, but typical of this investigation.

"Joanne Bates, the cleaning woman, thinks she heard a man's voice say 'Mom,' followed by the *F* word. Her vacuum was running, so she can't be sure. And Dee Walton, Payne Colton's administrative assistant, found an Arizona State Sun Devils pin in Payne's office."

Kerry nodded. "That was weird because Payne had no affiliation with Arizona State, and he wasn't much into football. There's speculation in the family that the shooter could have dropped it."

"Speculation seems to be all we've got right now." Frustration was a tight knot in Spencer's gut as he placed the pages back in order. "Thank you. This is a detailed account of the investigation so far."

"It's not much to work with, I know." Kerry looked apologetic.

"You can only report on what you're given. This isn't a murder case, so we don't have the same resources. But the shooter obviously meant for Payne to die, and the doctors aren't hopeful about his chances of recovery." Spencer took a slug from the hour-old cup of coffee on his desk. "This has the feel of a case that's going cold."

The case seemed to be bogged down in uncertainty and doubt. There was nothing which he could grasp and make a proper start. Used to being able to give his team direction, Spencer was irritated by the lack of activity. Determined to take back control, he had decided the forward momentum must come from him.

"Is there anything we can do to change that?" It seemed that Kerry was equally unhappy at the slow progress.

"As I said, the shooter wanted Payne dead. If he hears that his victim is showing signs of recovery, he may make another move."

"You're planning to flush him out with false information?" Kerry said. "Isn't that a risky strategy?"

"Payne won't be in any danger, and I've been working closely with the family on this plan. When I spread the word that his health is improving, I'll have him moved to a safe place and put a cop in his old room as a decoy."

With no leads, a sting operation felt like the only logical move. If Payne defied the odds and *did* start to improve, his attacker might decide to come back for a second try. This way, the police would be one step ahead in an inquiry that otherwise felt like it was going nowhere.

"I'll let the family know the details when they are finalized," he told Kerry. "For now, just keep me informed about any new developments."

When she'd gone, he glanced out of his office window, the bright afternoon sunlight catching him off guard. Maybe he should go out and get some lunch. A wry smile crossed his lips. Who was he kidding? When he had a caseload like his, lunch was usually a curled-up sandwich from the canteen and another cup of coffee that would grow cold by the time he got around to drinking it.

Although he hadn't said anything aloud, there was a grunt of agreement from under the desk. As far as Boris was concerned, the eating arrangements were never good enough. With a sigh, Spencer flipped over the Payne Colton report and opened another file.

THE AFFIRMATION ALLIANCE Group Center was surrounded by beautiful Arizona countryside. There was nothing around for miles in any direction, just acres of unspoiled land, palm trees and a shimmering hint of mountains in the distance. Katrina, having set out in response to Suzie's prompting, decided that, if this was isolation, she liked it.

After leaving the highway, she drove along a half-mile, tree-lined dirt drive to the main ranch house. The building had a woodsy, fancy log-cabin exterior and a large triangular roof, and was two stories high. Large, hunter-green gates were pinned back, as though always open, while big potted plants in front added to the welcoming feel.

Since the earthquake, she'd seen the AAG had been carrying out good work around the town, helping those affected. From handing out food parcels, to helping rebuild homes and offering accommodation to those worst affected, they had been highly visible in their efforts. Everyone Katrina had spoken to had been full of praise for the job they were doing.

She didn't know what she'd expected from their

headquarters, but it wasn't anything as warm and feel-good as this. Feeling slightly foolish now about her fears for Eliza, she parked her car next to a row of other vehicles. Her suspicions were the product of years of worrying about her sister. She should be glad Eliza had found this place. Even though she felt a bit reassured by the center's ambience, she was still worried for her sister. She might as well go inside and see if there was anything her twin needed from her. That way, she could see for herself how Eliza was doing in these surroundings.

At the same time that she crossed the parking lot, a man walked out of the building. As he strode across the porch and down the steps, his swagger and clothing drew Katrina's attention to him. *Skater dude.* That's how Eliza would have described him. He had handsome, rock-star features and shoulder-length hair peeking out from beneath a beanie. With his faded jeans and matching jacket, scuffed high-tops and graffiti-covered T-shirt, he was just the type her sister would have been drawn to. With a guy like him around, Eliza would *never* leave this place.

Although she told herself it was wrong to judge on appearances, she knew from experience just how good Eliza was at picking the wrong kind of guy. It was an upsetting thought, one that triggered a series of memories of rescuing her sister from bad relationships with men who strutted just like the one she'd just seen. Despair washed over her again as she headed inside the building. She had to find Eliza and see if she needed help.

The interior of the center was just as impressive as the outside. The wide porch led directly to a large, open lobby with wood-paneled walls, comfortable seating and a long table with complimentary beverages, muffins and fruit. Brass signs indicated the many guest and conference rooms. Beneath a long wooden desk, there was a large portrait of Micheline Anderson, AAG's founder. Blonde, blue-eyed and attractive, she had a warm smile that, even in a picture, seemed to be welcoming. The group's slogan—Be Your Best You!—was on display everywhere.

"Hi, there." The pretty young woman who approached Katrina was a blue-eyed blonde with a full-on smile. "I'm Leigh Dennings, the welcome manager here at the Affirmation Alliance Group Center. How may I help you today?"

"I'd like to see my sister, Eliza Perry. She's been living here since the earthquake destroyed her apartment."

There was a tiny pause before Leigh pursed her lips. "I'm not sure—"

"I just need ten minutes of her time." Now she had taken this step, it was important for Katrina to see it through. She needed to reassure herself that Eliza was okay. Perhaps they could even use this as a new start between them. Maybe next time she came, she would feel she could just call her sister instead of taking the formal step of going through the front desk. On this occasion, she wasn't sure how Eliza would feel about her sudden arrival and didn't feel comfortable with that approach.

"Oh, please don't think I would try to stop you

from visiting with one of our guests." Leigh lightly touched Katrina's arm. "It's just that I don't recognize that name. But let me check our records."

She moved toward the reception desk. Katrina trailed in her footsteps, confusion clouding her thoughts. She had seen signs for about twenty guest rooms. Surely, the welcome manager should know the names of all the people who were staying at the center. There was always a possibility that Leigh wasn't very good at her job. Or that Eliza had lied about where she was staying… It wouldn't be the first time her sister, under the guise of maintaining her independence, had misled Katrina about her whereabouts. In the past, once she needed money, or got into trouble, she'd eventually been forced to tell the truth.

After typing quickly on the keyboard of a desktop computer and then consulting the screen, Leigh looked up. Her smile remained in place, but her gaze shifted around instead of settling on Katrina's face. "Let me just talk to my colleagues."

Before Katrina could protest, the other woman had crossed the lobby and was talking to two men who were positioned close to the door. As Leigh spoke to them, they both turned to stare at Katrina. It was probably a natural reaction, but something about the way they looked her up and down left her with a crawling sensation along her spine.

Get a grip. Just because they look creepy, doesn't mean they are *creepy.*

It didn't matter what she told herself; the men gave

off an unpleasant vibe. After a few minutes of deep conversation, the three AAG members approached Katrina.

"Hi, I'm Bart Akers." In any other setting, Katrina would have figured Creep Number One was hired muscle. He was in his late twenties, big and brawny, with a blond crew cut. She sensed there wasn't much going on behind those light hazel eyes. "This is my colleague, Randall Cook."

Katrina briefly took in the older, taller man at his side.

"I don't know what's going on here, but I got messages from my sister saying this was where she was staying." She still spoke directly to Leigh.

"Maybe she meant another AAG ranch?" Leigh gave a slight giggle, as though inviting Katrina to share the joke.

Clearly, like the fireflies that lived in the Mustang Valley Mountains, the welcome manager was good to look at but not very bright. Even so, Katrina's instinct told her she was marginally more intelligent than the male AAG members.

"This is the place she came to," Katrina said.

"Yes, of course. We've been so busy since the earthquake, it's hard to keep track of everyone we've helped." Leigh had regained her composure and her smile was back to hundred-watt capacity. "Your sister did stay with us for two nights back in April. I wanted to check with Bart and Randall in case they had any information about where she went after she left us."

"We don't." Bart's smile was considerably less attractive than Leigh's. "She said she was going. Didn't say where."

For a moment, the solid tile floor beneath Katrina's feet felt springy. Then she realized her knees had started to shake. It was June. If Eliza had left this place in April, she had been absent for two months. It wasn't the first time her twin had gone missing. But it was the first time Katrina hadn't known about it and been actively looking for her. If she'd known, she would have followed her usual routine and contacted Eliza's friends, liaised with her counselors, and, if all else failed, reported her missing to the police.

"I'm sorry we can't help you." Leigh's gaze flicked toward the door.

Fighting the fog of panic that was threatening to engulf her, Katrina sucked in a breath. "I don't understand. Her apartment was destroyed. You offered her a safe place to stay. She had no money or belongings. Why would she leave? Where did she go?"

"We don't hold that sort of information on our database," Leigh said. "People who spend time with us are free to come and go as they choose."

"But you were out and about in the town offering people your help after the earthquake. That means you had a responsibility to care for them." Katrina wasn't concerned that the volume of her voice was rising. "You must have known Eliza was homeless and vulnerable. How could you have let her walk out of here without making sure she was okay?"

"Hey." Bart stepped closer. "You're clearly worried

about your sister, but Leigh has explained the situation. There's nothing more we can do for you."

If they thought she was letting this go, they were mistaken. Blank smiles and excuses weren't going to work. Katrina would talk to every person in this place if that was what it took to find even a sliver of information about her sister. With no other family and addicted friends who drifted in and out when she was part of their dependent lifestyle, Katrina was all Eliza had.

Just as she was about to tell Bart to take a step out of her personal space, a high-pitched yelp and the sound of claws scrabbling on tile made her turn her head. In a practiced move, she squatted in time to catch a squirming bundle of fur in her arms.

"Dobby?"

As she petted the excited dog and dodged the face kisses, her mind was whirling. How could her sister's pet be here if Eliza left in April? Because…

No. Just *no*.

Ever since Eliza had rescued the pup—whose face was not his prettiest end—when he was eight weeks old, the pair had been inseparable. Whatever else was going on in her life, Eliza made sure Dobby was fed, clean and healthy. The little guy's bed was always positioned alongside Eliza's, he ate ethically sourced food and he had access to the best training at Look Who's Walking, where, until Eliza had stopped coming around several months before the earthquake, he'd also attended play dates and gotten regular grooming.

Tucking Dobby under her arm, Katrina got to her feet, her resolve hardening. "Since my sister left you two months ago, perhaps you'd care to explain why her dog is still here?"

Dobby looked from Katrina to the two men as though he, too, was interested in the answer. For the first time, Leigh's pleasant mask slipped and she appeared nervous. It was a momentary lapse and she recovered quickly, but it was enough to fire up Katrina's suspicions.

"I remember now." The smile returned. "Your sister said she wouldn't be able to keep a dog where she was going, so she left him with us. We've adopted him at the center. He's become quite the AAG mascot, hasn't he, guys?" She threw a help-me-out glance toward Bart and Randall.

"Sure has. He's found his best self here with us." Bart reached out a hand to stroke Dobby's head, but the dog ducked away from him and tucked his head into Katrina's neck. The little guy always did have good taste.

"When I walked in here, you told me you knew nothing about my sister." Katrina kept her gaze on Leigh. "Now you're saying she left her dog behind and he's become your mascot? Call me skeptical, but I find it hard to believe you wouldn't have remembered that detail as soon as I mentioned her name."

Leigh looked down at her computer screen without replying. Bart and Randall also remained silent.

"I'm leaving now. Here's my business card, in case anyone remembers anything more about my sister." Anger stiffened Katrina's spine as she started to walk away. "And I'm taking your *mascot* with me."

Chapter Two

By the time Spencer made his way to the lobby, thoughts had moved on from lunch and he was already planning dinner in detail. His stomach, however, needed something fast and filling right now. Boris, ever hopeful of supplementing his carefully regulated diet with a few treats, trotted eagerly at his side.

Although Spencer and his K-9 partner were trained in search-and-rescue techniques and worked as a team, the other MVPD officers could use Boris if they needed him. The dog went home with Spencer at the end of each day and, when off duty, he was a pet rather than a working animal.

Spencer was crossing the lobby and heading for the canteen when a woman burst through the doors, barging straight into him. The impact had the effect of sending them both stumbling backward. She took the worst hit, however, and, for a moment, it looked like she was about to crash to the floor. But four years in the army had honed Spencer's reflexes, and he grabbed her by the upper arms, steadying her against his body. As he did, his mind registered a few details.

First of all, she was carrying some sort of exotic-looking rodent. Second, she was clearly distressed. And, finally, she was gorgeous.

Tall, with a slender, toned figure, she had dark blond hair that waved to her shoulders with the shimmer of silk. But it wasn't her flawless bone structure, her high cheekbones, or even her full lips that mesmerized him. It was her eyes. Huge and set under delicately arched eyebrows, they were a shade that was somewhere between green, gold and brown, but the color seemed to shift constantly as it reflected the light around her. Spencer figured it was what his mom used to call "hazel" and realized he'd never really seen it up close until now.

"Are you okay?"

She shook her head. "No, I—"

The creature she was holding that had been trapped between them when Spencer caught hold of her looked down at Boris and gave a friendly woof.

"Is that a dog?"

"Of course Dobby is a dog." Indignation seemingly startled her out of her distress, and she pulled away from him. "What did you think he was?"

"I was puzzled," he confessed. "I figured it could be a mutant rat. Or maybe a groundhog that had fallen on hard times?"

For a moment, he thought she was going to smile. He waited hopefully, but her expression clouded over. "I'm not here to talk about Dobby. I need to report a missing person."

Spencer thought about the mountain of paperwork

on his desk. He didn't have enough time in the day to get through his existing workload. Missing persons were below his pay grade…

"I'm Sergeant Spencer Colton. If you wait here while I get us both a coffee, we'll go to my office and you can give me the details."

His willingness to take on her case had nothing to do with the fact that she was possibly the most beautiful woman he'd ever seen. That was what he told himself as he dashed into the canteen. It had even less to do with the runt that was now skipping delightedly around Boris. No, this was about the troubled look in those amazing eyes.

Just keep telling yourself that, Colton, and everything will be fine.

Carrying the coffee and the last, sorrowful-looking sandwich, he led the way back along the corridor to his office. Boris, clearly startled by the antics of the overfriendly Dobby, but too well trained to show it, clung a little closer to his master's heels than usual.

After removing a stack of files from a chair, Spencer pulled it close to the desk and set one of the coffees in front of it. He reached into a drawer and took out a handful of creamers and sugar sachets. "Use plenty of them. Trust me, it's the only way to drink it."

His visitor sat down, and Dobby immediately jumped onto her lap. As she wrapped a protective arm around him, Spencer caught a glimpse of the logo on her T-shirt. He couldn't make out the words, but the picture was a silhouette of a woman and a dog high-fiving each other.

"Colton?" she asked. As Spencer took his own seat and pulled a pad and pen toward him, he was acutely aware of those full-beam eyes watching him. "As in *the Coltons*?"

"Yes and no. My dad and Payne Colton were distant cousins." He laughed. "I'm not part of the dynasty."

"I'm sorry. You must get tired of explaining that."

He shrugged. "If you live in Mustang Valley and your name is Colton, you get used to it. But we aren't here to talk about me. Let's start with some basics." He wrote the date at the top of a blank page. "Name?"

"Katrina Perry." She gave him her contact details and date of birth.

"And the person you wish to report missing?"

"My twin sister, Eliza Perry."

"You're a twin?" Spencer looked up from his notes.

"Yes." She frowned. "Is that important?"

"No. It's just that I'm a triplet. I guess it hit a nerve."

"Wow." For the first time, her expression relaxed. "I thought being one of two was hard. Can't imagine three."

They shared a brief, sympathetic smile. Giving himself a slight shake, Spencer returned to his notes. "We can go into details of Eliza's physical description, identifying features and personal information later. For now, I'd like you to tell me why you believe she's missing."

"If you check your database, you'll see this isn't the first time I've made a report of this type." Katrina took a slug of her coffee. She shuddered slightly as the acrid taste she knew so well hit. "But I'm not some eccentric who does this for fun. My sister is a drug addict… She *was* a drug addict." She pushed back her hair with a shaking hand. "She has lapses, lives on the fringes of the lifestyle, but she'd gotten herself clean—"

"I'm not here to judge your sister," Spencer said. "If she's in danger, it's my job to help her."

"Thank you." She chewed on her lower lip for a moment or two. He'd seen this inner battle so many times in his job. It was natural for a relative to want to protect the privacy of their loved ones. At the same time, the police needed to know the important details. "Eliza had been in a rehab program about twelve months ago, and she was doing well. Ours isn't an easy relationship."

"How could it be? Addiction is a cruel disease and people who suffer from it make bad choices. That has to be hard on both of you."

She shot him a glance that was half surprise, half gratitude. "Most people don't get that. What Eliza wants from me are the things I can't give her. Money, a shoulder to cry on, unlimited amounts of my time…" She shook her head. "Over the years, I've tried my best to get the balance right. If she needs help with living expenses, I make payments direct to her creditors instead of giving her cash. I've gotten expert advice every step of the way. Physicians, addiction counselors, therapists—I can list them all in the Mustang Valley region and beyond."

"From what you're saying, although Eliza has gone missing before, this situation feels different?"

Katrina nodded. "The other times I could sense it coming. This time, everything was fine. Until the earthquake."

Spencer frowned. "The earthquake was almost two months ago. Has your sister been missing since then?"

"I'm not sure what the time frame is." She hitched in a breath. "I hadn't heard from her for a few months prior to the quake, but that wasn't unusual. I knew she had an apartment and she was working with her counselors. When the earthquake hit, I texted and called her a bunch of times to check she was okay. Eliza finally responded that she was fine, although her apartment had been destroyed. She said she was being helped by a relief organization called the Affirmation Alliance Group and they had provided her with accommodation. After that, all my subsequent messages went unanswered. Today, I drove out to the AAG ranch to check on her."

"Why only today?"

"It sounds silly..." She shook her head. "I saw a dog that reminded me of Dobby and confided in a friend. She persuaded me that no matter how angry it might make Eliza if she thought I was interfering, I should go and make sure she was okay."

"Your friend was right. But I take it she wasn't there?"

"No. At first, the welcome manager at the AAG gave me an empty smile and tried to tell me she hadn't heard of Eliza. Then, she checked with a couple of security-type guys. They told me my sister stayed for two nights in April, then left without telling anyone where she was going."

Spencer looked up from circling "security-type guys" on his pad. "Is there a reason why you have a problem with that story, given that your sister has a history of taking off?"

"Dobby is my reason." At the sound of his name, the comical-looking dog wagged his tail. "He's Eliza's. They tried to tell me she left him behind." Tears filled her eyes. "But she would never do that. She'd die first."

KATRINA FIGURED THAT the good-looking police sergeant had probably written her off as trouble around the time she crashed into him in the lobby. But telling him she believed Eliza would die before she'd leave Dobby? Surely, that added up to a whole new layer of concern about her sibling's well-being.

At first glance, Spencer Colton's blond hair and blue eyes could have appeared boyish, but the strength of his features, combined with a tall, powerful body, confirmed his potent masculinity.

Yes, he was handsome, but why should she care what he thought of her? Her sister's safety was the only thing that mattered. And she was starting to believe that something bad had happened to Eliza. Even so, this would be a whole lot easier if she could convince Spencer to take her concerns seriously.

He continued making notes, apparently unshaken by her dramatic statement. When he looked up, she allowed herself to be reassured by the warmth of his smile. But then she remembered that life didn't work that way. Depending on other people was a waste of time and emotion. Although she needed his help to find Eliza, the only person she could *rely* on was herself.

"Based on what you've told me about the uncomfortable feelings you got from the AAG, I guess you'd like me to investigate the circumstances of your sister's departure from their ranch. And also, of course, try to discover her current whereabouts. Can you explain why you didn't try to reach out to her before now? And why you've only come to the conclusion that she's missing today?"

"As I've said, ours isn't an easy relationship. Although she depends on me for money and comes to me for help when she's in trouble, Eliza values her independence. If she suspects I'm trying to interfere in her life, I'm scared that she might disappear for good." Katrina sighed. "And, although I hadn't seen her for a few months, until the earthquake, I knew she was still in Mustang Valley because I got regular reports from her counselors that she was engaging with them. It was only when I went to the AAG Center and found out that she'd only stayed there two days that I realized she was missing.

"As for the AAG, *uncomfortable* doesn't come close to how I felt. That place was creepy." She shivered slightly. "I know that's probably not helpful from an investigative point of view."

Spencer tapped his pen on the table. "You'd be surprised how useful intuition can be. But the AAG is very visible in Mustang Valley and they seem to be doing a lot of good."

"But…?" She knew he was unlikely to tell her anything that linked to an ongoing investigation, but Katrina could sense a wariness in his voice that made her even more concerned.

"Let's just say, they are on my radar." He flipped his pad closed. "I hope to find they are as charitable as they appear."

She swallowed hard. "And you'll let me know what you find out? About Eliza?"

"Of course." There was that look again. Just the right side of sympathetic. "I know you'll have been given the standard speech in the past about how some people don't want to be found, but I can see how painful this is for you. I'm close to both my siblings, and I'd be worried out of my mind if either of them had gone missing in this way. We can't say for sure that Eliza is missing until I've undertaken further investigations, but I'll do everything I can to help."

Tears prickled the back of her eyelids again, and she blinked rapidly. Getting emotional over an offer of support from a stranger was a new experience, but it had been a tough day. She needed to get some fresh air and recharge her batteries.

"Looks like you've got yourself a cute companion. At least until we find Eliza." Spencer reached out a hand and ruffled Dobby's ears.

Dobby *was* cute. But it took a genuine animal lover to see past his imperfections. It was another reason to like Spencer Colton. Although, at the moment, he was staring at his desk in confusion.

"Did one of you eat my sandwich?"

"Ah." She felt the blush rise in her cheeks. "Dobby may be cute, but he is also a food thief."

To her relief, Spencer grinned. "Are you sure it was

Dobby?" He nodded to the dog, who was gazing into space, licking his lips. "He looks a picture of innocence."

Katrina sighed as she got to her feet. "To be honest, I'd forgotten about the food stealing. I'll have to theft-proof my kitchen. And my own dog might not be happy at the arrival of an unexpected house guest. Holly is a sweetheart. But she likes having me all to herself."

"You work with dogs?" He indicated her uniform.

"I'm a dog trainer. My business premises are over on Bridge Street—"

"Look Who's Walking? That's your place?" When she nodded, he laughed. "I drive past on my way to work each day and Boris always tries to stick his head out of the window to get a sniff at what's going on."

She stooped to pat the scent dog on the head. "You should stop by sometime when Boris is off duty. Play dates can be fun."

When she straightened, Spencer's blue eyes appeared brighter than ever. Had that offer sounded like something other than a doggy get-together to him? Was there a chance he thought the *play date* was for the two of them? She could either dig herself in deeper or leave.

"I should..." *Explain.* "Um..." *Go.* She pointed to the door.

"Yeah. I'll be in touch." He held the door open and she scooted around him to get through it.

Hurrying along the corridor toward the lobby with her face burning, she tucked the dog under one arm as she scrabbled in her pocket for her keys. "Great," she muttered under her breath. "Now he thinks I'm annoying *and* desperate. Such a good look, don't you think, Dobby?"

"Katrina?"

Spencer's voice just behind her startled her into uttering an undignified squeak. Swinging around abruptly, she found herself face-to-face with the person she'd just been talking about. From his expression, she was fairly sure he had overheard her comments to Dobby.

"You left your keys in my office."

IT HAD BEEN a long day. Spencer had a dozen cases that took priority over Katrina Perry's missing sister. But as he left the MVPD building and crossed the parking lot to his car, he couldn't shake the image of the pain in her beautiful eyes as she talked about her visit to the AAG ranch and her certainty that something bad had happened to Eliza.

"Can't hurt to pay a visit," he commented to Boris as he secured the dog in his air-conditioned compartment at the rear of the vehicle. "It's only ten miles in the wrong direction."

He'd hinted to Katrina that he had his own concerns about the AAG, but he hadn't shared any of the details with her. She hadn't been the first person to describe a feeling of creepiness about the organization, although she was the only one to make an outright allegation against anyone connected with a group that appeared to be doing nothing but good. Spencer's own suspicions centered on one specific AAG member named Harley Watts.

Following the attempt on Payne Colton's life, one of the Colton Oil IT guys had tracked down Harley through the dark web, finding rambling references that were troubling enough for the police to get a search warrant. They found the email to the Colton Oil board members about Ace Colton's birth on Harley's laptop, and then arrested him. His story was that he'd been asked to send the email by a friend, and since then, he had refused to say anything more. Spencer had tried making a deal for leniency with the DA to get Harley to talk, but the guy was adamant. He was no snitch. He pointed out that he'd been charged under interference-with-commerce laws for his implied threats of exposure regarding the secrets affecting the structure of Colton Oil. The evidence on his computer was enough to put him behind bars, so he may as well stay loyal.

Like everything else connected to the Payne Colton shooting, it was frustrating because it led nowhere. Spencer had no reason to believe that the friend who had asked Harley to send the email was a member of the AAG, even though he had used the organization's server. But where was the harm in exploring the theory that Harley's "loyalty" was to someone within the group?

Making inquiries about Eliza Perry would give him a chance to check out the headquarters. He could also ask the tough questions that might not have occurred to Katrina. Like what her sister's behavior had been in the days before she left town and whom she had been hanging out with. Spencer had seen many missing-persons cases that involved substance abuse and, privately, he suspected that Eliza could have drifted back into her old ways. As much as he hoped to be able to give Katrina other news, he doubted that would be the case.

When he arrived at the AAG ranch, he spent a few minutes behind the wheel of his car, checking out the exterior of the beautiful building. From this viewpoint, it was hard to understand the feeling of creepiness Katrina had described. On the contrary, it appeared the AAG leaders had gone out of their way to create an open, inviting atmosphere.

As he alighted from his vehicle, and released Boris from his compartment, it occurred to him that the place appeared almost deserted. The impression was reinforced when he entered the lobby and found it empty. Frowning, he approached some of the doors that led off the reception area. The delicious smell of cooking food and the sound of voices drew him along a corridor. As he reached the end, he could see into a large room with a long table, where about thirty people, including adults and children, were seated.

The sound of footsteps behind him caused him to turn. An attractive, well-dressed blonde woman, who he judged to be in her midsixties, was approaching him. As she closed the distance between them, Spencer could see her blue eyes sizing him and Boris up.

"Hi. I'm Micheline Anderson, leader of the Affirmation Alliance Group." Her smile was warm. "I don't think we've met?"

"Sergeant Spencer Colton, Mustang Valley Police." Spencer was used to reading people's reaction when he introduced himself. Micheline's open expression didn't change. "I'm trying to track down a missing person who was last seen on these premises."

"Oh, goodness." Her tone was sympathetic. "I got a message earlier today that a family member had been asking some questions. We'll do everything we can to help, of course." She waved a hand toward the dining room. "Please, ask anything you need to."

Although she gave the impression of being helpful, Spencer felt a twinge of annoyance. He was a police officer. He didn't need permission to do his job.

"Perhaps I could start with you? The missing woman is called Eliza Perry and she is known to have stayed at this ranch prior to her disappearance in April."

Micheline shook her head. "I'm afraid you are asking the wrong person. Although I'm the AAG founder and leader, I don't live on the premises. My home is nearby and I'm here most days, but I don't know the names of all our guests. Think of my role as that of CEO of a large business. You wouldn't expect me to deal with every client on a day-to-day basis, would you?"

Her manner was easy and natural and he could see how her group attracted so many people. He figured that Micheline would be good at making anyone feel comfortable. She had also skillfully closed down his line of questioning before he'd begun.

"And we've been so busy since April, when the earthquake struck." With the lightest of touches to his arm, Micheline guided Spencer into the dining room. A few glances were cast his way, but no one appeared troubled by his presence. “Let me introduce you to Leigh Dennings, our welcome manager.”

Micheline beckoned to an attractive young woman. As soon as Leigh got close, Spencer recognized the “empty smile” of Katrina’s description. Flipping back her hair, she gave him a measuring look from beneath the sweep of her long lashes.

“Why, Micheline, I hope you’re not planning to keep this handsome guest all to yourself.” The tone was flirty, but Spencer caught the questioning look that she threw her boss. It appeared that Leigh didn’t make a move without getting instructions first.

“The sergeant here wants to ask some questions about a missing person,” Micheline said. “I’ve assured him that we will cooperate any way we can.”

Spencer watched the way Leigh’s gaze flickered across the room to where two men were finishing up their meal. They were dressed casually, and there was nothing suspicious about their manner. Even so, he sensed they were watching him closely. He figured they must be the security types Katrina had described.

“I think you may already have spoken to the missing woman’s sister.” Spencer focused his attention on Leigh while also watching the two guys. “Katrina Perry told me she came here to inquire about her sister, Eliza?”

“That’s right.” Was he allowing his suspicions to get the better of him, or was there something a little rehearsed about her manner? “I felt sorry for Eliza’s sister, but she was very emotional and didn’t want to hear what we had to say. The truth is that Eliza only stayed here for two days. I asked around some more this afternoon and a few people remembered that, when she left us, she seemed a little strung out."

"Just like her sister was." Micheline's voice was soft and persuasive. "I guess it's a family trait."

The corners of Leigh's mouth turned down. "To be honest, the group members I spoke to told me that Eliza was something of a fantasist. She was inclined to be distrustful of everyone here at the ranch and… Well, she made up stories that people were out to get her. Apparently, she could be quite convincing."

Micheline shook her head sadly. "Not all actors are on the stage."

Although he was uncomfortable with the idea that Katrina might also be highly strung and may have been overdramatizing the situation, Spencer knew he had to keep an open mind. And she had been overwrought when she'd talked to him about Eliza. Not that he could blame her. He'd feel the same way if either of his siblings went missing. Even so, her emotional state, and this new information about Eliza, did cast doubt on the validity of Katrina's claims about her visit to the ranch.

"Was there anyone Eliza was particularly friendly with while she was here?" he asked Leigh.

"Not that I can recall. Randall and Bart may have some more information." She beckoned, and the two guys Spencer had noticed rose from the table and came to join them. Leigh quickly outlined the details of the conversation. "This is Sergeant Colton. He was wondering if Eliza Perry had any friends while she was here,"

The older of the two men scrubbed a hand along

his chin, his expression almost a parody of thoughtfulness. “A lot of people have been in and out of here since April. To be honest, I only remember her at all because of the dog.”

“Randall is our handyman,” Leigh explained. “He gets to know most of the guests. But anyone who only stays a few days—” She held her hands out, palms upward, in helpless gesture.

“What about you, Bart?” Micheline turned to the other man. “Did you see her with anyone while you were out tending the grounds?”

“Hardly saw her at all.” The guy’s job title might be “groundskeeper,” but his attitude reminded Spencer of a bodyguard. There was something threatening about the way he was frowning as he stood protectively between Micheline and Leigh, lowering his eyebrows as he watched Spencer, his glance dropping occasionally to take in Boris.

Spencer decided to try a different approach. “Did Harley Watts live on the premises?”

A swift look flashed between Randall and Bart, but Micheline heaved a sorrowful sigh. “Ah, Harley. Such a sweet, gentle soul, who was trying hard to be his best self. And he was devoted to me.” She placed a hand over her heart. “Which is why it hurt so much when he used our AAG server to send that awful email to the board members of Colton Oil.”

Leigh sent Spencer a reproachful look. “It wasn’t your fault, Micheline. You didn’t know what Harley was doing. None of us did.”

The three other AAG members moved closer to Micheline, as if forming a barrier between her and the outside world. Spencer knew when to call it quits. He wasn't going to get any more information from them, about either Eliza or Harley. Did that mean his suspicions had gone away?

He looked around the large, comfortable room, taking in the smiling faces and the homey atmosphere. No, he had more concerns than ever about the AAG. But with nothing concrete, and no evidence, all he could do was watch and wait.

He left the ranch house and headed toward his vehicle with the faithful Boris at his heels. Turning back, he caught a glimpse of Randall and Bart watching him from just inside the front door.

"Making sure we leave?" Spencer commented as he opened the rear of the car and Boris jumped in. "You know what this means?" The dog thumped his tail and rolled his eyes. "That's right. Now we have to go break it to Katrina that we didn't get anywhere."

While the thought of seeing her again was exciting, he wished it could be in different circumstances. His job meant he would have to be objective and explain that he had no reason to believe that there was any link between Eliza's disappearance and the AAG. In reality, he couldn't dismiss the feeling of discomfort that lingered as he drove away.

Chapter Three

Katrina knew about dogs. And her question, when one of her clients asked about getting a second pooch, was always the same. *What would your dog think of that idea?*

Like her customers, Katrina was a dog person. And dog people loved their fur babies. Sloppy kisses, wagging tails, furry snuggles and unconditional love were all very hard to resist. And if it was great to have one dog, why not double the magic?

Suppose your partner said, "I love you so much I'm thinking of getting another one just like you"? Usually, when she put it that way, her clients were able to see the situation from a canine viewpoint.

Now, after leaving the police station, she was taking Dobby home and expecting her own Holly to happily accept that she was no longer a single dog.

"You remember Holly, right?" She addressed the remark to Dobby, who was attached to a special harness on the rear seat of her car. "Long black ears? Cute face? Likes tummy rubs and chewing shoelaces? Hates motorbikes and mirrors?"

The two dogs had met once when Dobby had come to a grooming session at Look Who's Walking. Although they'd gotten on reasonably well, Holly had only been a pup and they'd met on neutral territory. This time, things would be different…

Luckily, her years of experience had taught her exactly what she needed to do in this situation. Having called ahead, she'd arranged for Suzie, who had a key to her house, to collect Holly and take her out to the yard. When she pulled into the drive, her assistant was already waiting on the front step. As soon as Katrina lifted Dobby from the car, the excited dog recognized an old friend and strained to reach Suzie.

"Hey, fella." Suzie slipped a treat from her pocket and Dobby scarfed it up like his life depended on it. "Holly's in the yard."

"Here's the plan," Katrina said. "We introduce them out there, let them play together for a while, then we take them into the house."

"Okay." Suzie sent her a sidelong glance. "How long will Dobby be staying with you?"

"I don't know." Having spent an emotional hour sharing her suspicions about Eliza's fate with Spencer Colton, Katrina wasn't ready to tell the whole story all over again. Not yet. "It may be some time."

"Then we need to do this right."

"We do." There was a path at the side of the house that led to the yard, and Katrina walked ahead. Before they reached the gate, she paused and glanced briefly over her shoulder. "And thanks."

"Anytime." Suzie briefly placed a hand on her shoulder.

At the sound of Katrina's voice, Holly let out a volley of barks and started hurling herself at the gate. Dobby, startled at such unseemly behavior, gave a yelp and tried to run away.

"Good start." Katrina rolled her eyes.

Giving Holly the "sit" command, she opened the gate. Her dog was an excitable, but well trained, youngster. Holly squatted, quivering all over, waiting for the moment until she was given permission to move.

Once Katrina, Suzie and Dobby were inside the training yard and the gate was secured behind them, Katrina told Holly to "come."

The dog, a nine-month-old bundle of black curls, scurried forward, wriggling with pleasure. Before she reached her mistress, she spotted Dobby, and did the canine equivalent of a double take. The two animals stared at each other as though unsure what to do next.

Taking advantage of their confusion, Katrina reached into a storage tub and withdrew a couple of balls. She threw them across the lawn and both dogs sped off. After they had played a few chasing games, she offered them a piece of knotted rope and was pleased with the way they responded. Grabbing an end each, the two canines tugged away, tails wagging happily. Although they made growling noises, there were no signs of aggression.

"Pack rules state that Dobby should be dominant, even though he's a neutered male," she said. "But this is Holly's house, so she shouldn't be expected to relinquish her place. And they both need to know that I'm the boss."

Suzie laughed. “They’re bright dogs. They know that already.”

“We need to reinforce the hierarchy by the way we enter the house,” Katrina insisted. “I’ll go first with Holly. You come next, making sure Dobby brings up the rear. Give me a minute to set up new food and water bowls. I’ll call you when I’m ready.”

The back door led from the yard directly into the kitchen. Blinking at the contrast as she stepped from the bright, early evening sunlight into the semidark house, she took a moment to adjust. After an instant of surprise, she quickly became aware that she wasn’t alone. Half-hidden in the shadows, a man was standing next to her refrigerator.

“What…?”

Before she could call out for Suzie, he crossed the room and shoved her hard on the shoulder. Katrina went sprawling onto the tiled floor, a cry of surprise escaping her. The sound triggered an immediate reaction from the two dogs, who started barking wildly. As the intruder ran from the room toward the front of the house, Katrina caught a glimpse of a male figure clad in jeans, sneakers and a hooded sweatshirt.

The front door slammed at the same time that Suzie burst through the back door with Holly on one side and Dobby on the other.

“What happened? Is everything okay?” She held out a hand to help Katrina to her feet.

“I’m going with no.” Katrina rolled her eyes as Dobby drained Holly’s water bowl before flopping down on her bed. The younger dog retreated under the table with her tail between her legs. "Not when we have an intruder situation, *and* a male-dominance issue."

"Never mind about the dogs." Suzie helped her to a chair at the table and eased her down into it. "Do you have any idea who he was? And, more importantly, are you hurt?"

Katrina took a moment to regulate her breathing. Although she was physically unharmed, the incident had shaken her. The knowledge that someone had gotten inside her house was bad enough. The fact that she didn't know what his motive was made it even worse.

She hadn't recognized him. Did that mean he was a robber who'd chosen her home at random? Or was his reason more personal and sinister? Her thoughts went to Eliza and she gripped the edge of the table hard. How could this have anything to do with her sister?

"I'm fine." She was pleased with the firm note in her voice. "And at least I disturbed him before he could take anything."

KATRINA'S HOME WAS in a new development just outside downtown and about ten minutes' drive from her workplace, off Mustang Boulevard. The Mustang Lake estate featured a collection of small houses with large yards and Spencer figured, as he approached the address she had given him, that the outdoor space would be useful for a dog trainer.

Having pulled up in front of the small house, he was just releasing Boris from the rear of the vehicle when Katrina's door opened.

"Wow." A small plump woman looked Spencer and

his police cruiser up and down with a critical gaze. "Is this a new MVPD policy? You guys turn up before a crime has even been reported?"

Just as he was wondering if he had the right house, Katrina stepped out onto the small porch. "Take no notice of Suzie. She likes to think she's funny." She kissed the other woman on the cheek. "Thanks for offering to stay, but I'll be fine."

"Call me if you need me. Anytime." Suzie patted her arm before walking down the steps. "Something needs to be done about the crime rate in this town." She addressed the remark to Spencer before stomping off toward her car.

"Has something happened that I need to know about?" he asked as he approached Katrina.

"Would you mind if we talked about this in the yard?" He raised a questioning eyebrow and she sighed. "Holly, my dog, hasn't taken Dobby's arrival well. If you bring Boris in here, too, she may have a complete breakdown."

"Outside is fine by me."

Stepping out of the house, she closed and locked the front door before leading him along a side path and into the yard. He noted the way the space had been divided. There was a large lawn, an area for the dogs to run free around the outside edge, an obstacle course and a small pool. Clearly, Katrina believed in bringing her work home.

As soon as they entered the yard, two dogs dashed up and gave Boris a thorough inspection. The well-behaved canine remained perfectly still until Spencer freed him from his leash. Then, with a groan, he dropped to the grass and rolled on his back before taking off at a run. After a few seconds, the other two followed.

"Actually, bringing Boris wasn't a bad move." Katrina's gaze followed the chase. "He's definitely an alpha, so Dobby will be forced to back off. It takes the heat off things for a while."

"Right." Spencer viewed her profile with pleasure for a moment or two, then reverted to a businesslike manner. "So, you want to tell me what your friend was talking about?"

"When I got back here, there was a guy in my kitchen."

"What?" The thought of her in danger made his pulse rate spike, bringing with it memories of another time, another place. "You mean, he'd broken into your house?"

"Not quite." She hung her head. "When I disturbed him, he pushed me over and ran away. After he'd gone, I checked to see how he'd gotten in and the window of the downstairs closet was open. I must have forgotten to close it when I left for work this morning."

"Or the intruder forced it open?"

"There aren't any signs that it has been forced," Katrina said. "I think he was probably an opportunist who saw an empty house with an open window. He was just unlucky that I came home and surprised him before he could take anything."

"That's a nice, neat scenario. And it may be true. But I'm going to take down the details and log this as a crime." He stepped back, viewing the small house through narrowed eyes. "And, before I leave, I'm going to check out your security system."

"Are you always this bossy?" There was a smile in her eyes and a teasing note in her voice. He liked them both. A lot.

"I'm a police officer. Bossy is what I do."

The smile faded at the reminder. "And you're here because of Eliza."

There was no way he could avoid giving her the bad news. "I went out to the AAG Center and asked a few questions. I got the same answers you did. Several members say she left two days after the earthquake. They said she may have been a little strung out around that time."

"No one mentioned that to me." Her smooth brow creased. "If she was upset, or in trouble, it seems kind of an important detail to mention, don't you think?"

"You were already worried. Possibly, they didn't want to share that sort of sensitive information with you in case it distressed you further."

"I was unhappy when I realized Eliza had left the AAG ranch and no one knew where she had gone. I wasn't hysterical." Her lip curled. "So what does this mean? You're telling me they're the nice guys?"

He held up his hands. "I'm not making a judgment. Just letting you know what I found."

"Which is a big, fat zero. Exactly what I discovered on my own." She watched the dogs for a few moments as they played a three-way game of chase. "What happens next?"

"You need to complete a missing-person-adult-waiver form. This form is essentially an affidavit that details your relationship to Eliza and states that you accept any civil liability for invasions of privacy that may take place during the course of the investigation. I have a copy here. If you fill it in and return it within seventy-two hours, Eliza will remain a missing person on our files and in the National Missing Persons System. We'll do what we can to find her."

She had told him that she'd filed a missing-persons report for Eliza before, so Katrina probably already knew how the investigation would progress. Inquiries would include speaking to friends, family and other known associates. It could also progress to checking with banks and a call history, and monitoring internet and social-media use. Even so, if Eliza chose not to be found, there were things she could do to keep her whereabouts hidden.

And, in the case of missing adults, the role of the police was only to verify the person's welfare. They would not reveal the whereabouts, or any other details, to the reporting person. Similarly, Spencer could not promise Katrina that he would "pass on a message" or provide contact information to Eliza.

"You'll take charge of this yourself?" Katrina asked.

An image of his overloaded desk came into his head. "I'll oversee the case, but I won't be able to undertake the routine tasks."

Her expression clouded. "But you're the investigating officer."

For an instant, he wanted to promise her he would

drop everything except this case. He would find Eliza if he had to work around the clock. Actually, when he looked into those incredible hazel eyes, he wanted to promise her the earth…

Try explaining that *to Chief Barco.*

"I'm in the middle of investigating the Payne Colton shooting—"

"Fine." She swung away from him, stooped to pick up a tennis ball and hurled it across the yard. "You have your priorities and clearly *your* family comes first."

"Katrina, it's not like that." It had been a long time since he'd tried to reason with an angry woman, and his skills were a little on the rusty side.

"It's okay. I'll investigate Eliza's disappearance on my own."

"No." She raised her eyebrows at the forcefulness of his tone. "You are not to do that. It's too dangerous."

Arms folded across her chest, she turned to face him. "So you won't assist me, but I'm forbidden to go it alone? Thanks, Sergeant Colton, you've been a great help."

"I'm offering you the best I can do with the resources available." It sounded like a lame official line even to his own ears.

"Well, I appreciate your input." She huffed out a breath. "If that's all?"

"It's not." He understood that she was hurt, but if she was trying to annoy him, she was succeeding. "I need to check out your security system, remember?"

"I SUGGEST YOU upgrade the locks on the downstairs windows," Spencer said after he completed his inspection of the house. "And I'd recommend a video-entry system for the front door."

"Thank you." Katrina's anger had started to fade and she realized she had been unfair to him. In reality, she was more upset with herself than with him. She had gone through her whole life relying solely on her own wits and judgment. Having been born to a teenage, drug-addicted mother, the twins had never known their father. Growing up, their maternal grandparents had been their only other family.

Mollie Perry had been unable to care for herself, let alone her daughters. She had been known to the police not only because of her substance abuse but also because of her attention-seeking behavior. As a result, Katrina's grandparents had been busy trying to keep everybody safe. As a child, Katrina had quickly learned that she was all alone in life.

Why had she suddenly broken her own rule and placed her trust in Spencer Colton? The only reason she could think of was that she was overwrought because of her fears for Eliza.

Conceding that she'd overreacted was one thing. Acknowledging it was another. She barely knew Spencer, and once they entered the house, he'd retreated behind a professional front. The sympathetic, helpful guy with the warm smile was gone, and in his place was a brisk cop who rattled off a checklist of security questions. Even if she'd wanted to apologize, she wouldn't have known how to get past the professional barrier he'd put up.

"Have you considered putting in motion-sensitive

lights in the yard?" Spencer asked. "It can be a deterrent to anyone snooping."

"I thought about it. But any canine visitors would probably keep setting the lights off and it would drive me to distraction."

"You could be right. In that case, I think I've covered everything." He clicked his fingers and the ever-obedient Boris moved quickly to his side. For an instant, as he looked down at her, Katrina glimpsed a return of the softer expression she'd seen at the police station. "Remember what I said."

She frowned. "You can't expect me not to look for my sister."

"Keep trying to make contact with her by all means. Just stay away from the AAG." He stepped out onto the porch. "And you know where I am if you need me."

She watched him as he walked to his car, wondering at the curious sensation of emptiness his departure brought. It felt like a connection had been severed. She shook aside the thought, labeling it foolish. How could you break something that didn't exist? She'd learned a long time ago that the safest attachments were to dogs. Apart from her grandparents, who had done their best to provide love and care against the odds, her only family had been her mother and Eliza, both of whom had depended on their addictions more than her. No, people were best kept at a distance. She had no bond with Spencer. And that was the way she liked it.

You know where I am if you need me. Had it been an invitation? More likely it was just a turn of phrase. The sort of casual remark he made at the end of every encounter. And why would she need him again? His intervention had hardly been helpful.

Stepping back inside the house, she checked the time. She was scheduled to teach a couple of evening training classes at Look Who's Walking, but she still had time to walk the dogs before dinner. Wandering into the kitchen, she removed a letter that she'd pinned to the cork noticeboard. Dog Daze was a new restaurant that had opened on Mustang Boulevard. Catering to pooch lovers, it featured a canine menu alongside the human one. The owners had offered Katrina a free meal in return for an honest review on her Look Who's Walking blog.

Tonight seemed like a good time to take them up on their offer. And while she was in town, maybe she could ask a few questions about the AAG.

Spencer's warning flashed into her mind and she tapped her fingers on the counter. How could he tell her in one breath that the message from the AAG was that Eliza had gone of her own accord, and then warn her to stay away, in case things got dangerous? Without giving her a reason to back off, he couldn't expect her to take him seriously. It was probably a standard police line.

Having called ahead to make a reservation, she found a split leash, attaching both dogs to it, and set off in the direction of Mustang Boulevard. The three-mile-long main drag was home to several restaurants, bars and coffee shops, and the warm weather had brought the town's residents out in large numbers.

After some initial reluctance, Dobby and Holly settled into a comfortable pattern of walking together on one leash. Holly was cute enough to attract attention and Dobby enjoyed fussing from humans. They were constantly stopped by admirers who wanted to pet them. The only problems occurred when Dobby smelled food and tried to drag Katrina and Holly with him to track it down.

Since there were AAG posters in almost every window, it was easy to strike up a conversation with people she encountered.

"I hear they've been doing good work since the earthquake." For the most part, she got positive responses to that comment. The AAG came across as popular and well-meaning. Katrina listened to several stories of people who had benefited from their good work.

It was only when she got close to the crossroads near Bubba's Diner that she came across anything different. A group of five AAG members had set up a stand on the sidewalk, and they were handing out leaflets to passersby. As Katrina approached, she could see that Leigh Dennings and her two goons, Randall and Bart, were among the group. The stand was covered in posters including a picture of Micheline Anderson and the slogan Be Your Best You! The information stated that Micheline was scheduled to give a series of talks about the group's philosophy over the coming weeks.

Although Be Your Best You! featured prominently in everything the AAG did, Katrina wondered for the first time about the philosophy underlying that slogan.

She'd never heard any detail about what it actually meant, but perhaps that was reserved for the paying customers?

Katrina drew level with them and shook her head as one of the group waved a leaflet in her direction. Just then, a car pulled up and the driver's door was flung open. A woman jumped out and dashed over to the AAG stand.

"You people are cheaters and I want my money back." Her voice was loud and a group of women who were just about to enter Bubba's Diner paused to watch what was happening.

Leigh took out her cell and started to make a call while Randall stepped forward. "Ma'am, this is not a good time—"

"I loaned my son a thousand dollars and I've just found out he used it for a seminar on 'becoming his best self.'" Her voice dripped with sarcasm and she made an air-quote gesture as she said the words. "What sort of mumbo jumbo is that?"

"I think you'll find that your son will have reaped the incredible rewards that come from an Affirmation Alliance seminar."

"My son just lost his dad in a horrible accident. He's sad and vulnerable." Katrina began to listen a little more carefully. Eliza had also been susceptible, and she, too, had become involved with the AAG. Was there a link? "You people preyed on his grief."

Katrina was close enough to hear Leigh as she ended her call. She spoke quietly to the group around her.

"Micheline said this is bad publicity. We need to close it down fast."

Moving swiftly, the other AAG members surrounded the irate woman, effectively blocking her from view. As she raised her voice, they started to talk loudly, drowning out her protests. Seconds later, she was being hustled into her car by Randall and Bart. Katrina didn't see them actually touch her. It was more that they invaded her space and gave her nowhere else to go.

She looked around. No one else seemed to have noticed what was going on. Should she film what was happening? Take a picture? Call someone? But who? An image of Spencer Colton flashed into her mind and she reached into her pocket for her cell. Even as her fingers began to swipe through her address book for his number, she hesitated. Why would he believe her about this incident when he had been lukewarm about her suspicions concerning Eliza?

"You're overwrought, ma'am," Randall said. "You should go home and rest."

Instead of calling Spencer, Katrina continued to watch. As she tucked her cell back into her pocket, she looked up and encountered Randall's gaze. The glare he gave her let her know he had recognized her, and it made her feel uncomfortable. Keeping her head down, she walked briskly away.

Chapter Four

Although Spencer wasn't close with the Colton Oil branch of the clan, he liked them well enough. Certainly, most of the board members had been cooperative during the investigation into the shooting of Payne Colton; only Ace had really seemed volatile.

To be fair, Spencer couldn't blame Ace for not wanting to help the police. Not only had he recently discovered that he wasn't a Colton by birth, it was also obvious that he was likely the chief suspect in Payne's attempted murder.

Now, Ace Colton was proving to be a problem when it came to setting up his sting operation. Technically, he didn't need the family's permission to proceed, but it would be smart to work with them, and the idea had come from a suggestion Asher and Jarvis had made. Since he would be moving Payne to another room, the Coltons could claim the police had been affecting their injured relative's care. With that in mind, he wanted to strike a balance. He wanted to keep the plan secret from Ace, who had been lying low since being labeled chief suspect—while making sure the rest of the family was well informed.

"You're absolutely sure that this sting operation can't backfire and place our father in danger?" Ainsley Colton asked. An attorney for Colton Oil, she glanced at her half sister, Marlowe, Colton Oil CEO, and seemed to be seeking her approval to question the police tactics. Marlowe gave an approving nod.

They were seated in Spencer's office and he had outlined the final details for the plan.

"As you know, I have a story ready to be put out to a few local busybodies and media outlets that Payne is recovering," Spencer said. "Once that news is out there in the public, we have to be on high alert. I'm counting on the fact that the shooter, assuming Payne will be ready to talk and reveal his identity, will want to finish the job."

"That's what we're worried about." Marlowe looked concerned.

"Before I even release the story, I'll have Payne moved to another floor of the hospital. He'll have a police guard." He looked around the table, making eye contact with each of them in turn. "The family can be involved in guarding him, as well, but there will always be a police presence." He didn't explain his reasoning. So far Ace had stayed away, but, if he was the shooter, there was no way Spencer was giving him a chance to be alone with his father.

"There will be an officer acting as a decoy in the original hospital bed with other cops hiding in the room. If and when the shooter arrives, we'll let him get up close before arresting him."

"You make it sound easy," Ainsley said. "Are you sharing these details because you need our permission to move him?"

"I'd like to think I have your agreement to this plan." He didn't want to get into a fight with Payne's family over this. "We're all on the same side and we want this guy caught as fast as possible. Which is why I need you to keep these details secret."

The siblings exchanged a glance and he knew what they were thinking. If the attacker was someone connected to the family, they needed to make sure he, or possibly she, didn't know about the intended sting.

Ainsley nodded. "You can rely on our discretion."

When they'd gone, he called Kerry into his office and relayed the details of the meeting to her. "Tomorrow we'll go ahead and inform our sources that Payne Colton is recovering."

She scribbled in her notepad. "I've contacted the technicians about the security-camera images from the night of the shooting. So far, they haven't had any more success with enhancing them."

"It feels like this shooter has either been very lucky or very clever. Either way, we don't have any firm leads." Spencer pushed away the case file and got to his feet. "We have to hope this plan to flush him out is successful."

After Kerry had gone, he plowed on with his backlog of administrative tasks, working through the morning until his stomach told him it was time to call a halt. When he paused and checked the time on his cell phone, he experienced a pang of disappointment that there were no calls or messages from Katrina.

It's a good thing. It means she hasn't had any further trouble.

For some reason, the reminder didn't make him feel any better. He'd told her to call him if she needed him. He said that to all victims, of course. But in Katrina's case, he just wanted her to reach out to him. And that was a problem. Because no matter how attracted he was to her, he would never act on it. He knew how it worked. First came an emotional pull. That was followed by the sweet, heady rush of falling in love. Finally, there was the jagged, knife-edge pain of loss. Spencer had been there before and he was never going back again.

He was just about to place his cell in his pocket and go in search of some tasteless but necessary food, when the display indicated an incoming call. Almost as if his thoughts had conjured up her name, he saw it was from Katrina.

"Is everything okay?" He already knew the answer. She wouldn't be calling him if it was.

"There's something I need to talk to you about. It may be nothing, but…" There was a note in her voice that told him it wasn't nothing. "Is there a good time to come to the station?"

"Have you eaten?"

"Um… No."

"Nor have I." Spencer got to his feet and clicked

his fingers at Boris. "I'll pick up some food and come to you."

Alongside his concern for her, the pull of excitement at the thought of seeing her again was more intense than anything he had ever experienced. For the first time, he wondered what would happen if he ignored his natural caution and explored his feelings.

Never going to happen.

His interest in Katrina was professional. If he kept telling himself that, everything would be just fine.

AFTER FINISHING HER morning training schedule, Katrina had decided to take Dobby and Holly to the nearby park. The dogs didn't need the exercise. There was more than enough to keep them occupied at Look Who's Walking. The reason for the walk was actually to clear her head.

She'd spent much of the previous night dwelling on the incident she'd witnessed with the irate woman and the AAG members. The more she thought about it, the more uncomfortable she became. It had been such an extreme reaction to a minor incident. And the way Randall and Bart had hustled the woman had looked practiced, something they'd done before. After musing over it for most of the morning, she had decided to put aside her reservations about Spencer and call him. When he'd suggested lunch, she'd turned around and headed back through the park the way she came.

The entrance to Mustang Park was at the southern end of Mustang Boulevard. It was a well-kept public space with picnic tables, paths and a large wooded area that was popular with dog walkers. Holly loved to run along with her nose to the ground, sniffing out creatures both real and imagined. After watching her for a moment or two, Dobby had enthusiastically joined in.

It was when she had retraced her steps, passing the picnic area and entering the woodland that Katrina became conscious of a man walking close behind her. Turning her head slightly, she saw out of the corner of her eye that he was just a few steps away. That shouldn't have been a cause for alarm and she tried to dismiss the prickly feeling along the back of her neck. It was just that too much had gone on over the last few days and she knew she was now feeling jumpy without any real cause…

When she sensed him drawing nearer, she called the dogs back to her and attached their leash. She'd wanted fresh air, but not at the expense of the theft of her wallet. Or worse. Swinging around, she prepared to face the guy, even challenge him, if necessary. To her surprise, though, the mysterious figure had gone.

Feeling relieved, and slightly foolish, she continued along the narrow track between the trees. She was in a lonely space, and at this time of day, there were few other people around. After she had walked for several minutes, she glanced to her right and into the denser tree cover. Her heart leaped when she saw the same hooded man moving among the tree trunks.

Coincidence. That was what she tried to tell herself as she increased her pace. But the image of Randall Cook's face as he caught her with her cell in her hand as she watched the scene with the unhappy woman persistently intruded into her thoughts. She had no reason to believe this man was connected to that incident—had no real reason to believe he was following her—but her nerves were stretched like a rubber band.

Abruptly, she changed direction. If this man was trailing her, she wanted to find out for sure. Once again, she lost sight of him and her fears subsided. Why would anyone follow her? She was allowing her worries over Eliza to spill over and affect every part of her life.

She took comfort from the fact that the dogs were with her. They hadn't shown any signs of sensing danger, and they would surely try to protect her if they had.

Forcing her breathing back to a normal rhythm, she continued in the direction that would lead her back to her starting point. And her breath caught in her throat as she saw the guy blocking the path ahead of her. His head was down, his face shadowed by his hood. He was tall and strong looking, without being obviously muscular, and she didn't think she knew him.

A glance over her shoulder confirmed her worst fears. They were in an isolated part of the woods and there was no escape.

She was trying to decide what to do next when he started walking toward her. Dobby, usually the friendliest of dogs, emitted a low growl. Like a gazelle in the path of a stalking predator, Katrina froze. Her eyes darted back and forth but her muscles were incapable of movement.

As he got within a few feet, an increase in background noise broke the spell. Distant at first, it became clearer and louder. It was the sound of children talking and provided the release Katrina needed. Breaking into a run, she darted through the trees, in the direction of the voices.

Becoming increasingly scared every second that a hand might suddenly grab her shoulder, she powered onward over the rough terrain with the dogs keeping pace. Up ahead, she could see movement and dashes of color. Finally, she broke through into a small clearing, where a group of what looked like kindergarten pupils and their teacher were spotting plants and bugs. It was close to a place where she and Eliza used to play as kids, and the warm memories comforted her.

Fumbling her cell from her pocket, she found Spencer's number. At first, her breath was coming so fast she was barely able to gasp out his name.

"Katrina? I'm just on my way to your place."

"In the woods… I thought he was, but I wasn't sure." She knew she wasn't making sense and forced herself to slow down. "I just got away from some guy who was following me."

"Where are you?" Spencer, it seemed, wasn't going to waste time on unnecessary questions.

"Mustang Park."

"I'm on my way."

AS HE HEADED toward Mustang Park, Spencer focused on driving safely but speedily, and tried to clear his thoughts of any comparisons of Katrina's situation with his own past. Four years ago, his fiancée, Billie Mikkelsen, a rookie cop, had been lured into a guy's apartment after answering a call about a suspected domestic dispute. Once there, she had been taken hostage and held for two days before being murdered.

Not again. Spencer gripped the steering wheel tighter. He told himself it wasn't the same. He wasn't close to Katrina. He never would be. Billie's tragic death was the reason why he had closed his heart to another relationship. Love was an incredible gift, but it brought with it the risk of loss and he couldn't put himself through that pain again. Until now, it hadn't been an issue. He hadn't gone beyond an initial attraction to anyone else in that time. Katrina had blown him away at first sight, but he couldn't let it go anywhere, couldn't take another chance with his fragile heart.

He would always miss Billie and mourn the closeness they'd shared. Sure, there were times when he craved love and intimacy. But the price of attachment was too high in any circumstances. With Katrina, a woman who was likely already in danger? It would be like stepping back into his worst nightmare.

After parking his vehicle at the side of the road close to the park entrance, he released Boris from his compartment and together, they dashed toward the main gates. As he ran, Spencer took out his cell phone and called Katrina.

He didn't bother with a greeting. "Describe your location."

When she spoke, he could hear background noise, almost as if she was surrounded by chattering children. "I've just left the park. There was a kindergarten class doing a nature study, so I stayed with them. I think the guy who followed me headed toward the old, disused gates on Western Drive, but I can't be sure. I'm at the intersection of Mustang Boulevard and Western. The kids are going back to school and I was going to head toward work."

Spencer paused for a moment while the tightness in his chest loosened. The location she'd described was busy, with shops and businesses on each corner and people passing by all the time. A man who had followed her would be stupid to try anything in such a public place. But he knew from experience that crooks played by their own rules and they weren't always the most predictable people.

"Stay where you are. I'm two minutes away."

Racing along Mustang Boulevard, Boris on his leash, he mentally reviewed all the reasons why someone would follow Katrina. It could be a dissatisfied customer, someone who had a grudge for another reason, or the guy could have noticed her because of her looks. He wasn't ruling out a link to her visit to the AAG and her sister's disappearance. Not yet—there were other possibilities to be explored first.

He was approaching the intersection and he was relieved when he spotted Katrina's blond hair and her two dogs at her side. She was standing on the sidewalk outside a drugstore. He was just about to call out to her when a squeal of brakes made him turn his head. He quickly registered the presence of a fast-approaching vehicle traveling along Mustang Boulevard. It was a black Chrysler sedan with tinted windows, and he checked out its license plate. As it sped closer, alarm bells started to ring inside his head.

Spencer broke into a run again and drew level with Katrina just as the car mounted the sidewalk a few yards away. He grabbed her around the waist and dragged her toward him, diving out of the path of the vehicle and into the shelter of a nearby doorway. Holding her down and shielding her with his body, he lifted his head to see what was happening.

Exhilaration pumped through his veins like a drug at the knowledge that he'd acted fast enough to save Katrina. A second or two later and the car could have plowed into her. The spark of fear in his belly that had been lit when she told him she was being followed now became an uncontrollable blaze.

She could have been killed...

As he cradled her close, his mind remained focused on the practicalities of keeping her safe. At the same time, his body insisted on taking note of how good it felt to hold her warm curves in his arms.

Having skidded to within feet of where Katrina had been standing, with its front wheels and most of the body on the sidewalk, the sedan veered sharply away. Bouncing wildly for a few seconds as it hit potholes in the road, it straightened before speeding off. He reached into his pocket for his cell phone and placed a call to the dispatcher at the station, giving the details of the vehicle and the direction in which it was heading.

"Are you okay?" He ended his call and drew Katrina to her feet, still holding her against him. Throughout the impending danger, Dobby had given the occasional bark, while Holly had hidden behind Katrina. Although they now appeared subdued, they were unharmed. Boris, who was used to difficult search-and-rescue and manhunt situations, calmly sat at his master's feet.

"I think so." She looked slightly stunned.

"Although the car came close, it was lucky that the driver managed to swerve at the last minute."

"But it was heading straight toward me." She raised frightened eyes to his face. "That wasn't luck. It was a warning."

Although he was inclined to agree with her, his police training had taught Spencer caution. Katrina had been making inquiries about her missing sister. Someone had broken into her house, she had been followed and a car had almost mowed her down. Those things could have been unrelated. Even though he didn't believe in coincidences, he would have to start from there.

"Not necessarily. The guy could have lost control of the car," he said. "He should have stopped if he was able to, but that doesn't make him an attempted killer."

She put her hands on her hips. "What has to happen for you to take this seriously? Do they have to carry a sign saying We Want to Hurt Katrina Perry?"

"I will investigate this, Katrina."

She pulled away from his arm, which was still around her. "You do that. And in the meantime, I'll try to find a stretch of sidewalk that's safe for me to walk on."

She was the most awkward, difficult and prickly woman he had ever encountered. She was also the most beautiful and desirable. As she stomped away, Spencer reflected that his life would be a lot easier if he wasn't getting more attracted to her each time they met.

KATRINA'S ANGER SUSTAINED her for most of her walk back to the dog-training center. Spencer's response had made her feel like she was overreacting, prompting memories of the dramas of her childhood. One of her worst fears had always been that people would compare her with her mother.

Even so... Do I have to get killed before Spencer Colton will listen to me?

That thought added a dose of fear to her anger, causing her to glance over her shoulder. Her gut instinct told her that the driver of the sedan had intended to scare her and not hit her. Not only that, but she was also convinced the incident was linked to Eliza's disappearance. She understood that Spencer had a job to do, and that there were police procedures he had to follow, but would he ever see her point of view before it was too late? It seemed as if a number of factors were conspiring against her. From her understandable distress about Eliza's disappearance at the time they'd first met, Spencer must have gotten the impression she was emotionally volatile. Then, it seemed that his visit to the AAG ranch left him wondering about Katrina's mental stability. It was no wonder his initial reaction was to treat anything linked to her with caution.

And, because events had overtaken them, she hadn't yet told him about the encounter between the angry woman and the AAG members. Clearly, it wasn't worth mentioning it to him now, but she couldn't let it go.

What was it that woman had said? *My son just lost his dad in a horrible accident.* Mustang Valley was a small town. It was possible that, by looking into that statement, she could find out more about the person who had challenged the AAG members. It was a long shot, but worth a try.

It had taken years of hard work to build up Look Who's Walking and its success was a result of Katrina's personal commitment. For the first time ever, the sight of her own business didn't soothe her spirits. Anxiety still pricked her spine as she stepped inside and she was barely aware of the quick, concerned glance Suzie cast in her direction.

"Have you eaten?"

Katrina shook her head. "I have some pasta in the fridge. I'll grab a few bites as we set up for the afternoon sessions."

"Sorry." Suzie jerked a thumb in the direction of the office. "A potential client stopped by. I asked if I could help but he insisted on seeing you."

Suzie had done the right thing. Although their business was thriving, they couldn't afford to turn away new customers. Even so, Katrina's nerves frayed a little more at the thought of pinning on a smile and going into corporate mode.

Got to be done. And it might give her a little distance from recent events.

She handed the split leash to Suzie. "Give these guys some water. I'll be with you as soon as I can."

When she entered her office, the man waiting for her was looking out of the window that overlooked the training yard. As he turned and smiled, Katrina took a moment to assess him. He was tall with pleasant features, and he stepped forward with a smile.

"Hi. I'm Aidan Hannant. Are you the person I need to talk to about my problem pup?"

"I'm Katrina Perry, owner and lead trainer here at Look Who's Walking." She moved to the chair behind her desk, and her visitor took the seat opposite. "How can I help you?"

"I have an eighteen-month-old rottweiler who thinks he's a puppy. In the last few weeks, he's eaten my digital camera, my game console, the baseboard from the kitchen cabinets and the legs from two wooden dining chairs."

Although Katrina laughed, she was slightly bemused. This wasn't an uncommon problem and Suzie could easily have assisted Aidan. His insistence on waiting for Katrina didn't make sense, but she'd been in this situation before. Some people just preferred to speak to the boss.

The customer is always right. Even when he's wrong.

"Okay. Chewing is often a sign of boredom. Give him things that he is allowed to chew, like sterilized stuffed bones and other toys that are too tough for him to destroy. That way, he'll spend his time on them and won't attack your belongings. If you can't trust him when you aren't home, I would suggest crating him. Rottweilers need plenty of exercise and play that challenges. If you can't meet those expectations, we offer a pet-walking service—"

His smile widened. "Did you get the message?"

"Sorry?"

"The car was a warning." He got to his feet, leaning forward as he placed his hands on the desk. "Your heroic rescuer could have saved himself the trouble of grabbing you. I wasn't going to hit you. Not this time."

Katrina stared blankly at him. Momentarily, her body shut down as she processed his meaning. When she finally surged to her feet, he was already headed out the door. Stumbling slightly, she ran after him. There was no one in the reception area and all traces of the seemingly nice guy were gone as Aidan turned to face her.

"Don't think about following me or telling anyone about this." There was a snarl in his voice. "Stay out of things that don't concern you."

He strode out the door and Katrina returned to the office. As she sank into the chair, she was shivering like a dog in a thunderstorm. Those sinister threats were bad enough. Even worse was the knowledge that if she went to the police, there was a chance she wouldn't be believed.

Yes, she could back up the fact that Aidan Hannant had entered her business. She had security cameras, and the footage would provide the proof she needed. The images of the parking lot should give a clear enough view of his vehicle to provide details of his license plate, so Spencer could verify his identity. While none of those things were proof of the threats he'd just made, they were evidence that the same guy who'd tried to attack her had entered her business premises…always supposing he'd used the same vehicle both times.

So why was her instinct telling her not to give Spencer another reason to write her off as a fantasist? The answer was simple, even if it wasn't rational. He had doubted her. Katrina didn't give her trust easily. And she never gave it twice.

Taking a deep breath, she reached into the desk drawer for her water bottle and took a long slug. So she was on her own. Wasn't that the way it had always been?

Chapter Five

The following afternoon, Spencer assembled his team for a briefing on the sting to flush out Payne Colton's shooter. They were discussing the final details before they set off for Mustang Valley General Hospital.

"I will be the decoy in the hospital bed that Payne has just vacated." He refused to let anyone else take the risk. "Kerry and PJ will be in the corridor disguised as orderlies. Lizzie and James, you'll be hidden in the hospital room. Dane, I need you in Payne's room."

"Even if we're in disguise, won't the shooter be spooked by a presence in the corridor?" veteran detective PJ Doherty asked.

"We've spread the word around that Payne's condition is improving and that he's being moved to a room on the second floor. His wife, Genevieve Colton, and Ainsley and Marlowe have approved the plan. The news that he could regain consciousness should be enough to bring the shooter to Mustang Valley General to check things out and probably to attempt to finish the job. If he sees empty corridors, he'll get suspicious," Spencer said. "With you guys pretending to be hospital staff, you can watch Payne's old room while maintaining an air of normality."

"What about the other rooms on that floor?" It was Officer Lizzie Manfred who spoke.

"All empty," Spencer confirmed. "The hospital manager is aware of the situation and has briefed his staff on a need-to-know basis. I'm not prepared to put anyone else in danger."

As he finished speaking, his desktop telephone buzzed. Since he'd given strict instructions that he wasn't to be disturbed, Spencer knew it must be important.

"I'm sorry to interrupt your meeting, Sergeant Colton," the front-desk clerk said. "But I have a man here who insists on speaking to you. He says he has information about the dangerous-driving incident that took place on Mustang Boulevard yesterday afternoon."

Spencer glanced at the clock. There was another hour before visiting hours started on the unit where Payne was being treated, and he needed to be there with half an hour to spare to set up the sting. He was already cutting things fine…

But this was about Katrina, and that mattered more than it should. "Put him in an interview room. I'll be right down."

Aware that his team members were looking at him with surprise, he got to his feet. "I need to deal with this. It's about an urgent situation that arose yesterday. I'll meet you at the hospital."

Confident that his colleagues would carry out his

instructions, he hurried to the reception area with Boris at his heels. The receptionist waved him toward one of the interview rooms and he went inside. The man seated at the table made a movement as if he was about to get to his feet.

"Please, stay where you are." Spencer pulled up a chair and sat down. "I'm Sergeant Spencer Colton. How can I help you?"

"My name is Aidan Hannant." He was quiet-spoken and appeared nervous. "I was driving the vehicle that mounted the sidewalk on Mustang Boulevard yesterday."

Spencer wasn't sure what he'd expected from this meeting, but it certainly hadn't been that. He picked up the pad of paper and pen that had been left on the table.

"I will need to ask one of my colleagues to take a full statement from you, Mr. Hannant. But I have a few questions to ask before that, starting with what caused you to lose control of the vehicle?"

"I sneezed."

Spencer glanced up from the note he was making. Hannant was offering a tricky excuse. It was a driver's responsibility to remain in control of his, or her, vehicle at all times. A sneeze, however, was an involuntary action—one that often could not be predicted or prevented.

"And your reason for not stopping at the scene, or coming forward sooner…?"

"I was scared." Hannant drummed his fingers on the edge of the table. "I mean, I closed my eyes for a second when I sneezed and the next thing I knew, my car was on the sidewalk. I could have *killed* someone."

"That's true. And, if your intention had been to harm someone—whether physically, or by scaring them—a sneeze is a very convenient defense."

Hannant sucked in a breath. "I—I don't know how to answer that. Except to repeat that it was an accident."

"So you didn't know the woman you nearly hit?"

"No!" The guy was either genuinely upset at the suggestion, or he was a very good actor. "I panicked and left the scene, but after I thought about it, I knew I had to come in here and tell the truth."

Spencer knew that appearances could be deceptive. Conducting a background check would give him a clearer picture of who Aidan Hannant was and might help him understand the reasons behind this visit. He couldn't quite figure out why the other man would turn up with this story if his intention had been to harm, or frighten, Katrina.

A quick glance at the screen of his cell told Spencer he needed to get moving. The operation at Mustang Valley General couldn't happen without him. Before he called in a colleague to take a full statement from Hannant, he had one more question.

"Do you have any connection to the Affirmation Alliance Group?"

"I don't understand." Hannant's forehead wrinkled. "Is that the group who've been helping people affected by the earthquake? What do they have to do with this?"

That was the key question. Spencer didn't have an answer. Yet. But he intended to find one.

Katrina had gone through the first training session of the afternoon on autopilot. Although every animal was different, most of the routines were the same and it didn't take much to adapt her approach to an individual dog. By the time the dogs were collected by their owners, the shakiness she had felt after yesterday's encounter with Aidan Hannant had returned and she was exhausted.

"I overheard something a woman said in the grocery store yesterday." She started the conversation before Suzie, who could be a little too perceptive sometimes, asked if she was okay. "She was talking about a man who had died recently in a horrible accident. I don't recall anything like that, do you?"

"Not here in Mustang Valley." Suzie could always be relied upon to be up-to-date with all the news, including the latest recent killings of beauty pageant contestants in two Arizona counties. "But my mom's friend Helen Jackson, who lives just outside of town, lost her husband recently. That was a tragic accident."

"How did he die?"

"He was an airplane pilot for a small commercial company operating out of Tucson. A month or two ago, his plane collided with another on takeoff." Suzie shook her head sadly. "Helen's son, Jonah, said they had to use dental records to identify the bodies."

Katrina stored the information away for later. It was possible that Helen Jackson was not the woman she had seen confronting the AAG members. But Helen *had* recently lost her husband in tragic circumstances, and her son could have borrowed money to spend on one of the group's seminars. She still didn't feel it was enough to take her suspicions to Spencer and risk being labeled as the same sort of attention seeker her mother had been. But it was a potential starting point and that gave her hope of finding a way forward.

By the end of the day, her fighting spirit had been restored. The panic brought on by Aidan Hannant's warning was still there, but she was able to push it aside and plan her next steps.

"You said Helen Jackson lives out of town. Where, exactly?" she asked Suzie as they locked up.

"She's a sculptor. Her studio is about ten miles out of town, close to the Mustang Valley Mountains. Why?"

"Just wondering why I never heard the story about her husband."

"There was an obituary in the *Mustang Valley Times*," Suzie said. "But it was just a few lines. I didn't talk to you about it because I figured you didn't know the family, and..." She shrugged. "You've had a lot on your mind lately."

They stepped out into the bright sunlight and Katrina resisted the temptation to laugh. She had a feeling that, if she started, she might be unable to stop. And her laughter could quickly turn to tears.

"You could say that."

"Look, I was going to see Rusty tonight." Suzie's on-off relationship with an old school friend was in one of its "on" phases. "But he'll understand if I call and cancel."

"Don't you dare." Despite their height difference, Katrina managed to drape an arm around the other woman's shoulders as they walked toward their cars. "I don't want to be on the receiving end of one of Rusty's dirty looks next time I see him."

Once she'd convinced Suzie that she really would be okay and waved her off, Katrina loaded the dogs into her own vehicle. Before she set off, she sat behind the wheel and spent a few minutes checking out Helen Jackson's website on her cell phone.

Although Aidan Hannant's words had frightened her, she wasn't going to let a thug stop her from finding her sister. It bothered her that an organization like the AAG could be behind sending a bully boy to scare her. Of course, there was always a chance that the leaders of the group knew nothing about the activities of some of its members. It was even possible that a few unscrupulous people had infiltrated a do-good group and were using it as a cover for their activities.

If that was the case, she was in over her head. She narrowed her eyes. Maybe she should contact Spencer one more time. She'd been threatened. And the warning had been specifically linked to the car that had come so close to running her down. Even Mr. Cautious Cop couldn't ignore *that*.

When she tried Spencer's number, it went straight to a voice-mail message that directed her to one of his colleagues. Since she wasn't going to start explaining the situation all over again to someone new, she decided to stop by the police station and ask to speak to him. It was on the way to Helen Jackson's place.

SPENCER HAD BEEN lying in the darkened hospital room for over half an hour. Visiting times were limited, and the hospital would soon close its doors for the day. If the shooter was going to make his move, he would need to act soon. The medical staff had played their parts, helping to make the scene appear authentic by positioning monitors and a ventilator close to the bed.

Beneath the bed covers, his right hand rested on his weapon. Under the bed, hidden from view by an overhanging sheet, James was lying on his stomach with his own gun trained on the door. In the corner, adjacent to the bed, Lizzie was concealed behind a folding screen. Outside, patrolling the corridor, PJ and Kerry were disguised as orderlies.

"No unusual activity." PJ's voice sounded overly loud in Spencer's headphones, but he knew the seasoned detective would be careful to speak quietly into his concealed microphone.

Because there were no other patients on that floor, the plan was simple. PJ and Kerry would observe the entrance. Once the suspect was approaching the room, they would alert Spencer. The team would let the shooter get through the door before surrounding him.

There were two entrances to Payne's second-floor ward. Either way, anyone entering was required to check in with the unit manager, whose desk was located a few yards from the room in which Spencer and his team were lying in wait.

The air was so brittle with tension it felt ready to snap. Spencer eased his limbs into a more relaxed position. With ten minutes left until the end of visiting hours, it was possible they'd struck out this time.

"Stand by. Looks like our guy just stepped out of the

elevator." At PJ's whisper, Spencer's heart rate kicked up a notch and his fingers closed over the butt of his gun.

Letting out a slow, controlled breath, he strained his ears. Sure enough, the faintest sound came from just outside the door. There was just enough light for Spencer to see the handle begin to turn.

Wait. Let him get inside. Those were the instructions he'd given…

A sliver of bright light appeared as the door started to open. Just as quickly, it was gone. Reacting to the loud slam, Spencer leaped from the bed and dashed from the room. He was in time to see PJ and Kerry running after a hooded figure. As the person reached the window at the end of the corridor, Spencer thought they had him cornered. There was nowhere for him to go.

"Halt! Mustang Valley Police."

As he shouted the warning, the intruder risked a glance over his shoulder. The fluorescent lights glinted off his shades before he turned away again. Moving swiftly, he opened the window, banged hard with the heel of his hand and forced it beyond the safety catch.

"Damn it. He's going to jump!" PJ was almost within grabbing distance, even had an arm outstretched, but the shooter nimbly leaped through the opening.

The three police officers reached the window and clustered together, gazing down at the scene below. The guy had landed on a grass verge. He scrambled to his feet, then cast a quick look around before limping to a vehicle. Before any of the cops could jump after him, he was driving quickly away.

Spencer muttered a curse under his breath as he pulled out his cell and contacted the officers who were watching the exits. Even though there was only a limited chance they would catch up with the shooter, he described what had happened and instructed them to make an attempt to pursue the suspect's car.

"I didn't get a good look at him," he said as he ended the call. "Did he match the description of the guy on the security cameras at Colton Oil the night Payne was shot?"

"Yeah." Kerry huffed out a breath. "He was pretty much identical."

"We need to get the hospital security footage to see if we can get a better description from it," Spencer instructed.

As they were talking, the other officers were emerging from their hiding places. The atmosphere was despondent. This had been their best chance of flushing out the shooter and he'd eluded them.

Although he told himself that they'd done their best and it had always been a long shot, disappointment gnawed at Spencer's gut. He didn't subscribe to that whole "it's okay to lose" philosophy. He believed if you didn't get it right the first time, you'd failed. And he didn't like feeling useless… Even so, he wasn't going to pass those emotions on to his team.

"We did our best, but right now, there's nothing more we can do here, guys. You may as well head back to the station while I report to the Colton family."

Spencer reached into his pocket for his cell phone. There were a number of missed calls from Katrina and a message from the MVPD dispatcher, saying that she'd called into the station looking for him. A frown pulled his eyebrows together. What now? He knew he was being unfair to her with the thought. It was only natural that she should be worried about her sister. And it wasn't her fault that trouble seemed to follow her…

As he made his way up the stairs toward Payne Colton's new third-floor room, he tried Katrina's number. The call went straight to voice mail. He left a short message, letting her know that he'd tried to return her calls.

He'd catch up with her later. Even Katrina Perry couldn't get herself into much trouble in the next hour or so.

DESPITE THEIR SORROWFUL EXPRESSIONS, Katrina decided to leave the dogs at home when she went in search of Helen Jackson's studio. As she drove along the winding drive that approached the property, Katrina saw a variety of life-size wooden animal sculptures. No wonder Helen had chosen to locate her home in this rural location. Her artwork was on a large scale and she clearly needed plenty of space.

At the end of the drive, a long, low building was split into three distinct units with signs over the door of each. They were a workshop, a sales area and a house. A woman was seated on the front porch and, with a feeling of intense relief, Katrina recognized her as the person who had confronted the AAG members on Mustang Boulevard.

As Katrina got out of her car, the other woman rose from her chair and came down the steps to greet her.

"Hi there." Helen—because surely it must be Helen—gave her a friendly smile. "I'm actually closed for sales at this time of day. But if you've seen something on the website that you're interested in, I'll be happy to give you a viewing."

"I'd love to look at your sculptures." Although Katrina felt it would be the easiest way to create a bond with Helen, she seriously doubted she would be able to afford one of the giant structures. Even if she could, she'd have to dismantle her canine-training equipment if she wanted to fit one in her yard. "But I came to talk to you about something else."

Helen's smile faded a little as she scanned her face. "I don't think we've met before."

"We haven't. But I was close by when you spoke to some members of the Affirmation Alliance Group on Mustang Boulevard the other day."

Helen's gaze shifted away from Katrina's face toward the nearby Mustang Valley Mountains. After a few moments of silence, she looked back again. "That was a misunderstanding."

"You seemed very certain of your facts. And you were unhappy with the way the AAG had treated your son," Katrina said.

"I don't want to talk about this."

The difference between the confident woman who had confronted the group two days ago and this uncomfortable, nervous figure before her now was striking. What could have caused this change in Helen? Although she was bemused, Katrina plowed on.

"I'm asking about this for a reason. Two months ago, my sister got involved with the AAG—"

"I said I don't want to talk about it." The words came out fast and sharp. Helen drew a breath before continuing in a calmer tone. "I was wrong to approach the AAG members the way I did. I made a mistake and I want to forget it."

"Please, let me just—"

With a determined shake of her head, Helen turned back toward the house. Defeated, Katrina walked back to her car. What else could she do? Something had caused Helen to change her mind. The anger she'd felt the other day had dissipated and there was this new… She searched for the right word. Resignation? Acceptance? It certainly looked like Helen had turned her back on her previous indignation.

As she drove away, she could see the other woman watching her. Helen was standing on the top step with her arms wrapped around herself, as if fending off a chill.

There is something very wrong here.

For the first time in her life, she was faced with a problem that she couldn't deal with. In the past, her biggest concern had been supporting Eliza through her addiction. Although she'd dealt with that by herself, it had never felt like an impossible task, or one that she couldn't deal with alone.

When she got home, she would try Spencer again. Even if he dismissed what she told him about Helen, he would be obliged to check it out. And that would at least get him asking questions.

As she headed home, she realized she was low on just about every household essential. She'd been putting off grocery shopping, but it had reached the point where starvation was looming. Drastic times called for a shopping trip.

As she pulled into the parking lot outside the convenience store, her phone buzzed. Checking the display, she saw it was an unknown number. She was halfway to declining the call when she paused. Helen Jackson didn't have her number, but what if she'd somehow gotten hold of it? What if she'd changed her mind and wanted to talk after all?

"Yes?"

"Is that Katrina Perry?" The voice sounded female, quiet and a little breathy. She was fairly sure it wasn't Helen Jackson.

It certainly didn't sound sinister, or like a cold caller trying to sell her a funeral plan, but Katrina wasn't prepared to confirm her identity. Not yet.

"Who is this?"

"I overheard you when you came to the AAG ranch." The voice had dropped to a whisper. "When you were asking about Eliza. I found your card and I've been trying to find the courage to call you."

Tears stung the back of Katrina's eyes. Was this it? Was this finally the breakthrough she'd been waiting for? Was she finally going to find out what had happened to her sister?

"Did you know Eliza?"

"Yes. Look, it's hard for me to talk over the phone. I don't know who could be listening."

"I can meet you anywhere." The groceries could wait. Who needed food, anyway?

"Mustang Park, by the slides. Half an hour."

"Wait—"

The caller had gone before Katrina could ask who she was, or how she would know her. With a combination of dread and excitement churning inside her, she left the parking lot and headed toward the park.

She arrived at the kiddie playground with ten minutes to spare and sat on a bench. There was no one else around and she figured most of the children who frequented this area would be finishing dinner around this time. It was family time. Homework, TV, bath, story, bed. The usual, familiar routines. The things she and Eliza had missed out on, unless they did them for themselves. Their mom had been more focused on her own needs. Vodka, dive bar, heroin, new boyfriend.

When darkness fell, this part of the park changed. Teenagers came down here to drink and make out. There had been a campaign in the *Mustang Valley Times* to get the park gates locked at night, but it hadn't gotten any momentum.

Maybe she should call someone. Suzie would bring the dogs over to help protect her. But that would mean explaining things to Suzie… Probably she should call Spencer. But he would take over, would try to talk her out of this meeting. She needed to hear what this mystery caller had to say about Eliza. That was the most important thing.

Lost in her thoughts, she gradually became aware that someone was watching her. A young woman clad in jeans and a lightweight sweater was standing across the other side of the slide area. She had dark hair pulled back in a ponytail. Her face pale, she appeared poised to run at any second.

Katrina got to her feet and walked toward her. "Hi. I'm Katrina Perry. Are you the person who called me?"

The other woman gulped, then nodded. "I'm Christie Foster."

"Shall we sit down?" Katrina indicated the bench. Together they walked across the playground and sat down. "Thank you for meeting me, Christie."

"I wanted to do it sooner. It's just difficult, you know?"

"Can you explain why?" Katrina was concerned at the other woman's manner. She reminded her of a bird, her jerky movements making her seem as though she was constantly ready for flight.

Christie ducked her head, then cast a quick glance around. "Because of what happened to Eliza. If anyone knew I was here, talking to you…" She pressed a hand to her lips. "I can't. I'm sorry."

Getting to her feet, she ran off in the direction of the park gates. Katrina started after her, calling out her name.

"Leave me alone!" Christie's echoing cry was like that of a wounded animal.

Torn between the need to know more about her sister's fate and Christie's obvious distress, Katrina let her go. What had just happened here? Christie was the one who had called her, yet within minutes, she'd run off. Torn between annoyance, frustration and sympathy, she dug her hands into her pockets and bowed her head.

At least she had a name and the number from where Christie had called her. What the other woman had told her made it obvious that something bad had happened to Eliza. It was also clear that Christie feared the same fate.

First Helen. Now Christie. It must be enough for the police to investigate the AAG further.

By the time she reached her house, Katrina's whole body was aching, as though tension had pulled every muscle a little too tight. She needed dinner—and since she hadn't gotten any groceries, that meant takeout—a hot bath and a good night's sleep. She got out of the car and stretched her arms above her head, then she headed toward the front steps. As she drew nearer, though, panic hit like a bucket of ice-cold water.

Her little house looked the same as ever, except for one key detail. The front door was hanging wide open, marks scarring its wooden surface as though someone had repeatedly kicked it. In the center, there was a white piece of paper, secured in place with tape. A message was scrawled on it in black felt pen.

From the yard, she could hear the sound of furious barking. Her mind registered that the dogs were angry but safe. With a pounding heart, she drew closer. Remaining poised to run, she read the words.

Stop poking your nose where it's not wanted, or next time your dogs will get steaks with antifreeze for dinner.

Chapter Six

By the time he left the hospital, Spencer was undecided whether to drive over to Katrina's place or leave it until the following day. His mood was already low after the failure of the sting, and his feelings about Katrina were confused.

From the first moment he met her, he'd experienced an instant attraction. Even though she had the ability to infuriate him, that pull had continued to grow. But, alongside the developing warmth, alarm bells rang when he thought about Micheline Anderson's warning. If Eliza was unsteady and attention seeking, wasn't it possible her sister had similar traits?

When Billie died, grief had caused him to lose some of his inner strength, and to shut down his feelings. He still did his job with the same expertise, and, until now, he'd never been unsure of his ability to judge the people he'd encountered. But he'd never come across anyone quite like Katrina…

It troubled him that he had no real evidence besides her word that she had been targeted. Her friend had been in the yard when Katrina had entered the house and told Suzie there was a man in the kitchen. When he'd asked how the intruder had gotten in, she'd talked vaguely about an open window. Then there had been the guy who'd followed her in the park. Had that really happened, or had she imagined it? Could it even have been another trick to get his attention?

Spencer had been there when the car mounted the sidewalk and almost plowed into her. But he hadn't been satisfied that the driver intended to hit her, or even warn her. After his meeting with Aidan Hannant, he was even less convinced.

Katrina seemed to feel that the Affirmation Alliance Group was connected to her sister's disappearance. Or at least that someone in the organization was involved in a cover-up. He reviewed the possibilities. First, there was a chance she could be right. But even if Eliza had encountered a problem during her time at the AAG ranch, why would the group's leadership, including Micheline, hide the issue? Surely, a socially responsible enterprise like theirs would want to assist if a crime had been committed.

That led him to the second option. Leigh Dennings had suggested that, prior to her departure from the AAG ranch, Eliza had appeared strung out. She'd implied that there were similarities to Katrina's own behavior. With their intense attitudes, the AAG members, particularly Randall and Bart, with their tough-guy act, were a little hard to take. It was possible that Katrina was simply overreacting.

Then there was the possibility that Katrina was right to be worried, but that the AAG was not the problem.

Eliza could be in serious trouble and, as a result, Katrina might be the target of the same unknown aggressor. If that was the case, Spencer needed to investigate further.

Finally, there was the option he didn't want to consider. What if the hint Micheline had dropped was correct? What if Katrina had made up all of this? He had no clue what her motive might be. Perhaps she was simply looking for attention.

But that would be one hell of a coincidence. And Spencer didn't believe in those. Experience had taught him that if there appeared to be a connection between events, there probably was. The simple truth was that victims of crime generally didn't lie.

These thoughts were going through his head as he drove from the hospital to the police station to collect Boris. As he pulled up in the parking lot, his cell phone buzzed. He alighted from his vehicle and checked the caller display. It was Katrina.

"Hi—" He didn't get a chance to say anything else.

"Someone has broken into my house." Her voice was so shaky he barely recognized it. "And left a note threatening to kill my dogs."

"I'm on my way."

Sprinting across the parking lot, he crossed to the side of the building where Boris's kennel was located. He unlocked the cage door and gave the dog one of his favorite treats. Calling Boris to heel, he headed back to his vehicle and was soon on the road toward Katrina's house.

His mind raced as he drove. What would he find

when he got to her place?? For the first time since Billie's death, he was attracted to another woman… And someone was trying to kill her! Or were they? He had no idea who Katrina really was.

When he reached her house, she was sitting on the front steps with Dobby on one side and Holly on the other. A quick look at her face told him she was either genuinely scared, or she was playing her part well.

What was it Micheline had said? *Not all actors are on the stage.*

As he approached, Katrina lifted a tearstained face to his. "I'm so glad you're here."

And in that instant, all of his suspicions disappeared. Her dogs bounded forward to greet Boris and Spencer sat next to her. When he placed a comforting arm around her shoulders, she leaned against him with a sigh.

"I haven't been inside. I was too scared."

"Do you want me to take a look? Or shall we go together?" he asked.

"I'll be okay if you're with me." She tilted her chin and some of her usual determination returned. "I won't let them beat me."

"Them?" He stood, then reached out a hand to help her to her feet.

"The AAG." She clicked her fingers to Holly and Dobby and the two dogs ran to her side. Boris trotted obediently to Spencer's heels and, as a group, they mounted the steps to the porch. Katrina cast a sidelong glance in Spencer's direction. "They sent someone to threaten me yesterday."

"What?" Aware that the word had cracked out like a whiplash, he tried for a calmer tone. "Where and when did this happen?"

"A guy came to Look Who's Walking pretending to be a client. He told me that the car was a warning and that I needed to stay out of things that don't concern me."

"Did anyone else witness this?"

"Suzie saw him, and the security cameras will have picked up his arrival. I wasn't there when he arrived, so Suzie asked him to wait in the office. But I was alone with him when he threatened me." She wrinkled her nose. "I don't know much about these things, but thugs don't usually make threats in front of an audience, do they? Naturally, he made sure we were alone."

How was he supposed to respond to that? He couldn't tell her the truth. That he was hoping another person had overheard so that he could finally put to rest a nagging suspicion…

"Anyway, he told me his name," Katrina continued.

"He did what?" Spencer frowned. Readily identifying themselves to a potential victim wasn't generally in the criminal handbook.

"He told me his name was Aidan Hannant. He said he hadn't planned to hit me with his car." She shivered slightly. "Not this time." Catching a glimpse of his expression, she frowned. "What is it? What have I said?"

"When did this happen?"

"Lunchtime. Just after I left you."

Spencer's mind was racing. None of this made sense. Why would Aidan Hannant threaten Katrina, then go to the police station and confess that he was the person driving the car? Unless Katrina wasn't being honest. But even if she was making up the story of the threats, how could she have known Hannant's name and that he was the driver of the car?

"When he threatened you, did this guy tell you he was from the AAG?" Spencer asked.

She paused, her expression thoughtful. "No. Now that I think about it, he didn't. But why else would he give me that warning?"

"There could be any number of reasons. He could be working for a client you've angered. It could be something to do with Eliza." Her eyes widened and he quickly hurried on. "Or maybe he's a stranger who saw you in the store one day and didn't like the way you looked at him. Sometimes these things don't need a reason. For now, let's go inside the house. We'll come back to Hannant later."

He turned his attention to the door, which looked like it had been given a few good, hard kicks. The wooden boards had splintered under the strain and the hinges had given way, leaving the door hanging from its frame. Katrina pointed to the note that was taped to the center panel.

"See? Another threat."

"Did you touch anything?" Spencer asked.

She shook her head so hard her ponytail swung wildly from side to side. "No way. I got close enough to read what that said, then I backed away and called you."

Instructing the dogs to stay, Spencer moved closer.

What he saw when he looked inside the house made his blood run cold. Katrina's neat living room had been trashed. Every item of furniture had been flipped over. Cushions and throws had been torn. Vases and mirrors had been smashed. Paint had been sprayed over her pastel walls. The place was an unrecognizable mess.

And yet, as Katrina placed a hand on his arm and peeked over his shoulder at the devastation, the doubts persisted. Could she have done this herself?

"Oh, no." She lifted a hand to her lips, the tears that filled her eyes quickly brimming over. "What am I going to do?"

"You don't need to do anything." There was one obvious way to silence his suspicions and get her the protection she needed. Only time would tell whether that protection turned out to be from herself or an external force.

"I don't understand." A frown furrowed her smooth forehead.

"I'm moving in."

KATRINA FACED SPENCER with her hands on her hips. "You can't just move yourself and your dog into my house. We need to talk about this."

Although Katrina's fiercely independent streak had kicked in, part of her was wondering why she was raising an objection. Surely, a handsome cop and his canine companion living with her while she was being threatened would be a good thing. Spencer had checked the rest of the house while she waited on the front doorstep. Although the intruders hadn't touched any of the other rooms, the damage they'd done to her living room was bad enough. She crossed her arms over her body as she surveyed the scene, a sick feeling starting low in her stomach.

"You can stay at my place instead, if you want. But the yard isn't really big enough for three dogs." Without waiting for her reply, he stepped onto the porch with his cell phone in his hand. A few moments later, he was deep in a conversation about fingerprints and handwriting analysis.

Sighing, Katrina took another look at the destruction that had once been her living room. Since Spencer had told her not to touch anything, she backed away carefully from the door and collected the dogs, then led them around the side of the house to the yard.

After spending about ten minutes encouraging Holly and Dobby to use the training equipment, while Boris watched her with interest but declined to join in, she took a seat on her favorite bench and left the three of them to indulge in a little canine free play. As always, her fingers strayed to her cell phone. She'd restricted herself to three calls a day to Eliza's number. Morning, midday and night. Anything else would be obsessive. Even though she had never gotten an answer, giving up on her sister would feel wrong.

Instead of calling Eliza, she sent a message to Suzie. She wanted to let her assistant know about the break-in. Doing it without causing Suzie to storm out of her date to come and check what was going on. It was a tricky balancing act. When her phone rang minutes after she'd sent the message, she wasn't sure she'd succeeded.

"I'm on my way over." Suzie sounded like a woman who wasn't going to take "no" for an answer.

"You don't need to do that. Sergeant Colton is here."

Suzie gave a snort. "You need your friends more than you need the police." Katrina decided now was probably not the best time to mention that Spencer might also be moving in. "You think this was the same guy who was in your kitchen the other day?"

"I don't know." Katrina's mind refused to process that line of questioning. It was as though her thoughts couldn't connect and were bouncing around in random directions. "All I know is that my living room looks like a herd of cattle stampeded through it."

"Hold on a second." Suzie engaged in a muffled conversation before continuing. "Rusty said don't worry. He'll be over tomorrow morning with his brothers to help repair the damage."

For a second or two, Katrina's throat tightened so much she couldn't talk. At some point, Suzie had stepped up from friend to family, becoming the sister Eliza had never been. It was a sweet feeling, but also a painful reminder of all the things her life had been missing. When she did speak, her voice was husky. "Tell Rusty thanks."

"What's the point of four grown men sitting around a hardware store all day?" Suzie's voice was breezy. "One of them can take care of the business while the other three come and straighten out your place. Now, are you sure you don't want me to keep you company tonight?"

"No. By the time the police have finished up, it'll be late. I'll see you at work in the morning."

It took a few more minutes to convince Suzie that she would be okay. By the time she ended the call, Katrina felt more tired than ever. When she looked up, Spencer was leaning against one of the fence posts, watching her. Although his expression was neutral, his eyes were shadowed.

"Are you okay?" He shook his head. "Stupid question."

She scrubbed a hand over her eyes. Somehow, the concern in his voice made her feel more vulnerable. "I, uh..." She searched for a distraction. "I just spoke to Suzie. Her boyfriend is Rusty Linehan. You know, from Linehan's Hardware Store? He's coming over tomorrow with some of his brothers to try to straighten the place out." She frowned. "If that's okay."

He came to sit next to her. "It'll be fine. My colleagues are on their way now to take fingerprints and take crime-scene photographs. Once those things are done, we can start to clean up."

We. She sneaked a look at him from beneath her lashes. "Did you mean what you said? About moving in?"

"Yeah." He leaned back, stretched his long legs and crossed his booted ankles. "I know a strange guy sleeping in your spare room is not what you signed up for when you reported Eliza missing, but we need to find out what's going on here."

"And is this standard police procedure?" She threw him a challenging look. "When a Mustang Valley citizen is in danger, one of your officers goes to live with them?"

"No." He appeared unfazed by the question. "But you are a special case."

"Why?" Suddenly, the answer to that question mattered almost as much as finding out who was behind the break-in.

"I'm not sure." Her heart started beating faster as he regarded her thoughtfully. "But that's one of the things I intend to find out."

PROPERTY CRIMES WERE not generally the highest priority for MVPD. But because Spencer himself had called in Katrina's break-in to Chief Barco, they gave it greater importance. Even so, by the time the investigation team had finished processing the scene, it was late.

Although Katrina reassured him that she was fine, Spencer had concerns about her emotional well-being. There was a lost look in her eyes, and she fiddled constantly with her cell phone as she spoke to his colleagues. It was as if she was expecting a call that never came.

The living room was still a mess and he decided it could wait until morning. If the Linehan brothers were planning to deal with it, the best plan of action would be to leave it to them. Linehan's Hardware Store had been established on Mustang Boulevard fifty years earlier by Clinton Linehan. After being extended and modernized by his son, Clinton's four grandsons now joint owned the thriving enterprise.

In the meantime, there were other issues to deal with.

"If you make coffee, I'll feed the dogs." He steered

Katrina in the direction of the kitchen. "Then we can order takeout."

She stared out of the window. "I'm not really hungry."

"When did you last eat?"

An impatient frown flitted across her features. "I don't know. Breakfast, maybe?"

He took her arm and led her to the table. "Sit down."

"I thought you wanted coffee?"

"I'm a multitalented guy. I can make coffee *and* give the dogs their dinner." He watched her face as she checked her cell. "Are you expecting a call?"

"Not really." She slid the phone into her pocket. "I keep hoping Eliza will get in touch. A young woman called me today. Her name is Christie Foster and she's an AAG member. She said she knew Eliza. We met in the park, but when she started to tell me what had happened to her, she got scared and ran off."

"That definitely sounds like it's worth investigating." He saw the flicker of relief in her eyes and was glad he could finally offer her some hope. Her kitchen was neatly laid out and he found everything he needed for the coffee. When it was made, he placed a cup in front of Katrina. "Where do you keep your bowls and dog food?"

"There's a storage box outside the back door. You'll find everything you need in there."

As soon as Spencer stepped outside, Holly and Dobby came bounding up and sat beside the box Katrina had mentioned. Boris, strolling over at a more leisurely pace, seemed to give him a questioning glance.

"I know what you're thinking." Spencer opened the box and took out three bowls. There was a large airtight tub of dog food and he read the label with approval. It looked like Katrina only bought the best products for her pets. "This could all go horribly wrong."

Two of the bowls were helpfully labeled with Holly and Dobby's names, and marks to indicate the level of their food. Since he had a good idea of how much to feed Boris, he was able to estimate the amount to give him. Once the dogs were all nudging each other out of the way and happily eating from any bowl they chose, Spencer went back inside.

Katrina was sitting where he'd left her with her gaze fixed on the window, one hand fidgeting with her cell. Her coffee remained untouched. The weight of his duty to this woman he barely knew hit him in that moment. He had a professional obligation to solve this case and ensure she was safe, but his responsibility to her went deeper and was more personal. After everything he'd been through in the past, the connection he felt should scare him, particularly as he had doubts about her emotional state.

What surprised him was that when he looked at her, none of that mattered. The initial attraction he'd felt for her had grown into a stronger bond that nothing, not his past or her potential vulnerability, could dent. Could he allow himself to explore that? He'd become so used to shutting himself down from the idea of another relationship that his thoughts automatically shied away from the suggestion. All he knew for sure was that he wanted to help Katrina.

And right now, that meant supporting her in a practical way.

"I'm craving burritos. If I order Mexican food, will you join me?" He picked up his coffee from the counter and came to sit at the table. "I hate eating alone."

A slight smile flitted across her face. "That must make living on your own a problem."

He grinned. "Boris is good company, but I prefer the human kind."

She laughed and the sound warmed a point in the center of his chest. "Since it's a favor to you, I guess I could manage some enchiladas."

He reached for his cell phone. "And maybe share some nachos?"

"Sharing sounds good."

She was right. For the first time in as long as he could remember, sharing sounded wonderful.

Chapter Seven

Later that night, Katrina was lying awake wondering why, among the many things that should be occupying her thoughts, Spencer's nearness had become the most important. She had gotten used to the idea early in life that she was on her own. Her mom and sister had been a tight little unit, excluding her because she didn't understand their choices, dramas and later their shared addictions. She'd had no choice. If anyone had asked her, she'd have said she liked it that way.

Now there was a man she barely knew sleeping a few yards away, and a new dog sharing the already overcrowded dog beds in the kennel. And it felt…okay. More than that. It felt right.

Until this point, her relationships with men had been superficial. She'd dated a few times, but always retreated if things started getting serious. Katrina understood why that was and, if she'd ever experienced an occasional pang of regret when she observed the deeper relationships that other people enjoyed, it had been fleeting. Trust was a basic requirement when it came to commitment.

Yeah. I don't do that.

So why did her feelings toward Spencer confuse her so much? From the moment she'd met him, he had made her feel secure. That alone made him different from any other man she'd known. Was security the same as trust? How could she tell, when she had never known what trust looked like?

Born to a teenage mom, she and Eliza had never known their dad. Mollie Perry had never had any hesitation about telling her daughters that she didn't know who he was.

"Could have been any guy in the bar that night." Mollie would switch to a familiar refrain. "If I hadn't been so drunk, I would've been careful. You think I wanted to be stuck with a couple of babies when I was only a kid myself?"

Growing up in the shadow of their mom's issues had been tough. Mollie's parents had given their daughter as much help as they could. Despite her grandparents' love and support, Katrina, older by three minutes, had always felt responsible for her younger fraternal twin. Sweet and pretty, but vulnerable, Eliza was a mirror image to Mollie. Living with a sibling and a mom who both had addictive personalities, and who could turn any situation into a drama, Katrina had felt out of place in her own home.

"You don't know what it's like to have feelings." It was an accusation both Mollie and Eliza had hurled at her regularly when, in the middle of one of their many crises, she would be forced to step in and deal with the practicalities. Let down time and time again by their sole parent, each twin had developed different coping strategies.

Eliza had done everything she could to please her mother. Katrina, on the other hand, had learned how to stand on her own two feet around the time she was studying her letters and numbers.

No matter how hard Katrina and her grandparents had tried, Eliza had taken the same route as her mother, spiraling into a life of addiction that started with alcohol and quickly progressed to drugs. Even Mollie's death from an overdose at the age of thirty hadn't halted her younger daughter's decline. Katrina had continued to care for Eliza as best she could. As they grew older, and Eliza became increasingly resentful of any interference in her life, it had gotten harder. It hadn't stopped Katrina from trying.

She had built up her own defenses. She'd put her head down and learned to blunt the noise and confusion of her home life with work and study. Her love of dogs had become her profession and her escape route. When colleagues commented that she was a workaholic, she knew she'd developed her own kind of addiction. It was just as intense as her mother's, but not as destructive. It had also become the way she kept the rest of the world at arm's length.

Go on a date? Sorry, I have to take care of the dogs. Meet friends? I have a training course to attend. Go away for the weekend? But who would take care of the business?

The only person who had broken down the barriers was Suzie. Somehow, Katrina's assistant had managed to keep trying until they had developed a lasting friendship. Until now, Katrina would have said she was happy with the way things were. Why had it taken Eliza's disappearance, a series of threats and a blue-eyed cop to make her question that? And, more importantly, what was she going to do about it?

You don't know what it's like to have feelings.

It was the old accusation, one she'd always believed to be true. She shivered. Sitting up in bed with her knees tucked under her chin, all of a sudden, she wasn't so sure.

"YOU CAN'T START the day without breakfast." Spencer shot a sidelong glance in the direction of Katrina's rear as she puttered around the kitchen in shorts and a tank top the following morning. He didn't want to come across as creepy, but her curves really were irresistible.

"Takeout last night. Breakfast this morning." She opened the door and shooed all three dogs outside. "Are you on a mission to feed me up, Spencer?"

He held up his hands in a "whoa" gesture. "One of the things my mom taught me and my siblings was to start the day right with a decent breakfast. I guess those habits stick with you."

"Of course. You told me you're a triplet." She came back into the room, regarding him with an intrigued expression. "What was that like, growing up?"

It was a question he got asked a lot once people knew about his family situation. Sometimes he dismissed it with a flippant remark, other times he gave a brief reply. For some reason, he wanted to provide Katrina with a more detailed answer.

"Naturally, my brother Jarvis, my sister Bella and I were very close. As I said, my dad was a distant cousin of Payne Colton, but he wasn't close with him. Although our parents were hardworking, they were low income. They both died in a car crash when we were ten."

"Oh, my goodness." Katrina placed a hand on his forearm. "I'm so sorry."

"It's okay. At the time, it was like our world had ended." He lifted a shoulder. "And it's still not a good memory. But I can talk about it. One of the worst things was that we didn't have any family we were already close to."

"What happened?" Her voice was soft. "Please tell me you were allowed to stay together."

"We were. But it was only because a childless aunt reluctantly agreed to take us in." His lips tightened as the contrasting memories came flooding back. "It was a big adjustment. The home we shared with our parents was full of love and warmth, but our aunt Amelia didn't like kids and she didn't know how to handle us. It wasn't a good time."

In the silence that followed, he caught a glimpse of Katrina's own emotional storms in the depths of her eyes. It shook him up to realize that she wasn't cold. The distance she kept from him wasn't to do with lack of feeling. It was about fear. Katrina was scared of feeling too much. Just as he was coming to grips with what he'd just discovered, she lowered her lids, shutting off her expression.

"Since I have nothing suitable in the house, how about I take you to Bubba's Diner for breakfast?" she asked.

He plucked at the front of his shirt. "I need to go home, shower and get a change of clothes first. It's still early, so I'll meet you there in an hour."

"Okay. But…" She gave him a confused look. "Don't you still have to go to work?"

"I need to speak to Chief Barco about protecting you. If he's okay with it, I can check in at the station each day, then do a lot of stuff from the office at your work premises."

"If you're planning on staying here until this is resolved, wouldn't it be easier if you brought some clothes over instead of going home to change each day?" Katrina asked.

"That's the plan." He went to the door and signaled to Boris. "I'll pack a bag while I'm there. Meanwhile, whenever I'm not with you, I want you to take your dogs with you if you go out and make sure you stick to public places at all times."

He headed for his vehicle, pausing briefly to look back at the house. The night had been uneventful, with no further attacks. That could have been for any number of reasons. Possibly, the person targeting Katrina was waiting to see what impact the break-in would have. Or Spencer's presence might have put him, or her, off. Then again, if Katrina had fabricated the harassment against her, she was hardly likely to continue when she had a police officer living in her home.

On the previous evening, as they'd eaten their takeout, he'd kept the conversation light while observing her closely. The only conclusion he'd reached was that Katrina was difficult to read. Now and then, he thought he saw some of the tension in her frame lighten a little. She was such a mystery it was hard to tell what that meant. Was she thankful that he was there to protect her, or relieved that her plan to gain attention had worked?

The Payne Colton case was soon occupying his thoughts. Payne had been moved back to his original private room. Although he wasn't in ICU, his family wanted to provide the best levels of care and security and these were available in the second-floor suites. Spencer figured the only way forward in the investigation would be to review what they'd already done. They needed to interview witnesses again, take a fresh look at security camera footage, and see if they could find a link that they'd missed.

The move from the shooting inquiry to protecting Katrina had happened so quickly that it had caught him unawares. It wasn't as if he wanted to give up on the Colton case, exactly. But if he thought about where he'd rather spend his time…

When he reached his vehicle, he checked his messages. There was a missed call from Kerry and a message asking him to get back to her.

"Harley Watts's lawyer has been in touch." Kerry got straight to the point. "Harley might be prepared to talk about who hired him to send the email. In return, he's asking for a very reduced sentence."

"Set up a meeting for later this morning with Harley and his lawyers," Spencer said. "Then ask Marlowe and Ainsley Colton if they are available to come into the station this afternoon for an update on the situation."

He was balancing a number of cases, including his new role of protecting Katrina. With careful planning, he could do them all. While Katrina was at work, she would be reasonably safe. He would have an alert put on her cell phone and make sure that, on the occasions he couldn't be at Look Who's Walking, he got a patrol car to do regular checks on the premises. He also figured Suzie would be a useful ally.

Was Harley's offer the breakthrough they'd been waiting for in the Colton Oil case? And, if so, would it lead them to the person who had shot Payne? He ended the call with Kerry and opened his vehicle door. It was too soon to feel optimistic, but this was the first glimmer of hope they'd seen in a long time.

BEFORE SHE MET Spencer at Bubba's Diner, Katrina took the dogs to the training ground and handed them over to Suzie. After finding the note threatening to feed them antifreeze, she wasn't prepared to leave them alone in the house. Not even for the duration of a meal.

"I'll be back soon," she told Suzie. "I'm meeting Spencer for breakfast."

Her friend gave her a thoughtful look. "Take all the time you need."

When she arrived at the diner, Spencer was already

there. He was seated at a table near the window and he waved a hand to make sure she'd seen him. As he did, her heart did a curious backflip.

Oh, my goodness. What was that?

He was a good-looking man, but she'd seen handsome guys before. None of them had ever had the ability to make her heart perform gymnastics.

As she took her seat, Spencer handed her the breakfast menu. Boris, who was lying under the table, wagged his tail against her legs. "Let's order, and then you can tell me about Aidan Hannant."

She frowned. "I didn't have much of an appetite, anyway. Now it's gone completely."

He pointed to the lighter options. "Try the avocado toast with poached egg."

She managed a smile. "You're very persistent."

"I am." He beckoned the waitress over. "And the fresh-squeezed orange juice is good, too."

"Since you know the menu so well, I guess you should order for both of us."

When the waitress had taken their order and left, Spencer turned his attention back to Katrina. "Let's do this before the food arrives. That way we can enjoy our breakfast."

She fiddled with a paper napkin for a moment, then nodded. "There isn't much more I can tell you. Aidan Hannant came into the training center asking for advice. Although Suzie offered to help, he insisted on speaking to me. At first, he seemed like a regular client. He introduced himself and told me about his dog. He said it was a rottweiler puppy that had some chewing problems. Then, when I started to give him advice, he asked if I'd gotten the message. That was when he said the car had been a warning."

"Those were his exact words?" Spencer's blue gaze lost any trace of humor and become very direct. "He told you that the car mounting the pavement and almost hitting you was a warning?"

"Yes." For a moment, she felt unnerved. Was he doubting what she was telling him? "He said my heroic rescuer could have saved himself the trouble. He wasn't planning to hit me. Not that time."

"Yet you didn't report this?"

"Hey—" anger started to bubble up inside her "—I'm not the one who did something wrong here. And I did try to report it. But every time I tried to call you, I got your voice mail, and when I stopped by the station, you weren't there."

"But you didn't tell another officer?"

"I didn't want to go through the whole story again with someone new," she explained. "I figured it would be better to wait and speak to you."

His expression remained stern. "I don't understand why, having delivered a warning, Hannant, or whoever was behind him, would follow through on it so fast."

"What do you mean?" Her anger faded a little. She knew exactly what he meant, and she wasn't looking forward to explaining her next actions to him.

"Usually, having issued a warning, the bad guys wait to see if it worked before they take action." Spencer's voice was calm, but that gaze probed her face. She imagined he was very good at interrogating his suspects. "In your case, the break-in happened soon after Hannant threatened you."

"Ah." She gave the napkin a good, hard twist. "That could be because I didn't listen to his warning."

"What?" He jerked into a more upright position. "Katrina, what did you do?"

Before she could answer, the waitress arrived with their order and the next few minutes were taken up with food-related matters. When the server had gone, Spencer took a slug of coffee and spoke in a calmer tone.

"Okay, let's eat and talk at the same time. What did you do to make Hannant, or whoever is backing him, trash your place and threaten your dogs?"

She took a bite of her toast and chewed it slowly before she answered. She might as well tell him everything. "As well as meeting Christie Foster, I went to visit a woman who I'd seen in a confrontation with some AAG members."

He frowned. "This is new information. When did this confrontation happen?"

"It was after I'd gotten home and found that guy in my kitchen. You remember? You came to tell me that you didn't think there was a connection to the AAG." She couldn't help giving him a hurt look. "After you left, I was going out for dinner to a new dog-friendly place on Mustang Boulevard and there were some AAG group members handing out leaflets in town. As I passed them, a woman started shouting about how they'd cheated her son out of money." As Spencer watched her, she told him the story of what had happened that evening with Helen Jackson and of her subsequent visit to the sculptor's home. "The difference in her demeanor was..." She searched for the right word. There was only one that fit. "Creepy."

"You think someone got to her?" He indicated her food as he spoke. "Told her to keep quiet about what happened?"

She took a few more bites as she thought about what he was suggesting. "It has to be a possibility."

He speared a piece of bacon on his own plate, then chewed it before lifting his gaze to her face again. "You know what this means?"

"The AAG must have been the ones who got to Helen Jackson?"

"It looks that way. But there's more to it." He reached across the table and lightly touched her hand. It was a casual gesture, but the impact powered through her like a thousand volts of electricity. "Someone knew you were at Helen's place."

"Oh." She lifted a hand to her throat. "You mean I was followed?"

He nodded. "And we're not dealing with amateurs. One person couldn't have been tailing you out to Helen's place and, at the same time, breaking into your house and leaving you that note threatening your dogs. It was a coordinated attack."

She looked down at the remains of her meal. "Now do you believe me that someone connected to the AAG is behind my sister's disappearance?"

"I'm prepared to consider it." His voice was serious. "In the meantime, Aidan Hannant has some explaining to do."

By the time he reached the station, Spencer felt like he was trying to juggle too many plates. If he wasn't careful, some of them were going to come crashing down around his head.

His biggest case was the shooting of Payne Colton and, since the sting operation had gone wrong, that was no further along than it had been at the start. Although there was no direct connection between the attack on Payne and the anonymous email that had been sent to the members of the Colton Oil board at the start of the year, he couldn't rule Ace out as a potential shooter.

Spencer's thoughts moved on to his first meeting of the day. Harley Watts, a dedicated member of the AAG, had admitted to being the sender. So far, he had resisted any attempts by Spencer to get him to flip on his backer in exchange for a reduced sentence. Although his lawyer was dropping hints that Harley was prepared to consider a reduced sentence in exchange for information, Spencer wasn't convinced. Someone had Harley in their clutches and his, or her, grip was tight.

And now, he had the issue of Eliza Perry's disappearance and the threats to Katrina to deal with. He was reserving judgment about what was going on there, but her revelations over breakfast made him less concerned that Katrina might be an attention seeker. They did, however, bring a new set of concerns for her safety.

His plans to keep her safe while she was at work were all in place and he'd run through them with her and Suzie. The MVPD dispatcher had placed an alert on both women's cell phones as well as on the business line. In addition, a police cruiser would check out the premises every half hour unless Spencer was there.

At least, unlike his colleagues in some neighboring counties, he didn't have the issue of investigating murdered beauty pageant contestants. He supposed he should be thankful for that, at least.

As he entered the building with Boris following close behind, his mind tried to untangle the threads of the different cases. Was he trying to make sense of something that had no logic to it? Or was he right in thinking that there was a common theme throughout everything he was dealing with right now? Each time he started to investigate a lead, it brought him to the AAG.

But what did that mean? Was the group being used as a cover for criminal activity? If so, where did Eliza Perry fit in? And would Harley Watts be able to help him with this inquiry as well as telling him more about the Colton Oil email? He quickened his pace, keen to begin questioning the AAG geek.

When he reached his office, Kerry Wilder was waiting for him. From the slump of her shoulders, he guessed she didn't have good news.

"Harley has withdrawn his offer."

Resisting the temptation to kick the wastebasket across the room, Spencer sighed. "Did he give a reason?"

"No. I think his lawyer was as surprised as we are," Kerry said. "Apparently, Harley had a prison visit from a very attractive blonde woman, an AAG member named Leigh Dennings. Since then, he's decided he won't talk."

An image of Leigh Dennings's face came into Spencer's mind and he wondered how her conversation with Harley had gone. He would never know for sure, of course, because neither of them would tell him. But it seemed likely that Leigh had persuaded Harley to change his mind about striking a deal with the police. The question was why? Leigh was Micheline's puppet. She didn't make a move without the boss lady's say-so.

Which led him to another question: What did Micheline have to hide?

"We didn't do any background checks on members of the AAG, did we?" he asked Kerry.

"No." She looked surprised. "Even though Harley sent the email from the AAG server, none of the other members have come under suspicion."

"Let's start with Micheline Anderson and Leigh Dennings," he said. "Run all the usual checks on those two and let me know if you come up with anything."

"Okay." Kerry scribbled a few notes in the pad she was carrying. "I take it you want this in a hurry?"

"You guessed right." Spencer reached for his cell phone. "I need to make a call to the AAG ranch, then, since Harley's no-show has freed up some of my time, I'm going to pay Aidan Hannant a visit."

When he called the AAG ranch, Leigh answered. Shc was her usual charming self. "Sergeant Colton, it's such a pleasure to hear from you."

"I'd like to ask you about one of your members. A young woman called Christie Foster."

It appeared that her default setting was vagueness. "I'm not sure..."

"Apparently she knew Eliza Perry."

He heard clicking sounds, as though she was typing. "I'm just checking our database. I'm sorry, but we don't have anyone called Christie Foster registered as having visited here. Not now, or in the past."

Chapter Eight

Katrina was in the Look Who's Walking office, trying to make sense of her business accounts, when Spencer walked in.

"Didn't I just have breakfast with you half an hour ago?" From the frown on his face, she wasn't sure her jokey tone had lightened his spirits.

"I'm going to Aidan Hannant's apartment and I want you to come with me."

"Why?"

"He came to see me on the day after he threatened you. He admitted that he was the person driving the car that mounted the sidewalk, but he said it was an accident," Spencer said. "I figure, if you're by my side when I ask him a few questions, he's going to find it hard to lie about what happened."

"Oh." She studied her computer screen for a moment or two before returning her gaze to his face. "Why didn't you tell me this when I first informed you about Aidan Hannant?"

"I wasn't sure if it was important." His manner troubled her. It was almost as if he had something to hide.

She told herself not to be foolish. He was busy, that was all. He had moved in to protect her, but he was dealing with other problems as well as hers.

She checked the time on her cell phone. "I need to be back in an hour for a training class."

"It won't take that long."

"To be honest, I'm glad to get away from the paperwork." She pushed back her chair, stood up and stretched her arms above her head. "Although I could think of more enjoyable ways of playing hooky."

She paused on the way out of the building to let Suzie and Laurence, the junior trainer, know she would be returning soon. As she stepped into the bright sunlight at Spencer's side, it felt like a long time since she'd relaxed. The thought made her smile. Had she ever been able to take it easy?

She'd spent most of her childhood waiting for the next crisis. The only times she'd been able to put aside her anxieties had been in the company of her grandparents. But, all too often, her grandma and grandpa would be drawn away by Mollie or Eliza, and Katrina would fade into the background.

Now, as an adult, much of her downtime revolved around her professional life. If she wasn't on training courses, she was researching new methods or honing her skills.

I don't know how to enjoy myself.

Why did it suddenly matter? She took a sidelong peek at the tall, muscular figure at her side. And found her answer. She might not like it, but Spencer had come into her life and changed it. He made her feel differently and he made her want more. She could fight it, but she wasn't sure if she wanted to. And that thought alone scared her almost as much as the idea of facing Aidan Hannant again.

Spencer held open the passenger door and Katrina got into the car. She heard the heavy thump of a dog's tail and twisted in her seat to pat Boris on the head. "Hi there, big guy." She turned to Spencer. "Can he have a treat?"

"Only if you want him to love you forever."

Reaching into the fanny pack she always wore when she was working, Katrina took out one of her own natural dog treats and offered it to Boris. The well-trained canine politely took it from between her fingers.

"What do you want to talk to Hannant about?" she asked as Spencer drove away from the training center.

"Apart from why he intimidated you?" Watching his profile, she detected a trace of tension in the muscles of his jaw as he spoke. "He told me he had no involvement with the AAG. I want to dig deeper into that."

She took a moment to consider that response. She should be experiencing a hint of triumph that he was finally taking her seriously about the threat posed by the Affirmation Alliance Group. Instead, her whole body felt curiously hollow. She recognized it as a heightened sense of her own vulnerability.

The man sitting next to her was a cop. An *experienced* one. If he thought the AAG might be dangerous, then she really was in trouble.

Spencer flicked a glance in her direction. "I'm not going to let anything happen to you."

His promise brought Katrina's emotions crashing over her head like a wave. The last time anyone had put her first and protected her had been when her grandparents were both alive. She had been ten when her grandmother died and, after that, her grandfather's health had quickly declined. When he passed two years later, she had replaced him as her mom and sister's caretaker. It had been a lonely life.

"And we'll find out what happened to Eliza," Spencer said.

Every other thought was driven out of her head at the implication of what he was saying. "What happened to her?" she repeated. "Don't you mean 'we'll find Eliza'?"

"I hope we'll find her." He didn't sound hopeful.

"Do you think she might have been involved in something shady that put her in danger?" When he didn't answer, Katrina shivered. "Or are you saying she could have been killed?"

"I really don't want to speculate."

"No." She shook her head. "You can't do this. I'm half out of my mind with worry already. You have to tell me what you're thinking."

"The reason that I don't want to make any assumptions is that I don't want to add to your concerns." He stopped the car outside an apartment block and turned in his seat to look at her. "Okay. This is just one train of thought. How do we know Eliza isn't behind the threats you've been getting? You said yourself she can get mad when she's feeling resentful."

"That wouldn't happen." Katrina bristled. "If I gave

you the wrong impression about my sister, I'm sorry. Despite her problems, Eliza would never be violent. And she wouldn't hurt me."

"Then we'll keep searching." He turned to face her. "I called the AAG ranch this morning. They've never heard of anyone called Christie Foster."

"But that's not possible. I have her number and the record of the call in my cell phone. She told me she'd heard me on the day I called there asking about Eliza. She said she knew her." Katrina rubbed a hand over her face. "I don't understand what's going on."

Spencer peered through the windshield at the building. "We'll find out. Starting right now with some tough questions for Mr. Hannant."

THE ADDRESS AIDAN Hannant had given Spencer was a second-floor apartment in a small building on the edge of town. Before he approached the entrance, Spencer looked around the exterior, focusing on the parking lot.

Katrina quickly glanced over her shoulder. "What are we waiting for?"

Spencer wished he could reassure her that she was safe when he was around. His desire to protect her was one of the most overwhelming emotions he had known. He knew it was partly because of Billie. He hadn't been able to save his fiancée when she'd needed him, so he was determined to be there this time for Katrina. But penetrating the wall of fear that surrounded her wasn't going to be easy.

"Can you see the black Chrysler sedan with tinted windows that drove at you?" he asked.

"Maybe Hannant isn't home? He could be at work, or possibly he's gone to the gym?" She sounded relieved.

"He damn well better be here. I got the officer on reception-desk duty to call and tell him I was coming. Hannant assured him he'd be here."

Leading the way to the apartment building, he keyed in the numbers on the security system for Hannant's apartment. When there was no response after a minute or two, he tried again.

"This isn't looking hopeful," he muttered.

As he was contemplating a third attempt, a young woman in sports gear opened the glass doors from inside of the building.

"Excuse me." Spencer held up his badge. "I need to gain access to the building."

She regarded him with a dubious expression for a second or two, then held the door wide. "Sure."

After thanking her, Spencer beckoned for Katrina to follow him. Once they were inside the small lobby, he looked around. There was no elevator, just a single flight of stairs directly opposite the door.

"Stay behind me," he told Katrina. "If there is any sign of trouble, get out and call 911."

Her eyes appeared bigger than ever as she stared back at him. "You think there's going to be trouble?"

"I don't have a good feeling about this."

She edged closer. Slowly, Spencer began to move up the stairs, checking for anything suspicious each step of the way. When he reached the second floor, he paused and scanned the empty hall.

"Hannant lives in apartment eight." He pointed along the corridor.

"If he's home, wouldn't he have answered when you tried his apartment buzzer just now?" Katrina asked.

"You'd think so. But there could be any number of reasons why not." He approached the door cautiously, listening for any sounds inside. When he heard nothing, he raised his fist and rapped hard on the panels.

"There's a bell." Katrina pointed out.

"I want to shake him up." As he spoke, the faintest sound from the other side of the door caught his attention. "Did you hear that?"

She nodded. "It sounded like a groan."

"Aidan?" There was no mistaking the sound this time. Someone inside the apartment whimpered as if in pain. "It's Sergeant Spencer Colton of the MVPD. Can you open the door?"

There was a shuffling sound followed by a scrabbling. Gradually, the door began to open. When he could finally see the person on the other side, Spencer was shocked. Aidan Hannant was unrecognizable as the person he had seen only the day before. He clutched his ribs and doubled over, his face a mass of cuts and bruises.

"Oh, my goodness! What happened to you?" Katrina started to move forward, but Spencer restrained her.

Yes, Hannant was a mess and he needed help, but they didn't know who, or what, they would find inside that apartment.

"I'm going to call 911—"

"No." Hannant's voice was muffled by his swollen

lips, but the word came out with enough force to be understood. "No medics. No law enforcement."

"You don't get a say in this, Aidan. I'm a police officer. If a crime has been committed, I have a duty to report it."

"Talk to you." Hannant shuffled to one side, indicating that they should enter.

"Wait here," Spencer said to Katrina as he drew his weapon. "And you, too," he added to Hannant. Although he seriously doubted the guy would be capable of moving without assistance.

The apartment was small, and once he was inside, Spencer was able to quickly check out each of the rooms. There was no one there and nothing that caused him any concern. The only thing that appeared out of the ordinary was an overturned coffee table and a mug smashed on the floor, its contents splattered across the rug.

Having satisfied himself that the place was safe, he holstered his gun and returned to where Katrina and Hannant were waiting.

"Lean on me." He placed a hand under the other man's elbow.

Katrina closed the door behind them and followed them into the sitting room. Spencer lowered Hannant onto the sofa and studied his face. "You need to get to a hospital."

Hannant shook his head, then moaned as if the movement caused him pain. "No."

"Do you have any painkillers?" Katrina asked.

"Bathroom cabinet."

She left the room, returning a few minutes later with a bottle, a glass of water and a damp facecloth. Shaking out a couple of pills, she handed them to Hannant, then held the glass to his lips as he washed them down.

"Hold this on your face." She handed him the facecloth. "It may soothe some of the pain."

He did as she instructed, nodding gratefully.

"Are you sure you don't want to talk at Mustang Valley General?" Spencer asked.

"Talk here," Hannant said. "Then leave town."

Spencer didn't like the sound of that plan, but he kept his thoughts to himself. He took a seat at the opposite end of the sofa to Hannant and Katrina moved to a chair.

"Sorry." Hannant spoke to Katrina. "The car and the warning. They paid me."

"Who paid you?" Spencer leaned forward, hoping for a name.

"Don't know."

"But you can describe them, right?"

Hannant shook his head, then winced. "Email. Money problems. Once I agreed, instructions sent to pick up car. Other details followed."

"So you were told to threaten Katrina, then come to the station and confess?"

"Yes. Make her look bad. Flaky." Hannant sucked in a breath. "If I came across as a good guy, she would look like a liar when she accused me of threatening her."

"What?" Katrina sounded outraged. "Why would anyone want to make me look flaky?"

Why indeed? Spencer remembered Micheline Anderson's smooth smile and her persuasive words. *Not all actors are on the stage.* It was looking more and more like Micheline and other members of the AAG were trying to make Katrina look bad to stop her, and the police, from searching for Eliza. It came back to the old question. Why?

He turned his attention back to Hannant. "How did you get paid?"

"Cash." After his burst of lucidity, Hannant appeared to be struggling to manage to speak clearly again. "Left on a bench in Mustang Park. Agreed time."

"If you did everything you were instructed to do, why were you beaten?"

Hannant twisted the facecloth in his hands. "More money."

"You asked for more?" Spencer queried.

Miserably, Hannant gave a single nod. "I emailed. Told them I'd go back to you and tell the truth."

Spencer sighed. "Bad guys don't like to be blackmailed. Did you see who attacked you?"

"No. Two men. Faces covered." He hitched in a breath. "Told me to leave town tonight. Next time… won't walk away."

Spencer glanced across at Katrina, who stared back at him with a mixture of anger and disbelief. Clearly, she was thinking the same as him. Someone had gone to a lot of trouble to frighten her off. But who?

He withdrew his cell from his pocket. "You won't be leaving town tonight, Aidan. You need medical attention, but, more importantly, a crime has been committed and I'm placing you under arrest."

KATRINA MADE IT back to the training center with minutes to spare before her next class started. Because Spencer needed to stay at Hannant's apartment, he arranged for another officer to give her a ride. It added to her stress that she hadn't been able to talk to him about what had happened. Losing herself in work was a bonus.

"You look like a soda bottle that's been shaken up and is about to pop its top," Suzie told her cheerfully as they grabbed a bite of lunch.

"And you say the nicest things." Katrina pulled a face at her.

"Rusty sent me a message. He said the intruder did a number on your place but they're putting it right."

Once again, Katrina felt a pang of gratitude for the big-hearted store owner and his brothers.

"That one's a keeper," she told Suzie.

Her assistant flapped a hand. "I sure like to keep him on his toes." She winked. "And his elbows."

"Oh, you are so naughty."

They were still laughing when the bell on the front door rang. After a moment or two, Laurence peeped into the room with an apologetic look. "Sergeant Colton is here."

"That guy can't stay away." Suzie gave Katrina a meaningful glance.

"He's trying to find Eliza." She felt a blush steal into her cheeks.

"He's trying to find *something*, honey." Suzie got to her feet. "I'll leave you in peace."

As she went out, Spencer came in and Katrina bit back a smile at the knowing look Suzie gave her behind his back. Trust her friend to start matchmaking as soon as a handsome guy appeared on the horizon. If only life was that simple.

"I wanted to make sure you were okay."

She knew he was busy, yet when she looked into his eyes, she saw concern for her well-being and a smile that was both gentle and caring. In that instant, she knew everything she needed to about Spencer Colton. He was a man who lived according to his values. A strong, honest, genuine man, who put others first and fought for what was right. And he took her breath away.

"I…" *Focus.* How hard could it be to answer a simple question? "Have you eaten?" Very hard, apparently.

"I'm headed back to the station for a meeting. I'll grab a bite when I get there." His smile widened. "*Are* you okay?"

"I've been busy, so I haven't had much time to process what Hannant told us." She bought herself a little thinking time by finishing her soda and tossing the can into the trash. "I'm still struggling with what he said about the person who paid him wanting to make me look unreliable. I don't understand why anyone would want to do that."

"I guess we'll find out when we know who's behind this." It was a vaguely unsatisfactory answer, but Katrina couldn't identify why she felt that way. "We're checking Hannant's emails to see if we can discover who made contact with him, but I don't hold out much hope. If, using his or her usual laptop in their own home, a person opens their main email account and sends a message to you, our police technicians will be able to determine where it came from with minimal effort. If, on the other hand, they buy a cheap electronic tablet for cash, take it to a bar, log in to their guest Wi-Fi, create a new email account and send the message from that… Well, it's almost impossible to trace."

"The person who first approached Hannant had to know he needed cash," Katrina said. "And how did they know he wouldn't go straight to the police? That took some confidence."

"You're right. Possibly, Hannant has acted on the wrong side of the law on other occasions in exchange for cash. It's worth checking out." He glanced at his watch. "I have to go. What do you want to do about dinner?"

She rolled her eyes. "This obsession with feeding me."

He laughed. "I make a mean Thai green curry."

"And with those words, you talked yourself into cooking tonight."

"I'll see you at your place later."

As she watched him leave, Katrina reflected on how easy it would be to start relying on his presence. But that wasn't her. She didn't do dependence. And she wasn't going to count on Spencer sticking around. By protecting her, he was doing his job. Once the person threatening her was caught, life would return to normal for both of them.

On that gloomy note, she cleared away the remnants of her lunch and headed toward the office to grapple with her annoying accounts for another hour or two.

Chapter Nine

"It's good news that Harley Watts is prepared to talk at last," Marlowe Colton said as she and Ainsley entered Spencer's office later that day. "We might finally start getting somewhere."

Spencer shook his head. "I hate to disappoint you, but Harley has changed his mind. He no longer wants a deal in exchange for giving us the name of the person who paid him to send the Colton Oil email."

He indicated two chairs on the opposite side of the desk to his own seat and his guests sat down.

"In that case, why are we here?" Ainsley asked. "I don't mean to sound rude, but you're busy and so are we."

"I wanted to give you an update on the sting operation we carried out at the hospital."

"I thought it was unsuccessful?" The half sisters exchanged a glance. "Is there anything more to be said?"

"Not much." Spencer shared their frustration, but he was determined to be honest about the investigation and not give them any false hope. "The slight figure who entered the floor where your father had been staying matched the one from the original video taken inside the Colton Oil building on the night of the shooting. He was caught on camera again, and I've watched it back a few times. He wore a hoodie with the hood up, sunglasses obscuring his face. He came close to the room—actually had his hand on the door handle—but then glanced around and seemed to get nervous. He ran off and leaped out of the second-floor window like an experienced free runner, landing on grass and bolting away."

"You're saying *he*," Ainsley said. "For all we know, the shooter was a woman. You just said the person in the original footage and at the hospital was slightly built."

"That's true. And I'm certainly not ruling out the possibility that it could have been a woman," Spencer confirmed.

"It could have been Selina who shot Dad." Ainsley's attractive face was severe as she talked about Payne's second ex-wife. "She's been out to cause trouble since the email arrived."

"I wouldn't put anything past Selina if she could gain from it," Marlowe said. "But we all know she's on the Colton Oil board because she has something hanging over Dad. Without him, she's nothing. She's not going to risk messing up her golden ticket."

"Man or woman, we lost him." Spencer did his best to maintain a businesslike approach and not allow his annoyance to show. "Or her."

"Do you think he—or she—will be back?" Marlowe asked.

"I know it. And he knows we're after him or her. That means he's worried."

There was a sense of defeat in the air as they ended the meeting. Although they knew that Harley Watts had sent the email to the Colton Oil board members, they didn't know who had paid him to do it. They were no closer to finding the real Ace Colton and they didn't know who had shot Payne.

There had been a recent distraction when a man called Jace Smith tried to pass himself off as the real Ace Colton. Although the con was uncovered, the last thing the police or the family wanted was any similar attempts to gain from the Coltons' misfortune.

In addition to everything else, Spencer was also dealing with the additional mystery of Eliza Perry's disappearance and the threats to Katrina.

Once Ainsley and Marlowe had left, he called Kerry into his office. "I know you haven't had much time, but have you gotten anywhere with your background checks on Micheline Anderson and Leigh Dennings?"

"I don't have anything of interest," Kerry said. "So far, they are both model citizens with records of good deeds."

"Keep digging. If there's anything there, I know you'll find it."

When he was alone, Spencer leaned back in his chair and studied the fluorescent light fitting. His mind kept returning to the issue of how he had been manipulated into doubting Katrina. The first seed had been planted by Micheline Anderson with her not-all-actors-are-on-the-stage remark. Then Aidan Hannant had fueled his suspicions with his nice-guy act.

And the mysterious Christie Foster? Where did she come into this? He made a note to ask Kerry to look into her as well. Was she genuinely scared and wanted to tell her story, or was she yet another attempt to make Katrina look like she couldn't be trusted?

There was no avoiding the truth. Spencer had been deliberately played. Guilt churned like acid in his gut and he needed to figure out why. So he'd fallen for a ploy to make Katrina look bad. He couldn't have known what was going on. Even so, his conscience continued to haunt him. And the reason was staring him in the face.

It was about Katrina. Right or wrong, she was not just another crime victim. In the brief time he had known her, she had come to mean so much more. He had let her down. The problem was that he had no idea how to explain to her how and why it had happened.

How could he tell her he had suspected that she might be making these threats up to get attention? Even if he approached it logically and explained that, as a police officer, he needed to keep an open mind, she would be hurt. And hurting her felt like the worst thing he could possibly do.

He shook his head, trying to restore some normality to his thoughts. Right now, he needed a little perspective before he called the hospital to see how Aidan Hannant was doing. He wasn't proud of the way he had fallen into the trap set by Katrina's enemies, but it was an issue he would come back to.

When Katrina arrived home, Spencer had used the spare keys she'd given him and was already there. The first thing she noticed as she entered the house was the delicious aroma of fragrant spices. The second was how much work the Linehan brothers had already done on her living room. They had done a good job of matching the color she'd used on the walls and had covered up the spray paint. Her furniture had been cleaned and Suzie had told her that Rusty had taken some items away to be repaired. The place was almost back to normal.

When she walked through to the kitchen, what caught her attention was the enticing rear view of muscular shoulders, a trim waist, long, strong thighs and a seriously touchable butt.

Where did that thought come from? And where did my headache go?

Spencer turned to look over his shoulder and the weariness and weirdness of the day drained away with his smile. "I took a chance that you'd like white wine. It's in the refrigerator."

"I'd better go say hi to the dogs first."

"Yeah." He pointed to the yard, where she could see Holly and Dobby racing around with Boris watching them like a kindly uncle. "I haven't fed them yet, but I've topped up their water bowls and given them a few treats. I've also checked that all the windows and doors are locked, and that the dogs' food hasn't been tampered with."

"Even when this is all over, I may never let you leave." Realizing what she'd said, she gave an embarrassed laugh. "I should, uh…" She pointed to the door. "I need to go see the pooches."

Spencer waved a hand as he turned back to his food preparation.

As she stepped outside, Holly and Dobby hurtled across the grass toward her. Squatting, she petted the two squirming canines. Boris, who took a more dignified approach, sat next to her and she stroked his head before resting her cheek on his broad back.

"I'm an idiot," she murmured into his silken fur. "I think I just invited your master to move in permanently. And you know what the worst thing was? He didn't even notice."

The big dog wagged his tail and, obviously feeling that something more was needed, gave a soft woof. Clearly feeling that this was some sort of signal, Holly and Dobby started dashing around in circles, then darting back to Boris as though inviting him to join in their game. The patient canine watched them like an indulgent nanny before charging after them. Laughing, Katrina watched their antics for a few minutes before returning to the kitchen.

"Boris is giving the kids a workout. You'd never know he was actually younger than Dobby." She went to the fridge and withdrew the bottle of wine. Although her knowledge was limited, it looked like Spencer had good taste. "Do you want some?"

He grinned. "Of course. And your timing is perfect because this is ready."

She poured two glasses and brought them to the table as he served dinner. As they sat and ate companionably, she was struck again by the ease with which they'd slipped into this new normalcy. Awkwardness had always come naturally to Katrina. Overthinking what she said, being unsure of what to do with her body, just generally high discomfort levels around other people, particularly new ones, was her default setting.

With Spencer, it was as if an invisible shield had been lowered. She could release her guard and allow him inside. Yes, that meant exposing her vulnerabilities, but she was fine with it. With him, it was okay to expose her true self. It even felt like maybe she could start to trust him. The thought caused her to gulp down too much wine and she spluttered.

"Is the food too spicy?" Spencer asked.

"No. It's perfect."

He quirked an eyebrow at her but didn't make any further comment. When they'd finished eating, Spencer carried the remaining wine and their glasses through to the living room. His presence made the room seem even smaller, but as she took a seat next to him on the sofa, Katrina decided she would sacrifice space for comfort. And he made her feel comfortable...

With his next words, her feeling of contentment became a memory. "I couldn't interview Aidan Hannant any more today. But I'm going to the hospital to speak to him tomorrow."

"He said he couldn't tell you who hired him."

"Maybe not. But what you said about his accessibility struck a chord with me. Someone knew he would be open to taking a job of that kind. How did they know he'd operate outside the law? Had he done that kind of thing before? If so, who knew about it? How would word have gotten around? If I ask the right questions and I can get Hannant to answer them, he might just lead me to the person behind these threats."

"It has to be the AAG," Katrina insisted. "This all started when I went looking for Eliza."

"You could be right, but I need to find a way to prove it."

"When I went to the ranch and asked about Eliza, they were covering something up. I could feel it," Katrina said. "But that makes me sound like a fantasist. The AAG has done so much good work in Mustang Valley. How could they possibly be involved in anything shady? Even supposing one of their members had committed a crime, surely the leaders of the group wouldn't hide it?"

"Even the most respectable organizations can be used as a screen." Spencer appeared lost in thought as he sipped his wine. "Maybe we should start looking at the key players in the AAG and find out if they really are on the up-and-up."

"Leigh Dennings is the public face of the group." Katrina thought back to her encounter with Leigh at the AAG ranch. "It seems to me that her job is to stop outsiders finding out about the AAG's activities."

His eyes narrowed. "Can you take some time off?"

"Probably. Suzie and Laurence know the training classes as well as I do and I'm pretty much up-to-date with my paperwork." She sipped her wine. "Why?"

"I think we should spend some time watching Leigh Dennings. Let's find out if she's as sweet as she appears."

"You want me with you?" She regarded him with surprise. "Why?"

"Because I can't trail her and protect you," he replied bluntly. "And your safety is my priority."

"Oh." She looked down at the sofa cushions as heat coursed through her body.

When she looked up again, the blazing look in Spencer's eyes turned the temperature even higher. Leaning closer, he removed her glass from her hand and placed it on the coffee table next to his own.

"Can I kiss you?"

"Yes, please."

Slowly, he reached up and placed his hands on both sides of her face. Katrina's eyelids fluttered closed. His lips met hers, and the world disappeared as she melted against him. Her brain closed down, rational thought deserting her as instinct took over and she responded to the magic of his mouth on hers. Their lips moved together in perfect choreography, as if they'd kissed a thousand times before.

It was the most wonderful feeling she'd ever known. Then it was over all too abruptly, and Spencer was getting to his feet.

"Good night, Katrina."

Bewildered, she watched him walk away toward the spare room.

EVEN THOUGH KATRINA'S spare bedroom was small and cozy, Spencer was still awake well after midnight. His insomnia had nothing to do with the furnishings, the temperature, or the noise level. The cause was simple. He couldn't get that electrifying kiss out of his head.

And yet you walked away.

Telling himself it had been the right thing to do hadn't eased the ache in his chest, or the corresponding tightness south of his belt buckle. There were so many reasons why the kiss should never have happened, and even more for why he couldn't take things further.

The first was straightforward. Although it was an unconventional approach, he was staying in her house as part of his job. Getting romantically involved hadn't been part of the agenda. And how would that look to an outsider? He would hate it if anyone viewed his intentions as sleazy.

Then there was the issue of Katrina herself. In many ways, she was a strong character. She had built up a successful business and she was good at what she did. This was despite a difficult start in life and the fact that she had to support her troubled twin her whole adult life. Her determination and drive had clearly carried her through some tough times. She was feisty and funny, and he admired her more and more as he got to know her better.

But right now, Katrina was vulnerable. She was fearful for her sister, and was also under attack from an unseen aggressor. It was a powerful combination. One that could make her seek protection. And if that protection happened to take the form of a strong pair of arms and a shoulder to cry on? Well, who could blame her? The problems would arise later, when the threat was gone and his presence was no longer needed.

In addition, he had added a whole new layer of fragility. By allowing himself to be duped into believing she might have been making up the threats, he had turned their relationship into a ticking time bomb. She barely trusted him now. When she found out he had doubted her, any trace of confidence she had in him would be shattered.

Putting Katrina's well-being first was his focus, of course, but there was more to it. When his fiancée had been killed, Spencer had retreated behind a wall of pain. The world had ceased to be a safe and reliable place, and he knew he would never risk his heart in the same way again. Nor would he allow grief to damage his capable and competent facade.

It would have been hard for other people to tell, but he had simply disengaged from life after Billie's death. He knew Bella and Jarvis had been concerned about his emotional disconnection, but he had shut down any attempt they made to talk about it. Throwing himself into work had been his coping strategy. The only guy who got to hear his problems was a certain large, chocolate-colored dog. And Boris was good at keeping secrets.

He knew love involved risk. No one could see into the future. Time and fate played their own tricks. But he'd known when he'd gone down on one knee and presented Billie with a diamond ring that they were both prepared to take a chance on a future together. Then she'd been snatched away and his feeling of loss had been so raw that he had dismissed the possibility of love in his future. He simply couldn't contemplate losing another loved one.

Until now, he'd never had cause to reconsider his decision. Then Katrina had come along and tipped his world off balance. Was he thinking of taking another leap of faith? He wasn't sure he'd reached that point. Not yet. But she'd awakened something inside him and reminded him of how it felt to be alive. When he was with her, he remembered that life had texture, color and meaning, and that it was full of excitement and joy. Did he want to walk away and retreat behind his wall once more? He wasn't sure, and that, in itself, surprised him.

He reached for his cell phone on the bedside table and checked the time. 2:00 a.m. Sleep seemed a million miles away. He sat up and pummeled the pillows in hopes of getting more comfortable. As he did, Boris gave a deep bark from the kennel outside.

Although Spencer's canine partner had a varied vocal range, the "woof" he'd just given was unmistakable. That was his warning bark. In response to the sound, Holly and Dobby had responded with a series of yaps, but Spencer ignored them. His own well-trained dog was telling him there was danger nearby.

Getting out of bed, he pulled sweatpants over his boxer briefs and padded barefoot to the window. He was able to open the slats of the blinds just enough to get a view of the yard. There was only a trace of moonlight and he remembered Katrina's comment about not wanting to install motion-sensitive lights in case her canine visitors triggered them.

After a moment or two, his alertness was rewarded.

Another bark from Boris was followed by a sudden movement close to the fence. Straining his eyes to get a better look, Spencer could make out a crouching figure moving slowly toward the house.

Lightning fast, he pulled his weapon from the drawer of the bedside table, where he'd placed it earlier. As he stepped from the room, another door opened, and he almost collided with Katrina.

"I was woken by barking." Although the hall was in near darkness, he could make out her pale features. "I thought something might be wrong."

She wore a tank top and shorts and, as he placed his hands on her shoulders, her flesh was cool beneath his touch. "I'm going to check out the yard."

She shivered. "I'll come with you."

"No. I'll only be a few minutes." His earlier thoughts about keeping his distance were momentarily forgotten as he drew her close and pressed a kiss onto the top of her head. "Stay inside. Lock the door after I've gone."

He moved toward the kitchen and she trailed after him. When he reached the door, she halted him with a hand on his arm. "You'll be careful?"

He smiled. "I'll do my best."

"Not good enough, Spencer."

It wasn't the words so much as the emotion in her voice that made his head spin. Even in the urgency of the situation, he was blown away by the knowledge that she cared. The timing was awful, but his heart had developed a happy new rhythm.

"I'll be careful."

Chapter Ten

When Spencer had gone, Katrina paced up and down the small kitchen for a few minutes before returning to her bedroom. Snatching up her cell phone and shoving it into the pocket of her pajama shorts, she returned to the kitchen.

Her mind was in turmoil. She knew Spencer would have to check out the yard when he heard Boris barking, but she had sensed there was more to this. He had been too tense, too impatient to get moving. The thought that he knew something was wrong had her on high alert, her nerves buzzing. With no idea what was happening outside, her fears for Spencer's safety were spiraling out of control.

An attempt to distract herself by drinking a glass of water didn't work. Maybe if she looked out the window, she would be able to see what was going on. She stepped up close, standing to one side and gazing out on the moonlit scene. She couldn't see any sign of movement, and the dogs had been silent since Spencer had left the house.

Even though the night was warm, after a few minutes of standing in one place in the darkness, she was feeling chilled. After shifting from foot to foot on the tiled floor, she decided to go in search of some footwear.

Turning away from the window, she let out a startled cry as she walked straight into someone who was standing behind her.

"What—"

His hand snaked out and he caught her by the arm, jerking her hard against him. The lower part of his face was covered with a scarf and he wore a hoodie pulled up over his head, with sunglasses hiding his eyes. Tall and strong, he held her easily despite her struggles.

"If you scream, I'll cut you." He held a blade up to her face, letting her feel the cold steel against her cheek.

It was as if a dark hole had opened in the floor beneath her feet and her bones turned to liquid, pulling her into it. She couldn't break free of his grip. Even if she'd been able to, she had locked the door after Spencer had gone and the key was on top of the cabinet across the other side of the room.

Should she defy this guy and cry out for Spencer? Even if he was close enough to the house to hear her, he was on the other side of that locked door, and this thug had a *knife*…

"We need to have a little talk."

Was it her imagination, or was he trying to disguise his voice? That gruff, growling tone didn't sound natural. She didn't think she recognized him, but her nerves were stretched so thin she barely knew her own name.

He hauled her roughly through to the living room and pushed her down onto the sofa. It flashed through her mind that this attack could be unrelated to anything that had happened recently, that this intruder's intentions were more sinister. Was she about to be subjected to a sexual assault?

Her cell phone dug into her thigh, reminding her of its presence, but she couldn't think of a way to sneak it out of her pocket without the intruder noticing.

"You haven't been listening to the warnings." He was an imposing figure, looming over her in the darkness.

"I don't know what you mean." Although her voice wobbled slightly, it came out stronger than she expected. The fact that her mouth worked at all under the circumstances was a bonus.

He grinned. "Yeah. I don't want to play that game. Let's get straight to the point. We tried the car. We did the break-ins. You still keep poking your nose in and now you have your very own cop security guard hanging around. You, lady, just don't know when to quit."

His use of the words *hanging around* made her wonder if he knew Spencer was living with her. If he didn't, he may not know just how close Spencer was at the moment. "Sergeant Colton wanted to make sure I was safe."

"That sounds good, except we know the truth is slightly different, don't we?" He leaned closer, catching hold of her chin and tilting her face upward. "The handsome cop is convinced that you are an eccentric who cries 'poor me' every chance she gets. He doesn't want to take care of you. He's staying close to stop you making up any more wild stories."

His words tore into her stomach and took over the beat of her heart. She tried counting to five, forcing herself to find the energy to breathe.

It's not true. But she knew it was. How many times had she noticed that odd response of Spencer's? A curious nonreaction to things she'd said and done.

"Why would he think that?"

Her tormentor laughed. "Because we wanted him to."

Gaslighting. Wasn't that what they called it? Perhaps it wasn't a classic case, since Katrina wasn't doubting her own memory, but she had been painted as something other than herself in Spencer's eyes. And the incident with Christie Foster had made her question her own recollection of events. Because of that, her sense of self had been damaged.

And Spencer had believed it. The thought left her trembling. With him, she had begun to take that first step into the chasm between fear and trust and this was how he had repaid her. Just hours earlier, he had kissed her, and her treacherous body had responded as though he was the only man in the world.

She had no idea who this guy standing over her with a knife in his outstretched hand was, or whom he represented. When he said *we*, he could mean the AAG, or he might be talking about someone else. Maybe this was a favor for a friend. Spencer had said these things could escalate from low-level encounters. Right now, it didn't matter. Someone had told Spencer that

Katrina was unreliable. Instead of coming to her with that information and checking it out, he had accepted it was true.

All her life, she had known what it was like to be let down. Why should it surprise her, just because this time it was Spencer Colton who was responsible for her disillusionment? She needed to put that hurt behind her and move on. Because at the moment, she had a bigger problem to deal with.

As she slid her fingers down her side and into the pocket of her shorts, she wondered if this guy knew Spencer was close by. From Boris's barking, it seemed likely that he'd gotten into the house through the backyard. That meant it was possible he hadn't seen Spencer's car parked out front.

She knew how to activate her cell's emergency function. Whether she could do it without the aggressive guy standing inches away noticing was another question.

Keep him talking. Right. How was she supposed to do that? Talk about the weather? Ask about his family? What kind of music he liked?

"Who persuaded Sergeant Colton that I was making up the threats against me? Was it Aidan Hannant?"

He snorted. "That guy? He's on his way out of town with his tail between his legs."

It was an interesting piece of information. Clearly, whoever was behind all of this didn't know that Hannant was in Mustang Valley General Hospital with a police guard on his door.

If she could trigger her phone's emergency function,

a prerecorded audio message warning that she was in immediate danger, and giving her precise location in GPS coordinates, would be sent automatically to two contacts. One of those contacts was Spencer and the other was Suzie. All she needed to do was press the power button on her cell three times in a row.

"So who did persuade him?"

With her heart almost pounding its way out of her chest, she got her finger onto the power button.

"Someone cleverer than the Hannant guy."

One. Two. Three. She released a long, slow exhale.

"But I'm not here to talk about that. My job is to give you another reminder, a painful one this time—"

As the blade arced close to her face, she flinched away from him and he caught her by the hair.

"Don't make it hard for me. I need to make it look like you could have cut yourself."

STEPPING FROM THE air-conditioned house into the June night was like walking into a furnace. Spencer remembered his father had a phrase to describe the Mustang Valley seasons. *Winter is warm, spring is hot and summer is hotter than hell.* At least Katrina had made sure the dogs had a large, state-of-the-art kennel, complete with its own AC system. *Kennel* wasn't a fancy enough name for the accommodation Katrina provided for her dogs. It was more like a small house.

He spoke a word of quiet reassurance to Boris and the obedient canine fell silent. Holly and Dobby took their cue from the top dog and Spencer was able to check out the yard without distractions. Silently, he made his way to the point where he'd seen the figure in the shadows. Although the yard was in near darkness, from his vantage point at the window, he'd gotten the impression from the person's size and physique that it was a man.

When he reached the place where he'd seen that person skulking, there was no one around. Reaching into the pocket of his sweatpants for his cell phone, he pulled it out and activated the flashlight. The yard was a large one, and scanning it using such a small beam would take all night. Luckily, Spencer had a far more effective method at his disposal.

She had given Spencer the code to open the kennel door and he used it now, stepping quickly inside. Holly and Dobby pranced around him in delight, clearly expecting some middle-of-the-night treats. After giving them a quick pat, Spencer reached for Boris's work harness, which he'd hung on a hook near the door.

His canine partner came quickly to attention. Boris understood exactly what was going on. Once he was in the harness, Boris became a police officer, a dedicated member of the team.

"Okay." Spencer finished fastening the clips in place. "Let's go."

The other dogs whined, but he was relieved that they didn't bark when he and Boris left them. When he'd locked the kennel door again, Spencer crouched beside Boris.

Boris was trained as a scent-specific search dog. If he was given something belonging to a person, he would discriminate that scent from the others around it and use it to hunt for the individual it matched. In this case, those skills were no use because Spencer didn't know who they were searching for.

Instead, because Spencer didn't have anything belonging to his target to give the dog to guide him, he would have to send Boris on an air-scenting search. This was a hard skill for a dog to learn, one that was taught after the animal had become proficient in trailing. Boris would probe the whole area, seeking human-scent particles. He wouldn't be detecting a precise scent. The dog would lead Spencer to any person he found. That was exactly what Spencer wanted him to do because anyone on Katrina's property was trespassing.

"Find." So long as the same instruction was used each time, it didn't matter what that word was.

This was what Boris did best and he loved his job. Quivering with pleasure, the dog took off with his nose to the ground. Although the light was poor and it was hard to see his dark coat, the reflective fabric of his harness made him easy to follow in the light of Spencer's flashlight.

The dog worked systematically, starting with the perimeter. When he reached the area where Spencer had seen the shadowy figure, he circled several times. Snuffling at the lawn, he wagged his tail before taking off toward the house. To Spencer, who knew his partner's signals, it was a clear indication that he had picked up a scent. When they reached the house, Boris halted beneath the window of the downstairs closet. It was the same one left open the first time an intruder had gotten into the house.

Back then, Katrina had believed she must have left the window unlatched by mistake. Now it hung wide. But Spencer knew for sure that he'd checked every door and window before he served dinner. Which meant this one had been pried open from the outside. On closer inspection, Spencer could see that the hinges appeared to have been damaged.

As he took in the implications of what he was seeing, his cell buzzed in his pocket. Snatching it out, he read the brief message. It was an emergency communication from Katrina's cell phone. He didn't know how she'd managed to activate it, but he knew what she was telling him. She was locked inside her own home with an intruder.

He drew the key from his pocket and broke into a run. Boris stayed at his heels and he knew his obedient partner would remain there until given an order to take down the target. When he reached the back door, he paused, trying to remember leaving the house.

Had the key grated in the lock? Had the door creaked? He didn't want to alert the guy inside to his presence, but acting fast was his priority.

To hell with it. Just get in there.

After unlocking and opening the door as quietly as he could, he stepped inside. After a quick scan of the kitchen, he noticed nothing out of place. Then he heard a man's voice, a low growl from the living room.

"I need to make it look like you could have cut yourself."

That was all the incentive he needed to propel him into the hall with his weapon drawn. Standing to one side of the living-room door, he took a quick peek inside. And the blood in his veins turned to ice.

Katrina was pressed into a corner of the sofa with her hands hidden at her sides. A tall man stood with his back to the door. Spencer could see the knife in his hand as he leaned close to her.

There was no way Spencer could get a clear shot at the guy without endangering Katrina. There was only one thing to do. Sending his canine partner up against a guy with a knife wasn't his preferred option, but there was no choice.

"Hold."

Before the intruder even had time to swing around, Boris had darted into the room and clamped his jaws around the man's calf. It was a paralyzing grip rather than a bite. The dog's teeth would not penetrate the flesh.

Spencer stepped into the room. "Mustang Valley Police. Drop the knife and put your hands up."

In a blur of movement, the intruder grabbed Katrina's wrist and dragged her up from the sofa. Shifting his hold so that one arm was around her neck, he pressed the tip of the blade to a point just below her chin.

"Call off the dog, or I'll cut her throat."

Spencer was faced with a stark choice. He couldn't guarantee any shot he took would incapacitate the intruder before he could harm Katrina. Nor could he be sure Boris would be able to take down the attacker in time to prevent that knife slicing into Katrina's tender flesh.

Reluctantly, he gave Boris the signal to come to heel. "Let her go."

"Okay."

Shoving Katrina full force at Spencer, the guy took off toward the kitchen. Reaching out to steady Katrina, Spencer was momentarily unbalanced. Although he managed to call out to Boris to give chase, he took a few moments before he followed his partner.

First, he steadied Katrina, holding her by her upper arms. "Are you all right?"

She nodded. "Just shaken."

"I need to—" He jerked a thumb in the direction of the kitchen.

"Go." She sucked in a shaky breath. "Catch him."

When he reached the kitchen, the door was open and there was no sign of the intruder or Boris. When he dashed into the yard, he caught a glimpse of Boris's reflective harness and headed in that direction. By the time he caught up with his trusty companion, Boris was sitting next to the fence with his head tilted back. As Spencer approached, the dog gave a soft whine as though expressing canine disappointment.

"I know. But it's not your fault he got away. And we will catch him." Spencer patted the faithful dog on his broad head. "That's a promise."

ALTHOUGH KATRINA WAS SHAKEN, by the time Spencer returned to the house, her fear had been overtaken by anger. The hurt she felt was like an inferno rising up inside her, trying to burst through her outer shell and scorch everything around her.

Having answered Suzie's worried text and reassured her that the emergency message was a mistake, she walked through to the kitchen and waited by the door. As soon as Spencer stepped inside, she was ready for him. Not caring what had happened in the yard, whether he had caught up with the bad guy or not, she turned on him. Unable to disguise the quiver in her voice, she faced him full-on.

"I suppose I imagined that? Made it up so I could look like a victim and get your attention? Like I did with Christie Foster and the speeding car and the other break-in…" Her breathing got the better of her voice and she paused for breath.

He gave her a wary look. "Katrina—"

She threw up a hand. "Don't even try to explain. I've already heard all about it from the guy who just pulled a knife on me. How you're here not because you want to look after me. No, you just need to make sure I'm not going to make up any more stories about being threatened. Isn't that right?"

"That's not how it is." For some reason, his calm tone fanned the flames of her rage.

"No? Then tell me he was wrong. Tell me you didn't think I was a fantasist who wanted you to believe I was a victim." When he didn't speak, she dashed a hand across her eyes. "Oh, it doesn't matter. Don't tell me anything. Just leave."

"No."

For the first time in her life, Katrina experienced full-on, wanting-to-throw-something fury. "What do you mean *no*? This is *my* house."

"And some guy just broke in here with a knife. You can be as angry with me as you want…and we'll talk about that some more when you're feeling calm. But I'm not going anywhere."

As if to illustrate his point, he leaned against the door frame with his arms folded across his chest. Even through her anger, Katrina could see the wisdom of what he was saying. She was in danger. If that hadn't been obvious before, it was now. A cop and his canine partner were about the best protection she could get. Even if the cop in question was the last man in the world she wanted under her roof.

Could she tolerate Spencer's presence until this was over? There was only one way to find out.

Huffing out a breath, she strode past him. "We will not be talking about this anymore. The subject is closed. Just do your job and catch whoever is doing this."

When she reached her room, she alleviated some of her frustration by slamming the door behind her. Leaning against it, she reviewed what had just happened with a sensation of disbelief. Not only had a stranger broken into her home and threatened her with a knife, but he had also told her he was going to do it in a way that made it look like she could have inflicted the injuries on herself.

Because that's how people are seeing me now.

As the sort of woman who was capable of self-harming to get attention. The fact that Spencer was one of the people who had viewed her that way felt like the worst kind of betrayal.

Her thoughts jumped a step ahead. If she felt betrayed by him, did that mean she'd *trusted* him? Spencer had offered her security. Now she knew how he really viewed her, that safety had been withdrawn. In the short time she had known him, she had come to rely on his support. Now it was gone and her chest ached with a combination of sorrow and humiliation.

Taking long, slow breaths, she forced herself to clear her mind and calm her nerves. She had learned a while ago not to take things personally. No one deserved to be hurt, but life didn't follow a nice, neat path. Even though she wasn't prepared to let Spencer get close again, she wouldn't let this negative experience have a destructive outcome.

She'd been living the life she wanted for herself before Spencer Colton came along. Through hard work and her own efforts, she'd built up a world where she could be comfortable. His blue eyes, dazzling smile and eye-popping muscles might have temporarily distracted her and made her wonder if she wanted more, but now she knew that he was shallow, she could dismiss him. She still needed his help to track down the person targeting her, and to find Eliza. But once that was done, she could relegate him to her memory bank.

Getting back into bed, she closed her eyes, determined to grab a few hours' sleep. Yes, she could dismiss Spencer Colton. She was almost sure of it.

Chapter Eleven

The atmosphere in Katrina's house the next morning could only be described as frosty. Although he couldn't blame Katrina for her anger, Spencer was determined to reason with her and make her understand his point of view. Since she wouldn't even make eye contact with him, he was clearly facing an uphill struggle.

"Coffee?" He held up the pot.

She pointed to her full cup without speaking.

"Ah." He jerked a thumb in the direction of the yard. "I'll go let the dogs out. Freshen their water—"

"It's done." She got to her feet. "I've been up for over an hour."

"I haven't been lying in bed." It was one thing to pledge not to let her get under his skin. It was quite another allowing her to deliberately rile him. "I was sending an email to my chief about the suspect who broke in here."

When she didn't answer, he assumed he was about to get more of the silent treatment. Then she frowned.

"Is something wrong?"

Great question, Colton. What could possibly be bothering her?

"Did you think he was disguising his voice?" she asked. "The guy who broke in here, I mean. It didn't sound like a natural way of talking to me."

"I didn't hear him speak much," Spencer said. "Was there anything about him that seemed familiar to you?"

She shook her head. "I don't think I knew him."

"If you remember anything, no matter how small, let me know." Her face still wore a blank, hurt look, and he wished he knew how to get past that. Instinct told him that now was not a good time to bring up the subject of what the intruder had revealed. "Are you ready to go soon?"

"Go?" Her forehead wrinkled. "Where?"

"We're trailing Leigh Dennings, remember?"

"You still want to do that?" she asked.

"Why not?"

"Well, you know. I wondered if you'd want to go ahead with that plan." She turned her head away, but not before he'd caught a flash of something that might have been pain in the depths of her eyes. "Given that you have doubts about my reliability."

"Katrina, I do not have any issues with you—"

It was pointless continuing. She had sprung up from her seat and left the room. Resisting the temptation to curse out loud, he finished his coffee and checked his messages. There wasn't anything that demanded his immediate attention, so he returned his cell to his pocket and went to the window to watch the dogs.

Professionally, he knew keeping an open mind had

been the right thing to do. Personally, it felt like he had screwed up. He didn't know how things could have worked out with him and Katrina. There had already been too many questions and barriers. But he had feelings for her, of that there was no doubt. And he was fairly sure she'd felt the same. Past tense.

By not being open with her, he'd created a gap between them so wide there was no chance of ever closing it. He'd known all along that she shied away from closeness. From now on, as far as emotions were concerned, he would be lucky if he caught a glimpse of hers in the distance.

He'd spent the rest of last night cursing fate and calling himself every name he could think of. Because, as it turned out, he knew exactly what he wanted going forward. He wanted her, and he was no longer afraid to admit it.

Finding your emotional courage when it's too late? Sounds about right. He ran a hand through his freshly washed hair. *So what happens next? You tell her why it's so hard for you to open up?*

He couldn't believe he was contemplating opening up to her. Not just about Billie, but also about his parents and how losing them had affected him.

He almost choked on his coffee at the thought. Katrina's face, when she looked at him now, was a mask of hurt and contempt. He figured any attempt to restore his reputation would result in digging himself into a deeper hole. He might as well face it; the romance ship had sailed. The best he could wish for was that she would eventually understand that he'd been led in that direction and none of this was a reflection on her.

When Katrina returned to the room and he caught a glimpse of her face, that hope soon faded. Her usual sparkling look had disappeared from her eyes. In its place, she regarded him with a wariness that made him want to reach out and hold her until she was reassured.

Never gonna happen.

Instead of her uniform, she was wearing jeans and a tight-fitting gray T-shirt. In her hand, she carried shades and a baseball cap. "I figured it's just too hot to wear a scarf or a hoodie, but I can tuck my hair up inside the hat."

He nodded approvingly. "From what I've seen of Leigh Dennings, she's pretty self-absorbed, so she's unlikely to notice us. I'm not wearing my uniform, obviously, and I'll put on a similar disguise to yours. I'll need to take Boris to the station. One of the other officers may want to take him out with them. If not, he will still need his usual training routine."

"I'll take Holly and Dobby to Look Who's Walking." For the first time, her composure slipped and her lip trembled slightly. "After everything that's happened, I'm not leaving them here alone."

Resisting the impulse to close the distance between them and take her in his arms was torture. How was he going to get through a whole day in close proximity to her, knowing she was hurting? And knowing he was responsible?

Find her sister. Find the people who are doing this. Make her safe again. That was how he could help her.

"How about I meet you at the station in half an hour? I'll pick up an unmarked police vehicle. We can head out to the AAG ranch and make an early start."

As they went out to the garden to collect the dogs, he reflected again on how easily they'd established a feeling of rightness. And how fast it had come undone.

KATRINA WAS STRUCK all over again by the beauty of the AAG Center. Everything about the headquarters was perfection, from the location to the building itself. There must have been some damage done by the earthquake, but there was no sign of it.

"I haven't met her, but Micheline Anderson must be a very smart woman," she said to Spencer.

They were seated in the bland police vehicle with its tinted windows. Spencer had positioned it at the far end of the parking lot at a point where they had a clear view of the ranch entrance. They had arrived at a time when they judged the group members would be finishing breakfast and preparing to start their daily activities.

From what she'd heard in town, those activities included growing crops, making furniture, and other items that were sold to raise funds. The members also spent time in reflection, learning to become the best versions of themselves.

He shifted slightly in his seat. "I think you're right about that, but what makes you say it now?"

"Just look at this place." She pointed to the beautiful golden structure that appeared to be slumbering in the morning sunlight. "It's stunning. When Micheline bought it, she must have seen the possibilities and known she could make it into a place people would feel welcome and supported."

She withdrew her gaze from the building for long enough to glance at Spencer's profile. His lips thinned briefly into a tight line before he answered. "Micheline is certainly an astute business person. She charges a thousand dollars for her seminars."

"I know. That was why Helen Jackson was so angry. She thought her son had been preyed upon when he was grieving," she said. "The thought of Helen, and the way she abruptly changed her mind, still worries me. I think she was pressured into doing it."

"I'll check it out, but if she sticks to her misunderstanding story, there's not much I can do." He drummed his fingers on the steering wheel. "As for Micheline, her seminars are just the start. At an additional five thousand dollars for each level, members can attain 'honest selfhood.'"

"What does that mean?"

"I don't know." He turned to look at her with a slight smile. "And I don't have enough spare cash to find out."

She didn't want to return the smile. She did everything she could to resist it. But her mouth refused to listen to the message. Despite her best efforts, she felt her lips turn up at the corners as her eyes maintained contact with his.

Spencer looked away first. Frowning, he focused on a dark-haired woman who was walking toward the center. "That's Dee Walton, Payne Colton's administrative assistant. I knew she was an AAG enthusiast, she offered their services after the earthquake, but she's here mighty early. Clearly, her links to the group are closer than I thought." He pulled out his cell phone. "I need to make a call."

Katrina continued to watch the center as he spoke briefly to one of his colleagues.

"Kerry? While you're checking out AAG members, look into Dee Walton…that's right. Payne Colton's assistant. And let's get her in for questioning. She may be able to tell us something about the other group members." He grinned at something the other person said. "Yeah, I know how you like to stay busy."

As he ended his call, Leigh Dennings stepped out onto the porch with Randall on one side and Bart on the other. The three of them had their heads close together and were clearly deep in conversation, but paused to exchange a greeting with Dee.

"I'd like to know what they are talking about," Spencer said.

Katrina shivered. "They give me the creeps."

He flicked a quick glance her way. "Can you explain why?"

"It's hard to put into words. In normal circumstances, it's the sort of sense you get from an individual, someone who chooses to ignore social cues. The sort of people who don't get the message that you aren't in the mood to talk, or who maybe stand a little too close for comfort."

"I know what you mean." Spencer continued to watch the three AAG members as he spoke. "They don't do anything outrageous, but they feel a little 'off.'"

"Exactly," Katrina agreed. "And, although your subconscious tells you something isn't right, you couldn't explain it to anyone else. That's how it is with the AAG. Only I get that feeling about an organization and its members instead of a person." She shrugged. "It's ridiculous. Right?"

"It might be if you were the only person to describe feeling that way to me. Since you're not, I think it must be a genuine vibe this group gives off." He straightened in his seat. "Looks like our target is on the move."

Leigh parted from the two men with a wave of her hand and headed toward a silver Toyota. Randall and Bart hung around on the porch for a moment or two, then went back inside.

"If Leigh is the welcome manager, shouldn't she remain here at the headquarters?" Katrina asked. "To, um, *welcome* people?"

Leigh, who appeared to be in no hurry to go anywhere, was checking her appearance in the rearview mirror. Spencer tapped his fingertips on the steering wheel as he waited.

"Part of her role seems to involve recruitment," Spencer said. "Micheline likes to send out the good-looking members to sign up newcomers."

He was right, of course. Leigh was good-looking. And it really shouldn't matter to Katrina what Spencer thought of the other woman. But for some reason, a spark shot through her at the words. If she hadn't been so angry at him, she could almost have believed it was jealousy.

A few minutes later, Leigh finished touching up her

lip gloss and gave her hair a last pat. Then she started up her engine and pulled out of the parking lot.

"Finally." Spencer gave her some space before following at a discreet distance. "She's turning right, so it looks like she's headed into town."

They completed the ten-mile drive into Mustang Valley in silence. Katrina reflected on the reason for that. Did their hat-and-sunglasses disguises provide an additional barrier to communication? She decided they didn't. The new boundary was all about the fragile trust that had been built between them and then shattered by the words of the intruder.

It was bad enough that she felt scared and threatened, but now she felt diminished by the lies that had been told about her. Throughout all of this, her sister was still missing. With each passing day, her fears for Eliza increased. It just didn't seem possible that her feckless twin could survive for this length of time without help. Not unless she was getting herself into real trouble.

She knew Spencer was one of the few people who could understand that, since he was a triplet and seemed to have strong feelings toward his own siblings. This new distance between them meant confiding in him wasn't an option, however.

Once they reached the center of town, Leigh drove along Mustang Boulevard and found a parking space near Java Jane's. Spencer pulled in across the street from the coffee shop and they watched the AAG welcome manager get out of her car. Going around to the trunk, she withdrew what looked like a paper tube.

She then locked her vehicle and walked away toward the nearest store.

"Any ideas what she's carrying?" Spencer asked.

"Posters of some sort?" Katrina suggested.

"You could be right." Spencer nodded. "The AAG likes to be visible. Let's go and take a look."

They left the car and headed in the same direction as Leigh. The store she'd entered was Nuts 'n' Grains organic grocery store. From the sidewalk, the large window gave Spencer and Katrina a clear view of the interior. Katrina's hunch was correct. Leigh was talking to a woman near the cash register and handing over a poster. A few seconds later, the two of them moved toward the entrance.

Spencer drew Katrina to one side, as though they were studying the list of prices displayed by the adjacent hair salon, taking her into his arms in the process. She wasn't sure the pretense was necessary, but the warmth of his arms around her and his chest muscles beneath her cheek was just too tempting to resist. And besides, if she'd protested, she'd have risked blowing their cover. Right?

When they sneaked another look, Leigh was leaving Nuts 'n' Grains.

"Thank you so much." She gave a wave of her hand to the cashier she'd been talking to. "The poster looks just perfect in your window."

As Leigh moved toward Java Jane's, Spencer released Katrina and took hold of her hand, leading her back to look at the window of Nuts 'n' Grains. On one level, her mind was processing the information on the AAG poster. On an entirely different level, all she could think about was the feel of his fingers between hers.

"Statistics." There was a slight sneer in Spencer's voice as he scanned the AAG notice now displayed in the store window. "It's basically a list of all the good deeds the group has done in Mustang Valley since the earthquake. How many people they've supported, how many buildings they've helped restore, how much money they've spent. It's replaced the one that was there telling us all to be our best selves."

"You have to admit, it does look impressive," Katrina said. "If I was in trouble and had nowhere to turn, I'd be tempted to go to them for help."

"They are very persuasive," Spencer agreed. "And high profile. But there are others in town who also have done positive work to care for earthquake victims. Savannah Oliver was in a prison van being driven to a state prison when the earthquake struck. The driver of the van was killed and Savannah escaped. It's a long story, but she was helped by first responder Grayson Colton. Those other groups are out there, they just don't shout about it. Let's check out what Leigh is doing in Java Jane's."

Still hand in hand, they strolled along the sidewalk. They were only doing this to maintain a pretense that they were a couple, Katrina told herself. Nothing more. There was no reason for her to like it, especially after everything that had happened…

Problem is... I do like it. Too much.

When they reached the coffee shop, Leigh was already helping one of the baristas to fix a poster onto the bare brick wall. She repeated the pattern all along the length of one side of Mustang Boulevard.

"The AAG now has free advertising space in every store she'd been in," Spencer commented. "Leigh sure is persuasive."

"She's also tireless," Katrina said. "We've been following her for two hours and, while she hasn't paused to even take a sip of water, I'm feeling exhausted and thirsty."

"Me, too." Spencer changed direction, turning back toward Java Jane's. "Let's take a break. We can catch up with her again later."

SPENCER OBSERVED KATRINA'S face as she sipped her fruit smoothie. There was no particular reason; he just enjoyed watching her. It was partly to do with her beauty, but also because she had such expressive features. As she looked around the coffee house at the other customers, he couldn't quite tell what she was thinking. But he could judge her mood.

It was clear she was still hurting, and he couldn't blame her for feeling that way. But she was talking to him. Sometimes amicably. Now and then, she'd even smiled. It wasn't enough for him to expect that she'd ever forgive him. The best he could hope for was that she'd come through this as emotionally unscathed as possible.

He glanced at the clock over the serving counter.

"Before we check back with Leigh, how about we go to the hospital to talk to Aidan Hannant?"

Katrina's eyes widened. "You want me to come with you?"

"If I'm not letting you out of my sight, you'll have to." He drained his soda. "And I'm *not* letting you out of my sight."

Mustang General was located at the far end of downtown Mustang Boulevard, just a short distance away. As he drove through the perfectly manicured grounds, Spencer recalled the last time he'd been here and the failed sting operation. Since then, there had been no change in Payne Colton's condition.

Aidan Hannant was being treated in the same unit as Payne. The hospital had state-of-the-art facilities, thanks to the support of Colton Oil.

The young cop who was seated outside Aidan's room got to his feet when Spencer approached.

"How are things here?" Spencer asked.

"All quiet. The medical staff have said the patient is responding well to treatment."

Spencer thanked him and entered the room with Katrina. Hannant looked smaller than he remembered and, if possible, his face looked even worse. The bruises had developed and become more colorful and the swelling made his eyes appear almost closed. The only reason Spencer could tell he was awake was by the way Hannant muttered something when he saw them.

"I didn't catch that, Aidan." He pulled two chairs close to the bed and indicated for Katrina to sit on one while he took the other. "What did you say?"

"Not fit for visitors," Aidan repeated.

"I won't keep you long. I just have a few follow-up questions for you." Although he didn't respond, Hannant twisted his scratched and swollen fingers in the sheet that had been pulled up to his chest.

"Already told you everything I know."

"Good to see you talking a little clearer," Spencer said. "That should make this easier. I want to ask you about the first email you got offering you money to give Katrina a warning."

"Like I said. I don't know who sent it." Even with features like raw hamburger, Hannant managed to look sulky. The guy had also developed an attitude since their last meeting.

"But you accepted the offer. How could the person who sent that email have been sure that you would?"

Hannant's hands stilled. "Don't know what you mean."

"Let me put it another way. Most regular guys, if they'd gotten an email like that, would have gone straight to the police with it. I could be wrong, but I'm guessing that the anonymous writer didn't just fire off dozens or hundreds of copies, then sit back and see who replied." Spencer leaned forward, his gaze probing Hannant's face. "I think he, or she, only sent one message, Aidan."

"I don't know who sent it, so I can't say."

Resting his elbows on the bed, Spencer invaded Hannant's space a little more. "I'm going to take my speculation one step further. I figure whoever sent that email knew they were on to a safe thing with you.

Why? Because they already knew what your answer would be. I'm guessing it was well known that you had money worries." Now there was a sheen of sweat on Hannant's brow, and Spencer decided to push him harder. "And you'd already spread the word around that you were available for a little dirty work."

"You can't prove that," Hannant muttered.

Spencer sat back. "You ever drink in Joe's Bar?"

With its greasy food, loud music and...*interesting* selection of adult beverages, Joe's Bar attracted a range of characters from serious pool players to those looking for a shady deal. Spencer and his colleagues often kept it under close scrutiny. Certainly bodyguard Callum Colton, Marlowe's twin, had been watching the bar recently after a suspicious character he'd been tailing was seen there. And it wasn't unusual for the police to be called out to deal with a breakout of rowdy behavior.

"Now and then."

"Have you ever told anyone in there that you needed money and you'd be willing to do anything to get it?"

Hannant puffed out a breath. "Jeez. Am I supposed to remember everything I say when I've had me a few beers?"

Spencer grinned. "I like that, Aidan. You should try it on the judge." As Hannant squirmed, he became serious again. "Even if you've forgotten, can you be sure your drinking buddies will have such short memories? Especially when some of them may need their own favors from the police."

"Look. I may have said a few things." Hannant sounded miserable. "Boasted a little about some stuff

I'd done in the past and not gotten caught. And yeah, I needed cash. Got into a few games of poker, and was having trouble paying my tab."

"I'm going to need some more details from you in a statement. For now, I'm more interested in *who* you spoke to in Joe's."

"You make it sound like I sat down with some guy and talked one-on-one, but it wasn't like that," Hannant said. "I was just shooting my mouth off, you know? Talking to anyone who'd listen."

That was what Spencer had been afraid of. Drunk and with an out-of-control mouth, Hannant could have been overheard by anyone who was in the bar that day. Spencer was right back where he'd started.

"Do you remember who was around?" *Anyone from the AAG?* He didn't want to give Hannant that sort of prompt.

"The usual guys." Hannant attempted a shrug, then winced. "And a few from that self-help place."

In the chair next to Spencer's, Katrina shifted slightly. Before she could speak, and jeopardize the inquiry, Spencer continued his questioning. "I need you to be more specific. Who were these people?"

"Give me a second. Some water would be good."

"I've got it." Katrina reached for the specially adapted bottle and held it to Hannant's lips. Spencer was in awe of the way she could help a man who had put her in danger and then threatened her. It took a remarkable person to show that kind of compassion. He was figuring out fast just how special she was. And what a jerk he'd been for doubting her.

"That's better." Hannant leaned back. "Yeah. They started hanging around the place. What were their names? Randy? No. That's not right. Randall. And his buddies. The one with the muscles and the cool dude."

So Randall Cook had been visiting Joe's Bar? It was an interesting piece of information. That made it seem likely that the "one with the muscles" was Bart Akers. But the "cool dude"? Spencer had no clue who that could be.

"Ken? Kenny?" Hannant mused. "I'd had too many beers by that time. Now I think of it, he was the guy who was doing the buying."

"And this Kenny, you're sure he was with the other two? The one called Randall and his buddy with the muscles?" Spencer asked.

"Could have been. Like I said, it's a blur. I'm tired." Hannant was starting to whine. "I need to sleep."

Figuring that he'd gotten about as much information from him as he could, Spencer decided to leave it there. If he was honest, he hadn't expected as much. Would what Hannant had revealed hold up in court? A man who'd admitted he was drunk had said two guys who could have been Randall and Bart might have heard him boasting about past misdemeanors. It was a big leap from that to linking the AAG to the threats against Katrina.

And the mysterious Kenny? If he existed at all, he could be anyone.

When they got outside the room, the expression on Katrina's face told him she shared his frustration.

"He didn't tell us anything we hadn't already guessed," she said. "What do we do next?"

"I don't know about you, but I'm hungry. Let's grab some lunch, then go back and check on Leigh, as planned. After that, we can find out if there are any AAG members called Ken or Kenny."

"Police work is not as interesting as I imagined it would be," she commented as they headed toward the exit.

He laughed. "Believe me, you don't want to be around when things get exciting."

Chapter Twelve

After they'd shared a pizza in Lucia's Italian Café, Spencer suggested they head toward the opposite end of Mustang Boulevard. His reasoning was that Leigh had been working to a system that morning and, if he was correct, she should have reached Bubba's Diner by that point.

"What if you're wrong and we've lost her?" Katrina asked.

"Then she's probably up to no good and we were right about her all along. Plus, we know where to find her. She'll turn up at the A AG Center sooner or later." His cheerful mood was unrelenting, even though trailing Leigh was proving to be boring and unproductive. "But I'm not wrong."

Katrina followed the direction of his gaze. Leigh was standing on a shady corner near Bubba's, studying her cell phone. Every now and then, she glanced up and down the street in both directions.

"She has the look of a woman who is waiting for someone," Spencer said.

"Maybe she has a hot date?"

"Or a meeting with the boss lady?" He lightly gripped her shoulders and turned her to face the other way. "That's Micheline Anderson."

The woman approaching Leigh looked to be in her midsixties. She was blonde, attractive and well groomed. Nodding and smiling to people who called out as she passed, the AAG leader clearly knew plenty of people and was very sure of herself.

"She's not what I expected," Katrina said. "I thought she'd be tougher, more hard-edged. She looks like someone you'd want to confide all your problems to. Although I guess that's a prerequisite in her job."

"You know what they say about appearances."

When Micheline reached Leigh, the two women embraced and exchanged a few words. Leigh excitedly showed her boss something on her cell phone and Micheline patted the younger woman's shoulder.

"Pictures of the posters she's been putting up?" Katrina said, hazarding a guess.

"You could be right."

When Leigh tucked her cell into her purse, the two AAG members walked arm in arm toward the silver Toyota that was still parked near Java Jane's.

"I guess we're on the move," Spencer said.

They were heading toward their own vehicle when a man coming out of Java Jane's almost bumped into Micheline and Leigh. He halted immediately, holding his hands up in apology. As Spencer and Katrina got closer, they could hear the conversation.

"Sorry, ladies. I hope I didn't startle you."

Leigh giggled. "Just watch where you're going next time, Kenyon."

He gave a mock bow before walking away.

"Kenyon?" Spencer kept his voice low. "Sounds enough like 'Kenny' to be worth checking out." When he saw her expression, he frowned. "Is something wrong?"

"I've seen that guy before. It was the first time I went to the AAG Center." A cold sensation started in the pit of her stomach and spread outward. "I noticed him because he looked just like the sort of guy Eliza would be attracted to. I remember thinking she'd have stuck around just to get close to him."

Spencer narrowed his eyes, watching Kenyon as he strutted along the sidewalk, then paused to study his reflection in a store window. "I think we may have found our cool dude."

"I have a bad feeling about this," Katrina said as they got into the car. "Eliza had poor judgment when it came to men. She always had a thing about bad boys. Even in kindergarten, she'd be drawn to the kid who pulled her pigtails."

"What about you?" he asked, glancing her way as he pulled out into the traffic. "Were your choices any better, or did you bond with a rebel over the sandbox?"

The teasing note was almost irresistible. Almost. Just in time, the hurt he'd caused her kicked back in and she turned away. "I didn't bond with anyone."

An uncomfortable silence followed, lasting for a few minutes. When Spencer spoke again, any trace of humor was gone. "You think Eliza could have gotten mixed up with this Kenyon guy?"

"I think he's the sort of man she'd have been drawn to. And if he was involved in getting Hannant to intimidate me…" She turned her head to look out of the window. Did she want to put her darkest fears into words? It felt like saying them out loud would somehow make them more real. "That doesn't look good for Eliza."

He reached out a hand and briefly touched her knee. The fleeting contact warmed and comforted her more than she cared to admit.

"If there's one thing I've learned, it's not to jump to conclusions. Although you haven't heard from your sister, you shouldn't assume the worst. Although that guy may be her type, that's a big step from her hooking up with him and him harming her."

"You're right." She relaxed a little into her seat. "I know it. I just wish she'd get in touch."

"If my siblings ever did what I wanted, I think I'd pass out from shock," he said. "Twins, triplets—people assume that bonding thing means you do everything in perfect harmony."

"I read somewhere that fraternal girl twins are supposed to have the second strongest bond after identical girls. Eliza and I must have missed that class in twin school. We were always fiercely individual. We didn't hate each other." She managed a smile. "We just never had that real closeness that other people told us we should."

"Me, Jarvis and Bella were close—and we grew more so when we went to live with our aunt Amelia—but we still have our differences." He nodded at Leigh's vehicle, which was a few cars in front. "They are headed in the wrong direction for the AAG ranch."

As he spoke, Leigh turned left. She was following the road toward Mesquite Canyon, a development of low-budget houses and apartments that had been hit hard by the earthquake.

"Are they on another recruitment drive?" Katrina asked.

"It's possible they're being more caring than that." Spencer indicated a delivery truck that had pulled up outside a row of houses. Leigh stopped her car behind it and she and Micheline alighted. "We'll get the best view from that incline over there."

He drove past Leigh's vehicle, turned around at the end of the short street and parked under a clump of trees. They watched as a few home owners emerged and shook hands with Micheline and Leigh. After a few minutes, more cars arrived and other AAG members, including Randall and Bart, got out. Everyone donned hard hats, then the truck doors were opened and kitchen fittings and appliances were off-loaded.

"I think we just spent a day trailing Leigh Dennings only to stumble on her and her fellow AAG members' deepest secret. They're rebuilding the kitchens of some earthquake victims," Katrina said.

AS THEY DROVE back along Mustang Boulevard, Spencer was lost in thought. If the AAG was a cover for something, he had no clue what criminal activity was being hidden. On the whole, Mustang Valley was a run-of-the-mill southern Arizona town. Crime rates were average for the region, although there had been a recent upsurge of unusual activity. The police force was busy, but not stretched beyond capacity.

Of course, hiding a criminal enterprise behind a respectable organization was a clever way of duping law enforcement. He'd have to check it out with his colleagues in other local police departments and find out if there was any new activity he should be aware of. Drugs, firearms, the usual organized-crime stuff…

"Stop!"

Katrina's exclamation startled him out of his thoughts and he slammed on the brake.

"What is it?"

"That woman." She craned her neck to get a better look at the house they'd just passed. They were almost out of town now, and the last few houses straggled along a final stretch of road with a clear view of the Mustang Valley Mountains.

Katrina turned to him with a stunned expression. "It's Christie Foster, the woman who said she knew Eliza at the AAG ranch."

The highway behind him was clear, so Spencer put the vehicle into Reverse and went backward until they were almost alongside the house she had indicated. There was a woman standing by the front gate, shielding her eyes against the sun as she looked along the road. A suitcase sat at her feet.

"Are you sure?" Spencer asked as he looked in the rearview mirror. "You said she looked nervous and bedraggled."

From what he could see, the woman at the gate was

well dressed and wore full makeup. She certainly didn't look like the insecure waif Katrina had described.

"It's her." Katrina was already on her way out of the car.

"Hey—"

He was talking to a closed passenger door. With a resigned sigh, he followed her. Katrina was walking briskly toward the other woman. When she reached her, she stopped in front of her.

"Remember me?"

The woman at the gate flicked her a glance, then looked past her at the road. "No."

Katrina's outraged gasp lasted several seconds. "You pretended to know my sister. You pretended to be scared out of your wits. I felt sorry for you, Christie—"

"My name isn't Christie."

Spencer decided it was time to intervene. "What is your name?"

"I don't have to answer that."

"You can answer it here, or you can answer it down at the police station," he told her. "I don't mind which."

She gave an exaggerated sigh. "My name is Cordelia Mellor. I'm an actress. I was hired to approach you and pretend to be this Christie Foster girl." She shrugged. "I'm sorry about your sister, okay? I didn't know that was part of the deal until I'd already agreed."

Katrina shook her head. "You did it to trick me?"

"Hey, it wasn't my idea. Blame the guy who hired me and paid me five thousand dollars in cash."

"Who did hire you?" Spencer asked.

"It was in a bar at a recruitment fair." She gave a bitter little laugh. "I haven't made it into the movies yet."

"And who lives here?" He gestured to the house.

"I have no clue. This is where my cab is meeting me. No offense, guys, but small towns are not my scene. The guy who hired me made me stay hidden at that ranch place for a few days. When he said it would be okay to leave, I walked as far and as fast as I could." As she was talking, a cloud of dust in the distance signaled the approach of a vehicle. "This is my ride."

"Not so fast." As the cab pulled up, Spencer signaled to the driver to keep going. "That 'ranch place' is going to seem like a palace compared to where I'm taking you."

DARKNESS WAS FALLING as Spencer sat on the bench in Katrina's yard and watched her put Holly and Dobby through their paces on the training course.

"Suzie said they did some good work today demonstrating techniques to the dog owners in her classes, but they haven't had their usual walk," she explained.

"Boris doesn't have the same problem." He stroked his partner's ears and the dog rolled his eyes with a blissful expression. "He has a daily workout routine whether I'm there or not."

When the dogs had completed their drill, she gave them a treat as a reward, then tossed a few balls across the yard for them to chase. Spencer's heart gave a glad little leap when she came to sit next to him.

"Did we learn anything today?" she asked. "Because I'm feeling more confused than ever."

He considered the question. "We only spent one day following Leigh, so it was a snapshot of her activities. From what we saw, she—and Micheline—are on the up-and-up."

"Are you saying we have it wrong about the AAG? Cordelia said she stayed at the ranch when she was pretending to be Christie Foster."

"But Leigh Dennings denied that they had any record of Christie as an AAG member and, to be fair, Christie didn't actually exist. It's possible that whoever hired Cordelia could have kept her hidden, even from the other AAG members. Right now, the next great actress to hit our screens is sulking and refusing to talk."

"She didn't strike me as the sort of person who could keep that up for long," Katrina said.

"I've always said we should be objective." Dobby dropped a ball at his feet and Spencer threw it across the yard. All three dogs bounded after it. "The AAG could be the socially responsible organization it appears on the surface, or it could be a cover for something darker."

"Forget being objective. Just this once, tell me what you really think is going on," Katrina said.

"Right now, with the limited evidence available, I think it's possible a few shady characters have been drawn to the AAG. They could be using a genuine do-good group to disguise their own criminal activities."

"Do you develop this open-mindedness during your police training?" she asked. "Do they teach you to give everyone the benefit of the doubt? Oh, hold on. I didn't get that, did I?"

The words stung, but it was the look in her eyes that felt like someone was holding a knife to his skin. There must be something he could say to undo the hurt he'd caused, some way of showing her how much he was regretting his stupid mistake.

"Katrina, let me explain."

When she remained silent, he almost didn't dare breathe. Was she going to let him speak, or was she preparing to walk away? And, now that he had a chance, what the hell was he going to say?

"You're the most beautiful woman I've ever seen."

Not what I expected...

Katrina was staring at him as though he'd sprouted horns and he couldn't blame her. He had no idea where the words had come from. "*That's* your explanation?"

"No." He smiled. "But I thought it was worth mentioning."

"You're impossible."

"I know." He hung his head. "Can we just pretend I haven't been thinking straight since I met you because I was dazzled by you?"

She gasped. "No, Spencer, we can't. Trying to get me to fall for that is almost as bad as believing I made up those threats."

He sneaked a peek at her face. Her tone was outraged, but her features were less rigid. Clasping his hands between his knees, he stared down at them for a moment or two, trying to find the right words. One chance. That was all he had. She was already halfway to hating him. If he blew this…

"I didn't believe you made up the threats, but I did

harbor some doubts for a while. And I have no excuse to offer you for that."

She remained silent for a moment or two. "I felt sure you'd tell me it's your job to consider all possibilities."

"Would it make you feel better if I did?"

"I don't think anything could make this better." He heard the quiver in her voice and something deep inside his chest snapped like a twig. "You made me feel worthless, Spencer. You went ahead and believed the worst based on what you were told about my sister's volatility. That was information I freely gave you. I was at least owed a question or two about who *I* am."

"I got it wrong. I'm sorry."

For a long time, they observed the dogs' antics without talking. When the heat got too much for the canines, they drank noisily from the water bowls and flopped down in a shady corner.

"That guy, the one who broke in here with the knife, said you wanted to move in to stop me from making up any more stories." Katrina's voice was soft, her face half-hidden by the curtain of her hair. "Is that true?"

"I wanted to protect you." He closed the distance between them, taking her hands in his. "And be near you."

There was a sheen of tears in her eyes as she raised them to his face. "When you kissed me, it felt real."

"It *was* real." The realest thing he'd felt in a long time.

"Kiss me again."

He leaned back slightly, studying her face. "You're still hurting. And I'm the person who hurt you."

"Are you saying you don't want to kiss me again?" Her lower lip trembled.

"I want to kiss you more than I want my next breath. I'm just saying that this might not be good timing."

"I don't care." She wrapped her arms around his neck. "Make me forget all of this."

Her lips were sinfully, temptingly close. He clutched the remnants of his sanity while he could. "We have enough going on. Let's not complicate things with regrets."

"I agree. We shouldn't have regrets."

Her lips lightly brushed his and rational thought became a thing of the past. It was just a kiss. A reassurance that his feelings for her hadn't been colored by foolish doubts…

He crushed her against him, his lips hard and demanding as his tongue parted her lips and swept inside, caressing and probing. Katrina wrapped her arms around his neck and tightened her grip, pressing her body closer as she used her own tongue to explore Spencer's mouth in return.

Instantly, he tangled a hand in her hair, turning her head to the angle he wanted, deepening the kiss to bittersweet intensity. The fire in his body increased and became concentrated at a specific, exhilarating point. They were heading toward the point of no return and Katrina seemed happy to drive them over the edge.

Breaking that kiss was one of the hardest things he'd ever done. Resting his forehead against hers, he drew in a breath. "Some thinking time would be good about now."

She gave a shaky laugh. "Who knew restraint could be so sexy?"

He ran a hand through his hair. "It's not the hottest image in my mind right now. But I don't think we should rush into anything."

"You're right." She cast a look into the darkened corners of the yard. "It's just... I don't want to sleep alone tonight."

He groaned. "Is that what this is about? You want me to be your teddy bear?"

She laughed. "No. But I could use some company. If that wouldn't be too hard?"

He got to his feet and reached out a hand to help her up. "If I share a bed with you, it would definitely get hard, Katrina." He waggled his eyebrows in a mock lewd expression. "But I'll risk it so you can get a good night's sleep."

KATRINA KNEW SHE was playing with fire. She wasn't a virgin, but she was sexually inexperienced, having had only a few meaningful encounters. She'd seen at close range the damage that recklessness could do, and she'd always kept it safe in relationships. Yet here she was, wanting to throw caution to the wind and act on impulse. For the first time in her life, she understood a little of Eliza's untamed nature.

Getting ready for bed had become like a strange new ritual in which everything had taken on a double meaning. For the last hour, Spencer, who was clad in sweatpants and a T-shirt, had lain still as a rock on one side of the bed, while Katrina clung to the other side.

Even though they had their backs to each other, she was fairly sure he was awake.

She was in bed with a glorious man whose touch made her melt and, instead of pressuring her, he was determinedly keeping his distance. His restraint had gone a long way to reassuring her that he did value her and that he genuinely regretted his doubts over her reliability.

Just my luck. I finally discover my wild side, only to fall for Mustang Valley's last remaining gentleman. The thought made her stifle a giggle.

"Are you okay?" Spencer asked.

"Fine." She shifted to her other side, facing his back in the darkness. "Is this too weird? Is that why you can't sleep?"

"It feels a little…unusual." He mirrored her action and, in the darkness, she could just make out his outline. "It's been a long time since I've shared a bed with someone."

Although she knew he was single, she hadn't given his prior relationship status much thought. There was a desolate note in his voice, and she wondered what had put it there.

"I'm sorry. I was thinking of myself when I suggested this. I didn't know it might be a trigger for you."

"How could you know? It's not something I talk about."

"Do you want to talk about it now?" Was she being presumptuous? Then again, they *were* in bed together. And neither of them appeared to be sleepy. "I'm a good listener."

When he didn't respond, she figured she had her answer. Yes, she was being forward. Why would he want to tell her his secrets? There was an undeniable physical attraction between them. On her part, that attraction could turn into something more, but why would she assume it meant the same to him?

"Billie was my fiancée." His voice was so quiet, she had to strain to hear. "She was murdered four years ago."

"Oh, my stars." She moved closer and placed a hand on his arm. "What an unbearable burden for you."

It explained so much about him. That air of sadness she'd always sensed, the way he deliberately kept other people at a distance, how he stepped back every time they were getting close.

"She was a cop. Just a rookie. There'd been a call to go to an apartment because of a domestic dispute. The caller said there was a kid screaming for help. Billie ignored the golden rule and went in alone without waiting for backup." The words were coming out fast now. It was as if, having started to tell the story, he couldn't stop. "It was a trick. The guy who placed the call had a grudge against the police. He took her hostage—"

Even though her touch on his arm was light, and there was still space between them, Katrina could feel the tremors that shook his body. Scooting over, she wrapped her arms around him. "Don't do this to yourself. Not if it hurts too much."

"It's all in my mind, anyway. Talking about it doesn't make it worse." He rested his head on her shoulder. "He held her for two days before he killed her. I was nearly out of my mind picturing what he was doing to her. Had to be restrained from going in there a few times. In the end, it was almost a relief to know she was dead. Except those images wouldn't leave me."

"I'm so sorry." She stroked his hair as silent sobs wracked his body. "Did you get help? You must have needed someone to talk to."

"I was diagnosed with PTSD and I had counseling." He breathed deeply, clearly using a technique he'd been taught. "In the end, it was my brother and sister who pulled me through it. Late-night chats, long walks, film nights, jokes that no one else understood… They were in tune with what I needed in our unique triplet way."

"They sound amazing."

"They have their moments." He gave a half laugh. "If you ever meet them, don't tell them I said that."

She rested her cheek against his hair and smiled. If she ever met them? Why would that happen?

"Maybe we should try to sleep now?"

"Yeah." Spencer pulled her closer. "This feels good."

Holding him, comforting him, caring for him: those things had replaced the earlier awkwardness between them. This new closeness had nothing to do with the heat they'd generated. Yet the attraction was still there, waiting to resurface.

And he was right. It did feel good.

Chapter Thirteen

"Can anyone explain to me why there is a good-looking cop in our office?" Suzie asked the next morning. "If he was dating anyone here, I'd understand." She rolled her eyes in Katrina's direction. "Or if there was a problem that needed the police, one only a friend could help with."

Katrina sighed. "Sergeant Colton is investigating the break-ins at my house. He's working here temporarily until the perpetrators have been caught."

"Do you call him Sergeant Colton when you're eating breakfast together?" Suzie asked.

"Stop it." Katrina cast a nervous look over her shoulder. "Laurence will hear you. I don't want him to think there's something going on."

"Why? *Isn't* there something going on?" her friend whispered. "What is wrong with you?"

"It's a long story."

Suzie shook her head. "Don't let that one get away."

They were on familiar territory here and Katrina snorted. "Isn't that what I keep saying to you about Rusty?"

"Who keeps saying what about me?"

They both turned to look at the tall man who was leaning on the door frame. Rusty Linehan wore a cowboy hat and a grin a mile wide.

"How long have you been standing there listening to us?" Suzie demanded.

"Long enough to know you talk about me when I'm not around."

Suzie's hand-on-hips stance wasn't fooling anyone. Katrina could tell how pleased she was to see the hardware store co-owner. "Shows how much you know. It was Katrina who started talking about you, not me."

"That's good, since it was Katrina I came to see," Rusty said.

"Oh." Suzie pouted. "Shall I leave the two of you alone?"

Laughing, Rusty tipped his hat in Katrina's direction. "I wanted to show you some fabric samples for the cushion covers we're replacing."

Katrina was about to thank him again for everything he'd done, when Spencer stepped out of the office. "This Kenyon guy—" He broke off as he noticed her companions. "Oh, excuse me."

"Is that Kenyon Latimer you're talking about?" A frown descended on Rusty's pleasant features.

"I don't know," Spencer said. "But I'd like to hear more about anyone called Kenyon."

"If we're talking about the same guy, he's bad news." Rusty shook his head. "He's not from around here and I don't know him personally, but he caused some trouble in Joe's Bar a few weeks ago. He threatened to punch one of the female bartenders when she wouldn't serve him because he was drunk."

"Wait." Spencer frowned. "That happened in Joe's? I've never known anyone to be refused in there."

"Yeah." Rusty nodded. "That's how bad he was. The guy couldn't even say his own name."

"Was this reported to the police?" Spencer asked.

Rusty choked back a laugh. "We're talking about an incident in Joe's on a Friday night. If everything that went on in there got reported, you guys would never deal with anything else."

"True." Spencer nodded his head in acknowledgment. "Do you know anything else about Kenyon Latimer?"

"I don't know if he's a member of the AAG, but he hangs out with their security guys."

Katrina exchanged a glance with Spencer. So to an outsider like Rusty, Randall and Bart appeared to be security. Was that intentional? Micheline and Leigh hadn't introduced them that way, and it didn't seem to be their main role in the group. Even so, they took on a protective role and could come across as intimidating. Perhaps this was yet another way in which the AAG wasn't all it seemed.

"That's been really helpful, Rusty. Thank you," Spencer said. "If you think of any other details about Kenyon Latimer, please let me know."

"Yeah. The sergeant works here now." In response to Katrina's glare, Suzie batted her eyelashes. "Did I say something wrong, honey?"

Spencer had started to turn away when Rusty spoke again. "There was one other thing, but I don't know how true it is and I don't want to speak about a guy I don't know."

"I'm not going to arrest anyone on the strength of some gossip, but anything you can share will be useful to give me a broader picture of this man," Spencer said.

"Okay. After this Latimer guy told Candy, the barmaid at Joe's, that he'd smash her face up if she didn't pour him another beer, a few of the regulars helped him through the door. Maybe they made sure his feet didn't touch the ground on the way out. I remember overhearing someone say Latimer had been hanging around Mustang Park, trying to sell drugs to the teenagers."

"Drugs?" Katrina lifted a hand to her lips.

The very first time she'd seen Kenyon Latimer, she'd known he was the sort of man to whom Eliza would be attracted. Since then, everything she'd heard about him had been bad news. Now, the missing ingredient had been added into the mix. Drugs. Her sister would have been a helpless prey in this man's clutches. Like a butterfly on a cart wheel, he'd have crushed her and walked away without noticing.

"Just what I heard." Rusty shrugged.

Suzie shot a quick glance in Katrina's direction before grabbing her boyfriend's arm. "Hey, lover, why don't you leave those fabric samples and come back for them in a day or two? And, while you're here, you can come and take a look at that flickering headlight on my car."

She hauled Rusty away.

Katrina smiled at Spencer. "She's not subtle."

He moved closer, his gaze scanning her face. "Rusty

could be right. The story about Latimer selling drugs might be gossip."

"You don't believe that."

He ran his hands lightly up and down her upper arms. "We still don't know that Eliza had any contact with Latimer."

"*I* don't believe that."

"Let me check him out before we jump to any conclusions."

She nodded, briefly resting her head against his chest. "Thank you."

"What for?"

Tilting her head up, she smiled. "I seriously don't know where to start."

"Well, that makes two of us." After pressing a quick kiss onto her cheek, he returned to the office and closed the door behind him.

"Nothing to see here, folks." The sudden sound of Suzie's voice from behind her startled Katrina so much that she jumped. "Hugs, kisses and starry eyes. Why would anyone believe they were signs that there was something going on?"

STILL UNWILLING TO allow Katrina out of his sight unless it was necessary, Spencer had decided to take her along to the Colton Oil offices with him when he met with the board members. He left his vehicle in the parking lot, next to the spaces that were reserved for Colton Oil staff, and they passed security cameras to enter the imposing building.

"Won't they wonder why you need a dog trainer to

be with you at their board meeting?" she whispered as the concierge checked Spencer's badge.

"After everything that's happened in this family lately, I don't think they'd notice if I brought a dancing pony into the boardroom."

"Nice." She followed him into the lobby. "That's the first time I've been compared to a performing animal."

Since Payne Colton's shooting, security had been increased, so a uniformed guard escorted them to the boardroom. When they were shown into the elegant room, there were two people waiting for them.

The first was Ainsley. With her was Rafe Colton, who was also Kerry Wilder's fiancé. Rafe had been adopted as a young child at Payne's first wife's insistence. Payne had grudgingly accepted the boy, but had later recognized that Rafe was a financial wizard. As a result, he was now CFO of Colton Oil.

The Colton siblings both rose from their seats behind the polished desk as Spencer and Katrina entered.

"We've informed Dee Walton that this is an informal meeting, but that she can have representation if she chooses," Ainsley said. "So far, she's declined. She said that as Dad's loyal administrative assistant, she wants to help any way she can."

"She may change her mind about that when she knows you've invited a police officer along," Spencer said.

"We'll see." Rafe indicated seats alongside theirs. "I don't think we've met...?"

"Katrina is observing." His tone of voice and expression didn't allow for challenge or further discussion. In her dark pants and white blouse, Katrina could have been a plainclothes cop, or serving in a clerical role. Spencer wasn't going to enlighten his companions about the real reason why she was there.

"I think we're ready." Ainsley glanced around for confirmation. "I'll ask Dee to come in."

She left the room and returned a few moments later with another woman. Dee was an attractive woman in her midthirties, with chin-length brown hair neatly styled in a bob. She was professionally dressed and, although she appeared a little nervous, she nodded a greeting to Rafe as she took a seat.

Ainsley returned to her own place on the opposite side of the table. "You understand that this meeting is not an official one, Dee?" Very much the attorney, Ainsley clearly wanted to set the record straight before anyone started talking. "You don't have to answer our questions and you are free to leave at any time."

Dee's brown eyes opened wide. "Why would I do that when I'm as anxious as you are to find out who shot your dad?"

"Thank you. That's good to know." Ainsley indicated Spencer and Katrina. "This is Sergeant Colton of the MVPD. He is here in an advisory capacity to the board and his companion is observing. Are you okay with that?"

"Of course. I'm happy to go along with whatever needs to be done."

Watching her, Spencer couldn't pick up on any clues that she had anything to hide. Beyond a natural unease generated by the situation, she appeared genuinely eager to help.

"The main reason we wanted to talk to you is that we know how close you are with members of the Affirmation Alliance Group," Ainsley said.

"That's right." Dee clasped her hands beneath her chin, her eyes shining. "It's the most wonderful, life-affirming place. Discovering how to live my best life—"

"How well did you know Harley Watts?" Rafe asked, interrupting her praise for the group.

Dee's sparkling expression faded. "Oh, Harley. That poor boy. So misunderstood."

"Dee, that 'poor boy' sent an email via the dark web to the members of the Colton Oil board telling us that Ace is not a Colton by birth." Ainsley leaned forward in her seat as she spoke. "He used the AAG server to do it."

"It's so sad that an AAG member would get mixed up in something so awful. And that he would direct his feelings at Colton Oil." Dee shook her head. "I still find it hard to believe."

"Do you know how he got hold of the names of the board members?" Rafe asked.

It was a good question and Spencer observed Dee's reaction closely. Her hands dropped to her knees and she bent her head.

"I've thought about it a lot." Her voice was little more than a whisper. "I may have inadvertently given the names to Harley in casual conversation."

Rafe shot a fiery look in Ainsley's direction, but she signaled for him to stay calm.

"Did you give that information to anyone else in the AAG?" Ainsley asked. "Is it something you could have shared with Micheline Anderson, for example?"

"Oh, no." Dee looked up again, shaking her head. "And, even if I had, Micheline is the most trustworthy person I know. Why, she's like a mother to me. She's my mentor, my friend. She makes me feel so positive about the future—"

"Do you think Micheline knew in advance that Harley was planning to send the email to the members of the Colton Oil board?" Rafe asked.

"Absolutely not." If Dee was faking the horrified look she gave Rafe, she was the best actress Spencer had ever seen. "Micheline would never get involved in anything like that. Harley is gullible and I think someone preyed on him, hiring him to send that email without warning him of the consequences."

Spencer stepped in with a question of his own. "Do you have any idea who could have done it?"

"I wish I did, but I truly don't."

"What do you know about Kenyon Latimer?" Spencer asked.

"Kenyon?" Dee frowned. "He's new to the group. We don't turn anyone away, but…" She gave a little shrug. "He's a very troubled young man." She turned back to Ainsley. "Will I lose my job over this? Because I gave Harley the names?"

"It's a breach of confidence and something the board

will need to discuss," Ainsley said. When Dee gave a sob and covered her mouth with one shaking hand, Ainsley continued in a gentler tone, "It's in your favor that you've been honest."

"Please. You have to believe me when I say this job means everything to me."

"We won't keep you waiting long for a response," Ainsley assured her. "The other board members will already be arriving for another meeting. We'll discuss this with them and let you know the outcome as soon as possible."

She got to her feet and led Dee from the room.

"What do you make of her story?" Rafe asked Spencer.

"If she's lying, she's good," Spencer said. "But this whole situation is tough to call. Nothing is how it seems."

"I know." Rafe leaned back in his chair with a weary air. "As soon as we think we're getting somewhere with one angle, it leads us nowhere and a new problem arises."

As he was talking, Ainsley returned, and the remaining members of the board followed in her wake. The group had been reduced in size since Payne was in the hospital and Ace, the chief suspect in his father's shooting, was lying low. The other two members were Marlowe and Selina Barnes Colton, VP and public-relations director. They were accompanied by Genevieve, who, in Payne's absence, had his proxy.

"We never have outsiders present when we discuss company business." Selina was Payne's second ex-wife.

"True. But we've never had Dad lying in a hospital bed unlikely to recover from gunshot wounds before," Marlowe said, firing back. "We need to hear from Spencer about how the investigation is going, and we can tell him if any new information has come our way."

Selina pouted. "I'd have thought updating the police about new information was the duty of every good citizen."

Ignoring her, Ainsley got straight to the point about Dee and outlined the details of their earlier meeting with Payne's assistant. "I think there's little doubt that she breached company rules by sharing confidential information even though she's stressed it wasn't deliberate. The question is whether we feel the offense was serious enough for us to fire her."

Selina drummed long, red fingernails on the table. "Setting aside the breach of trust, she should be fired on the spot for being a member of that creepy do-gooder group. Let's not forget it was an email from one of them that caused chaos in *our* company. Plus, they hit me up for a donation twice today as I was on my way here. In two different locations. You can't walk down the street without encountering those people lately."

"But with Dad in the hospital, Dee is only part time, anyway, and it may be better to have someone on the inside with the AAG, someone whose brain we can pick if need be," Marlowe said. She glanced around the table at her siblings. "On those grounds, I'm saying we keep Dee in her job."

Ainsley and Rafe nodded their agreement.

"I have Payne's proxy." Genevieve spoke quietly but firmly. "And I spoke to Ace a few days ago. Although he's no longer CEO, he is still a board member. He arranged for me to have his proxy as well. Since I agree with Marlowe, there's no more to be said on this subject."

Her words prompted Selina to shoot up from her seat like a scalded cat. "So the Colton team have made up their minds to stick together and veto anything I suggest. If that's the case, I really can't see any point in wasting my time here any longer."

With a flip of her long hair, she flounced from the room.

Marlowe sighed. "Storming out within five minutes. That's a record, even for Selina. Dad's influence usually keeps her under control for at least half an hour."

"We're all too busy to spend time on dramatics," Ainsley said. "Does anyone have anything that might be of interest to Spencer before we move on to business matters?"

"I do." Rafe's words drew everyone's attention. "One of my contacts has tracked down a man who was born forty years ago on Christmas Eve at Mustang General."

"We're sure that the baby switch was carried out by a maternity ward nurse named Luella Smith. Only three baby boys were born that night at Mustang Valley. One of them was Ace, and her son was another. Luella went into labor late Christmas Eve, but she left with her sickly baby on Christmas morning. This happened after the fire that destroyed the maternity records," Spencer said. "What's the name of this guy you've tracked down?"

"Sebastian Clark." Rafe held up his hands. "I know what you're going to say. It's not Smith, but who knows what Luella did with the baby she stole? Maybe she put him up for adoption?"

"We have to investigate every lead. We've already had one impostor, Jace Smith, try to pass himself off as the 'real' Ace Colton. We need to avoid a repeat of that." Spencer wasn't particularly hopeful about this line of inquiry, but he couldn't afford to let it pass. "Arrange to meet Sebastian Clark and see if he's willing to have a DNA test."

"Okay. I'll set up the meeting." Rafe typed a note on his electronic tablet.

"Does anyone have any other information for Spencer?" Marlowe asked.

When there was no response, Spencer and Katrina said their goodbyes and left the room. Once they were outside the building, Katrina drew in a deep breath. "I don't know how they deal with that pressure every day."

"It can get pretty full-on," Spencer agreed.

"It's made me glad I'm not a Colton." She paused, a

hint of color staining her cheeks as she realized what she'd said. "I don't mean you…"

"It's okay. I know what you mean." He grinned. "There are days when I wish I could change my name."

Chapter Fourteen

"When did you learn to cook?" Katrina asked as she watched Spencer prepare a dish of noodles and prawns.

"I taught myself when I left the army." He stir-fried vegetables and added a dash of chili sauce. "My aunt Amelia couldn't cook, and we existed on a diet of grilled cheese and store-bought apple pie. When I grew up, I wanted a more varied menu."

"How long were you in the army?"

"I joined when I was twenty and enlisted for a four-year term. I was stationed in South Korea for much of that time, and while I was there I decided I wanted to be a cop." He looked up from what he was doing. "I guess I could have joined the military police, but I was also a little homesick. I like living in Arizona, and I missed my brother and sister. It was while I was in South Korea that I developed my love of cooking Asian food."

"I'm glad you did. It smells amazing."

"It will taste even better."

They shared a smile that caused her stomach to flutter. For once, she let it happen. The dogs had been exercised and fed. They were chilling in the yard. Beer was cooling in the fridge and Katrina had downloaded a movie they both wanted to watch. The night was theirs.

Okay, so they still didn't know who was behind the threats on her life, or who had shot Payne Colton, or where Eliza was… But, right now, she was going to try to put her fears to one side and come as close to relaxation as she could.

They ate in front of the TV, drinking beer and watching the movie in silence at first. When it turned out to be a disappointment, they began to pick apart faults in the script, laughing over the stilted dialogue.

"That was fun, even though it wasn't meant to be." Spencer inched closer.

It was a now-or-never moment. Katrina knew if she backed away now, he wouldn't approach her again. They'd rebuilt a little of their fragile faith in each other, but was it enough to take the next step? She figured there was only one way to find out.

Slow and steady...

As he leaned in and touched his lips to hers, slow and steady became a distant memory. Kisses with him were better than anything she'd ever experienced. Spencer knew how to seduce her with just his mouth.

Katrina didn't kiss him back immediately. She was too busy trying to think straight. But, no… That wasn't happening.

Wrapping her arms around him, she eased back as Spencer ran his tongue over her lips, teasing the sensitive flesh before kissing her once more. This time, she raised her right hand and clasped the back of his head, holding his mouth tighter to hers. She responded to his kiss and their tongues twined together. Her mind left the building.

She managed to grab hold of the last remnants of reason. "Spencer, I don't know…"

"How about we just stay here and make out?" He shifted position so they were lying side by side on the cramped sofa. "No pressure. This doesn't have to be anything more."

"That could be fun." She ran her fingers through his hair. "I've never done that."

"You never just made out?" He looked shocked. "You don't know what you've missed."

She wound an arm around the back of his neck as he ran one hand up and down her body. He was so incredibly sexy, it dazzled her to look at him. Instead, she closed her eyes, giving herself up to sensation. His tongue was so hot against hers, his lips alternately hot and insistent, then soft and caressing.

His body felt hard against hers as he slipped a hand down to her hips, stroking them before moving to her ass, his tongue still deep inside her mouth. Pressed up against hers, his muscular thighs felt tight against her own. His arms were strong and warm against her bare skin. It was an incredible turn-on to know that this didn't have to lead anywhere.

Unless we want it to...

Because she already knew that she wanted to feel him closer than this. She needed him deep inside her. Slowly, she began to grind her pelvis against his. He was already hard, and he groaned softly, encouraging her to keep moving. He slipped his hand up her shirt, squeezing her breasts through her bra until she whimpered into his mouth. He was working his hand into the cup when she opened her eyes…

And saw the outline of someone looking in at them through the window. Because of the way the light fell, the details were unclear and she couldn't see the face, but it was possible the person wore a hood.

"Spencer!" As she jerked upright, the shape vanished.

"What is it? What's wrong?" Spencer was looking down at her in bewilderment.

"There was someone watching us through the window." She lifted a shaking hand and pointed. "We didn't close the drapes."

He frowned. "But the dogs are loose in the yard. They didn't bark."

"Oh, no." She was on her feet, running through the kitchen toward the back door. "The antifreeze warning."

Ever since the most recent break-in, Katrina had started leaving a flashlight near the back door. Spencer snatched it up and they headed outside together. Her worst nightmare came crashing down around her when she saw the three dogs lying motionless on their sides. Giving a little moan, she clutched Spencer's arm.

He ran over and checked each dog in turn. "They're breathing normally. My guess is they've been drugged rather than poisoned. I'll call the police veterinarian."

Katrina's knees began to act like Jell-O, but she managed to stay upright while Spencer made a call. On the grass close to the dogs, there was a piece of half-chewed meat. When Spencer had finished talking, she pointed it out to him.

"That's not the sort of thing I give my dogs."

"It doesn't belong to Boris, either." He put an arm around her shoulders. "The veterinarian is on his way."

She couldn't control the trembling in her limbs. "My dogs…"

"I know." His expression was grim. "The person who did this is going to pay."

BY THE TIME the veterinarian arrived, Boris was already showing signs of recovery. His tail was twitching, and he was whimpering as if he was having a bad dream.

"That's because he's a larger dog," the doctor explained as he examined him. "All three of them probably consumed similar amounts of the drug, but it has had less of an effect on him, so he's able to shake it off faster."

"And what is the drug?" Spencer asked.

"It's impossible to say for sure without a detailed analysis, but I'm thinking the meat they were given has been laced with some sort of sedative. Concerned owners are increasingly turning to such drugs to calm nervous pets during storms or fireworks displays. They are relatively easy to obtain and don't do any long-term damage."

"So they'll be okay?" Katrina needed to double-check.

"They may feel a little disoriented when they come around, but that won't last for long. Don't expect to see much activity from them until morning. When they wake up, give them plenty of water and let them do things in their own time. Call me if you have any concerns." He left, taking the meat with him for analysis.

"Let's get these poor puppies to bed," Spencer said.

Carefully, he carried Holly, then Dobby, into the kennel. By the time it came to Boris, the big dog got to his feet and staggered into the shelter himself, collapsing onto his dog bed with a groan like a drunk after a night on the town.

Spencer turned to Katrina. "You are *not* staying out here with them tonight."

She managed a shaky laugh. "I didn't know you were a mind reader."

"You heard what the veterinarian said. They'll be fine."

"But there was a guy who deliberately did that to them—"

Firmly, he led her out of the kennel and locked the door.

"And now they're safe here." Once they were inside the house, Spencer held out his hand. "Why don't we go to bed?"

His meaning was clear and, this time, Katrina didn't hesitate. Their growing closeness made it feel like this was the right time. She wasn't going to agonize over "what next" or where it was leading. She'd just take this. One perfect moment. An antidote to all the fear and anxiety. And if that was all there was? Well, how cool would that be?

She placed a hand in his. "Yes, please."

With that, he lifted her off her feet, holding her against his chest with her feet five inches from the floor. Kissing her so hard she felt like her whole body was on fire, he walked with her through to the bedroom.

After kicking open the bedroom door, he drew her with him to the bed and flicked on the lamp. Sitting on the mattress, he pulled her close to him. From her vantage point, standing between his muscular thighs, Katrina was able to rest her chin on the top of his head. She breathed in his delicious scent and lightly stroked the short hair at the nape of his neck. The texture felt softer than she'd expected, like rough velvet beneath her fingertips.

His breathing was warm against the top button of the white blouse she still wore and he wrapped his arms around her waist. They remained still for long minutes, each savoring the closeness, his hands gliding down her spine, just skimming the top of her ass.

"You're beautiful." When he looked up, the blue of his eyes appeared darker than ever.

"And you're overdressed." Moving her hands down his sides, she tugged at his T-shirt, easing it up. He helped her by raising his arms, and she pulled it over his head and dropped it to the floor.

As he lowered his hands, he ran his fingertips over her lips and kissed them before drawing one finger into her mouth. With an indrawn breath, he pushed a second finger between her lips while cupping her cheek with his other hand. She ran her tongue over the pads of his fingers before nipping lightly, then taking them deeper into her mouth.

The way he was sitting there, looking up at her as she sucked on his fingers, was incredibly sexy. She could tell he was as aroused as she was, yet he was letting her set the pace. Katrina could feel the heat between them shimmering in the air, penetrating her bloodstream. Her every nerve ending was alight with need.

His eyes were pools of naked need, inviting her into their depths. Releasing his fingers, she darted her tongue between his lips, lightly teasing. Demanding more, he caught hold of her hair. Pulling her head down to his, he filled her mouth with his tongue, energy and desire arcing from his body to hers.

Gasping, she broke free and leaned back. Nothing had prepared her for this moment. She was trembling with need and exhilaration. She wanted him so much, her whole body ached with longing. Knowing his need for her was just as intense… That was the most powerful feeling she had ever known.

Brushing her hair aside, he moved his lips to her neck, sucking and nipping at the taut skin just below her ear, and her knees weakened. He pulled her blouse out of the waistband of her pants, his fingers fumbling with the buttons, finally getting them undone before he slid it down her arms and let it fall. Sucking in a breath as he gazed at her, he pressed his lips to the curve of her breasts above the lace of her white bra.

Reaching around behind her to unhook the garment, he dragged it up above her breasts, lowering his head to dance his tongue across her skin. The sensation was almost too good to bear and she dropped her head to look at him, drinking in the sight of his face against her flesh as he took one nipple into his mouth.

When he sucked and nipped the sensitized bud, Katrina almost went into orbit. He paused and, with a soft whimper, she pushed herself against his mouth again. Glancing up with a wicked smile, he moved to the other breast and repeated the sweet torture.

With a final tug on her nipple, he took hold of her hands and moved them to his belt. Eagerly, she unbuckled him, feeling his stomach muscles tense as her fingertips brushed against them.

She leaned closer and whispered in his ear, "I think you should take your boots off now, don't you?"

He grinned. "Only if you get rid of your pants and shoes."

"Deal."

The gleam in his eye made her smile as he kicked off his boots. She removed her shoes then unzipped her pants and slid them down, kicking them off and adding them to the growing pile of items on the floor. Her bra followed. Standing before him in nothing but her panties felt deliciously exciting.

His gaze was serious as he looked up at her. "Before we go any further, I want to make sure you're okay with this."

"In case you hadn't noticed, I want this. I want you." She placed her hands on his face. "And I'd like you to be naked."

"I can do naked." His voice was gruff as he raised

his hips and removed his boxer briefs. "If that's what you want."

Katrina tilted her head to get a better look at him. "You're beautiful."

"I think I'm supposed to say that." His attempt at a laugh faded when she ran a hand along his length.

His eyelids fluttered and she exulted in her power over him as he twitched and grew against her fingers. When she withdrew her touch, he groaned and lifted his hips.

"Don't tease me, Katrina."

In response, she kneeled between his knees, taking him firmly in one hand. Spencer's low growl of anticipation made her smile, then she lowered her mouth to his head. Flicking out her tongue, she savored the first musky, salty taste of him. His breathing quickened and she fastened her lips over his tip.

Pulling him into her mouth slowly, she slid her other hand up and down his straining shaft. His thigh muscles tensed and quivered, and his breathing quickened until the sound of panting filled her ears.

"I won't last much longer..."

Ignoring his warning, she continued at the same pace, pleasuring him with her mouth and hand as his gasps became moans. His hips began to jerk and his hands gripped her hair as the warmth of his climax filled her mouth.

She was easing away from him when he reached down and lifted her with his hands on her waist. Hugging her to his chest, he held her close as his breathing subsided. After a minute or two, he turned his head to kiss her, his hands sliding down her body.

"I think we should both move onto the bed."

He rose and helped her to her feet, slipping his hands into the elastic of her underwear at the same time. Katrina wriggled as he tugged and, between them, they got the garment over her hips and down so she could step out of it.

Catching her by surprise, he swung her around until she had her back to him. Flattening his hand over her belly, he drew her firmly back against him until her ass was pressed tight against his pelvis. At the same time, he moved a hand around to the front of her body.

Katrina gasped as she felt his growing erection press into her spine. "Didn't you just...?"

"Yeah. But if we keep doing this, I could make a quick recovery."

KATRINA FELT WONDERFUL. Her nipples had been puckered and erect ever since she'd removed her bra. Now they hardened more as Spencer's fingers and thumbs closed around them, and he tweaked, pinched and rolled them.

Moving lower, he reached between her legs and gently brushed the tip of his index finger over one of her outer lips. The action coaxed a soft sigh from Katrina. Using his fingers, he parted her delicate inner folds. Dipping his fingertips into her cleft, he ran them gently around the opening, teasing her wider. She gave another moan, this one deep throated and hungry as he slid two fingers deep inside her.

She was soft, warm and very wet. Spencer wanted to take his time and explore her body at his leisure. But as he slid his fingers in and out of her, she was already squirming and rotating her hips in time with his movements, and he figured that, this time, slow was not a good option.

Dropping his head to nip at her neck, he pulled her down onto the bed with him, making sure he broke her fall with his body. When she shifted into a kneeling position, he took a moment to admire the perfect globes of her ass before shifting into position behind her. Moving her hips backward, Katrina sat on his thighs.

Her legs parted as he dipped his fingers between them to find her core.

"You're so hot and tight." He whispered the words into her hair and she moaned softly.

Her breath was coming fast, catching in her throat as he drove two fingers into her. Leaning forward, she pushed herself down onto them. He could feel her muscles already starting to tense and her hips were bucking. Her head dropped lower, and Spencer nuzzled her neck again.

He couldn't get enough of her. Of her satiny skin, her seductive natural scent, the way her body quivered in response to his slightest touch. But there was a deeper connection between them, an emotional intimacy more satisfying than anything physical.

"Feels so good." She ground out the words between clenched teeth.

Her hips ground against him and she leaned forward to give him better access. He found her clit with the thumb of one hand. She gasped and her back arched as he painted tight circles and figure eights over and around her bud. At the same time, he continued driving into her with his fingers, strumming her body until she was taut with pleasure.

"Let go and show me how good it feels," he murmured.

Feeling her whole body begin to stiffen, he withdrew his fingers. Katrina fell forward. Spencer pressed his palm flat against her clit and rocked against it gently, bringing the fingers of his other hand along the crease between her buttocks. When he finally thrust his fingers back inside her, she gripped them tight, her whole body shaking as she contracted around them. For an instant, it was like trying to hold onto a wildcat as she writhed and thrashed against him before she slumped forward.

Spencer watched in fascination as her shoulders and hips shook and her spine bowed. Silently, she trembled through her orgasm. Then, she stilled. Twisting to one side, Spencer pulled her with him, drawing her into his arms and kissing her gently.

After a few minutes, he raised on one elbow, watching her face. With her eyes closed, she could have been asleep, but she lifted one hand and traced lazy circles around his chest. He was lost in the wonder of her. He wanted her again so badly it was a physical ache.

"That was wonderful. Thank you."

He shook his head. "Thank *you*."

Her gaze traveled down his body. Lightly kissing him, she wrapped a hand around his length. "I guess that recovery you mentioned wasn't a boast. So there's just one other question..."

He pressed a kiss onto her lips. "In the pocket of my jeans."

ONCE SPENCER HAD the condom in place, he lay back against the pillows and Katrina straddled him. Dipping her hips, she held him at her entrance, letting him feel her tight heat. His groan made her heart skip a beat. Easing back, she slid along his length, still stunned at the ease with which they'd achieved this level of closeness. Her craving for him had only increased with greater intimacy.

When she kissed him, his response was instant and passionate, his tongue making love to her mouth. Lifting up her body, she held him in place beneath her. Tongues of fire darted outward from the point where their bodies connected, licking up her spine and along her limbs. Every part of her was aware of him, of them, of the promise of what was to come.

Slowly, mesmerized by the look in his eyes, she eased down. His eyes widened and he gasped as she pushed onto him and rotated around, then rose up again. Each time she repeated the action, she took more of him.

"That feels..."

"Too teasing?" she asked.

"Too perfect."

Encouraged, she lowered herself farther. The combination of stretching, tingling and heating was maddeningly good. Too good. He pressed a fingertip to her clit and thrust up into her. Having taken all of him inside her, she paused to catch her breath. The sensation of him filling her was stunning and exhilarating and new heat powered along every nerve ending.

His gaze claimed hers and refused to let go. Warm, feeling slightly rough against her softer flesh, his palms traced a path from her waist to her hips and back again. Shifting his pelvis beneath her, he increased the rhythm, and almost blew her mind.

"Ah." She dropped her head, curtaining them with her hair.

Spencer grinned. "You like that?"

"So much."

He repeated the action and she tightened her muscles around him, holding him more firmly. Claiming him. He increased the pace, his upward thrusts becoming less gentle, and Katrina tipped forward, bringing them into even closer contact. The look on his face was delicious. A clear indication of his enchantment, it made her feel wanted, appreciated and sexy as hell.

Wrapping his arms around her waist, he moved down the bed, pulling her with him. Keeping Katrina clamped tight to him, he rolled until she was beneath him with her back to the mattress.

"Is this okay?" He put his weight on his elbows. "I don't want to squish you."

"Maybe I like the idea of being squished by you." She arched her back suggestively.

He groaned, leaning down to kiss her before thrusting deep.

Katrina gasped. "Yes. Like that."

She tightened her legs around his hips and moved in time with him, grinding her pelvis into his, driven on by the exquisite friction of his hardness moving high inside her. He pulled out, almost completely free of her tight heat, before slamming back in. Pinned by his weight, her arms flung wide, Katrina strained against him, her body convulsing with pleasure.

The sound of ragged breathing filled the room as she came down from a high she'd never dreamed possible. Watching Spencer's face as he continued to thrust, she could see his concentration and sense him getting closer to his own release. Then his breathing changed, hitching and almost stopping, his neck muscles corded and his face blank. After one final thrust, he tilted forward and rested his head in the curve of her neck. She could feel the sheen of sweat on his skin and the shaking of his muscles.

A few minutes later, he turned his head and pressed his lips to hers, his eyes smiling. The kiss was soft and sweet and lasted for a long time. At some point, the shared peace turned to laughter about the cramp in his leg and the ache in her arm.

"Where are you going?" Katrina grumbled when he eventually pulled away. She didn't want to lose the feeling of his skin on hers, his muscles beneath her fingertips, his breath on her cheek.

"I'll be right back. Just need to lose the condom."

There was no awkwardness attached to the remark. For the first time in her life, she felt she could be completely open with another person.

Spencer headed to the bathroom, returning a few

minutes later to draw her back into his arms. "In case I forget to mention this before I fall asleep, you are amazing."

She smiled against his chest. "You're okay, too."

"Just okay?" He pretended to be hurt. "You're hard to please."

"I'm glad you figured that out. Get some sleep, Spencer." She reached up and patted his cheek. "Maybe next time you can please me enough to upgrade from 'okay' to 'good.'"

Chapter Fifteen

Although Katrina woke early, it was light enough for her to see Spencer's face on the pillow next to hers. His face was softened by sleep, some of the pressures of his work life and the pain of his past soothed away.

Or maybe it was the amazing sex?

She smothered a laugh at the thought. But it had been beyond amazing. She'd never experienced anything approaching the sexual energy between them. It had generated a connection so intense she could still feel it now. The intensity was a lot like an unbreakable bond. The thought was scary and exciting at the same time.

It also meant there was no chance of her going back to sleep. Slipping quietly from beneath the bed covers, she grabbed some clothes and headed for the bathroom. When she emerged, she checked the time on her cell. Five thirty.

She headed out to the kennel, nervous about what she would find and worried that she should have checked on the dogs earlier. Despite the veterinarian's reassurances, a night of passion was no excuse for not monitoring their condition.

Boris seemed fully awake and wagged his tail when she entered. Holly lifted her head and licked Katrina's hand when she stroked her, but flopped down and went back to sleep. Although he snored loudly, Dobby didn't stir at all. Katrina decided that figured. The greediest of the three dogs, he had probably consumed most of the drugged meat. She placed a bowl of water close to him, ready for when he did wake, then left the kennel.

Remembering Spencer's comments about starting the day with a decent breakfast, she decided to head to the twenty-four-hour convenience store and stock up on provisions. Snatching up her keys and purse, she headed out. Only as she was driving did she spare a thought for what Spencer would say about her recklessness in leaving the safety of his protective presence.

Were bad guys early risers? She knew being flippant wasn't a good attitude given the situation, but she was already midway between home and the store. She may as well keep going, get her breakfast supplies and put this lapse down to the distractions of the previous night. The combination of frightening and delightful distractions.

When she reached the store, the parking lot was almost empty and she pulled into a space close to the entrance, casting a wary glance around. There was no one close by and she dashed from the car to the entrance. Once inside, she grabbed a basket and tried not to look like she was sprinting as she snagged pastries and juice from the shelves. She was just heading toward the deli section, when the sight of a familiar figure stopped her in her tracks.

The answer to one of her earlier questions was standing with his back to her, clutching a bag of chips and a family-size pack of cookies. Some bad guys clearly were early risers. Either that, or they didn't go to bed at all. Judging by the munchies-busting foods in Kenyon Latimer's hands, Katrina figured the up-all-night option was more likely.

A wave of anger surged through her. Her sister was likely in deep trouble. For all Katrina knew, Eliza might be dead and this guy could be the cause. Yet he was able to do normal things like buy cookies and chips, while she didn't know what had happened to her twin.

Forgetting to be afraid, she marched up close and tapped him on the shoulder. He swung around fast. A little too fast for a man who had nothing to hide. Up close, he wasn't quite so good-looking. His skin was bad and the dark shadows beneath his eyes looked like bruises.

He frowned down at her from his superior height. "Do I know you?"

There was a nasty note in his voice that should have frightened her, but concern for her sister kept her anger level high. She was going to do this for Eliza and not be intimidated by some nasty AAG thug.

"No, but I think you knew my sister. Eliza Perry?"

She could almost see his mind working, assessing how to respond. In the end, he smiled. She found the expression even scarier than his scowl. "Oh, yeah.

You've been asking about her at the AAG ranch. I think I met her a few times."

He wasn't as polished as most of the other AAG members. As he spoke, his gaze wandered away from her face and he shifted from foot to foot. She tried to judge whether he could have been the man who broke into her house and threatened her with a blade. Although his build was similar, the voice was different. But she had been certain that the guy with the knife had been disguising the way he spoke.

Keep him talking... Maybe she could learn something and see if she recognized him.

"You think you met her? Most people in the AAG remember her because of her dog, Dobby."

"Oh, yeah. So many people have been through the center lately, it's hard to remember them all." He took a couple of steps back, as though trying to get away.

"So you did know her?" Katrina persisted.

"I think it's too much to say I knew her. If she was at the ranch, I'd have met her." His eyes darted toward the checkout counter. "Look, I have to—"

"Did you ever speak to her?"

"Hey." Although he still looked cagey, she could sense him getting annoyed. "I already told you, I don't remember. Just stay out of things that are none of your business."

The attitude switch from nervy to nasty happened so fast it almost unbalanced her. In an instant, he became someone she wouldn't mess with. Turning his back, he stalked away from her. Tossing aside the chips and cookies, he headed toward the exit. Moments later, she caught a glimpse of him crossing the parking lot with his head down and his hands in his pockets.

Although Kenyon's attitude wasn't proof that he knew anything about Eliza's disappearance, he wasn't behaving like an innocent man. None of her business? Eliza was her *sister.* If her welfare wasn't Katrina's business, she didn't know what was. She sensed she'd just taken a step closer to discovering what had happened to her twin. She also felt she'd just poked a hornet's nest and put herself in even more danger.

As she paid for her purchases, she glanced out the window at the dimly lit parking lot. The last time she'd seen him, Kenyon had been walking away. He could easily have doubled back and be waiting for her in the darkness…

"Can someone carry these to my car?" she asked the cashier.

"Sure." She pressed a buzzer and a minute or two later a young man appeared from the back of the store. "This lady needs you to carry her bags."

Feeling slightly embarrassed at asking for help when she was perfectly capable of lifting the light weight of her purchases, Katrina followed the guy out to her vehicle.

"Could you load them into the trunk and, um…" She extracted a generous amount of cash from her purse and handed it to him. "And would you mind waiting here until I've driven away?"

"No problem." He nodded sympathetically. "My sister had a stalker problem a few years ago. I hope it works out for you."

Anxious to get away, she didn't want to get involved in explanations. After thanking him for his help, she got into her car and drove away. When she pulled up outside her house, Spencer was headed down the front steps in sweatpants and a T-shirt with his hair standing on end.

"What is it? What's wrong?" she demanded as she dashed from the car. "Have you heard something about Eliza?"

"No. I woke up and you were gone." He caught her by the shoulders as she almost hurtled into him. "Don't ever do that to me again, Katrina."

Looking up at his face, she saw panic etched in the fine lines around his eyes and understood its cause. Four years ago, he'd lost the woman he loved. And she'd disappeared without letting him know where she was going, just as there was a faceless figure out there threatening to harm her.

Although she was angry with herself for being so thoughtless, a tiny part of her exulted in the knowledge that he cared. Really cared. For now, she stored that little piece of information up for later. Right now, they had more important things to talk about.

"I got juice and croissants." She held up the bag.

"In that case, let's go inside."

AFTER CHECKING ON the dogs, who were all sleepy but recovering well, they ate breakfast and Katrina gave Spencer an account of what had happened at the store. When she'd finished, he put his head in his hands.

"Tell me you didn't really approach Kenyon Latimer."

She tossed back her hair defiantly. "I didn't see why he should be walking around without a care in the world while Eliza could be in trouble. Or worse. If he knows where she is, he should be made to tell us. And I wanted to look him in the eye while I asked him about her."

"I agree with you, but you need to leave this to me and my MVPD colleagues. Someone has already driven a car at you, broken into your house, drugged our dogs and threatened you at knifepoint."

"I tried to keep Latimer talking to see if I could tell whether he was the person who broke in here," Katrina said. "It could have been, but I'm not sure."

"Katrina."

"Hmm?" She was buttering a croissant and didn't glance up from her task.

Spencer placed a finger under her chin and tilted her face until she was looking at him. "You are not to go near Latimer, or any other member of the AAG, again without my permission. Is that understood?"

"I like it when you're strict." Her smile was full of mischief and promise.

He laughed. "I'll bear that in mind. Right now, I need you to agree that you'll do as I ask."

"Don't worry. I won't be going anywhere near Latimer again." She shuddered. "The way he turned nasty so fast was frightening. Even though he denied knowing her, I think he had something to do with Eliza's disappearance."

"If he did, we'll bring him to justice. But we'll do

it by the book. The MVPD book." He took her hand. "Trust me."

Something flickered in the depths of her eyes. For an instant, he saw years of unhappy memories, tears that never fell and cries for help that had never been uttered.

"I do trust you." Although she smiled, her lip trembled. "You're the first person I've ever said that to. Or even about."

It would have been easy in that instant to feel the weight of his responsibility toward her. But he wasn't concerned about letting her down. That wouldn't happen. She had become too important to him. With everything that was going on, it probably wasn't the right time to tell her that, but it was the truth. And it was a powerful feeling.

Breakfast was interrupted by the ringing of his cell phone. He checked the display.

"It's Rafe Colton."

He answered the call, and Rafe launched into an account of how he, Ainsley and Marlowe had met with Sebastian Clark, the guy born the same night—and in the same hospital—as Ace.

"He was clearly his parents' child, that much was obvious from his resemblance to them, but we asked him to have a DNA test to be sure," Rafe said. "We paid to have it done and it was expedited. The results, which were available within twenty-four hours, were as expected. He's not Ace Colton."

"So we keep trying," Spencer said.

"Of course." Rafe sounded dispirited. "But it's like looking for a needle in a haystack. The real Ace Colton could be anywhere in the world, for all we know. He could even be deceased. He was born a bit frail, remember?"

"That could be true, but something tells me he's out there somewhere. Waiting for the chance to bring himself into your lives."

"Yeah, as long as we can avoid any more Jace Smith style impostors," Rafe sighed.

Spencer ended the call and turned to Katrina. "You heard that?"

"I got most of it." She crumbled the remains of her croissant. "What you said about the real Ace Colton waiting for his chance. Does that mean you believe in fate?"

He gave it some thought. "I suppose I do. Life seems to have a way of unfolding over time in unexpected ways. And, with hindsight, a belief in destiny helps us make sense of things that have happened in our past. I'm not sure I can apply that to all of the things that have come my way, but it's useful to straighten some of them out."

She nodded, seeming satisfied with his answer. He didn't ask her what she was thinking or why it mattered. They hadn't had any deep conversations about their beliefs. Maybe this would be the first of many.

"What are the plans for today?" Katrina asked.

"I want to call in at the station and find out where Kerry is with her background checks into the AAG members. When I know what she has for us, I'll decide where to go from there." He got to his feet. "And I need you to follow my rules."

"What are they?"

"You stay with me at all times. No leaving my sight."

Her smile was brilliant. "Suzie and Laurence are covering my classes, so I can follow those rules."

So Spencer believed in fate. Katrina had always felt that destiny played a part in the way life panned out. In a world where there were so many people, she thought how unlikely it was to randomly meet that one person who would make a difference in your story. In a certain place, and at a certain time, making a connection to someone you were intended to meet… No, there had to be an external force at work.

If Spencer felt the same way, did that mean he thought they were meant to be together? She pulled herself back from that idea. Why was she even thinking that way? It was way too soon to even picture them together in any long-term sense. The connection between them might be beyond anything she had ever known, but it was too much, too sudden, too scary.

Still, it didn't hurt to know they were on the same wavelength…

With her dogs—who were both fully restored to health—safely deposited at the training center, they were headed toward the police station with Boris in his compartment at the back of Spencer's vehicle.

"With luck, Kerry will have discovered where Latimer is from," Spencer said. "She should also have found out if he has a criminal record."

"If Rusty is right about him selling drugs, it doesn't sound like the sort of thing he just started recently."

Katrina thought again about Eliza, and how easy it would have been for her to get drawn back into that lifestyle. Her sister was vulnerable and a man like Latimer would be able to easily persuade her to do what he wanted.

"Latimer hasn't been around Mustang Valley for long." Spencer pulled into the parking lot at the MVPD building. "He's not known to us here as a drug dealer, but that doesn't mean he hasn't been arrested in another area."

"He could still be trouble and not have a criminal record," Katrina pointed out.

"Unfortunately, that's true. If he's like Aidan Hannant and has slipped beneath the law-enforcement radar, there's not much we can do about it."

They left the vehicle, after having released Boris. Skirting around the building, Spencer took his canine partner to his training session before returning to the front entrance. In the lobby, Katrina recalled their first meeting with a shudder. She'd flown through the door, almost knocking him off his feet, yet he'd treated her with courtesy and respect. Was it any wonder he'd questioned her reliability when she'd been so close to the edge of her control?

When they reached Spencer's office, he used the internal telephone system to contact his colleague, Kerry. When she arrived, she was carrying a file of papers and she wore a harassed expression.

"I still can't find anything on Micheline Anderson or Leigh Dennings," she said. "I think we have to accept that they are who they say they are. Hardworking, dedicated to the good of the community, both of them willing to go the extra mile to help those less fortunate than themselves."

"When did Micheline found the Affirmation Alliance Group?" Spencer asked.

"Forty years ago. She's a gifted self-help guru and healer, who quickly built up a following and grew the AAG into a thriving business." Kerry consulted her notes. "Leigh is twenty-six. She's worked for the group for a few years and appears to be devoted to Micheline. Using her looks to her advantage, her role appears to be to charm new males into becoming members and stop any others from drifting."

"And Kenyon Latimer?" Spencer asked.

"He's a different story." Kerry's expression changed to one of distaste. "He was arrested for possession of heroin last year in Tucson—his hometown—and is a small-time troublemaker. He has a record of low-level offenses up and down Arizona, dating back to the age of eighteen. I haven't started on out-of-state records yet."

"Is there any information on my sister's whereabouts?" Katrina asked. She didn't hold out much hope but figured it was always worth asking.

"I'm sorry," Kerry said. "We don't have anything more to report."

"I'm going to check my messages, then Chief Barco has given me permission to spend the rest of the day working from Katrina's office," Spencer told Kerry. "You can reach me there if you need me. I'll be back to collect Boris after lunch."

As they left, Katrina turned to him. Nothing in what she'd heard gave her any hope for her sister. If anything, her spirits were lower than ever.

"If Eliza got mixed up with Latimer, she didn't stand a chance."

Spencer hooked an arm around her shoulders, drawing her into a quick hug. "We still haven't established any connection between them."

"But we both know you will."

He didn't answer and that was all the confirmation she needed.

THAT EVENING, THEY walked the dogs in the park.

"They get along," Spencer said as the three canines snuffled along the ground together, excitedly chasing the same scents.

"That's good, isn't it?" Katrina asked. "I mean, if we liked each other but our dogs hated each other, it wouldn't make for an easy life."

He didn't answer and she wondered if she'd said too much. Did he think she was pushing him into an admission that they had a future? Or was she just overthinking, as usual?

Holly brought her a stick, dropping it at her feet and wagging her tail as she invited her to throw it and Katrina focused on the game. She could overthink anytime.

When they left the park, Spencer suggested ordering pizza, then he checked his cell and groaned. "I'd completely forgotten."

"Hot date?" she teased.

"Sibling date. I'm supposed to be meeting my brother and sister at Mustang Valley Steak and Seafood in ten minutes."

"It's not a problem. I can take the dogs home," Katrina said.

"Hey." He caught hold of her hands, swinging her around to face him. "The rules about not letting you out of my sight haven't changed. That's if you're okay with dinner for four instead of for two?"

"I guess so. As long as your siblings won't mind?" He had mentioned her meeting his brother and sister at some point, but she'd thought it was just a throwaway remark. Suddenly, it had become a reality.

"Mind?" He started to laugh. "They'll be delighted to be able to gossip about me. There's just one problem." He pointed to the dogs.

"I could call Suzie and see if we can leave them with her for a few hours," Katrina suggested. "She lives close to the restaurant."

"Sounds perfect."

By the time they'd dropped off the dogs at Suzie's place, they arrived a little later than planned. Spencer's brother and sister were already seated at a table for three, and there was an initial fuss as the captain changed the arrangements to make room for Katrina. She was aware of Jarvis and Bella exchanging a couple of meaningful glances while this was going on.

"Are you going to introduce us?" Bella asked, when they were finally seated. She was petite and pretty with reddish-blond hair and green eyes. Katrina got the impression that appearances were deceptive and that she was nobody's fool.

"This is Katrina Perry," Spencer said.

"Oh, I know who you are." Bella flapped a hand. "You own the dog-training place. The one with the cute name."

"Look Who's Walking." Katrina smiled at her enthusiasm.

"Yes. I'm a lifestyle blogger but I did an exposé on dog thefts. One of the people I interviewed mentioned your classes."

"In a good way, I hope?"

"Oh, yes. She raved about how you taught her dog to sit and stay and not chase the mailman," Bella said. "She even showed me the graduation pictures."

"Graduation pictures?" Jarvis sounded bemused as he joined in the conversation. "Are we still talking about dogs?"

Katrina nodded. "We have a graduation ceremony at the end of our puppy classes. It started out as a joke, but the owners love it, so now we give out certificates and we take pictures of the dogs wearing a ceremonial cap."

They continued talking about dogs and training as they decided on their food, and Katrina was surprised at how quickly she'd relaxed around the other two Colton triplets. Spencer had talked about the way they made jokes that no one else understood, but Jarvis and Bella appeared to be on their best behavior around her.

"I know the focus is all on the AAG and the work they're doing to support the earthquake victims, but

I've been hearing about how much the police and first responders have been involved in the rebuilding efforts," Jarvis said as they were eating.

"Chief Barco was keen for his officers to get involved in the community and be hands-on in helping people who'd been affected," Spencer explained. "Rather than simply fund-raising."

"All we hear about these days is the AAG. You'd think no one else ever did any good work in Mustang Valley. I know they have worked hard and what they've done has benefited the community but..." Bella pulled a face. "All the publicity feels a bit *icky*."

"Icky." Spencer looked across the table at Jarvis with a straight face. "It's one of those intellectual words. Taught in only the best schools."

"Oh, you." Bella gave him a shove that nearly knocked him off his chair. "Does he tease you like this, Katrina?"

It was a blatant attempt to find out more about their relationship and Katrina snagged Spencer's gaze. His eyes were brimming with laughter and she hid a smile. "Sometimes."

Bella pouted. "Okay. I get it. You're going to be as secretive as he is."

Jarvis, who was a ranch hand at Payne Colton's Rattlesnake Ridge Ranch, talked about the shock waves that had hit after the shooting of his boss. "Hope you catch the guy who did it soon," he told his brother.

"That's the plan." Spencer nodded wearily.

The time passed quickly, and when they'd finished eating, Katrina felt like she'd known Jarvis and Bella forever. For someone who didn't make friends easily, it was a good feeling. Like coming home after a long, hard day.

"We must do this again soon." Bella hugged her as they parted at the restaurant door.

"We must," Jarvis said. "It's nice to see my brother with a smile on his face again."

Chapter Sixteen

The following day passed slowly with no new developments. That evening, once the dogs had been fed and settled for the night, they ate at the kitchen table.

"Goodness, you must be hungry," Katrina commented when she saw how fast Spencer was consuming his meal.

"No. I just want to finish eating quickly so I can take you to bed."

She gasped, then started to laugh. "I appreciate your honesty."

He leaned across the table to kiss her. "I want that to happen a lot. All the time."

"Sorry?"

"This feeling that I have to finish my food quickly so I can make love to you. The first time was wonderful. Last night was equally perfect, but I'll never be able to get enough of you."

"Oh." She wasn't sure exactly what he was saying, but his words had a permanent ring to them that she liked the sound of. Right now, she was more focused on the gleam in Spencer's eyes and his delicious kisses. "I'm finished eating now."

As he got to his feet and held out his hand, heat raced through her body. When they reached the bedroom, Spencer pulled her tight against him, running his hand up and down her spine. "I've been thinking about this all day."

"Me, too." She melted against him with a sigh.

"In that case, I think we should get rid of these clothcs."

Within minutes, they had both discarded their garments and were lying on the bed. Spencer moved to lie between Katrina's thighs, then smoothed a warm palm along her body from shoulder to hip. After a few minutes, when she was totally relaxed beneath his touch, he began to stroke along the inside of one thigh.

When his fingers found her, she jerked with a combination of pleasure and surprise. His touch was magical, instantly making her whole body melt with desire.

"I want you now," she murmured.

The look in his eyes was a perfect balance between vulnerability and strength. He reached for the condom he'd placed on the nightstand and quickly sheathed himself. After pushing apart her thighs, he placed a hand beneath her and lifted her to him. Pressing up against her, he dipped into her briefly, then pulled back.

Desperate for more, Katrina wriggled her hips closer, wrapping her legs tight around his hips. Tilting up her pelvis, she reached a hand between them and guided him to her. Spencer's breathing changed, and when she looked up, his gaze was bright on her face.

He entered her so slowly she thought she might pass out from anticipation. His smooth, hard length moved inside her just a little way, pulled out slightly, then came all the way out to glide over her clit before pushing back inside again.

"So good." Her back arched and her head tilted back.

His fingertips dug into her ass as he lifted her higher, drawing her closer and sinking deeper into her. His mouth found her shoulder, nipping and sucking as he drove into her hard and fast.

"The way we fit together feels perfect." His voice was harsh, his eyes glazed. There was a sheen of sweat on his face, neck and chest.

He changed his rhythm, using his hips to grind against her, pounding into, pulling out and grazing up against her clit. Her release was beginning, coiling low in her belly, tightening her muscles and igniting her nerve endings.

"More, please." Her voice was little more than a whimper.

Pushing her knees up and back toward her chest, he powered into her, hard and fast. Instantly, she tightened and vibrated around him. And then she was falling over the edge, bucking her hips into him, contracting so hard around him her muscles ached. Her body felt like it was being flung around by a giant hand, like it was turned inside out and then pulled back again.

As she struggled to breathe, she was barely aware of Spencer's continuing thrusts. As she was taken over by another series of pulsing contractions, she sensed his peak as he held himself deep inside her. He bowed his head into her neck, growling against her skin as his muscles began to quake.

Eventually, they both stopped shaking and started to breathe normally. Spencer turned until they were lying on their sides and he could cradle her in his arms. Exhausted, Katrina felt her mind empty of anything other than the sound of his breathing and the feel of his heart beating against her cheek. She felt completely relaxed in that perfect moment of intimacy.

Sleeping next to Spencer had quickly become her new normal and she wanted to do it for a very long time. When she lifted her head to tell him how she felt, he was already dozing.

SPENCER WOKE WITH a start when his cell phone buzzed in the middle of the night. It didn't happen often and he knew it must be important. The sound hadn't disturbed Katrina, and he eased her away from him, trying not to wake her.

Even in the urgency of needing to check his cell, he took a moment to appreciate how incredible she was. How amazing things were between them.

Call me pls.

The message was from Kerry Wilder.

He gathered up his clothes, then carried them through to the living room and started pulling them on as, with his cell awkwardly held against his ear, he made the call.

"What's going on?"

"There was some trouble at Joe's Bar a few hours ago. One of the responding officers was injured."

Images of what he had pictured when Billie was captured flashed through his mind. "Who was it? What happened?"

"It was Officer Donovan. He was punched as he tried to arrest a guy. He's fine, just a cut lip and a few bruises, but the guy who hit him got away..." Kerry paused. "I thought you'd want to know who it was."

Spencer could have taken a few guesses, with one obvious name at the top of his list, but he played along. "Go on."

"It was Kenyon Latimer. Other customers reported that he appeared drunk, or high, and that he was looking for trouble from the minute he walked into the place."

"Where is Latimer now?" Spencer asked.

"We don't know his exact location. After he hit Officer Donovan, he ran off toward Mustang Park. I've posted a lookout at the AAG ranch in case he turns up there," Kerry said. "I've also got a vehicle patrolling the area, but it seems he's lying low in the park. I'm reluctant to send officers on a manhunt when we don't know if Latimer could be armed."

She was doing everything right and her caution was understandable, but Spencer could feel her frustration. Latimer had proved to be tricky so far and they already knew he could be violent.

"There is another reason why I called you. Latimer left his jacket in Joe's."

Spencer was on his feet and moving toward the door.

"Bring it to the park entrance. I'll meet you there with Boris in ten minutes."

As he released Boris from the kennel and gave pats to the other sleepy dogs, he considered the situation. He was leaving Katrina alone, something he'd sworn he wouldn't do. But there was a police officer watching the AAG ranch and Latimer was pinned down in Mustang Park.

She was safer now, in her own bed with the doors and windows locked, than she'd been since this whole thing started because Latimer, the person who'd threatened her, had other things on his mind. If Boris was his usual efficient self, they could have Latimer in custody before she even woke. In the meantime, Spencer would get a patrol car to do a regular check on the house.

When he reached the park entrance, Kerry and Detective PJ Doherty were waiting for him. Spencer's body armor was in the rear of his vehicle and he donned it before releasing Boris from his compartment and getting the dog into his own protective gear. Although Boris was calm, his eyes were shining and his tail was wagging. He knew he would soon be needed on a job and that was his favorite thing.

When Spencer joined his colleagues, he overheard a radio message from Lizzie Manfred reporting that there was no change out at the AAG ranch.

"Nothing new to report here, either," Kerry confirmed. "As far as we're aware, Latimer is still in the park."

"It's a big area for Boris to cover." PJ's expression was skeptical.

"He's an experienced dog." Spencer had complete faith in his partner. "And, if he has a scent, he should be able to track Latimer easily."

Kerry had covered Latimer's jacket with a plastic evidence bag. Spencer pulled on a glove before removing the jacket to ensure he didn't confuse the dog. Although a number of other people could have handled the garment since Latimer had worn it, he wanted Boris to get as much of the target's scent as possible.

He crouched and snapped the fingers of his ungloved hand to Boris. The dog obediently came to sit in front of him. Spencer held out the jacket and Boris sniffed it. The dog didn't need a command; the presence of the garment was enough. After a moment or two, he gave a snort as though indicating he knew what he needed to do.

Spencer attached a tracking line to the canine's harness. He didn't always use one, but at night and in a large open space, he didn't want Boris to get too far ahead and risk the possibility of losing sight of him.

"I'll maintain radio silence, as I don't want to alert the target to my presence, but I have it with me if I need to contact you in an emergency," he told Kerry and PJ.

With that, he and Boris took off in search of Latimer. The park was a different place at night, darkness altering its familiar tracks and forms and giving them a sinister twist. Nose to the ground, and pulling hard on the line, Boris almost flew along the central path. He reached a row of large shrubs and paused, snuffling along its length. This was a danger point for Spencer and he eased his weapon from its shoulder holster.

If Latimer was armed and hiding in those bushes, it could be a trap.

After a minute of sniffing, Boris moved on, straining in a new direction. His eagerness was a clear indication that he knew exactly where Latimer had gone. The next time the dog paused, it was next to a large willow tree. Standing at the base of the trunk, Boris looked up and began to eagerly sniff the air.

Could Latimer be hiding among the branches? The willow was sturdy, but Spencer wasn't sure a person would be able to climb it. Squatting beside his canine partner, he removed a flashlight from his utility belt and shone it up into the leaves. He couldn't see anything unusual.

"If he was here, he's gone," he whispered to the dog.

Boris didn't seem convinced. His sturdy body bristled with excitement and he stood to attention, his ears pointed and his eyes bright.

As Spencer straightened, he noticed that the earth around the tree had been disturbed, as though it had recently been dug up. Shining the flashlight beam wider, he caught a glimpse of something more alarming. A few feet away, he could see what might be a shallow grave.

Before he could investigate, the slightest sound behind him made him turn to look. It was enough to ensure that the blow meant for the back of his skull caught him on the side of his head. As he fell forward onto the sandy ground, he dropped the flashlight and its beam illuminated Latimer standing over him, a rock in his hand.

Letting go of Boris's line, he managed to utter one slurred word. "Leave."

The dog's instinct would be to remain with his handler. Overriding that was one of the hardest things to teach a police dog. Even now, as Latimer raised the rock again, Spencer couldn't be sure what Boris would do. Would he obey and go for help, or stay and try to save his master?

It was his final thought before pain seared through his head and darkness engulfed him.

STRETCHING SLEEPILY, KATRINA reached out a hand for Spencer. When she found that his side of the bed was cold, she frowned and sat up. It was still dark. Where could he have gone at this time?

Doubt instantly flooded her. Was he regretting getting so close, so fast? The hints he'd dropped about wanting to make love to her all the time had sounded like he wanted a long-term relationship. Was this his way of backing off, of telling her that what he actually wanted was only physical, and his sweet-talking her was just a part of that?

She knew what was happening. Her old trust issues were too raw to lie down and die completely. When she was with Spencer, she felt sure of him. It was at times like this that the doubts crept in and prodded her. What she needed was to feel his arms around her.

Maybe he was in the living room, working on his laptop. She slid out of bed, pulled on her clothes and headed through to the other room. The small house was too quiet for him to be anywhere else and she frowned.

She checked her cell phone but there were no messages. Surely, he would have let her know if he'd had to go out in the middle of the night?

With almost perfect timing, the display on her cell lit up. Every other thought went out of her head when she saw who the message was from. *Eliza...*

I need you. Come quick. Where we used to hang out as kids in the park. E x

Hope bubbled up inside her like an underground spring rising to the surface. It was exactly the sort of message Eliza always sent when she was in trouble and she wanted money from Katrina.

The easiest way to get to the place where she and Eliza used to play was to enter the park using the old gates on Western Drive. She remembered how they used to sneak in that way as kids and how her grandpa would scold them and ask how he'd know where to start if he needed to come looking for them.

But it was nighttime, and Eliza's message sounded urgent, so Katrina was going to take the quickest route, even if it wasn't the safest. Before she headed out to her car, she spared a thought for Spencer. He'd been so worried when she'd gone to the store without letting him know where she was. Although she had no clue to his whereabouts right now, she sent him a message letting him know that Eliza had been in touch and that she'd gone to meet her. That should reassure him.

After pausing to find a flashlight in one of the

kitchen cabinets and to put on boots instead of her sneakers, she set off. Because of the time, the roads were quiet and she reached her destination in minutes. It was only as she left her car and looked up at the old gates that the first doubts hit her.

She was alone in the early hours of the morning, about to enter an isolated but enclosed outdoor space, and if Spencer didn't pick up her message, no one knew she was here. It was taking recklessness to a whole new level.

Inside her, caution went to war with her responsibility to her sister. The time she'd spent agonizing over her twin's welfare had taken its toll on Katrina's own well-being. She *had* to know how her sister was, for her own sake as well as Eliza's. She'd come this far; the final few steps would be easy.

The night air was stifling and sticky, and sweat coated her skin as she followed the tracks. The route from the main entrance was familiar, but her childhood memory soon kicked in and she easily found her way to the dip in the ground where she'd seen the kids several days earlier.

Shining her flashlight around, she picked out the trees she and Eliza used to climb. And over there was the big willow tree. They used to sit beneath its overhanging branches and tell stories about princesses and knights. But there was no sign of her sister. Instead, the silence was unnerving. She turned in a circle, trying to pick out a figure in the darkness.

There! A faint movement caught her attention and she heaved a sigh of relief.

"Eliza?"

She took a step back, stumbling slightly on tree roots as Kenyon Latimer appeared in the circle of her flashlight with a gun in his hand.

"Sorry to disappoint you." His grin made her flesh crawl. "But I did warn you not to poke your nose in."

"I don't understand." Katrina looked around her wildly. Could Spencer have been right all along when he speculated that Eliza might be the one who was threatening her? Was her sister working with Latimer? "Where's Eliza? That message came from her cell phone."

"You mean this one?" He held up a familiar pink, sparkly cell. "I had fun reading her messages. She sure knew how to play you, twin sister."

From nowhere, it felt as if an invisible gale was blowing, pushing Katrina back, numbing her brain and forcing her body to slow down. Despite the summer temperatures, her teeth chattered as though she was chilled. "You did know her."

"Yeah, I knew Eliza." He looked over his shoulder. "We had a good thing going on for the short time she was at the ranch. I even liked her. I thought we could have made something of the start we had."

Katrina choked back a sob. If Eliza had left behind Dobby *and* her cell phone, did she really want to hear the answer to her next question? "What happened to her?"

His expression changed, becoming sad and furtive at the same time. She didn't like those quick glances he kept taking over his shoulder. "She told me she was a former addict and I tried to get her hooked on heroin again."

"Why would you do that?" Katrina momentarily forgot her fear of the gun pointing her way and let shock show through. "After all the trouble she'd gone through to get clean, why would you want to drag her back down again?"

"Hey." His voice was sharp. "You think I don't want the same things you do? Someone to come home to each day? To care for me and be by my side as I grow older? But I know that won't happen with a person who isn't addicted. Although Eliza liked what she saw in me, she wasn't going to stick around if she was clean. So I tried to remind her how good drugs can feel. When I asked her to get high with me, she refused."

Katrina experienced a fierce pride in her sister. She knew how hard it had been for Eliza to fight her cravings, yet, not only had she beaten her habit, but she had also managed to refuse this man to whom she had been attracted…and the allure of relapsing. That had shown incredible strength.

"I may have done a little more than usual because I was showing off to Eliza, so when she turned me down, I got a little crazy," Latimer continued. "I held her down and forcibly injected her. But the stuff I gave her was bad."

Katrina swallowed hard. "Are you saying she's dead?"

"I'm sorry. It wasn't what I wanted." He looked over his shoulder again. "She told me about this spot where she used to spend great times with her twin as a kid. She talked about how she hoped the two of you could start fresh one day. I thought this would be the best place for her."

Risking a movement of her flashlight, she illuminated the area behind him. It became clear what he kept looking at. A few feet away, just behind him, there was a disturbed patch of earth, the exact size and shape of a body.

"Is that…?" She lifted a hand to her lips.

"Yeah." He nodded. "I buried her where I thought she'd be at peace. I come here most days now, even keep my stuff buried here. It's like she's guarding it for me."

Katrina bit back a sob. Her troubled sister had known so little peace, but to be robbed of her life in such a way? By a selfish man who wanted to use her as his partner in addiction… She choked off her anger, turning her thoughts in another direction.

"So you were the person warning me off all this time? It was all you?" She was having trouble with that. Somehow Latimer didn't seem competent or organized enough to have orchestrated the threats that had been made against her. "You did it all on your own? You hired Cordelia Mellor to pose as Christie Foster? You got Aidan Hannant to warn me off? You were behind the break-ins? You drugged my dogs? And the plan to discredit me, so no one would listen to me? You came up with that?"

Even as she listed all the things that had happened since she started searching for Eliza, she got the feeling he wasn't really listening. His focus was on Eliza's grave.

"Look, I didn't want to do that. But I had to try to stop you from finding the truth." He ran a hand through his hair. "You think I like threatening women?"

She still couldn't see this man, this shaky, *weak* man, having enough energy and intelligence to go through with the plan to intimidate her. But that wasn't the most important thing she needed to think about right now.

Although he genuinely appeared to feel bad, Katrina reminded herself that he had killed her sister. And now *she* knew everything. The thought struck fresh terror into her. There was no way she was getting out of this alive. Unless…

"Sergeant Colton knows where I am," she said, bluffing. It was true. Sort of. If only Spencer had checked his messages…

"Him? I'd almost forgotten."

He pointed to one side of Eliza's grave. There, slumped on the ground like a pile of dirty laundry, was Spencer. He wasn't moving, and from the dark slick covering the left half of his head and face, it appeared that he was bleeding heavily.

Forgetting the danger, she started forward. "What have you done to him?"

"I hit him with a rock when he found my drug stash and saw where I'd buried Eliza," Latimer said. "I think he's dead."

Chapter Seventeen

"What have you done to him?"

Even though it sounded like it was coming from a long way off, Spencer knew that voice. If he could just move past the persistent drumbeat inside his skull, he might be able to figure out whom it belonged to.

The person who answered wasn't as helpful. It was a man, but he didn't speak clearly and the only words Spencer could make out were "drug stash" and "Eliza." They should mean something, but his head felt like it had been filled with cotton balls and rational thinking wasn't an option.

He should probably try moving, but it was easier to stay like this with his cheek resting on the sandy ground and leaf litter. He wondered why he couldn't feel any pain. Liquid, sticky and warm, was oozing from the wound on the top of his head and trickling down his face. He didn't know how much blood he'd lost, but it felt like a lot…

Katrina!

That was whose voice he'd heard. And the person replying had been talking about Spencer finding the stash of drugs and the shallow grave. A brief memory came back in a rush and he saw Kenyon Latimer lifting a rock, about to bring it crashing down on his head.

Did Boris get away? He couldn't ask the question out loud, but he pinned his hopes on his canine partner's experience and resilience.

Pain kicked in along with his memory. It felt like his head had been accidentally placed into the sort of machine that compacted junk cars into tiny metal cubes. Even so, he should try to move. Katrina was facing her sister's killer. He couldn't leave her to do that alone. But how could he help her when even blinking made him nauseous?

There was a change in the air around him as someone drew closer. He remained still, playing dead until he knew for sure what was going on. A whiff of Katrina's scent filled his nostrils and then she dropped to her knees beside him. Her nearness comforted him, but now she had her back to Latimer. That made her vulnerable to the guy who had hit Spencer on the head with a rock. He could try the same tactic he'd used on Spencer and hit Katrina…

Through half-closed eyes, Spencer observed her turning to talk over her shoulder to Latimer. "If you're right, and he's dead, there'll be no hiding place for you. The police will make sure they hunt down a cop killer."

She lifted Spencer's hand, holding it to her cheek. As she did, he shakily lifted his other hand, holding his middle finger over his lips in a "shh" gesture before reaching for the gun that was lying at his side. At first, he wasn't sure she'd seen what he did, but then he noticed the sheen of tears on her cheek and she gave a tiny nod. Holding her flashlight steady, she made sure the scene was illuminated.

"No way is that happening." Latimer's voice shook as he cocked the gun. "None of this was my fault. I can't go down for accidentally killing Eliza or bashing a cop over the head because he saw where I hide my drug stash."

Summoning every ounce of strength he had, Spencer rose suddenly, pushed Katrina to the ground and angled his body up to get a clear view. Shooting to wound was a risky tactic and most police marksmen were not skilled enough to take that chance. Luckily for Latimer, Spencer was army trained, plus he wanted Eliza's killer to face a court and answer for his crimes.

With a single shot, he caught Latimer just above his right elbow. The guy's lower arm swung loose as he cried out and dropped the gun. Katrina darted forward and grabbed the weapon at the same time that a large, familiar figure burst through the trees with an excited bark.

Latimer was staggering around, wailing and clutching his arm, as Kerry and PJ appeared with their weapons drawn.

"MVPD. On your knees with your hands behind your head," PJ ordered.

"I can't. He shot me. Broke my arm," Latimer whined.

"I can't see anything wrong with your legs." PJ wasn't known for his sympathetic nature.

Still complaining, Latimer got to his knees. Through

a haze of pain, Spencer heard PJ telling him he was under arrest and Kerry calling for medical help.

Katrina took Spencer's gun, made it safe and placed it on the ground with the one she'd removed from Latimer. Then she leaned closer. "Can you talk?"

"No." He pulled her down to him. "But you can still hold me."

She made a sound that was halfway between a laugh and a sob. "I don't want to hurt you."

"I'll take my chances. I've been finding out lately that love comes with risks."

Her body was warm around his for a few seconds, then a wet nose was thrust into Spencer's hand and Boris's tail thumped hard on the ground between them.

"I guess even the most well-trained dog can be forgiven for wanting to know if his master is okay," Katrina said.

"Boris is a hero." Kerry came to kneel beside them. "We didn't know what was going on when he emerged from the park without you. But he started charging up to us, barking and wagging his tail, then running back toward the park entrance. It was clear he wanted us to follow him. He led us straight to you."

A few minutes later, they heard the wail of an approaching ambulance siren.

Katrina turned to Kerry. "Can you take Boris with you?"

"Of course. Why do you ask?"

"Because I'm going with Spencer to the hospital." She lifted his hand to her cheek. "These are the new rules. *I'm* not letting *you* out of my sight."

SPENCER STARED UP at the tree canopy as the paramedics put a brace around his neck. A faint glimmer of light was beginning to shine through. Or maybe his eyes had been damaged. He felt as though an iron girder had been smashed across the entire left half of his head. Had it? He thought it was something to do with Kenyon Latimer and a rock, but his memory could be playing tricks. Now and then there were flashes of clarity, but everything that had happened since he and Boris entered the park felt fuzzy, like a TV screen with too much static.

The two men on either side of him carefully lifted his upper body to finish with the brace, giving him a view of his legs. As they did, he wiggled his toes. His injuries couldn't be that bad, he decided. His spinal cord was still working.

He was vaguely aware of being immobilized and carried to the ambulance on a stretcher. From the emergency vehicle, he was taken to the ER at Mustang Valley General. Then, a female doctor asked him where he hurt, and he gestured to the back and left side of his head.

By then, his skull felt like it was trying to pound its way out of his head through the skin. The drugs the doctors gave him didn't stop the pain completely, but they made him drowsy and less inclined to care. The whole time, he clung tight to Katrina's hand. Her face reassured him. He only let go of her when he was taken for a CAT scan.

After the scan, he was wheeled into a small room

and lifted onto a bed. By this time, he was feeling nauseous and shaky.

"Where's Katrina?" he asked the nurse who brought him water. "I need her."

"Is that your girlfriend? She went to make some calls."

Spencer lay back on the pillows, just the effort in conducting that brief conversation draining all his energy.

Is that your girlfriend?

His brain wasn't working at full capacity, but he knew how he wanted to answer that question. After everything they'd endured, he wanted to keep Katrina in his life. He wanted her to be more than his girlfriend. He wanted her forever.

When she entered the room a few minutes later, there was a doctor with her.

"The CAT scan showed no major damage." Spencer found he was too weary to react to the good news. Even his smile muscles refused to respond. "You have a concussion, which means you'll need to rest and avoid stimulants. But you can go home as soon as we have your medication ready."

"That's wonderful news." He saw a glimmer of tears in Katrina's eyes. When the doctor had gone, she gripped his hand tightly. "I can't believe this nightmare is finally over."

"Not for you." He returned the clasp of her fingers. "Eliza is dead."

She hung her head. "I've spent my whole adult life waiting for something bad to happen to her, knowing she was likely to fall for the wrong man or get into bad company. This is a sad day and I guess I'll always wonder if I could have done more to help her. But I'm also relieved that she did turn her life around and that she was strong enough to resist Latimer when he tried to get her back on to drugs. Because of that, I feel I'll eventually be able to make my peace about what happened to her once I've laid her to rest in a more suitable place."

"You're so strong. I can't believe how lucky I am that you came into my life when you did."

"When I nearly knocked you over, you mean?" Her voice was teasing.

"I've never enjoyed being almost slammed to the ground more." He studied her face. "If I could change the way I reacted—"

She pressed a finger to his lips. "You can't. And what happened tonight has taught me that life is too short for regrets."

"In that case..." He took a breath. "I love you, Katrina."

"Oh."

"That's it? Just 'oh'?"

She smiled, a hint of her usual mischief peeping through. "I'm just not sure you should be allowed to tell someone you love them when you have a concussion."

He laughed. "*You* don't have a head injury."

"True." She leaned closer. "Which leaves me free to say that I love you more than words can say."

He hooked a hand behind her neck, pulling her down for a kiss. "That's good enough for me. For now."

"For now?"

"We'll continue this conversation when I'm of sound mind." He gestured to his clothes, which were folded on a chair. "Let's go home."

"Whose home? Yours or mine?" she asked.

"*Ours.* The one where our canine family will be waiting for us."

A FEW DAYS LATER, Kerry called to say that Eliza's body had been moved from the shallow grave in Mustang Park to the coroner's office. Spencer put her on speakerphone so Katrina could listen to the conversation.

"Latimer has confessed that he killed her right there by the willow tree when she took him to show him the place that was so special to her in her childhood," Kerry said. "He's refusing to say any more about whether he involved anyone other than Hannant in the threats to Katrina."

"Keep pushing him on that," Spencer told her. "Ask him about drugging the dogs, about hiring Aidan Hannant, about the break-ins at Katrina's place. Most importantly, ask him if he had any help with those things, particularly from anyone inside the AAG.

"Latimer is facing a murder charge. Revealing the names of any helpers in the intimidation against you isn't going to help him," Spencer said when he ended the call. "If he did have support, I guess he'll continue to protect his friends."

Spencer was making a good recovery. The headaches he'd been suffering were almost gone and the wounds on the back of his head and his temple were healing well. Although he still felt tired occasionally, his energy was returning. Katrina could tell he was starting to feel restless at his enforced inactivity.

"I want to go and lay some flowers at the place where she died." She was determined to honor her sister's memory.

"Are you sure you feel ready to go back there?" he asked.

"I thought maybe we could take the dogs for a walk in the park. That way it will be more natural and less formal," she said. "That's if you feel able to walk that far?"

He nodded. "I'll be fine."

It was early afternoon when they reached the park; there were a number of families enjoying eating in the shade of the larger trees.

"Will Dobby be okay around all this food?" Spencer asked.

"Dobby will be a model of good canine behavior," Katrina assured him. "Suzie and I have given him plenty of additional training and he can resist food even if it's right under his nose."

As if to demonstrate his newfound ability to ignore temptation, Dobby trotted past the picnickers with his stubby snout in the air.

"Good boy." Katrina rewarded him with a treat.

They followed a turn in the track, coming across a group engaged in a yoga session in a clearing. They were in the middle of doing the downward-facing dog pose. Holly, normally the most well-behaved canine of the group, clearly thought this activity looked like great fun. Charging over to the group, she jumped on top of the people who were holding their positions, causing several of them to topple to one side. Although most of them were amused by her antics, the instructor angrily shooed her away.

"I guess Holly also needs some additional training?" Spencer's shoulders shook with laughter as they hurried away.

"Why can't they be more like Boris?" Katrina asked.

"Don't forget that he's had intensive training," Spencer reminded her. "His skills are honed with personalized daily sessions, and… What is that smell?"

"I think that smell could be Boris." Katrina's eyes danced with amusement. "I have a feeling he may have missed the personalized session about not rolling in fertilizer."

Chuckling at the bizarre twist that meant Dobby was now their best-behaved dog, they continued deeper into the trees until they reached the dip in the ground and the large willow tree. There were signs that the earth had been recently disturbed, and Spencer held Katrina's hand as she stared at the place where her sister had been buried by the man who'd killed her.

"Tell me about Eliza," Spencer said. "You've told me some things about her personality, but you must have other memories."

Katrina thought for a minute or two. "Oh, she was the nosiest person you ever met. There was no such thing as privacy with Eliza around. Everywhere I went, she was right there behind me, snooping around in my business. That was how she found out I couldn't dance."

"You can't dance?"

"I can now." She smiled reminiscently. "Instead of making fun of me, Eliza showed me some moves. It really helped improve my self-esteem."

"It sounds like you had a good time together." His voice was gentle.

"Sometimes we did. Other times the sibling rivalry kicked in. No one could get to me like her, but no one could get to her like me. And, in a way, the fact that she could drive me to distraction meant that she knew me better than anyone. We understood each other, and although she had her problems, we were there for each other." She bowed her head, letting the tears fall. "I never grudged looking out for her, and I always wanted her to know that I'd be at her side in a second if she needed me."

"I think you just rehearsed your speech for her funeral." Spencer slid an arm around her shoulders.

She stepped forward, placing the bunch of flowers she'd brought with her on the mound of earth. "I'm so proud of you, Eliza."

Turning her face into Spencer's chest, she began to sob. His arms tightened around her and they remained locked together for a long time. Eventually, Katrina drew a tissue out of her pocket and dried her eyes.

"I'm ready to go."

"Are you sure? We can stay as long as you like," Spencer said.

"No. I know I can come back anytime. When the time comes, I'll arrange to have her buried in the cemetery next to my mom and grandparents." She looked around for the dogs. "Maybe we should avoid the yoga group and the fertilizer on the way back?"

He grinned. "And expecting Dobby to behave around the picnickers on two occasions is just tempting fate."

"Let's use the old Western Boulevard gates."

"I knew I was getting involved with a rebel." As they walked, he shot her a sidelong glance. "About getting involved... Is today bad timing? We said we'd talk some more once you were sure my head was mended."

She laughed. "I'm satisfied that your head is in working order."

"Good."

When he didn't say anything else, she looked at him in bemusement. They reached the gates and called the dogs over. Spencer wrinkled his nose.

"Seriously, Boris. When you decided to stage a rebellion, did it have to be a stinky one?" He groaned as a thought struck him. "We still have to get fertilizer boy here home in the car."

"Deep breath in, hold it, exhale through the mouth," Katrina advised. "I've traveled with a lot of smelly dogs."

By the time they'd gotten home, bathed Boris, fed all three dogs and eaten dinner, it was late. Katrina was ready to curl up in front of the TV, but when she reached for the remote, Spencer halted her with a hand on her arm. "I want to talk to you, remember?"

The look in his eyes was so intense it made her throat constrict. "Okay."

"I've thought of a dozen different ways to say this

and none of them sound right, so I'm just going to talk and see where it takes me." He took her hands in both of his. "I was in a dark place when we met. I'd been there for a long time. Then you came along, and you showed me that I didn't have to be scared. It took me a while to admit it, but you had me completely almost from the moment I saw you. I love you, Katrina. I need your hand in my hand, your lips on mine, your body next to me at night—" He broke off as his voice started to shake.

"Spencer, it's okay. I get it. I didn't know I was lonely until I found you to make my life complete," Katrina said. "I thought I could hide behind my fears and pretend I didn't need another person at my side but when I'm with you, I feel at peace. I've learned to trust you, but loving you came naturally."

"And I know that love requires risk, but I'm happy to take chances if that means I have you next to me from now on." He kissed her. "I thought it might be too soon, but we've been through so much together, I know we can face anything. Will you marry me, Katrina?"

She caught her breath, stunned at the sheer rightness of the unexpected question. "Yes, Spencer. I would love to marry you."

"Even though you said you were glad you're not a Colton?" His smile was teasing.

"For you, I'll live with it."

He crushed her to his chest in a tight embrace. "And you know what one of the best things is? I get part ownership of two cute dogs."

She rested her head against his chest with a groan. "And I get a share in a stinky one."

THE FOLLOWING MORNING, Spencer was planning to go to the AAG ranch to interview Micheline Anderson about Kenyon Latimer. It signaled the start of his phased return to duty.

He was still undecided about the role the AAG and its leader had played in Eliza's death and the threats against Katrina, but he felt the matter required further investigation.

Just as he was about to leave the house, his cell phone buzzed. He frowned as he saw the name on the display. Holden St. Clair was his former army buddy who was now an FBI agent. Spencer couldn't remember the last time they'd spoken.

"Holden? It's been a while."

"Yeah. You know how it is. I've been meaning to call you, but things have been busy. I've been working on the beauty-pageant killings," Holden said.

"I've been hearing about that. It sounds nasty."

"Yes. Two contestants have been killed in the past month in two Arizona counties. The Ms. Mustang Valley Pageant is the only one taking place in July and I have a bad feeling about it. The killer may be in town, or on his way there, waiting to strike. That's the reason I'm calling. I'll be in Mustang Valley working undercover at the pageant next month."

Spencer frowned. A killer at a beauty pageant? It was the last thing the town needed with everything else that was going on. "You can count on me and my team to be available if you need us."

He ended the call to Holden and headed out to his car. Katrina had returned to work that day and they planned to go shopping for a ring on the following weekend. Everything in their personal life was perfect.

Professionally, there were still so many loose ends. They were no closer to discovering who had shot Payne Colton, or who had hired Harley Watts to send the email to the Colton Oil board members. And one of Spencer's biggest concerns was the way the AAG appeared to be involved whenever there was a problem. But was that true, or was he just seeing trouble where there wasn't any?

When he arrived at the AAG Center, he was immediately enveloped in the calm atmosphere. Micheline Anderson was a talented lady who knew how to use her skills to create a haven for people to feel wanted. The fact that she had turned this skill into a successful business was to her credit.

When Spencer entered the lobby, Leigh Dennings was waiting for him with her pretty smile already pinned in place. "Micheline is in her office."

She escorted him to a room at the rear of the reception desk. Holding the door wide, she indicated for him to step inside. Micheline was seated behind a large antique desk and she looked up with a smile as he entered.

"Sergeant Colton, how nice to see you again." The bright expression faltered a little. "Although I wish the circumstances were different."

"So do I." When she gestured toward a chair on the

opposite side of the desk, he sat down. "Eliza Perry, who stayed here at your center, and whom I was assured had left to go elsewhere, was murdered by a member of your group."

Micheline shuddered. "A terrible tragedy."

"I'd like to ask you some questions about her time here and the possible involvement of members of your group," Spencer said. "You may wish to have a lawyer present."

She opened her eyes very wide. "Why would I do that? We have nothing to hide."

"In that case, can you explain how you and your fellow group members got it so wrong?" Spencer asked. "I was told that a number of people remembered Eliza moving on. Leigh even said she remembered Eliza telling her she could take her dog with her to the place she was going. That can't have happened. Eliza had made no plans to leave."

Micheline spread her hands in a helpless gesture. "I have no explanation. All I can offer is a suggestion that because we have so many people passing through the center, we confused this poor woman with someone else."

"Yet there's the issue of her distinctive dog," Spencer said. "It's hard to get Eliza mixed up with someone else when she always had Dobby with her."

"There's also the fact that Kenyon spread the story around that she'd left," Micheline continued in her smooth tone. "The two of them were friendly, so there was no reason to disbelieve him."

"You're telling me now that they were friends, yet

when I visited last time, I asked if there was anyone she was close to and no one could remember." Spencer didn't bother trying to keep the frustration out of his voice.

"But of course. Now we know what happened, it's all come back to us."

She was too tricky. Spencer decided to try tripping her up with a direct question. "Did you know about Kenyon Latimer's drug problems?"

"Oh, goodness, no." Micheline appeared genuinely horrified. "He joined us in April, just after the earthquake and around the same time as poor Eliza. He's been living here ever since and has really kept a low profile. I had no reason to believe there were any issues until your colleagues told me what had happened. I've never been more shocked or saddened."

"Latimer threatened Eliza's sister when she tried to find out what had happened to her. It's possible he had help, even that the help could have come from someone within the AAG. Do you know anything about that?" Spencer asked.

"Absolutely not. I would never condone such behavior from our members."

"Do you know the sculptor Helen Jackson?"

Micheline appeared bewildered by the abrupt change of subject. "I can't say—"

"A little while ago, she confronted a group of your members who were handing out leaflets on Mustang Boulevard. She was angry that her son had paid a thousand dollars for a seminar that she felt was a waste of money. When her complaints attracted attention, Randall and Bart escorted her to her car." Spencer watched Micheline's face as he spoke. She seemed mildly interested in what he was saying. "Soon after that, Helen unexpectedly changed her mind and said she'd been mistaken. She didn't have any problems with the AAG, after all."

"That's nice to know." Micheline flashed him a smile.

"The thing is, when Helen was shouting about how crooked your organization is, Leigh was overheard speaking to you on her cell phone. Apparently, you told her it was bad publicity and she should shut it down."

"Oh, goodness, I don't remember that. Well, if this lady you've mentioned isn't happy, I'd be glad to talk to her." She frowned. "But… I think you said she *is* happy now. So I'm not sure what the problem is?"

"Another troubling aspect of this case is that an actress named Cordelia Mellor was hired to pretend to be an AAG member who knew Eliza. In the guise of a young woman called Christie Foster, she tried to fool Katrina Perry into believing she had information about what had happened to Eliza but that she was scared to pass it on. It seems that Cordelia was hired by someone who kept her hidden here at the AAG ranch."

"Well, that can only have been Kenyon, can't it?"

"Can it?" Spencer asked.

Micheline opened her eyes very wide. "Why, whoever else could it have been?"

"That seems to be the unanswered question," Spencer said as he got to his feet.

There didn't seem to be any more to say. Although

she was slippery, her distress at Eliza's death and the guilt of an AAG member appeared to be real. As he left the ranch, Spencer couldn't help wondering if there was more to Micheline than met the eye. She'd said no one from the group had helped Latimer cover up what had happened to Eliza.

Maybe that was true. But the AAG did like to keep its secrets, and the group was not comfortable with adverse publicity. Would he ever know for sure if Latimer had been the one threatening Katrina, or if Randall and Bart had decided to get heavy on behalf of their boss? Or could it have been a combination of both? He guessed the answer to his own question was easy. Unless Latimer had proof, and was prepared to use it, he'd never know for sure.

And there was still Payne Colton's shooter to be caught...

Before he drove away, he checked his cell. There was just one message and it was from Katrina. He smiled as he read it.

What do you want for dinner tonight? And do you want to eat it fast?

* * * * *